Elizabeth Missing Sewell

A Glimpse of the World

Elizabeth Missing Sewell

A Glimpse of the World

ISBN/EAN: 9783744728980

Printed in Europe, USA, Canada, Australia, Japan

Cover: Foto ©Andreas Hilbeck / pixelio.de

More available books at **www.hansebooks.com**

A GLIMPSE OF THE WORLD.

Ballantyne Press
BALLANTYNE, HANSON AND CO.
EDINBURGH AND LONDON

A

GLIMPSE OF THE WORLD

BY

ELIZABETH M. SEWELL

'I have chosen the way of truth, and thy judgments have I laid
before me.' PSALM cxix. 30

NEW EDITION

LONDON
LONGMANS, GREEN, AND CO.
1886

A GLIMPSE OF THE WORLD.

—◆—

CHAPTER I.

'DON'T, Juliet; just see what a stroke you have forced me to make; and I asked you to draw at the other table.'

'And I told you I couldn't see there. What does the stroke signify? Mr. Brownlow never scolds.'

'But, Juliet, I must have it right; I can't bear an untidy drawing.'

'Then, if you please, Annette, it is time you should learn to bear it. There is Myra, who never finished a drawing decently in her life, and is quite happy without it.'

The assertion was made at random, at least if it was permitted to judge from Myra's countenance. She was at that moment seated before a writing-desk, one hand supporting her head, the other playing idly with a pen, whilst her face was so expressive of anything but happiness, that even Annette forgot her annoyance at the false stroke, and joined in Juliet's laugh at her sister's despairing attitude, as she pored over her German exercise.

'I don't see why you are to laugh,' exclaimed Myra, and she turned round petulantly; 'you have neither of you begun German yet; when you have, see if you won't feel just the same.'

'It is not feeling, but looking,' said Juliet. 'If I were going to be hung, I wouldn't look so crestfallen.'

'Wait till you are tried,' was the retort, as Myra gave a push to her writing-desk, which nearly upset the ink.

Juliet rushed to the rescue of the German exercise-book.

A

Annette carefully removed her drawing to a distant part of the room.

'Good-bye to my chance of a mark to-day,' exclaimed Juliet; 'there is a blot on the left ear of the left hand figure, in the left hand corner. Look, Myra!' She held up the drawing good-humouredly, but Myra was not to be soothed.

'It would not have happened if you had not laughed at me,' she said; 'but you and Annette are always making fun of me—and from younger sisters I won't bear it. Every one makes fun of me,' she added in a lower tone.

'Only when your collar is awry,' said Juliet provokingly.

'Or when your cuffs don't match,' added Annette from the distant corner where she had settled herself.

Myra glanced at herself in the glass over the mantelpiece; then, without vouchsafing a reply, went and stood before it, and tried to put her collar straight.

'You had better let me do that for you, Myra,' said a voice which had not been heard before.

A very pretty girl, tall, and dressed in good taste, but in the height of the fashion, stood in the doorway. There could not have been a greater contrast to Myra. Her smile was so sunny—her voice so cheerful—her movements so graceful—even Myra's ill-humour was mollified by her soothing tone and manner. 'Mamma wants you in the drawing-room, so you must let me put you to rights,' she added, as Myra seemed at first inclined to resist any interference with her toilette.

'I can't go; I have not finished my exercise, and Herr Werther will be here at three,' exclaimed Myra, the cloud returning again to her face. 'Who is in the drawing-room?'

'The Verneys; at least Mrs. Verney and a niece. Mrs. Verney wants the niece to walk with you, only she is too shy to come into the schoolroom with so many strangers; and you are just her age, so you are to go and make acquaintance.'

'It is very unkind in you, Rosamond, not to bring her in here yourself; you know I can't bear going into the drawing-room; and Mrs. Verney always looks me over from head to foot, and talks to mamma about me as if I was a doll.'

Rosamond only replied by gently forcing her sister into a chair, arranging the collar, smoothing the ruffled hair, taking off the unmatched cuffs, and sending Juliet for another pair.

Myra submitted, but neither cheerfully nor gratefully. There was an expression in her face which, if the cause had been more important, might have called for sympathy. It was not annoyance, nor, at that moment, temper. It was a look of inward trouble—restlessness; in an older person it might have portended a settled despondency; and it did not leave her even when Rosamond pronounced that she was all right now, and Juliet came forward and declared that she looked quite a different person—almost pretty. The only change then was in her manner. It had been natural before —it was constrained now; and as she left the room, Juliet's comment to Annette was—'I think it is worse when she is on her best behaviour, because then she is affected.'

Myra was correct in her account of Mrs. Verney. She did look at her from head to foot as she entered. 'Myra is much grown, I think,' was her remark, addressed to Mrs. Cameron; 'and she really is more like Rosamond than I ever thought she would be.'

The voice was so gentle and refined, it was wonderful what made the speech so unpleasing. Perhaps it was the sharp criticising glance which accompanied the words.

'Myra does very well when she chooses to take pains with herself,' said Mrs. Cameron languidly. 'My dear, don't drag that chair so awkwardly. Madame Dupont was in despair about her for some time, but I think I see some improvement. Place your chair by that young lady, Myra, and make acquaintance with her; she is Mrs. Verney's niece.'

Myra moved her chair. The two girls looked at each other, but neither uttered a word beyond the first necessary question.

'Myra has such a very awkward way with strangers,' observed Mrs. Cameron in an undertone. 'Rosamond, do try and help her.'

'Rosamond is so sweet and kind; she makes everything go smoothly,' said Mrs. Verney. And certainly it did seem as if Rosamond possessed some magical influence, for she had no sooner made a commonplace remark, than the spell was broken. Catharine Verney, who had just come from a London school, began to pour out anecdotes—very amusing, if not always in good taste; and Myra listened, and asked questions, and ventured at length to propose an adjournment to the schoolroom.

'Don't drag one foot behind the other,' said Mrs. Cameron as Myra walked across the room; and before the door was closed, she added, 'It is so odd that she should be awkward and affected too.'

Then Mrs. Cameron was not fond of Myra, and treated her unkindly? Not at all. Mrs. Cameron only gave utterance to her thoughts, without considering their possible effect. And she said what was quite true. Myra was affected at times, under certain circumstances. She was unquestionably awkward, and had, moreover, a very unpleasant temper—extremely irritable, and very often passionate. No mother, anxious as Mrs. Cameron was for her child's good, and perhaps it should be added, for the world's approbation, could help being fretted by her. But there was another, a very special cause for vexation in this instance. Myra was such a contrast to Rosamond, and Rosamond was Mrs. Cameron's stepdaughter. It was scarcely in human nature to see the grace and sweetness of manner which marked the one, without feeling mortified at the deficiencies of the other. To do Mrs. Cameron justice, she never showed her annoyance ill-naturedly. She had adopted Rosamond and her two brothers as her own children, when Rosamond was six years old, and had always treated them with affectionate consideration. The claims of her own children had never been allowed to interfere with theirs. And she had been in one respect well repaid. The first family—as her step-children were often called—were remarkably good-tempered and manageable. The boys, indeed, had early passed beyond her control; they had been sent to a public school, and now Godfrey, having gone through college, was studying for the bar, and Edmund was preparing to enter the army. Nothing in their career had ever caused her any uneasiness. Mr. Cameron might have had his anxieties about them, but they were not shared with her ; and Mrs. Cameron was not a person to go out of her way to seek for trouble. What came before her she accepted ; but she had married in order to escape from the worries of a large household, conflicting bills, and a small income ; and when she found herself in affluence, and free from the tyranny of a domestic democracy, her naturally indolent mind at once succumbed to the temptations of her position, and all thought of duty being concentrated in the one idea of obedience to her husband, she suffered everything beyond the sphere of his expressed wishes to pass unnoticed. What might have been her course if Rosamond had been of a different disposition, it is needless to inquire. Resistance at an early period of her married life might have roused her energy. But Rosamond's sweet temper was a marvel. She accepted her stepmother from the first with a kiss, and a smile, and a promise to be very good, and the promise was carefully kept.

Servants, governesses, masters, all bore the same testimony. Miss Cameron really gave no trouble. She was very willing to learn, equally willing to play. Nothing seemed a grievance or a difficulty to her. That she formed no very strong attachments, and, though always welcomed by her young companions, was never deeply regretted by them in absence, might be partly the result of her reserve, partly of an unacknowledged feeling of envy at her superiority. For wherever Rosamond appeared competition ceased. Others might be second, but she was always first. A sweet voice, a good touch, and a perfectly correct ear, made her an excellent musician. If her drawings did not show any original genius, they were always artistic and carefully executed ; and for information, Rosamond gained, apparently without reading, a knowledge which others after months of toil were never able to make their own.

Poor Mrs. Cameron! It was all very pleasant at first, when Rosamond was the one child in the schoolroom, and the little ones in the nursery were only brought down to be exhibited for a few moments to some particular baby fancier,

and sent away at the earliest intimation of a cry; but it was
very different when they were all to be displayed as one family.
The difference between Rosamond and her sisters was then
evident to every one—Mr. Cameron included. Juliet and
Annette, indeed, were passable; they had not Rosamond's
grace and beauty, but they might grow into something presentable, and at any rate there was nothing in them that could
be remarkably the reverse; but that unhappy Myra! 'My
dear, if she can't look good tempered she must stay in the
nursery,' was the short and stern dictum issued by Mr. Cameron
to his wife, when the child was about seven years old; and
his words being taken literally, Myra was constantly irritated
with injunctions to look bright and pleasant when she went
down to dessert, till she lost all control of her temper, and in
consequence was pronounced the naughtiest little girl in England, and left upstairs for the remainder of the evening.

The governesses, and they were many (for Mrs. Cameron,
much as she disliked exertion, could never be satisfied without
trying a new plan upon Myra every two years), gave rather a
different testimony. Myra, indeed, was very fretful and passionate, but then she would work. Whether it was obsti-
nacy or industry no one ventured to decide, but certainly
whatever she took in hand she finished;—untidily, perhaps,
and not in a way which showed any great talent, but in a
fashion of her own, which, after all, was better than not at all.
And Myra would read too, which was what Rosamond never
did. Give her a book and she was happy; and in this taste
was found the peace of the schoolroom. Crouched in a low
chair, in an ungainly attitude, with her feet on the fender,
Myra could sit for hours absorbed in some tale—which,
probably, she had read half a dozen times before—and Juliet
and Annette were then allowed to pursue their own occupations
undisturbed. But the moment the reading was over—the
moment there was anything to be done jointly, and in consequence any difference of opinion, or question of conflicting
rights—Myra started up, full of complaints, eager to assert
herself, and ready to do battle with the first who opposed
her.

It was no wonder that the disposition was expressed in the face. Myra had only a very moderate share of beauty by nature, and certainly at sixteen it had not been increased by the softening influences of education.

'My stepdaughter and my own daughter—if they could only be reversed!' was Mrs. Cameron's unexpressed thought, as Rosamond, after accompanying Myra and Catharine Verney to the schoolroom, returned to wish Mrs. Verney good-bye, and prepare for a ride. And Mrs. Verney's after-comment—'How sweet and charming Rosamond is!'—by no means soothed her wounded maternal vanity.

CHAPTER II.

'FAITH has brought the tonic, Doctor; don't you think you had better take it at once? And here is a biscuit all ready.'

The speaker was an elderly lady with a very clear complexion, and rather a bright colour, quiet blue eyes, and grey hair dressed in large curls. She wore a dark puce-coloured silk dress, by no means expensive, and rather short; so short, indeed, as to exhibit a pair of square-toed shoes, made very high in the instep, and, if one might judge from the loud footstep, very heavy-soled. Her voice was rather hard, her utterance rapid, only the pure accent told of the refinement of good society.

The Doctor was an old gentleman with strongly-marked features, which in youth might have been called handsome. The brown wig, pushed rather to one side, gave them an incongruous expression now. It cut off a portion of his forehead, and tended to exaggerate the length of his nose—a very remarkable nose, long, rounded, and cogitative, in which the chief expression of the face was concentrated. Without it the mouth might have been almost weakly benevolent, whilst the eyes were decidedly irascible.

'A quarter of an hour before your time, Patty,' was his reply to the medicinal offer which had been made him. The grey eyes, twinkling through spectacles, were still kept fixed upon the folio open before him, and he turned a page with one hand, whilst motioning away the intruders with the other.

'I am going out, Doctor, and you will forget. Faith, pour out the medicine.'

Faith, a diminutive counterpart of her mistress, having attained that singular family resemblance which is often to be remarked in servants who have lived long in one household, came forward with a tray, a bottle of brown liquid, a wine-glass, and a plate containing one small biscuit.

'It will do you good, sir; you have been much better since you took it. Hasn't he now, Mrs Patty?'

'Of course he has. The notion of those pins' heads doing any one good! But Miss Medley is out of her mind, poor thing; there is no doubt of that. I hope it is not wrong to say so. I hope not. Now, Doctor, dear!'

The affectionate epithet did its work. The Doctor gave a slight sigh as he made a memorandum on a sheet of paper which lay on his desk, and then confronted his medical advisers.

'It isn't so very bad, after all,' said Faith, looking at Mrs. Patty; 'not half so bad as the black doses my grandmother gave me when I was a child.'

'I wish, Faith, your grandmother was here to give you this, then,' said the Doctor. 'Patty, what have you done with my globules?'

'Locked them up, Doctor. They are a temptation to you. Don't think about them now.' She put the glass into his hand.

'Only one biscuit!' exclaimed the Doctor. There was an evident hesitation for a moment; then the nauseous mixture was swallowed, and the empty glass laid upon the tray, with a look which Faith seemed instantly to understand, and answered by conveying the obnoxious objects as quickly as possible from his sight, whilst Mrs. Patty handed him the solitary biscuit, saying, as she saw him glance at the empty plate, 'Two would spoil your appetite.'

'Patty, I shall keep the globules myself,' was the Doctor's rejoinder; 'mind you let me have them.'

'We will see, Doctor, dear; don't think anything more about it; there is some nice porridge for dinner. Shall you want anything more before I go out?'

'Nothing,' was the irritable reply; but the very next moment the old man looked up and repeated gently, 'Nothing, thank you, Patty; only, if you meet Mr. Baines, tell him I should be glad to see him.'

'Mr. Baines dines with the Camerons to-day, so I hear,' said Mrs. Patty; 'I don't see clearly what makes him like to go there so often.'

'He is dull, and there are young people there,' replied the Doctor abstractedly; and he turned to resume his studies with an eagerness which seemed to show that he trusted to St. Augustine to help him to forget the nauseous flavour that still lingered in his mouth.

Mrs. Patty stood for a moment in thought, and then trotted rather than walked out of the room, muttering to herself, 'I dare say she is very good; I ought not to say a word; no, I ought not; and perhaps he never thinks about her, only it might be better for him not to be always laughing and talking with her.'

Mrs. Patty Kingsbury followed Faith into the kitchen, a pleasant-looking room, bright with well-kept pewter covers, and a dinner set of real china, of the old-fashioned willow pattern. The lattice windows were open upon a back court, kept in perfect order, and made really pretty by a few pet plants. An arm-chair stood by the window, and Mrs. Patty seated herself in it, and summoned Betsey, the cook, to a consultation with herself and Faith.

'Your master won't take kindly to the porridge much longer, Betsey; you must think of something else for him.'

'He has had it but three days, ma'am, and my father took it for a fortnight.'

'Dr. Kingsbury is of a different constitution to your father,' observed Mrs. Patty, with a slight tone of offended dignity.

'Mr. Harrison says his case is peculiar. You know, Faith, he objects to gruel also.'

'Quite, ma'am,' replied Faith, shaking her head. 'He objects to everything now, except the pins' heads. To think of Miss Medley's deluding him so ! But he'll give in, ma'am; don't take on so, pray now don't. He took down the draught quite good, like a baby, Betsey ; he did indeed.'

'He did indeed,' repeated Mrs. Patty ; 'but, Betsey, I think I should have a mutton-chop ready, in case the porridge does not suit. They are very good—are men—very good indeed ; you know, Betsey, we ought to look up to them, and we do ; but they like their own way in eating and drinking, and very natural.'

'You mustn't let master be asked out yet, Mrs. Patty ; if you'll forgive my boldness for saying so,' said Betsey. 'There's been Colonel Verney's man down since breakfast, and he says they are likely to have a gay time there before long, for the Colonel's nephew is expected back from India, and there will be dinner-parties for him.'

'Your master requires no check but a sense of duty,' was Mrs. Patty's reply ; whilst Faith added quickly :

'One would think, Betsey, that master ate and drank like a tiger ; but he has no more appetite than a chick just out of its shell.'

'May be,' replied Betsey ; 'but if't was a saint, I wouldn't put him down to gruel at one end and turtle soup at the other. Those grand dinners at the Colonel's are a perfect sight. How do you wish the mutton-chop dressed, Mrs. Patty ?'

'Quite plain, Betsey ; it can't be too plain. Did the butler say when Mr. Charles Verney was expected ?'

'The day after to-morrow, ma'am ; and Conyers, at Mrs. Cameron's, says that her mistress and Miss Rosamond are asked there for next week. She does not quite know what day.'

'Miss Myra must be getting nearly old enough to go out now, surely,' said Faith. 'I wonder nobody ever asks her.'

'Such a wee whimpering child as that !' exclaimed Betsey ; 'why, if anything went wrong she would burst out storming in the middle of dinner. I never did see any one so queer, for her age—no, never.'

'Yet there's something good about her too,' said Faith. 'There is not one of the young ladies as pays master half the respect Miss Myra does.'

Mrs. Patty had been sitting with rather an absent air during this short colloquy between her servants, but the last sentence caught her attention. Perhaps the discussion struck her as somewhat unfitting, for she rose up and said gravely, 'Mutton-chop, then—quite plain—at four o'clock.'

A burst of laughter was heard at the open window.

'Faith, is that you?—do come here, please do, Faith.' The voice was Juliet Cameron's; her round merry face appeared at the lattice; she evidently did not see Mrs. Patty. 'Myra has slipped down the bank into the pond; she is not hurt, she is only wet, and a little frightened; and she wants to know if Betsey will let her come and dry herself at the kitchen fire.'

'Myra can come into the parlour, my dear,' said Mrs. Patty, advancing.

'O Mrs. Patty! I beg your pardon. I didn't know you were here. Myra told me not to go to the front door, because of the Doctor's being unwell; and she said it would be making a fuss. There is nothing the matter. Catharine Verney is there—that is Mrs. Verney's niece, you know; and she and Myra were talking, and not looking where they went, and Myra fell and rolled over, that was all. It was so very odd to see her; she went down the bank like a ball: you can't think how droll it was.'

'Young ladies should learn to walk straight,' observed Faith before Mrs. Patty could reply. 'Is Miss Myra very wet?'

'Faith, if you please to fetch my garden-bonnet, I shall go and see about it,' said Mrs. Patty. 'It may be better that Myra should go home.'

'Myra won't do that till she is dry, if she should have to stay in the sun all the afternoon,' said Juliet, her laughter breaking forth again. 'Mamma would scold her. You know, Mrs. Patty, she always says Myra is no better than a child of five years old; and she did roll over just like one.'

Faith brought the bonnet, a very remarkable one—a deep curtain behind, a kind of pent-house before—at the far end of which Mrs. Patty's face appeared somewhat like the sun in a mist.

'We will go and see, my dear,' was her reply to Juliet's remark. 'Betsey, remember the mutton-chop; and, Faith, if I am not back to take the Clothing Club pence, when the women come at two o'clock, you must begin.'

'So like her, that is—looking after things so long before-hand,' observed Betsey to Faith, as Mrs. Patty joined Juliet in the court; 'why, she may walk to Marston and back before two o'clock comes.'

'It is because she wouldn't run the chance of neglecting,' was Faith's reply.

Mrs. Patty did not encourage Juliet's communicativeness. She walked on at a steady quick pace, to which Juliet found it somewhat difficult to accommodate herself. The Rectory stood on a rising ground, with a smooth piece of sloping lawn in front. At the foot of the lawn was a little wooded dell crossed by a rustic bridge, and rising from the other side of the dell were the gardens and fields attached to Yare Hall, a moderate-sized, square, red-brick Elizabethan house, with stone mullions and facings to the windows, and a thick shrub-bery round it. Mrs. Patty crossed the lawn and the bridge, and then turned into a gravel path which skirted the dell. Presently she paused.

'The large pond, I suppose, my dear?'

'Yes, Mrs. Patty; they were walking along the terrace at the top.'

'Very good. Run on, my dear, and tell them I am coming.'

'But, Mrs. Patty, Myra never thought of troubling you; she will be so vexed.'

'Run on, my dear; you can go quicker than I can.' And Mrs. Patty nodded her head good-naturedly, but moved for

Juliet to pass her in a way which showed that she had no intention of having her will disputed. Juliet was out of sight almost immediately. Mrs. Patty followed at the same pace as before—not at all hurried, only determined. Three minutes more brought her in sight of the pond. It was, in fact, a pretty piece of water; the banks were clothed with birch and elms. To the right was an extensive wood; to the left, the village and the church. The three girls were grouped picturesquely upon the turf; and the glancing sunlight which fell upon them made the whole a picture for an artist. But Mrs. Patty was not artistic; she walked straight up to Myra, placing her foot fearlessly as she went upon bramble and stinging nettle, and said—

'My dear, home is best for you; you will go back to the Hall with me.'

Myra started up, exhibiting, as she rose, a dress covered with mud, and still dripping with water.

'Oh! no, Mrs. Patty; no, indeed I can't. Please, you must let me come to the Rectory. But it was so ill-natured of Juliet. I told her not to make a fuss. I begged her to go to the back-door. I can't go home. It is impossible.'

Myra's face, usually pale and woe-begone, became crimson with excitement. Juliet looked at Catharine Verney, and laughed. Catharine shrugged her shoulders, and cast up her eyes; and Myra caught the expression of surprise, and was upon the point of storming again, when Mrs. Patty quietly drew her arm within hers, and said—

'We will come, my dear. You two girls go to the Rectory, and tell Faith not to trouble herself, for Myra is going home to change her clothes.'

'We must go, I suppose,' whispered Catharine to Juliet.

'Yes, I suppose so; but poor Myra is in for a scolding.'

'Never mind the scolding, my dear,' said Mrs. Patty, overhearing them. 'Run off as fast as you can, and then come up to the Hall; and, Juliet, you may tell Faith I shall certainly try and be back in time for the Clothing Club.'

Myra walked by Mrs. Patty's side silently. It would have been difficult to say whether she was most cowed, frightened or ashamed. For a girl of her age it certainly was rather humiliating to be taken home with a wet dress, after having tumbled into a pond. As they drew near the house she sidled a little away from Mrs. Patty, with the evident intention of making her way into the house by a back entrance, while she said apologetically, 'There may be company in the drawing-room. I know there is some one. Mrs. Verney is there. Mamma would rather not see me.'

'Your mamma had better see you, my dear; then she will know what to do for you. You are wet through, and I should make you go to bed.'

'What! in the middle of the day? For punishment— like a baby? Mrs. Patty, I won't; I never heard any-thing'——

Mrs. Patty gently tapped her on the arm. 'A warm bed, and a little hot wine and water, will keep you from taking cold, my dear. I always send the Doctor to bed when I think he is likely to take cold, and he says he quite enjoys it; only he can't go on with St. Augustine's Commentary. So now we will just rap at the drawing-room door, and tell your mamma all about it.'

'There is Annette in the drawing-room; I can't go in, Mrs. Patty, indeed I can't.' Myra slunk away, and nearly burst into tears.

'Well, then, I will, my dear; wait here for a moment, and I daresay your mamma will come out to you.'

As the drawing-room door was opened by Mrs. Patty, Myra stole to one side so as not to be seen; and the moment it was closed again, she rushed up the stairs, and bolted herself into her own room.

CHAPTER III

FAITH and Mrs. Patty were singularly alike in outward form, but there were great divergences in their minds, greater than Faith would have been willing to allow. Faith knew nothing of such profound reverence as Mrs. Patty felt for the Doctor; perhaps for that reason she required more sympathy from other persons. She liked a little gossip, and was not fastidious as to the quarter from whence it came. Great as was her virtuous horror of homœopathic globules, she did not deem it at all necessary to shrink from communication with the one inhabitant of Yare who had been guilty of introducing them into the village; and even the startling fact that her master had been cajoled into the use of them was not sufficient to make her dread any similar influence upon herself. Strong in her own convictions, she often made an excuse, when sent on an errand into the village, to pay a few moments' visit to Miss Medley, just for the pleasure of triumphing over her, by informing her how 'Mrs. Patty had persuaded the Doctor to try a tonic, or a cup of coffee, or even, sometimes, a little brandy, which had done him a world of good; and how he had had quite a sweet nap afterwards in his arm-chair, and woke up as fresh as a bird, and no pain.' The triumph was increased by the fact that Miss Medley's father had been a physician—by some called a quack, because he had late in life adopted the new system of medicine; anyhow, he was a gentleman, and Faith, never forgetting that Miss Medley was born a lady, was all the more happy in her self-gratulation, when she could, as she thought, prove, to the confounding of all gainsayers, that port wine, or water gruel, as the case might be, would be found to be worth all the whimsies which clever gentlemen or clever ladies had ever invented or encouraged.

'You don't happen to be wanting anything I can get for you at the grocer's, ma'am?' was her inquiry, as she knocked at, and then immediately opened, the door of Miss Medley's little parlour. 'I have been at the Hall, on a message from Mrs. Patty, and now I am just going on a step farther down the village.'

'I don't want anything that I know of, Faith, thank you; but don't stand in the draught of the passage.'

Faith willingly obeyed, though draught there was none from the passage, for a very good reason, that no passage existed. The little steep staircase went up directly from the street-door. The landlady, Mrs. Haynes, had the parlour to the right; Miss Medley herself the parlour to the left, with the bedroom above. It was a comfortable little lodging upon the whole, and tolerably well furnished. There was a dark puce-colour leathern arm-chair, a sofa with a chintz covering, a chiffionier and some bookshelves, a mahogany slab and a little writing-table; not to mention a rosewood cabinet piano, which Miss Medley's friends voted a great encumbrance, but which Miss Medley herself looked upon as the one only important piece of furniture in her possession, since on it she diligently played chants and psalm tunes on Sunday evening, singing at the same time with a cracked, though originally good voice, to the great edification of Mr., Mrs., and Miss Haynes, who, besides listening and approving, were not unfrequently summoned to join.

'Anything the matter at the Hall, Faith?' asked Miss Medley. She was a brisk little woman, and her bright black eyes twinkled and glittered incessantly. They made her look quite young at a distance, especially when it was not seen that her brown curls had no natural and necessary connection with her head.

'I can't say, ma'am. I wouldn't undertake to say. Mrs. Patty recommended that Mr. Harrison should be sent for; but Mrs. Cameron—I don't mean any disrespect—but she is very slow; and fever is sometimes fearful rapid.'

'Fever! infectious? scarlet? typhus? gastric?' Miss Medley stretched out her hand to a large green book which always lay on her table.

'Dear heart! no, ma'am. How can one say? fevers are like babies; there's no knowing them apart when they are born. And who can tell what this will turn to? or it might not turn at all. But anyhow, they have some common sense up at the Hall, and will know what to do. I said so to Mrs. Patty, and great comfort it was to her to think of it.'

Common sense could not mean globules ! Miss Medley was quite sure of that fact ; but under what nauseous form it would be likely to exhibit itself, in the emergency so vaguely hinted at by Faith, she did not stop to inquire. 'Mrs. Cameron has fever, then—low fever, I suppose? It is going about a good deal.'

'Mrs. Cameron, ma'am ! No, surely. I didn't speak of her, did I ? If I did, I was wrong. Mr. Cameron must be home by this time, and he may know better what to do. Miss Myra is greatly in fear of her papa, they say ; and well she may be, for his one word goes further than other people's dozens.'

'His word, and his wish, and his will, of course !' observed Miss Medley, and her thin lips curled satirically. 'When was there ever a man that had not his will? But what about Miss Myra ?'

'Why, that she is likely to die of fever, if she does not get better soon, ma'am,' replied Faith ; 'and it is her own doing too ; a wilful young lady she was always.'

'Aconite ! aconite !' murmured Miss Medley. 'Three globules every hour ! it would quite save her.' She gave a deep sigh, and for a moment she seemed lost in some sorrowful meditation. 'But, Faith,' and she looked up as briskly as ever, 'what is the cause ?'

'A child's folly, ma'am,' replied Faith, 'which never would have been if her papa had been at home. She tumbled into the pond, and got wet through, and when she went home locked herself up in her room, and would not let any one in ; and there they stayed outside, begging and begging, and she inside, in her wet things, for nearly an hour. So of course there is a cold and fever ; that is all, Miss Medley. But Mr. Cameron will be home by and by, and then there will be some one to manage her.'

'I don't see what good a man is to do in a sick-room, unless

B

he is a physician,' observed Miss Medley. 'As a race, Faith, men are noisy.'

'Very true, ma'am.'

'And impatient.'

'Yes, I suppose so, ma'am.'

'You need not suppose it, Faith, it is a fact; they are awkward, also.'

'Well! yes, perhaps.' Faith thought for a second, and added, ' Master is not.'

'Noisy, impatient, awkward—and selfish, Faith; selfish—don't think of denying it ! they are selfish ; and what good can they do in illness ? '

'They can have things their own way, ma'am,' replied Faith bluntly; 'and I take it that is what is wanted in all households. And if you will forgive me for saying it, you would think the same if you had heard Mrs. Patty's account of what went on at the Hall this afternoon.'

'If Mrs. Patty had done right,' replied Miss Medley, 'she would have taken the responsibility upon herself, and not have waited for Mr. Cameron. It has been my rule through life, Faith. I have never hesitated to accept any responsibility. I should have given aconite directly, and Myra Cameron's life would have been saved.'

'Please, ma'am, she is not dead yet,' observed Faith.

'But she is going to die—there can be no hope,' exclaimed Miss Medley impatiently. 'I am half inclined —— But Mr. Cameron is not a man to listen.'

'To listen, but not to answer, ma'am,' replied Faith ; 'and if you are thinking of the pins' heads in the little bottles, you might as well talk to a stone wall as to him about them. I heard him say one day myself, when he was dining at the Rectory, and I was waiting at table, that it was—I forget the word—but it was something very unpleasant.'

'Humbug ! It is his favourite word. You need not be afraid to repeat it, Faith. I know Mr. Cameron well.'

'If you do, ma'am, it is more than any one else does,' answered Faith. 'An oyster in his shell isn't more close.'

'I know him, Faith, as I know all men. Two or three

general principles are all which is required to enable one to find the key to their characters. If one does not fit, another will. But you cannot understand that.'

'I don't know about keys and principles, ma'am. I dare say they might be useful, if one had to live with Mr. Cameron ; but master, you see, is different.'

'Dr. Kingsbury is a remarkable—not exception—he has the faults of his sex : but, upon the whole, he is enabled to rise superior to them. But Dr. Kingsbury is being spoilt ; and Mrs. Patty will live to repent it. However, we will avoid unpleasant subjects. Miss Myra Cameron, you say, is dying ?'

Faith pretended not to hear ; she was searching in the corner of the room for her umbrella.

'Will it be many hours, do you think ?' continued Miss Medley, adopting the sorrowful and sympathetic tone.

Faith, leaning with both hands upon the umbrella, confronted Miss Medley with open eyes.

'Many hours or few, Faith ?'

'Just as many, or as few, as is willed above, ma'am. And as far as I can tell, Miss Myra is as yet no nearer dying than you—nor so near, if I may make bold to say it,' she added, glancing at the green book ; 'and so, if you please, I wish you good evening.'

CHAPTER IV.

FAITH was not quite correct in her assertion. Myra Cameron was nearer dying at that moment than Miss Medley—at least, according to human calculation. An hour and a half in wet clothes would alone have been sufficient to give her cold ; when passion and excitement were added, no one could be surprised that she was seriously ill. Myra had locked herself into her room, and resisted both commands and entreaties to open her door. If Mrs. Patty had been there, she might, perhaps, have been more easily persuaded ; but Mrs. Patty had no idea of neglecting her own duty for the sake of attending to that of others. She was wanted at home for the Clothing Club, and it was Mrs. Cameron's business to attend to her child; so Mrs. Patty went back to the Rectory, somewhat vexed at Myra's wilfulness, but never supposing for an instant that she would hold out her citadel against the attacks of the besiegers for any length of time. Great was her surprise then to learn, when in the course of the afternoon she called at the Hall again, that Myra had carried on her resistance for nearly an hour, and had only yielded at last upon being told that, if she did not, the door would be broken open.

'I think, Miss Greaves, I should have broken it open at once,' was Mrs. Patty's observation to the daily governess, whom she found watching in Myra's room; and the timid young lady whom she addressed ventured to add:

'I said so once to Mrs. Cameron, but she was too nervous to answer me.'

And thus, between nervousness and timidity, Myra had been given up to her own will. Now she had no will except to be quiet, and have the room dark. Her head throbbed with excruciating pain, her lips were dry, her tongue parched, her hands burning. She had decided fever; not as yet infectious or dangerous, but in a degree which might soon become so.

It was nine o'clock, and Mrs. Patty was again at the Hall, though not in the capacity of head nurse, for she was conscious of being near-sighted, and what is termed unhandy, and Conyers, the lady's maid, was fully able to do what might be required. Neither did she consider her society any particular advantage to Juliet and Annette. They were suitable companions to each other, and did not need her; whilst Rosamond was, or ought to be, a comfort to Mrs. Cameron. It was nothing but sympathy and anxiety which made Mrs. Patty linger in the library, keeping out of the way, and rather avoiding than offering help. She had walked up from the Rectory at eight o'clock, after her brother's tea, and when she had settled him comfortably in his arm-chair, with a lamp and a book of travels by his side; and hearing from the servant that the doctor was to see Miss Myra at ten o'clock, and that Mr. Cameron was expected home every minute, she sent a message to Mrs. Cameron, saying that she was there, but did not wish to disturb any one, and then waited to hear the last report. Most persons would have occupied themselves with reading under such circumstances. Mrs. Patty took some knitting from her pocket, and her fingers worked as busily as her thoughts, though, happily for the result, more connectedly. Fifteen years had passed since she first knew the Camerons. Such was the commencement of her meditations. Myra was a baby when Dr. Kingsbury became rector of Yare. Mrs. Cameron was very pretty then, very sweet and amiable; every one liked her, and thought she would make such a good wife. Every one said also that Mr. Cameron required a good wife, for he would not put up with a bad one. That had been Mrs. Patty's report of him, and it had excited her interest in him, perhaps awakened some fear. People said other things of him, that he was cold, selfish, exacting; but also that he was a very just man in business matters, and a good landlord. Mrs. Patty had speculated about Mr. Cameron then; she speculated about him now—for she was not quick at making up her opinion about any one; and after an acquaintance—it might be termed an intimacy—of fifteen years, she did not feel that she knew him, or that she could even be quite sure what he would say or do. What would he feel about Myra? Would he be anxious? Was there anything tender in his nature? Were his children really much to him? He was very proud of Rosamond, and he was proud of his sons; he liked Annette's drawings, and would sometimes laugh at Juliet's quick sayings. But was that real affection—the affection which would stretch itself to include Myra? Mrs. Patty did not put the question to herself definitely—it would have seemed wrong to suppose that a father could be indifferent to any one of his children;—but she felt it—it pressed upon her uneasily; and a saddened feeling awoke in her heart a troubled tender yearning for the poor little girl whom no one liked, who was entering upon life with such grievous faults, such fierce self-will, passion, vanity, and selfishness, destined, it would seem, to be her own torment, and the torment of her friends. And Mrs. Patty laid down her knitting, and standing up, folded her hands, and said a prayer for Myra Cameron—a prayer like that of a child in its simplicity, but like that of a saint in its earnestness.

The wheels of a carriage were heard; it drove up to the door. Then followed a determined ring, and a rush amongst the servants. Mr. Cameron was come. It was just the hour at which he might be expected from London by the last train, but Mrs. Patty was taken by surprise. She had meant to have left the library before he arrived, lest she might be in the way; but there was no mode of escape now without meeting him. She caught a few words which passed between him and the butler, and hoped he would go upstairs at once, for Mrs. Cameron was in Myra's room. But no; he came into the library first. Mrs. Patty's candle had burnt low, and the wick was long. Mr. Cameron failed to recognise her till she went forward to greet him.

'I am afraid I am in the way, Mr. Cameron; I know I ought to have gone, but I was a little anxious, so I stayed to hear Mr. Harrison's report. I will go directly now.'

'On no account; pray seat yourself. Mrs. Patty Kingsbury can never be in the way.' Mr. Cameron placed a chair on one side of the table for Mrs. Patty, and another opposite for himself, carefully snuffed the candle, rang the bell, and sat down, his head bent forward a little, in the attitude of listening.

He was a very handsome man; dignified in person, and courteous though stiff in manner. And he was very young-looking; no one would have imagined him to be fifty, or have supposed that so many years had been spent in the exhausting mental work and excitement of a barrister's profession. He might have been a bachelor of forty, without a care beyond himself, instead of a man who had been twice married, and was called upon to take thought for six children. His stillness, and slowness of utterance, no doubt contributed somewhat to this impression. He always seemed to be at leisure, and now he looked at Mrs. Patty with an inquiring gaze, which implied that no doubt she had something to say, and he was prepared to give it his full attention ; not allowing himself to be at all disturbed by the fact that he had been engrossed with business since ten in the morning, and had returned home weary and hungry, with his head full of the news of the day, to find his whole household in disorder, and one of his children seriously ill.

Mrs. Patty, however, could think of nothing to say. She nervously gathered up her knitting, and felt greatly relieved when one of the needles fell on the floor, and she could stoop to look for it.

'Allow me ;' Mr. Cameron bent down after her. 'This candle is not enough ; I have rung for a lamp.'

'Oh ! not for me : indeed, Mr. Cameron, it can't signify ; I am only staying just till Mr. Harrison comes ; if you would only kindly leave me ; our gardener is here, and is to walk back with me. I really don't want anything, and you will be longing to go upstairs and see Myra.'

'Poor little Myra ! she unwisely fell into the water, I hear. Was Miss Greaves with her, can you tell me ?'

'No, not that I know of ; I am sure not, indeed. The three girls were down at the Rectory pond.'

'Oh ! The accident was untoward. I am afraid it has occasioned you trouble.'

'Not me, Mr. Cameron ; if you just won't think of me, but of Mrs. Cameron and the poor child. Myra is very ill, and fevers are going about ; and no one knows what this may turn to.'

The servant entered to answer the bell. Mr. Cameron took no notice, but continued : 'The accident happened at the Rectory pond, you said ; and I suppose Myra was brought home directly.'

'Not brought, but walked,' replied Mrs. Patty. 'The accident would have been a trifle, only—but it does not signify now ; I would not on any account keep you from going upstairs. Mrs. Cameron will tell you all about it much better than I can.'

'A lamp, John ! and the round table cleared for supper,

Mrs. Patty, you will excuse me, but a man who has been fasting for ten hours feels somewhat hungry.'

'No doubt, and you will wish me gone; and as Mr. Harrison is late, I suppose I ought to go. But poor little Myra!'

'We must hope that she will be better to-morrow. Have you any commands for Mrs. Cameron before you return home?'

Mr. Cameron rose, and as the servant came back with the lamp, took up the solitary candle preparatory to going upstairs.

Mrs. Patty had many commands, at least in the way of imaginations and wishes, but they had fled, and left her brain a blank.

'Good-night, Mr. Cameron; good-night!' She held out her hand to him. 'I know I ought to go, and the Doctor will wonder what has become of me.'

'My compliments to the good Doctor,' said Mr. Cameron, his mouth betokening a first effort at a smile. 'Permit me to inquire if your servant is ready?'

Mrs. Patty's longings to run upstairs and see Mrs. Cameron, or at least the lady's maid, and just to look at Myra, and perhaps—if she could but hide herself in some corner—to wait a little longer, in the hope of having Mr. Harrison's opinion, were completely quenched. To get out of Mr. Cameron's way—that was all she desired; and that was all he desired likewise.

CHAPTER V.

'ROSAMOND, mamma says that if Myra is not better, you can't dine with the Verneys on Tuesday.'

Rosamond only smiled.

'She does say so,' continued Juliet, 'so I don't see why you should trouble yourself to practise so much; it must be disturbing to every one.'

'It does not disturb me,' said Annette, 'I like it. Rosamond, do you think this shade is too heavy?'

Rosamond left the piano directly, and looking over her sister's shoulder, gave her opinion with an air of interest.

'A little, dear! at least at the edge; it should melt off, you see. Can I touch it for you?'

'Mr. Brownlow dislikes any touching,' said Juliet.

Rosamond made no reply, but took the brush from Annette's hand.

'Myra is worse this morning, Mr. Harrison says,' continued Juliet, as she walked to the window. Leaning forward, she looked out into the sunshine. 'I wish she had not been so silly. I wish we had never gone to the pond.'

'I wish Miss Greaves would come downstairs, and give you something to do,' said Rosamond playfully. 'You are like a disturbed buzzing bee, Juliet.'

'Very likely,' replied Juliet; 'but Mrs. Patty looks so grave.'

'I am glad I never put myself into such a passion as Myra,' said Annette; 'I heard Mr. Harrison telling Mrs. Patty, as they were talking outside my door this morning, that half the mischief came from her being so excitable.'

'People always now call being in a passion being excitable; don't they, Rosamond?' asked Juliet.

'Generally, in polite society,' observed Rosamond.

'At Colonel Verney's, for instance,' continued Juliet. 'Myra and I were talking the other day about the new words Mrs.

Verney uses. Self-appreciation, she said, was Catharine Verney's characteristic.'

'I suppose a characteristic is not a fault,' remarked Annette.

'If it is not, it is so like one that I should never know the difference,' observed Juliet. 'Catharine Verney is as conceited a girl as I ever met.'

'She has a fair share of self-esteem,' replied Rosamond; 'but she will do very well by and by.'

'You like all the Verneys,' said Juliet.

'So would you, my dear, if you knew them.' And the 'my dear' silenced Juliet—for the moment; it showed such immeasurable superiority.

'Henrietta and Elise dress beautifully,' said Annette. 'It nearly made Myra cry the other day when they came to call. She said that if she were to live a thousand years she could never look like them.'

'No, never,' said Rosamond, with a quiet smile. 'See, Annette, won't that do better?'

'Oh! thank you, yes. That is quite different. But '—— Annette eyed her palette with a look of dismay.

'It is not quite as clean as when I took it from you,' said Rosamond; 'but it is not the business of a palette to be very clean.'

'Or for an artist to have a very tidy table,' said Juliet. 'Poor Annette! how I pity you.'

Annette collected her colours and brushes, and wiped the table with a piece of rag; but when the operation was ended she looked at her fingers with great disgust.

'You must go and wash them, dear,' said Rosamond; 'there is no help for it. And I know you won't be happy till they are washed.'

'And you won't make the table untidy again while I am gone, will you?' said Annette caressingly. 'You know, Rosamond, if you do I shall have forfeits.'

'Don't be afraid, dear child. I will take my sin upon my own shoulders. Just run away, and make yourself happy.' Rosamond still kept her place, and went on drawing.

Annette was gone a long time; so long, indeed, that Rosamond was able to do wonders in improving the drawing. Annette had great natural taste, but very little practice, and she was only just beginning water-colours ; whilst Rosamond drew remarkably well.

' Here she comes ! ' exclaimed Juliet, when nearly half-an-hour had elapsed. ' I wonder what she can have been doing ? '

' It is not Annette, it is Miss Greaves,' observed Rosamond ; and she rose from her seat rather hurriedly, and going to a distant part of the room, appeared to be looking for a book.

Juliet rushed up to Miss Greaves. ' Any news of Myra ? Is she better ? '

' Rather—at least we hope so. I have been sitting with her, or I should have come to lessons sooner. But of course you have been busy. I knew you could set to work without me.'

Juliet scarcely heeded the last remark ; she caught hold of Miss Greaves's dress, and said, in a voice broken with agitation—' Then they don't think——they are sure now she will get well ? '

' Mr. Harrison thinks the fever has turned.'

Two large tears rolled down Juliet's cheeks, but she walked to the window to hide them.

Rosamond sat reading, and Miss Greaves examined Annette's drawing. Rosamond heard her murmur to herself, ' Wonderful talent, certainly ! Mr. Brownlow will be immensely pleased. Do come and look, Miss Cameron,' she added, addressing Rosamond. ' Did you ever see anything more clever for a beginner ? '

Rosamond's mouth curled with amusement ; but she walked gravely up to the table, and began expressing her astonishment quite naturally.

' Such a correct eye, and such a very decided touch,' continued Miss Greaves. ' And the drawing is a difficult one.'

' Difficult and pretty,' observed Rosamond, turning the conversation. ' It must be a view of Mont Blanc from the bridge of St. Martin. Mr. Brownlow travelled in Switzerland last year.'

'Annette must go some day,' continued Miss Greaves, 'she would make such charming sketches.'

'Wonderful; if they continue to improve at that rate,' said Rosamond, still with a lurking smile, which Miss Greaves failed to perceive.

Juliet had left the room. Probably the two tears had multiplied faster than she was prepared for. Miss Greaves found herself without either of her pupils.

'I will go and look for Annette,' said Rosamond; 'her fingers must be clean by this time, and it is too tiresome for them both to run away.' She persisted in her offer, though Miss Greaves entreated her not to trouble herself. And a few minutes afterwards Annette returned alone, full of apologies for being absent;—but the paint had stained her fingers, and there was a spot on her dress; and, in fact, Annette had been so unhappy in her untidy schoolroom condition, that she had not been able to resist the temptation of putting herself, as she called it, thoroughly to rights.

'Thoroughly to rights' meant wearing a silk dress instead of a cotton one; but a love of neatness was so unusual a virtue at Annette's age that it was difficult to find fault with it. Miss Greaves accepted the apology, and praised the drawing; and Annette in like manner accepted the praise, and giving her little governess a kiss, declared she was the most good-natured, dear Miss Greaves that ever lived, and she should never like any one to teach her half as well. So governess and pupil were equally well satisfied with each other; and the lesson in history, which succeeded the drawing, was satisfactory and pleasant:—all the more so, probably, because poor Myra was lying on her sick bed, and Juliet had in consequence no temptation to exercise her powers of teasing.

Three days elapsed after the fever had, as Mr. Harrison had stated, begun to turn, and during that time a messenger was sent to the Hall regularly every morning, with 'Dr. and Miss Kingsbury's compliments, and they would be glad to know how Miss Myra was;' but Mrs. Patty herself carefully remained in the background.

'If persons don't do good where there is illness, they do

harm—so keep out of the way, Patty,' was Dr. Kingsbury's injunction, when his sister expressed a wish that she could hear more details. And the advice was by no means new; for it was but carrying out the principle on which Dr. Kingsbury had acted, and had compelled his sister to act, ever since he came to Yare.

With a different rector Mr. Cameron would probably have been at daggers drawn. If he lived at peace with his country neighbours, it was only because he so awed them by his politeness that they never approached him within offending distance. But with the clergyman of the parish he was forced to be on terms of more familiar intercourse, and disagreement would have been inevitable if Dr. Kingsbury had not at once taken up similar weapons of defence, and by entrenching himself in unsociability courteously, put it out of Mr. Cameron's power to compel him to do so uncourteously. Yet it was a line of conduct adopted unwillingly. Dr. Kingsbury, though dry and argumentative when questions of theology were presented to him, was at heart a genial, friend-seeking, kindly old man, who desired to accept his parishioners as his children; or, if they were too old for that, at least as his brothers and sisters. And Mrs. Patty was more than kindly. Except when on rare occasions she took some strong prejudice, philanthropy was her failing. As a general rule, she could have lovingly embraced the whole world—heathens and sinners—Mr. Cameron included, if only he would have permitted it. He, however, needed no tenderness, for he was neither a heathen nor a sinner, but a most high-minded, liberal, upright English gentleman : a little stiff, a little cold, but respectable, trustworthy, estimable, from the crown of his head to the sole of his foot. His was a reputation which had never known a flaw; for from the period when Mr. Cameron had reached the age of discretion, until the present moment, no one had ever known him commit an action which could be termed imprudent. Mrs. Patty could not possibly expect to be on a familiar footing, and to pass uncriticised and uncontemned by such a man. And criticism is not pleasant; unspoken, but felt criticism, is indeed peculiarly the reverse; and even Mrs. Patty's simplicity

was not proof against it.   The check which unconsciously she
placed upon herself in Mr. Cameron's presence—the care she
took to avoid any expression of wonder, or interest, or affection
—to do or say nothing which could shock or surprise him—
was the result of a self-control, which in another person might
have been the preparation for martyrdom.   And yet she
offended, quite unknowingly, quite inadvertently, and very frequently, and was so conscience-stricken in consequence—so very
penitent—the burden would really have been too great but for
the power of confessing to her brother.   Dr. Kingsbury never
transgressed—nothing that he ever said or did excited the
courteous sneer which thrilled through poor Mrs. Patty's veins,
like a blast from an iceberg; but then, as Mrs. Patty once
observed to Faith—taking a personal rather than a theo-
logical view of her brother's character—' The Doctor was born
to go straight to heaven, with no one to stop him—not even
Mr. Cameron.'

It was an infinite relief to her to be told, on the fourth day
of absence from the Hall, that Mr. Cameron was not only as
usual gone up to London, but was likely to remain in town
that night.   She had then the whole day before her, and might
manage her business in the village, and inquire for Myra as
late as she liked, without any fear of being thought intrusive ; and
for once Mrs. Patty even considered it might be possible to leave
the Doctor to drink tea alone, if Faith would but take care
that his toast was buttered upon one side only.   ' Too much
butter was so very bad for him ; and he was so absent he ate
whatever was given him, and might kill himself any day with
new bread, and never be a bit the wiser.'

' You won't let your tea be too strong, Doctor, dear ? ' was
her last admonition, as she fidgeted about in his study, wishing
to make quite sure that everything was just as it should be,
and that whilst she was gone he could not possibly need anything which she could get for him.

' Faith can make it,' said the Doctor, without looking up
from his book.

' Yes, Faith can make it ; but I fancied you might not like
that.'

'I like anything, my dear. Are you going now?'

The Doctor was just then very deep in thought.

'And you won't worry yourself if I am not home before half past nine? I may be, but if they should want me it might be awkward to come away.'

'Stay as long as you like, my dear, and'—Dr. Kingsbury looked up and smiled—'tell the little girl to get well as soon as she can.'

'And to come and see you,' added Mrs. Patty. 'Ah, Doctor, dear, she likes that; so do most people.'

The Doctor put up his hand, twisted his brown wig, settled his spectacles, and looking at Mrs. Patty with his head a little upraised, said simply, 'Patty, you talk nonsense;' and then he returned to his book, and Mrs. Patty went her way to the Hall.

CHAPTER VI.

'Myra is really better, dear Mrs. Patty,' said Mrs. Cameron, as the butler announced Miss Kingsbury; 'she has left me free to-day, and so you see I am resting.'

Mrs. Cameron generally was resting; she was not strong, and really needed rest; but the occasion present was always, in her own eyes, an exception to the general rule of exertion.

'Won't you sit down?' she continued, pointing to one of the many luxurious chairs with which the boudoir was furnished.

'I should never be likely to get up again, if I did,' said Mrs. Patty, drawing near the sofa, 'and I am not tired, thank you; I have only been into the village and back to-day.'

'Ah! you are such a Hercules, and so benevolent. My poor little Myra has taken up a great deal of my time, Mrs. Patty, and my thoughts too, I may say. Do sit down; it will make me more comfortable.'

Mrs. Patty sat down, though with evident unwillingness.

'Mr. Cameron is gone to town; he won't return to-night. I daresay the servants have told you; and perhaps it may be better he should not: he rather frightens poor Myra.'

'No doubt,' escaped unconsciously from Mrs. Patty's lips.

'And she is a trouble; she has been a great trouble to us always. Mr. Cameron feels this; he is very considerate. We have been talking a good deal about Myra. This illness has been quite brought on by her own wilfulness; and at her age—she will be sixteen next month—it is too childish. I could not have imagined it possible; now could you, dear Mrs. Patty?'

'No, indeed,' was Mrs. Patty's earnest reply. Myra had been to her for years an unsolved problem.

'And when she has been treated quite like a grown-up girl,' continued Mrs. Cameron; 'brought forward as the eldest of my own children—even confirmed. You know we had her confirmed last year, when we were at Hastings, because we thought it might help to make her more of a woman in her ways and tone of mind.'

It was a new view of the object of Confirmation, but Mrs. Patty only said, 'The Doctor was sorry she was confirmed away from home.'

'Ah! he was very good and thoughtful for her; but you see the opportunity came; Elise Verney was there, and she was a companion, and there were two or three other young people about the same age, and as it was to be done, it was as well it should be when there were several of them together. And then the Bishop was not likely to be here for another year—altogether, I knew dear Dr. Kingsbury would understand; and, as I said before, I did hope that the examination, and the ceremony, and the whole thing, would have made an impression—but I cannot see that it did.'

'When I was young,' observed Mrs. Patty, 'I remember I never liked to tell anybody what made an impression upon me. So, perhaps, Myra thought more of her confirmation than you imagine.'

'Perhaps so; no one can tell. But to confess the truth, I have been disappointed, and so has Mr. Cameron, and he is not a man to be trifled with; in fact, things can't go on as they are.' Mrs. Cameron looked so mysterious, that terrible visions of threats and punishments floated through Mrs. Patty's brain. 'I should not have mentioned the subject, except to prepare you,' continued Mrs. Cameron. 'You will find Myra much distressed. Her father has been talking to her.'

Mrs. Patty rose suddenly from her seat : 'Perhaps I might go to her; I can find my way, and I shall knock very gently —indeed I won't disturb her.'

'Oh no, you never can disturb any one! Would it trouble you to move that screen, so as to shade my eyes? And—I beg ten thousand pardons—but if you could just ring the bell for me, I can't stretch my arm far enough; my coffee must be ready, and I really feel quite exhausted. Poor little Myra, she is too much for me always! We shall expect you to stay to tea, dear Mrs. Patty; or will you have anything now?'

The present invitation was declined, the future left uncertain. Mrs. Cameron ordered her coffee; and Mrs. Patty found her way up the soft-carpeted stairs, and along the well-lighted corridors of the first floor, to the narrower steps and dimmer passage which led to what were known as the young ladies rooms.

Myra's apartment was small, but by no means uncomfortable. It had a book-case, and a writing-table, and a high-backed chair—sometimes designated easy—with shelves for curiosities, and a recess, with a chintz curtain before it, which made a closet for hanging dresses; and the window—though so high that it could only be reached by a step—commanded a view over the church, and the village, and the wood by the side of the ill-omened pond, which had been the cause of so much trouble. To the right of the window was the little bed, the curtain being drawn round it so as to exclude the light; and Myra was lying with her face to the wall, so that she did not see who it was that came in.

Mrs. Patty was as noiseless as she could be; but the heavy square-toed shoes would creak, and Myra uttered a rather impatient and complaining moan.

C

Mrs. Patty drew near the bed. 'Did I disturb you, my dear? I am so sorry; but these shoes are so tiresome; and I am afraid you were asleep.'

'No!' was all the reply.

'But trying to sleep, perhaps; and so I might be better away? I only wanted just to give you one little kiss.'

Myra turned herself round now, though with some difficulty, for she was very weak considering the short time she had been ill. Mrs. Patty assisted her, not very handily; but the good-will could not be mistaken. Myra looked up, and said : 'Thank you ; won't you sit down?'

'Just for a minute, my dear, if I may. And you really are better? Going to get well now? I am so thankful for that, and so is the Doctor.'

'Nobody else cares,' said Myra.

'My dear ! what will you say next? Poor mamma is quite worn out with anxiety about you.'

'Worry,' said Myra; 'she and papa think I am the greatest trouble in the house.'

'Perhaps you are,' replied Mrs. Patty. Myra's head turned angrily. 'But you don't mean to be so any more. Why, Myra, this is the last silly thing you intend to do all your life.'

'How do you know, Mrs. Patty? I can't help it; and papa declares I am wicked.'

'For that matter, so are we all, my dear. Papa declares what is very true.'

'But really wicked—different from your wickedness—so wicked that I can never be better,' exclaimed Myra.

'There is a good deal to be said about that,' said Mrs. Patty; 'only, my dear, I won't talk to you about it now, because you are not strong enough.'

'Yes, I am quite strong enough!' exclaimed Myra impatiently. 'I lie here and think, and no one comes near me, and that tires me; thinking is a great deal worse than talking.'

'That depends upon what the thoughts are,' replied Mrs. Patty. 'Anyhow, my dear, it is quite a new notion to me

about your being so wicked that you can never be better ; '
and as she spoke, Mrs. Patty began to search about the room
—for what, she did not say.

' Do you want anything ? ' asked Myra.

' Only a Bible, my dear, just to make quite sure whether
what you said is true. It certainly strikes me that it is not ;
at least, it is not what I was taught.'

' Papa says it,' persisted Myra ; ' and the Bible can't mend
matters.'

' Can't it, my dear ? I find that it mends most things.'

' But then papa says it,' repeated Myra, evidently almost
angry at the thought of having such a dictum disputed, especially when she had built an edifice of self-pity upon it.

' Mr. Cameron is very clever,' replied Mrs. Patty ; ' but you
know, Myra, no one could say that he was cleverer than the
Bible. Besides—you can say your Catechism, my dear ? '

' I said it when I was confirmed,' replied Myra ; ' of course
I don't say it now.'

' Well, but you remember you were taught there that you
have been made "a member of Christ, and a child of God, and
an inheritor of the kingdom of Heaven." And to my mind, the
Bible says the same.'

' I don't know where,' answered Myra in a perverse tone.

' There is a great deal about it in the Epistle to the Ephesians,' said Mrs. Patty. ' It is the Doctor's favourite epistle ;
he always makes me read it to him when he is ill. It is just
like the Catechism, only that seems to put the meaning of the
Bible into few words. I confess, Myra, I don't understand how
any one who is God's child can think as you do about never
improving.'

' All that is for you good people,' said Myra ; ' and, Mrs.
Patty, you may just as well talk to the wall as to me, for I am
made to be bad ; and I have been bad all my life, and I shall
be to the end of the chapter.'

' Well, I can only say that it is very strange,' said Mrs. Patty ;
' and that I never heard any one talk so before.'

' But it is true ! ' exclaimed Myra. ' If it never was true of
any one else, it is of me. I have tried, and tried, and made

such a number of resolutions, and they have all failed.   Mrs.
Patty, I did wish to be good when I was confirmed, but I was
not able to be, and '—Myra waited a moment, and added with
hesitation—'I prayed to be helped ; but I don't think I was
helped.'

'Don't you?' said Mrs. Patty ; 'but now I should have said
just the contrary.'

'What ! when I was always doing wrong again?'

'And yet always wishing and praying to be able to do right,'
said Mrs. Patty.

'Wishes ! what are wishes?' asked Myra contemptuously.

'I suppose it is the Holy Spirit who gives them to us,' said
Mrs. Patty ; 'because you know, my dear, every good thing is
His gift.   And if the prayers don't come from Him, where can
they come from?'

'I don't understand ; it is all puzzling,' persisted Myra.
'You talk about people being God's children, whether they are
good or wicked, and that can't be.   And, Mrs. Patty, if I am
wicked, God cannot love me, and it is no use to tell me that
He can.'

'I don't find that in the Bible,' said Mrs. Patty.   'I always
thought it said there that "while we were yet sinners God
loved us."   And certainly, dear, when you were made His
child at your baptism, you could not, so far as I see, have
been a good child, because you did not know anything about
being good or wicked.'

'Well !' said Myra, looking still more perplexed.

'Then isn't it that God makes us His children, and because
we are His children, gives us His love and His Blessed Spirit
just out of His great kindness?' said Mrs. Patty.

'But He takes His help away if we are wicked,' exclaimed
Myra eagerly.

'Nay, not so, surely.   He does not take it away, but we
don't choose to accept it.'

'It comes to the same thing,' said Myra ; 'anyhow, we
don't have it.'

'But we may, at any moment, if we only go and ask Him
for it again.'

'At any moment, if we only go and ask Him for it!' Myra repeated the words in an undertone.

'Surely, surely,' continued Mrs. Patty. 'He would not be our Father if He was not always ready.'

'But wicked people—people who deserved to be punished?' said Myra.

'I don't think we were talking of people's deserts, but of God's forgiveness and help,' said Mrs. Patty. 'It isn't pleasant, dear, to think of deserts, so we won't do it, except when we remember what the Blessed Saviour did to save us from them. Don't you see now,' she added more earnestly, 'it is all wrong to say you can't, and you despair, and you are out of God's favour; and very dreadful to say He won't help you? Because there God stands, close to you—close to you and me now, Myra—waiting, and waiting, and putting it into your heart to pray, and making you wish to be better, and forgiving you however many times you do wrong, if only you are sorry; and you turn away to the wall, and will declare that God won't love you, and won't hear you, and won't help you; and, Myra, that is the devil's teaching.'

Myra's eyes opened widely, as she said, 'Sometimes I thought it was being humble.'

'I daresay you did, my dear. The devil is very clever, and makes us fancy a great many things good which are not so; at least, that is what the Doctor tells me. But though I don't know much in the way of learning, I can see quite plainly, that to be always telling God that He does not mean what He says, is a very odd kind of humility.'

'So I am worse than ever, then,' said Myra, in a tone which was half angry and half desponding.

'Well, yes, to be sure, if you continue to say what you do, and to think it; but perhaps, Myra, after this little talk you may have a different notion.'

'I can't; it is not in me; I must always be wicked,' persisted Myra.

'Very well, my dear, let it be if you wish it,' said Mrs. Patty. 'But anyhow, you are God's child, and there is the fact, and it can't be altered.'

'I shall not go to Heaven at all the more for that,' observed Myra.

'Certainly not, if you don't wish to go. I never heard that God means to take any persons to Heaven against their will.'

Mrs. Patty stood up and drew her shawl together, as if she was going away.

Myra caught hold of her dress. Tears stood in her eyes. 'Mrs. Patty, I do wish it ; I wish it so very, very much ; you can't tell how much.'

'Then, my dear, Heaven is ready for you, that is all I can say ; and, please God, I hope we shall spend many a long day there together.'

'Not days,' said Myra, and a smile came over her face. 'You know, Mrs. Patty, there will be no days in Heaven.'

'Which is one of the things I don't understand, my dear, as there are a good many things about Heaven which are a puzzle to me. But, Myra, let it be days or not days, it will be very pleasant ; and if you and I should be so happy as to be there together, I can't but think that we shall recollect this talk we have had, and you will wonder how you could ever have had such doubts of the Blessed Saviour's kindness. Now, good-bye, my dear, and if nothing should come in the way, I shall hope to see you again to-morrow.'

'Only one more word, Mrs. Patty—please stay ; because— I don't want to distrust, but wicked people are punished—they must be punished. If I were going to die now, I could not escape being punished.'

'I don't see it,' was the reply.

'O Mrs. Patty !' and Myra looked quite shocked.

'I thought that Saviour means to save,' continued Mrs. Patty, 'and that all the punishment was borne just because it should not come upon us ; and I know, Myra, if I did not think so, I should be just as frightened as you are.'

'But you would have no cause,' replied Myra ; 'every one says that you are so very good.'

An expression of real pain crossed Mrs. Patty's usually bright face. 'It does not do to talk so, my dear, but we will let that pass. Only, if the Blessed Saviour is so kind to us, it is not in nature not to try and be good and to please Him, or not to be dreadfully sorry when one is not good. I think, Myra, if you will just lie quiet a little, and think about it, you will understand it better—especially, do you see, if you could say a prayer to Him. It is wonderful how He makes things clear to us when we do pray.'

Mrs. Patty stooped down and kissed Myra, and as the kiss was returned, Myra whispered, ' O Mrs. Patty ! I love you dearly ; ' but whether what had been said had also been received and accepted, was left doubtful.

CHAPTER VII.

MRS. PATTY remembered as she went downstairs that she was hungry, and that a substantial tea was most likely going on in the dining-room. Mr. Cameron being away, she ventured to find her way there. Rather a merry party was assembled— Mrs. Cameron and Rosamond, Juliet, Annette, and the young curate. Rosamond was making tea. Mr. Baines was handing about the cups, perhaps a little officiously ; at least with a manner which made Rosamond laugh at him in a very quiet way. She never was anything but quiet—and simple too, many persons would have said. She made room for Mrs. Patty directly.

' By me, please, dear Mrs. Patty,' and she pointed to an empty seat. ' Mr. Baines, may I trouble you ? If you would bring a plate from the sideboard, and a knife and fork too. Mr. Baines is new in his employment, Mrs. Patty ; you must forgive his awkwardness.'

Whether awkward or not, Mr. Baines was evidently in the seventh heaven of felicity—ordered about, and permitted to make himself quite useful and at home. Mrs. Patty began talking about Myra—a very natural subject. ' It was so plea- sant,' she said, ' to see her better, and to find her, upon the whole, really making rapid progress.'

'Delightful; quite a relief.' Rosamond looked into the teapot and shook her head. 'Mr. Baines, be charitable once more, and ring the bell. Mamma, do you hear that Mrs. Patty thinks poor little Myra's improvement wonderful?'

'I don't see why she should always be called little Myra,' said Juliet rather sharply. 'She will soon be as tall as you, Rosamond.'

'Not quite, I think. Mr. Baines, do you recollect our all being measured when your sister was here?'

Mr. Baines remembered it perfectly. Miss Cameron was the tallest of the young ladies. He had been measured also himself on that occasion.

'And I think you were just the height of my brother Godfrey?' observed Rosamond.

'Half an inch taller,' and Mr. Baines almost involuntarily elevated his head. Rosamond was remarkably tall, and he did not wish her to look down upon him.

Mrs. Patty turned round upon him quickly. 'Mr. Baines, you were at the school this morning, I can be nearly sure, unless you have changed your day. Did you see Betsy Ford's tall boy there?'

'The one who is half an idiot?' asked Juliet, breaking suddenly into the talk, which could scarcely be called conversation.

There was a laugh from several of the party; merriest of all from Rosamond. Mrs. Patty retained her gravity. 'The Doctor thinks him quite an idiot; and I was going to ask you, Mr. Baines, if you would kindly see Betsy about him, and if it should turn out that he is so, enough to be sent to the Asylum, something could be done about it.'

'I don't want him to be sent there,' said Rosamond; 'he makes himself so useful in sitting to be sketched. Don't you recollect,'—and again she turned to Mr. Baines—'that day when I was drawing him, as he stretched himself on the bank by the churchyard? It was the day of the terrific thunder-shower, and when you lent me your umbrella.'

Mr. Baines recollected it perfectly: it was not likely, he said, that he should forget it; and he was rejoiced to find Miss Cameron's memory so good.

Rosamond looked quite unconscious, and begged Mrs. Patty to take a little marmalade.

'None, thank you, my dear. But I think, Mrs. Cameron, you have a vote for the Idiot Asylum.'

'I had last year—Mr. Cameron had, at least; but I am not sure now—it involved so much trouble; every one was writing and begging for it. I know we talked of giving it up.'

'That would be a pity,' said Rosamond; 'if I can't spare my pet idiot, there will be many others to take his place.'

'It must be that same boy whom Mr. Brownlow has put into the drawing he offers us for a prize,' said Annette; 'he told me he had sketched the figure from nature.'

'Are you drawing for a prize, my dear?' asked Mrs. Cameron; 'I never heard of that before.'

Annette slightly blushed. 'Not a prize, mamma, exactly; but Mr. Brownlow said that if either Juliet or I could do another drawing as good as my last, his copy should be a reward.'

'I think every one has finished tea, mamma,' said Rosamond abruptly, and half rising. 'Shall we go to the drawing-room?'

There was a general move, and in passing out of the room, Rosamond whispered to Annette: 'What a silly, little, conceited thing you are! Why could you not let the drawing alone?'

Annette looked disconcerted, and just then Juliet also came up to her, and said, 'You need not reckon upon Mr. Brownlow's drawing, if you are to do another of your own like the last, seeing that was more than half Rosamond's work.'

'Nonsense!' exclaimed Rosamond; 'there were not more than half-a-dozen strokes of mine.'

Juliet held up her hands in astonishment.

'My love, you know nothing about it,' continued Rosamond. 'You have been waiting upon Myra, and have never seen me touch the drawing, except that one day when I showed Annette where she was wrong in the shading. You should not be envious, Juliet.'

Juliet's face flushed crimson, and she ran upstairs. Rosa-

mond entered the drawing-room with that indescribable air of
subdued virtue which naturally accompanies the consciousness
of giving merited reproof.

A little more conversation about the drawing went on, but
all of a very safe kind.   Mr. Brownlow's picture and Annette's
copy were brought forward and compared, and Mr. Baines
and Mrs. Patty admired, and did not venture to criticise.
Annette was pronounced a most promising artist, and in the
eagerness of excitement at the praise she was receiving, engaged some day to do a drawing for Mr. Baines.   Rosamond
kept at first in the background, only now and then putting in
a little remark, which showed how much more she knew about
drawing than any one else; but it was curious to see how by
degrees she brought round attention to herself.   At length her
own portfolio was produced, and her little scraps, as she called
them—the trifles which she had just thrown off on the spur of
the moment, which really were not worth looking at—were
turned over.   And as Mrs. Patty did not care much about
them, and was anxious to talk to Mrs. Cameron about the
Idiot Asylum, it was, of course, quite natural and right that
Rosamond should be polite to Mr. Baines, and give him all
the explanations which were necessary to enable him to understand the little scraps.   Mr. Baines was remarkably interested
by them, and hinted, at last, that it would be such a great
favour—one he could scarcely venture to suggest—but if, some
day, Miss Cameron would give him an outline—he asked
nothing more—a mere outline of the village street, with the
curate's lodging,—it would be such a valuable reminiscence—
invaluable indeed.

Rosamond's answer was cold: 'her time was much occupied
—she never liked to promise; but, no doubt, Annette would
try the sketch for him.'   Poor Mr. Baines !   It was very cruel
upon him; he was really a very shy and modest man, and it
was evident he had been guilty of a misdemeanour.   He murmured something not quite intelligible about pleasure, and
hope, and forgiveness, and was interrupted in the middle by
Mrs. Patty.

'Mr. Baines, I must wish you good evening, for the gardener

is waiting to go home with me, and the Doctor will want a little looking after before he goes to bed.'

The curate, in his eagerness to escape from his position at the table, stumbled over a footstool, and nearly fell at Mrs. Patty's feet. 'Oh! but, indeed, Mrs. Patty, I can't let you walk home alone. I was just thinking that I ought to be going, and I shall be so happy if you will let me take charge of you.' He glanced at Rosamond, but she was busy tying up her portfolio.

'We meet on Tuesday at Colonel Verney's, I suppose?' said Mrs. Cameron.

'Yes, I hope to have that pleasure;' and there was another glance at Rosamond. 'I conclude, of course, you all dine there?'

'Mamma, I should prefer going in the evening, if I go at all,' observed Rosamond indifferently. 'Dear Mrs. Patty, may I fetch your cloak and bonnet?'

'They are in the hall, my dear; I will go and put them on there; and Mr. Baines can join me, if he will be so civil to an old woman.'

'Good-night, Mr. Baines;' Rosamond held out her hand very coldly. The poor curate scarcely dared to take it. If he might only have endeavoured to make his peace. But his was such a very small offence—he did not quite see why it should have been one; but then he knew nothing about ladies. He only felt they were made of wax, and were liable to be broken at a touch; so he tried to say, 'Good-night,' just in Rosamond's tone—and hoped he had succeeded. But if he had watched Rosamond's smile, as she followed Mrs. Patty to the Hall, he might have discovered that he had failed.

CHAPTER VIII.

MYRA CAMERON was called 'little Myra,' and treated like a child. A strange inconsistency, when she was sixteen. No one felt it more than Myra herself. And it might have been even more strange if she had understood herself. But if Myra was a problem to her friends, still more was she one to her own heart. Of all the inmates of Yare Hall, there was not one who thought so much, read so much, or felt so much, as Myra. Even when she fed her imagination with fiction, the fiction was digested and reproduced so as to become her own possession—to be part of the world in which she lived. She never simply received ideas ; they were pondered upon, and analysed, though quite unconsciously, and the experience of daily life was brought to bear upon them and to be their test. No one was a keener observer of inconsistencies, no one more quick at discovering discrepancies between principle and practice ; but this very quickness was a stumbling-block in Myra's path. She was so alive to the peculiarities of others, that she thought very little of her own, except when they brought her into public notice. Then she shrank from them with a sensitiveness which was morbid. To be told that she was awkward was distressing, but to be accused of being affected was almost torture. There were times, and those not few, when Myra would willingly have rushed away from the pleasantest party and the most amusing companionship, and shut herself up in solitude for hours—not from temper, though it certainly would have been called such ; neither from wounded vanity, though it might have borne such an appearance ; but from the mere desire to be where no one could make a remark upon her, even in the way of praise. Not that Myra was insensible to praise. When implied, she could enjoy it ; when written, it was delightful to her ; but spoken praise was suffering. And Myra had not sufficient self-esteem to support her against the consciousness of her own external defects. What she was told of herself she received as undoubted truth ; and certainly there were facts within her own consciousness to corroborate what she knew to be the general impression of her character. Bad temper, and that not merely a passionate, but a fretful and peevish temper, was a fault which it was impossible to deny. Selfishness also was an accusation not to be gainsayed, for Myra knew perfectly well how alive she was to what she called her own rights, and how determined upon asserting them, whether they interfered with those of others or not. And vanity also she would at once have pleaded guilty to, only she would not have allowed that it was vanity which made her what people called affected ; but the thing which perplexed her, which gave her a sense of injustice—a wounded, isolated feeling of being misunderstood by others, and not even understanding herself—was the nobler spirit beneath. Child she was, wayward, and foolish, and ungoverned in temper and in wishes ; but even as Myra owned herself to be such—even whilst she talked and acted as if she neither professed to be nor wished to be anything better—a truer voice whispered to her in the depths of her own heart, that she was not a child ; that she had longings and aspirations, dreams of goodness and beauty, an appreciation of all things 'just, and pure, and lovely, and of good report,' which, if examination were made, would be found wanting in those who were the most keen-sighted to her defects, and the loudest in her condemnation.

So up to this hour had Myra lived in the weariness of this perpetual conflict between her opposite characteristics. It can scarcely be wondered at that her existence was for the most part solitary. It was only when alone that she was her better self, and therefore only when alone that she could find rest—such rest, at least, as could be obtained from the opiates of study and imagination.

The two may seem somewhat incompatible ; an imaginative is generally considered to be the opposite of a studious mind : but that one faculty, which perhaps had saved Myra from being cast off as hopeless by all who undertook to manage her—the faculty of persevering industry—had, through the whole of her short life, been curiously co-existent with a vivid delight in poetry, and an enjoyment which even amounted to what might be termed revelling in fiction. It seemed, indeed, as if a portion of the same excitement which made her lose herself in the story which she was reading, was awakened also by the stimulus of study.

What Myra once undertook to learn, absorbed her as though it had been a novel. And she did undertake many things in an irregular way. Her education had been imperfect and desultory; she had been taught by a succession of governesses, and in spite of her temper and constant punishment, had managed to acquire such an amount of information as would enable her to pass well in society; but this was not sufficient to satisfy her. She had a craving for more knowledge, and a consciousness of being superficial, and since no one else undertook to teach her thoroughly, she was compelled to teach herself.

A strange medley of old books was to be found in Myra's room. Withering's 'Botany,' and a Spanish Grammar and 'Don Quixote,' side by side with Watts on 'The Improvement of the Mind,' Abercrombie on 'The Moral and Intellectual Powers,' Bacon's 'Essays,' Russell's 'Modern Europe,' Miss Burney's novels, Sir Charles Grandison, De Foe's 'History of the Plague,' 'The Old English Baron,' and 'The Arabian Nights' Entertainments'—not all very desirable reading, but seized upon by Myra because she had heard the books spoken of, and was determined to find out for herself what they were like. And they were all read and studied in turn. Myra was gradually emerging from schoolroom restraints, and was allowed to manage her time, upon the whole, very much as she liked; and with her love of solitude she was always making an excuse to escape from public engagements, and praying to be allowed to enjoy herself in her own way. Of course no one was admitted to a share in her occupations, or even told anything about them. Myra would have endured no small amount of physical pain rather than confess to any one that she liked reading deep books, and she was thoroughly ashamed of her love of fiction; and as for asking for any particular

author, she would far rather have been supposed to be playing
with a doll. The volumes she had in her possession had been
collected surreptitiously in her wanderings about the house,
and whilst searching into the contents of bedroom book-cases
and old closets. Mr. Cameron had a very excellent library,
but his children were never allowed to touch a volume. It
was one of his strictest rules. The moment a child handled
a book he considered it spoilt, and only fit to be given up to
the nursery; and it was to this rule that Myra owed the
possession of the 'Arabian Nights,' a very handsome copy in
four octavo volumes, which in some moment of weakness had
been taken from the shelves by Mrs. Cameron, during her
husband's absence, in order that she might read a story to the
children, and being carried off into the schoolroom, had been
found there on Mr. Cameron's return, and from thenceforth
abandoned to its fate. The enchantment of the 'Arabian
Nights' was over, however, now; Myra knew the tales by
heart, and thought of them only when—as sometimes happened
—she was called upon to entertain a stray little visitor by
telling a story. Then the histories of Prince Houssain, Prince
Achmet, and Prince Ali, the Little Hunchback, and the Forty
Thieves, to say nothing of the Wonderful Lamp, were invaluable; whilst the Pilgrimage of the Prince who was sent to
fetch the Golden Water, and was compelled to stop his ears
to the taunts of the unhappy travellers who had on previous
occasions been turned into stone, and were resting on the
mountain side, lingered in her memory, she knew not why,
but perhaps to come forth at some future time with that im-
pressiveness of a deep moral, which we all feel so keenly
when, as years roll on, it is discovered by ourselves as inherent
in some childish legend.

And Myra gained something also from the library, debarred
from it though she was; it gave her the titles of books, a
knowledge which at first sight may appear absolutely useless,
but which can never really be so. She learnt, for instance,
that Sir John Malcolm had written a History of Persia; and
Boswell a Life of Johnson, and Middleton a Life of Cicero;
she recognised Bossuet and Bourdaloue, and Massillon and

Fenelon, as French standard writers; she knew Fielding and Smollett by sight, and was quite aware that Hume had written something besides the History of England. And her respect for dictionaries—generally regarded as the meanest species of school-book, and delivered over to any amount of ink and dog's ears—had been nurtured till it had actually become veneration, by seeing the goodly array of splendidly-bound volumes, from the Dictionnaire de l'Académie Française, to those of Spanish, Portuguese, Chinese, Hebrew, Sanscrit, and all other known and unknown languages, which it had been Mr. Cameron's pride to collect, and which were always pointed out to his friends as the choicest collection in England.

This mere acquaintance with facts might no doubt have been useless to the majority of young girls, but with Myra a fact was the material by which the soil of her mind was gradually becoming enriched. The outsides of books were only one degree less real than the outsides of the persons who wrote them. The names which would have made no impression when learnt as a schoolroom list of celebrated authors, became realities when they daily met her eye on the library shelves. And so, when at any time a reference was made to these authors, either by Mr. Cameron or the friends who visited him, Myra's attention was arrested. She would sit in the corner apart, working perhaps at some never-ending piece of embroidery, which was always her company-work, whilst listening to the arguments or discussions which were going on, and gaining more by the working of her own powers, the struggle to understand what no one thought of explaining to her, than she could have done from the lecture of the most learned professor, who would have solved her difficulties in a conversation of a quarter of an hour.

Even the outward appearance of the library books was not without its effect upon her. In these days we are ceasing to regard external richness as any tribute to the internal merits of a volume. Whilst our best writers are content with sober-coloured cloth, we array 'Tom Thumb' in morocco, and dress 'Puss in Boots' in calf and gilding. The outward signs of reverence are no longer recognised. But in this respect Mr.

Cameron was a gentleman of the old school. He prized his rare editions, and large paper copies—he loved to trace the pedigree of his time-stained volumes—he delighted in broad margins, and detested small type ; and when he laid his old quarto on the table and carefully turned every leaf at the top, and then, opening it further, pointed out the manner in which the book, so perfectly well-bound, lay back of itself, requiring nothing to keep it open, there was somewhat of a personal tenderness for the material form, apart from the thoughts conveyed by them, which it was impossible to watch without being impressed by it. Every man, it is said, has some soft place in his heart. Mr. Cameron's softness was shown towards his books.

He had no idea of influencing Myra ; he was not a man who troubled himself about influencing any one, except when he was pleading in court ; but he did influence her very materially. She was growing up unconsciously with much of his feeling upon this point ; and the reverence, which was not very strongly developed in her naturally, was fostered by this one exhibition of it in a degree which will probably be unknown to the next generation. The cheap editions of Bacon's 'Essays' will scarcely become the heirlooms of memory to our children.

Yet, with all this love of study and appreciation of books, Myra was not considered clever, in the ordinary sense of the word ; nor, indeed, had she any strict right to be so called. Cleverness, though its definitions are various, is, perhaps, generally accepted as meaning quickness in receiving ideas, and aptness in making use of them. Myra was neither very quick nor very apt ; in some things she was decidedly dull, and in the opinion of society, Rosamond would undoubtedly far excel her. And she had not even that fair appreciation of her own powers which would enable her to make the most of them. She had no dreams of distinction, no youthful visions. of authorship and fame. Not being aware of having thoughts or ideas worthy of preservation, it was impossible for her to put them down upon paper. And then she had a vague sense of its not being a woman's business to write. One thing she was quite sure of, that no woman had ever attained to the dignity of a quarto edition in morocco, much less in Russia leather, and any dignity beneath this would not have been worth striving for.

So Myra listened, and studied, and thought, and gave way to her temper, and selfishness, and vanity, and was a child in her own estimation, and a very troublesome and disagreeable one in the estimation of her friends ; because she had not yet learnt the truth which, sooner or later, must come home to us all, that the moral powers are the multipliers of the intellectual —that the cleverest man, or the most gifted genius, unable to govern his own temper, and control his own impulses, is, so far as he yields himself to those impulses, nothing better than an infant ; and that in the race of life he will most certainly be outstripped by men far inferior to himself in mental capacity, but able to keep the balance which he has lost, and to exemplify those deep words of Scripture—' He that ruleth his spirit is greater than he that taketh a city.'

But a new phase of inward existence was dawning upon Myra.

We all have granted us, from time to time, fresh starting-points in life ; but there is not one so marked as that which is associated with our first vivid apprehension of the fact that God loves us. Men call this apprehension by different names; they attach to it different degrees of importance. This is not the place for entering upon such a controverted subject ; but one thing is known and acknowledged by all alike, that to confess such a belief by the lips is one thing, and to receive it into the heart another ; that in the one case it is a mere formula, whilst in the other it becomes the most powerful of all motives—the one all-embracing principle which meets every difficulty and every temptation in life. Myra Cameron did not hear Mrs. Patty's declaration of her religious creed for the first time in that one conversation after her illness ; she had been told the same truths often before, as applying to mankind generally, but it had always seemed as if some special exception had been made to her own disadvantage. When a very little child, she was assured that God loved good children ; but the assurance was always accompanied by the reminder that she was a very naughty one. It was as if a mirror was continually being held before her, in which she might see her own misdeeds ; and her poor little weak efforts to do better were not perceptible amidst the mass of evil ; or if sometimes it crossed her mind that she was not quite so bad as people thought her, that when she was alone she did wish to be good, though when she was with others she was always doing wrong, her comfort was checked by the recollection that wishes were nothing, prayers even were nothing, actions were the only test; and her actions—it was better not to think about them.

What comfort could it be to Myra to be called upon to repeat, Sunday after Sunday, that she was 'a child of grace,' when the fact impressed upon her by every one in the house, and confirmed by her own consciousness, was that she was 'a child of wrath ? '

People do not often get rid of such an impression about themselves suddenly ; young people especially do not. Myra felt when Mrs. Patty left her that she was not quite so unhappy as she had been before, but she had no idea that there was any real change in her own principles. It was only that Mrs. Patty was so good and kind, and thought well of every one ; and if she could believe that God would be as merciful as Mrs. Patty, there would be some hope. But then He knew so much better what her faults were. To be sure He knew also how miserable they made her, and how much she longed to get rid of them ; but that was all nothing ; her father had said so only that very day, before he went off to London, and of course he knew much more about her than Mrs. Patty.

Thus Myra tried to reason herself out of comfort, and in spite of her reason was comforted. The mere thought that some one believed she could do right, was like a strengthening cordial to her crushed spirit. For this last failure and folly had completely crushed her. Pride alone rendered her ashamed of herself, and her natural morbid shrinking from observation caused the thought of the remarks which would, she was sure, be made upon her, to be almost unendurable. But for Mrs. Patty's few words, Myra would have been

despairingly wretched.   As it was, she lay still, trying to recall
the conversation ; and finding herself unable to recollect all,
she turned, as an assistance to her memory, to the epistle
which Mrs. Patty had said was Dr. Kingsbury's favourite.
Certainly, so Myra thought, if he liked it, it could have
nothing to do with her, for he was standing on the highest
pinnacle of perfection, whilst she had not even begun to
ascend the lowest step of the ladder which led to it ; but, at
any rate, there would be some interest in reading it, and people
were always told to read the Bible when they were ill.

Myra read ; and as she read, thought of Dr. Kingsbury and
Mrs. Patty, and, for the first time, the words excited her
imagination—that imagination which was always ready to be
worked upon by stirring descriptions or appeals to the heart.
They carried her into far-off worlds,—the heavenly places,
which, it might be, were to be found among the stars that
night after night she was accustomed to watch as she lay in
bed.   They told of glory, and greatness, and power ; of a
dominion above all other dominion ; of the ' exceeding riches
of God's grace ;' and of those who, from being ' strangers and
foreigners,' were now ' fellow-citizens with the saints and of the
household of God.'   Myra laid down the book, for she was
weary, and much there was which it was hard to understand ;
but as she closed her eyes, and thought became more and more
an effort, there mingled with the recollection of the words she
had been reading, others—sounding as their clear and most
sweet echo—which brought faint visions of a golden city, and
jewelled gates, and the river of the water of life ; and Myra
fell asleep.

CHAPTER IX.

'DR. AND MISS KINGSBURY'S compliments, ma'am, and if you are going to Colonel Verney's they will call for you at twenty minutes past six, and give you a seat in their fly.'

Faith put her head in at the door of Miss Medley's parlour, and surprised that lady in the act of taking off her cap and arranging her grey curls.

'Wait a minute! dear me!' (Miss Medley's eye sought for her cap in the far corner of the room), 'where can it be? On the floor? In the chair? Where can I have put it? One minute, Faith! On my head, to be sure! What shall I do next? Come in; pray come in.' Faith entered—so far at least as she could, whilst still holding by the handle of the door.

'Please to shut the door, Faith; draughts are so dangerous. Twenty minutes past six, did you say? It is very kind of Dr. Kingsbury. I really think I must accept the benevolent offer. But is the Doctor well enough to dine out?'

'He is better than he has been for this month past, ma'am. He has been ordered to take a little brandy with his dinner, and it does him a world of good.'

'Alas! A man so excellent! not to perceive the necessity of abstaining, if only for example's sake. But it is like all men; quick as lightning to see others' duties, slow as snails to see their own. Dinner parties are sad temptations, Faith.'

'To be sure, ma'am. May I tell the Doctor, then, that you mean to go?'

'You may assure him I will be ready. Time was, Faith, when I avoided dinner-parties, but it is different with me now. So it would be with the good Doctor if only he would persevere. But brandy! it is very sad—very sad indeed.' Faith compressed her lips, evidently not trusting herself to reply. Miss Medley continued—'The Doctor, I suppose, will leave early; late hours are so very injurious.'

'The Doctor and Mrs. Patty most times leave at ten, ma'am; but somebody said there was like to be some dancing at the Colonel's to-night.'

'What! with the Doctor there! O Faith! indeed you must be mistaken!'

'As to that, ma'am, I don't know why I should be. I've heard Mrs. Patty say, that in his young days the Doctor could show off in a hornpipe with the best, and, indeed, danced so well that he was had out before all the company at a dancing-school ball, and did the toe-and-heel step and the shuffle in a way as was quite surprising.'

'But not now, Faith; Dr. Kingsbury has to consider the dignity of his cloth.'

Faith's countenance showed a little perplexity, as she replied: 'Well, to be sure, I did think of that myself! The Doctor's coat is just new, and dancing is very dusty work; and it did come across me that the brushing and rubbing afterwards wouldn't be good for it. But if I could be quite sure, ma'am, that dancing was to be, I'd persuade Mrs. Patty to give him his second-best; he doesn't know one from the other, good man, himself.'

'And so far he is an exception to his sex. Men are vain, Faith—much more vain than we have any idea of. I have a nephew, who used to spend half an hour every day arranging his neck-tie: but he is in India, poor fellow!' and Miss Medley sighed heavily. 'Dr. Kingsbury, you say, will leave before the dancing begins?'

'Dear me, ma'am, no; just the contrary. He takes pleasure in seeing the young people merry: and it's my belief, that if the dancing is late, he may be late too.'

The possibility was so alarming to Miss Medley's regularity, that she found herself compelled to sit down; and as Faith turned, apparently with the intention of going, she said, in a hurried tone: 'Pray wait—one moment only; I won't detain you, but I must consider. If the fly were to come for me first, if I were to return alone—eighteenpence they would charge—it would be eighteenpence, I think, Faith?'

'I can't say, ma'am; but the Doctor would be very sorry

for you to trouble yourself upon such a matter as that. He
and Mrs. Patty would be sure to let you come away whenever
you choose. It's not like the Doctor to be putting his own
pleasure in the way of other people's.'

'Not at all. He is a very remarkable instance of masculine
unselfishness. You will appreciate such an exception more
and more, Faith, as life brings you experience. But this matter
of returning—it may be better to leave it. Possibly——You
said, I think, Faith, that there would be a large number of
dancers ? '

'I don't know that I said anything about it, ma'am; but
there's Mr. Charles, the Colonel's nephew, just come from
India, and the young gentlemen, Master John and Master
William, home for Easter—that makes three ; and then there's
Mr. Edmund and Mr. Godfrey Cameron come down to the
Hall—so I heard just before I came in here ; and what with the
Miss Verneys, and the niece who is there for the holidays, and
Miss Cameron, and the other young ladies as are sure to be asked
to the Colonel's—there will be such a number of young folks
that Mrs. Patty said to me, as she gave me the message for
you, they would be pretty nearly certain to dance ; and if they
did, the Doctor had such a fancy for music, and for seeing
the young folks enjoy themselves, he'd be sure to be late.
That's the long and the short of the matter, ma'am : but to
think of its coming in your way never entered anybody's head ;
and I make bold to say you can leave at half-past nine if you
wish it.'

'Oh no, Faith ! To break up the party—I could not do
that. And I should like to see Mr. Verney. I am deeply
interested in everything connected with India : yet it perplexes
me. Are you going into the village ? '

'I've been thinking of it, ma'am ; but I had not quite
decided.'

'If you were going,—perhaps four yards of ribbon, peach-
coloured satin—or gauze and satin might be best ;—Lane has
some, I know ;—it would brighten my cap. I am not used to
gay parties, Faith ; and they don't agree with me. But camo-
milla is very soothing : it enables me to do many things now

which I never could do before: I never go anywhere without it.' Miss Medley dived into her pocket and took out a tiny bottle. 'Tinctures are best; but in their absence, globules.'

It was like presenting a pocket-pistol to Faith : she turned suddenly round, and, with a hasty 'Good morning, ma'am ; I will leave the ribbon as I return,' departed.

Stormont was the name of Colonel Verney's house. It was a mile and a half from Yare, and was considered rather the show-place of the neighbourhood ; for it had a grand hall, a very fair gallery of pictures, and a museum of Chinese curiosities, all exhibited to the public on certain days. Otherwise it was an uninteresting place, with but a few acres of park about it, and possessing no remarkable beauty either in the grounds, the gardens, or the view.

Colonel Verney was the most open-hearted and hospitable of country gentlemen ; in politics a Whig—so far, at least, as Whiggism can still be considered to exist ; in religion a professed Churchman, with as kindly a leaning towards dissent as was necessary for the sake of consistency with his political creed. He was a very popular man in the neighbourhood ; indeed all the family were popular, except, perhaps, Mrs. Verney, and she was an exception only in the eyes of a few persons, amongst whom Myra was included. Mr. Cameron and Colonel Verney differed in politics, and this antagonism might have resulted in an open feud, had not the punctilious politeness of the former served as a check upon the ebullitions of temper of his good-natured though irritable opponent. Mr. Cameron was once heard to say to his boys, when, after an open fight and very abusive language, they were brought before him to be punished : 'Quarrel, boys, if you will : at your age I did it myself; but quarrel like gentlemen.' A very worldly-wise man was Mr. Cameron. This principle of quarrelling like a gentleman had served him in good stead on many trying occasions, and none more trying than when he was brought into open opposition to his nearest neighbour, Colonel Verney. One of the very few boasts which he had ever been heard to utter was, that throughout the many electioneering and magisterial contests in which they had been engaged, he had never uttered a word for which he could be called upon to make an apology.

Not so Colonel Verney ; his words were hasty, his language strong, his epithets far from choice. He prided himself upon saying what he thought, it was the privilege of a free Englishman ; but then, unfortunately, he very often said what he did not think, and it was on such occasions that Mr. Cameron gained the advantage. 'I leave to Colonel Verney the command of words, and reserve to myself the command of temper,' was his reply to a very violent speech made by the former at an important public meeting : and the Colonel succumbed to the sarcasm, and not being gifted with that most rare and noble characteristic, the power of owning that he had been wrong, never recovered the ground he had lost, nor was again able to hold a position in the county of equal influence with that of Mr. Cameron.

The two Miss Verneys, or, as Miss Medley always took pains to call them, the Misses Verney, were bright and pleasant in manner, and partook of much of their father's goodnature. Henrietta, who was about one-and-twenty, was the useful— Elise, who was three years younger, the ornamental—sister. And there were, as Faith had said, two brothers at Eton, rather commonplace, but perhaps all the more likely to be favourites in general society, since they excited no envy and aroused no criticism. Colonel Verney's family might, indeed, have been a pattern of prosperous ease and self-content if only Mrs. Verney would have consented to leave it to itself; but the elements of ambition and energy which were wanting in her children existed strongly in herself. The world, her own little world especially, was regarded by her not as it was, but as it should be. She had an ideal for everything and everybody, and, unlike the generality of idealists, she spared no efforts to convert her fiction into a reality. Good, sensible, rather blunt Henrietta, essentially practical and matter-of-fact, was to be the deep-thinking studious daughter ; and pretty bright little Elise, with her rather sentimental drawl, and taste for flower-painting and English ballads, was to be the graceful and artistic one. Both were treated accordingly. And so with all her

friends. To hear Mrs. Verney converse, it might have been
supposed that she lived in the midst of the most peculiar and
attractive specimens of her fellow-creatures. Such germs of
genius, and thought, and beauty, and taste were to be discovered amongst them; only all requiring development, and
that not in the course of God's Providence, in the ordering o
their lives, but from her own especial dictation. The Stormont neighbourhood, with some few exceptions, such as Dr.
Kingsbury, Mrs. Patty, and Myra, submitted to this dictation.
All neighbourhoods will in course of time submit to any dictation, if it is accompanied by a little flattery. How, for instance,
could Mrs. Cameron resist Mrs. Verney's influence in her
family arrangements, when she was always hinting to her that
she had a susceptible poetical temperament, and that her
indolence was the reaction of intense feeling jarred upon by
the roughnesses of life? Mrs. Cameron quite fell in love with
herself as she lay on her sofa, pondering upon the vision
which Mrs. Verney had presented to her. And the generality
of Mrs. Verney's friends were equally self-enamoured. Even
Mr. Cameron had been surprised with the consciousness of his
'self-sustained, elevated individuality' (Mrs. Verney delighted
in long words), and had learned to regard himself as an obelisk
of virtue, and, in consequence, bore from Mr. Verney observations and suggestions which would not have been tolerated for
a moment from any other person.

Mrs. Verney was just now on a pinnacle of happiness. She
had a new specimen of human nature on which to make dis-
coveries, a new mind to develop, that of her nephew,—the
son of her husband's elder brother,—who had been left an
orphan at an early age, and having been sent to India, had
returned on account of his health. Report said that Mr.
Verney's career had not been very satisfactory; but report
is proverbially ill-natured, and Mrs. Verney rejoiced in con-
tradicting it. A man holding a civil appointment in India
ought to be highly intelligent, therefore her nephew must be
remarkably clever; and not only clever, but his mind would
certainly be well balanced,—strictly just. He would have en-
larged views of human nature generally. He might have a

taste for luxury and magnificence ; and as he had lived in the
constant sight of diamonds and rubies, gold tissue and embroi-
dered shawls, he could not be expected to tolerate the poverty
of our English style of dress and ornament ; but with this
fastidiousness, he would be extremely lavish and even princely
in his generosity. Mr. Verney might indeed be expected to
appear in the character of a munificent genius, scattering
blessings on all sides. Mrs. Verney had so often said all this
to herself, and so often repeated it to others before her nephew
arrived, that she did at last actually believe it ; and if any one
had ventured to throw a doubt on her assertion, she would
have sighed over 'that painful tendency to censoriousness,
which must always endeavour to detract from excellence, however evident and acknowledged.'

But, notwithstanding all this romance, the drawing-room at
Stormont Park did not present any features of unusual interest
when, on the day fixed for the dinner-party, and precisely as
the hands of the French clock over the mantelpiece pointed to
half-past six, Dr. and Miss Kingsbury and Miss Medley were
announced. The room, not a very large one, and rather
crowded with tables and fancy chairs and tiny ottomans, was
nearly full. Colonel Verney was standing in the recess of the
window talking to Mr. Cameron ; and Mr. Baines and two or
three other gentlemen were congregated near, whilst the ladies
had collected in a circle round the fire, which was pronounced
scarcely needed, but very pleasant to look at. They had
scarcely advanced beyond this fact, because it was necessarily
stated upon every fresh arrival, and, indeed, was the only
remark which a nervous lady could venture to make upon
being brought suddenly into contact with the circle of wide-
spreading dresses which half-filled the room. When the
friends whom we are accustomed to see in dark, high, close-
fitting gowns, appear before us arrayed in silks made to stand
alone, and muslins of the colours of the rainbow, inflated to
the size of a balloon, to say nothing of ribbons, jewels, and
feathers—the transformation, however we may have been
prepared for it, must always have somewhat of a subduing
effect upon the spirits ; and the only person who in this in-

stance appeared thoroughly at her ease was Mrs. Patty, who
had forgotten the time when she wore low dresses, and considered her Sunday gown all that was needed for any party.

'So glad to see you, dear Mrs. Patty,' said Mrs. Verney,
as she held out both her hands. 'You know I consider it a
privilege to have you with us. So seldom as you leave your
home nest, and those absorbing duties! It is quite a privilege!—And Miss Medley, too. I could not have asked you
out, knowing your delicate fragile state, only I was sure you
would be interested. My dear Doctor, my nephew longs to
see you. He looks to your advice for the furtherance of his
benevolent schemes for India.'

'He will consult some one who knows something about the
matter, if he takes my advice,' said the Doctor shortly. 'Is
your nephew here, Mrs. Verney?' and Dr. Kingsbury looked
round the room.

'He will be here in a moment. He is so accustomed
to order everything his own way, that I think he scarcely
recognises the necessity of an observance of our English rules
of society.'

'By which I suppose you mean that he is always late for
dinner,' said Dr. Kingsbury, laughing. 'Young men learn to
be that without going to India.—How do you do, my dear?'
—he turned away from Mrs. Verney and addressed Rosamond
Cameron, who was sitting, rather hidden by a screen, which the
Doctor in his haste to speak nearly upset.

Catharine Verney, who was opposite, showed her school-
girl ill-breeding by a laugh, but Rosamond caught the screen,
and then stood up and continued standing whilst Dr. Kingsbury was speaking to her. It was very respectful, and
Rosamond looked so pretty and interesting with her hand
resting upon the mantelpiece and slightly leaning forward in
a deferential attitude, Dr. Kingsbury was quite attracted by
her.

'And your two brothers are with you, my dear, are they
not?' he asked. 'They are quite strangers in this part of the
world.' Dr. Kingsbury looked round the room, but his eyesight was bad, and he could not see them.

'Yes, both came the day before yesterday, and are to stay with us some little time,' was the reply. 'Godfrey! Edmund!' Rosamond's gentle voice could not be heard amidst the murmurs of the group of gentlemen, and it was only courtesy to put aside her chair, and draw a little nearer so as to try and attract the attention of her brothers. If they did not hear, Mr. Baines did, and had the satisfaction of receiving—in answer to his bow of recognition—one of Rosamond's very sweetest smiles. But she had no thought to give to him, none at all: she was such a very affectionate sister, and these two brothers were such treasures!

'Godfrey, Dr. Kingsbury is asking for you.' Godfrey came up directly. He was very good-looking. He had his father's cut features, and a good deal of his father's manner, only without stiffness. How should a young man with such prospects at the bar, such knowledge of the world (including a bowing acquaintance with some of the leading men of the day), who had a fund of law anecdotes at command, and could argue upon remarkable cases with gentlemen, and talk about music and the opera with ladies, be stiff? The only difficulty with Godfrey Cameron was to prevent other persons from being stiff and ill at ease with him. He really did not intend to dazzle them with his brilliancy; he always tried to imagine that every one, like himself, knew everything, but it was impossible to prevent the ignorance which was nearly universal from appearing now and then in a way which was awkward. He came up to Dr. Kingsbury instantly, with his most beaming gracious manner. The Doctor was an old friend, and Godfrey liked old friends, especially those who lived in the country, and whom he could gratify without effort by the exhibition of his talents.

'I meant to have called upon you, sir, yesterday, but they told me you were ill and rheumatic, and I was afraid of being scolded by Mrs. Patty. But you are better, I hope, as I see you here?'

'I can't say much for being better,' replied the Doctor. 'I believe I should have been wiser if I had stayed at home. But Patty said I was to come, and I came.'

'The influence of the ladies!' exclaimed Godfrey. 'It is the same everywhere, sir. I was talking about it to Rigby the other day—you know Rigby, of course, a quick-witted fellow, just made Queen's Counsel, but superficial,—decidedly superficial.'

'They tell me that all classes are superficial now,' said the Doctor.

'Well, it is so. It is a painful fact, but there is no denying it. To give you an instance—just one; I could give you hundreds. A man brought his son to me the other day to be examined. He wanted to have a notion of his general abilities; in fact, he desired me to see what he was fit for; and I tried the boy. I went through the elements of Euclid and put him upon Lyell's geology; then I tested him as to the theories of ethnology and comparative philology; and at last, when I found he really knew nothing, I asked him a mere simple geographical question—what was the distance from the North Cape to Timbuctoo? Would you believe it?—he was completely floored. Of course I gave in then, and advised his father to send him to the colonies.'

'I should be interested to know myself what the distance is,' said the Doctor, with perfect simplicity.

'Excuse me, my dear sir, you mistake. The answer was the boy's business, not mine. Do you want a practical illustration of the art of questioning? Edmund '—he touched his brother on the shoulder, and the young officer, a great contrast to Godfrey, for he had a square figure, and a plain though honest face, not yet shrouded in moustaches and whiskers, turned round.

'Tell us, will you, what was the plan of Wellington's defences at Torres Vedras? Now, sir, there is a question which I put, but which my brother will be required to answer; I leave him in your hands.' And Godfrey walked off, just as the door opened and Mr. Verney entered the room.

The defences of Torres Vedras were, happily for Edmund Cameron, forgotten in the little stir which followed. Mr. Verney was the hero of the party, all the more of a hero because the dinner had been kept waiting till he appeared. Yet he was not a hero in appearance : he was tall, thin, and middle-aged ; there was nothing in the least martial or striking in him, and his face was one about which it would have been difficult to make a remark, except that it was not handsome, and that the eyes were grey. Rosamond glanced at him, and then sat down and began talking to Elise Verney. Edmund Cameron took advantage of the opportunity to remove as far as possible from Dr. Kingsbury, fearing, no doubt, lest Torres Vedras should again be brought upon the *tapis ;* whilst the Doctor moved forward, as quickly as his rheumatic infirmities would allow, and begged to shake hands with the nephew of his old friend.

' A very intellectual face, you must allow,' whispered Mrs. Verney to Miss Medley, who was seated beside her on the sofa. ' Do you observe that peculiarly quiet movement of the limbs ? The whole being is equally balanced, and there is such an air of thought ;—you see it even in the complexion, in the absence of colour, or any flush of excitement.'

' Mr. Verney looks as if India had not quite agreed with him,' said Miss Medley. ' I should like to have a little conversation with him. Perhaps he may have known my nephew, and there are many interesting facts connected with the hospital treatment, which I should like to ask him about.'

' He will be able to give you any information you may require, I have no doubt,' replied Mrs. Verney. ' It is a mind which gathers as it goes, and that insensibly ; but you would like an introduction—'

Dinner on the table ! Introductions and conversations were cut short ; and following each other, according to some theory of Mrs. Verney's, which no one but herself seemed to understand, since all appeared bent upon doing exactly what they ought not, the party moved into the dining-room.

Rosamond found herself seated with Dr. Kingsbury on one side, and Mr. Baines on the other ; Mr. Verney was opposite. It was a good position for studying a stranger, but she could not make up her mind that there was anything worth studying in Mr. Verney, except his quietness, and a slight air of melancholy, which possibly might have something to do with his bilious complexion. She tried in the intervals of the parochial talk with Mr. Baines, which was the style she always adopted with him when wishing to attend to something else, to hear what Mr. Verney was saying; but he had such a low voice, it was impossible to catch more than a few words, and his manner gave the impression of his being weary. It was very vexatious to Rosamond, for it made the dinner dull. If she had been left to amuse herself with Mr. Baines, it might have been all very well; but to be distracted with watching Mr. Verney was too tiresome. Suddenly, however,—the consciousness came upon her, just as she had roused herself to a little exciting banter with the young curate,—Mr. Verney's voice was heard more distinctly; he was addressing Dr. Kingsbury, and the Doctor was leaning forward with an air of attention; Mr. Cameron also was listening. Mr. Verney, singularly enough, had gained the attention of the table, though Godfrey Cameron was attempting a diversion at the other end by a loud argument with Elise Verney upon the comparative merits of Italian bravuras and English ballads

'You say, sir, that the future of India depends upon its colonisation more than its Christianity, if I understand you rightly?' said Dr. Kingsbury. The words were accompanied by a little impatience of manner, which might have been caused by his deafness, or his disagreement from the principle enunciated.

Mr. Verney repeated his statement with a kind of indolent gentleness of tone, but his glance went rapidly round the table.

'Charles had a quarrel with the missionaries,' said Colonel Verney. 'Indeed, I never heard that at any time there was much love lost between them and the Civil Service.'

Mr. Cameron remarked sententiously that the government of India had done wisely in allowing the missionary work to develop its own features. The duty of government was, in all cases, to guide rather than to create.

Mr. Verney seemed to weigh the observation, and then he spoke, rather slowly at first, but becoming rapid as he grew interested.

'He quite agreed with Mr. Cameron ; it was the principle which, if he might be allowed to speak of himself, he had always advocated, and upon which he had always acted.' And then he went on to give illustrations of its practical working. He told of what he had himself seen, of the intercourse which he had held with the natives ; and in answer to a question of Dr. Kingsbury's, he became more distinct in his description of the various races ; tracing their numerous divisions, their religious and geographical distinctions, giving a great deal of new and important information upon points on which almost all present were ignorant. The original question was quite lost in the variety of topics introduced, and not one of which was left by Mr. Verney, without some notice worthy of being treasured in the memory. And this without the least effort, or endeavour to engage or retain attention, but rather like a man who has to rouse himself from some physical disinclination to conversation ; but who speaks because he feels that he is called upon to please others. Dr. Kingsbury was no longer impatient, and not at all inclined to be argumentative. Mr. Cameron, in a very well-set sentence, expressed his satisfaction. Mrs. Verney again repeated to Miss Medley—'Such a mind and such thought !' Miss Medley murmured to Mrs. Patty, 'If men could but act as they talk, my dear Mrs. Patty ; but alas !' whilst Mrs. Patty in reply observed, 'It seems to me, my dear Miss Medley, that we might all gain a good deal from what we hear if we could only understand it ; and I dare say the young folks do ; but you know I am a little deaf, which must be my excuse for not taking it in properly.'

And all this time Mr. Verney's dinner was apparently such a secondary consideration, that it was nearly forgotten. Happily the Indian conversation had begun rather late, so that it was carried on with the greatest energy at dessert. But first, second, and third courses, wine or dessert, seemed equally indifferent to Mr. Verney, who took or refused what came before him with an absent air, which was very imposing, and slightly rebuking to persons who, like Mr. Cameron and Colonel Verney, were conscious that, to them, dinner was a very important affair.

'India has spoilt your appetite, Charles,' said the latter,

after listening to a succession of noes, quite dispiriting to a host on hospitable thoughts intent. 'We would have ordered curry and mulligatawny, only you Indians are so particular, you never will touch them unless they are cooked in your own particular fashion.'

'Thank you, but I have rather given up eating lately,' was Mr. Verney's answer; and as though annoyed at having attracted observation, he addressed a paradoxical remark to Dr. Kingsbury, which brought a decidedly argumentative reply, and the conversation was carried on as brilliantly as ever. The good Doctor grew highly excited. He was hearing principles laid down incidentally, to which he could by no means yield consent; but when, according to his wont, he attempted to stop the fluent speaker with 'Stay; let me understand; you think so and so,' he found himself blown off, as it were, by a puff of repeated assertion, ending with, 'My dear sir, excuse me, but first principles must be assumed; if you had been in India, you would know that I am correct;' and away went Mr. Verney again; the Doctor, eager to follow him, lest he should lose something important, yet longing to stop and treasure up in his memory the points open to dispute, that he might have them all out, as he would have expressed it, on another occasion. It was an amusing scene at last, for the conversation was left in the hands of the two who were all but combatants. Rosamond's attention was fully gained; she turned from one to the other, and every now and then laughed gaily with that sweet, soft, yet clear laugh, which is heard so rarely, but which, when it is heard, rings on the ear like music. Mr. Verney answered the laugh by addressing her, so as to bring her into the conversation; and Dr. Kingsbury, who always accepted even a child as a fit subject for explanation and argument, seized upon her in order to state his views to a person who, at least, would listen to them. Rosamond was most deferential, quiet, and interested then; she looked prepared to discourse upon Indian politics with the Governor-General, but— a most untimely interruption—Mrs. Verney from the top of the table bowed to Mrs. Cameron at the bottom, and all opportunity for Rosamond to shine forth in her new character was lost.

Yet the effects of that momentary display of interest were not quite lost. About three-quarters of an hour afterwards the gentlemen appeared in the drawing-room, Mr. Verney being one of the first. The array of ladies had in the meantime been increased by the addition of the three young daughters of Mr. Harrison, the surgeon, who were chaperoned by their governess. Catharine Verney also, who had retired before dinner, not being considered old enough to dine at table, was again stationed at the comfortable sofa-corner, and the boys, who in like manner had been exiled to the schoolroom, had reappeared. The party was just such as would be likely to enjoy an impromptu quadrille, and Mrs. Verney proposed it. Mr. Verney escaped from his aunt just as she was about to introduce him to Miss Medley, and walked across the room to Rosamond with a languid step and the air of a martyr.

'Miss Cameron, may I have the gratification of hearing your opinion upon India in the interstices of a quadrille? I am not likely to have the opportunity in any other way.'

Rosamond was properly humble, and yet dignified. 'She knew nothing about India, but she would be happy to dance a quadrille, if they were really going to dance.'

A glance showed her that Mr. Baines was standing near, and she immediately addressed him : 'Mr. Baines, I am always so sorry for you when dancing begins ; I know you don't think it clerical.'

'Not quite, Miss Cameron ; but I am very happy, I assure you. It is too good of you to waste your pity upon me.'

Rosamond smiled still more kindly, and Mr. Verney, as he led her to the top of the quadrille, said carelessly, 'Too good indeed ; you don't know the value of your pity, Miss Cameron.'

The tone was doubtful. It might have been that Mr. Verney intended to be sarcastic ; but, if he did, he had no opportunity given him, for he was instantly taxed with a question about India, which compelled him to leave the region of personalities for that of politics. He made several efforts to escape, for his former zest on the subject was evidently gone, but Rosamond mercilessly drew him back to it ; till at last, as he led her to a

seat, after the quadrille was ended, he said, ' I shall think you
are preparing for the office of Governor-General, if you persist
in this thirst for information. Do you really never talk about
anything but politics and government ? '

' Sometimes ; when I am quite sure of the sympathy of the
person with whom I am conversing,' was the reply ; and before
Mr. Verney could seize upon the opening thus given him, Rosamond had turned away from him, and was insisting upon having
a galop with young Harry Verney. Mr. Verney retired to an
arm-chair in the corner, and watched the scene with the quietly
amused, but slightly melancholy air of a man of forty, whilst
two or three of the young girls, delighting in the absence of
formality, danced together merrily.

' Now, that is what I call pretty,' said Miss Medley, who,
having failed in her purpose of being introduced to Mr. Verney,
and discussing homœopathy with him, had thrust herself forward so as to intercept Mrs. Patty's view of the dancers ; her
peach-coloured ribbons waving, as she nodded her head to keep
time to the music. ' It is just what it should be,—dancing for
dancing's sake. What do you say, Doctor ? '

The Doctor's attention was absolutely engrossed. He had
almost a childish pleasure in graceful and rhythmical movement.

' You will do best not to interrupt him,' said Mrs. Patty ,
' he says that looking at dancing is to him like reading his old
Greek poetry books.'

' And Mrs. Cameron is so good-natured in playing, and
keeps such excellent time,' said Miss Medley. ' It is a pity,
though, that she can't see her own eldest girl.'

' Not hers,' replied Mrs. Patty ; ' Myra is her eldest.'

' Oh yes ! Myra—I forgot ; but I always put her aside, she
is so unlike the rest ; much more of her father in her ; now,
don't you think so, Mrs. Patty? Just that kind of odd, shut-up
way about her—the man's way, in fact ; nothing open-hearted
and woman-like, and get-on-able with.'

Mrs. Patty was a little quick in her reply : ' I don't think
that we know what any young girl, or young boy either is, or
is likely to be, till time proves it, Miss Medley ; and so I

would rather say nothing, except that poor little Myra has a vast deal of good about her.'

'Oh! no doubt; and it is not like a boy, with whom there are ten chances to one against his turning out good for any-thing; with a girl, as you say, there is hope always. But you must own, Mrs. Patty, that Rosamond Cameron shuts her sisters out like sunlight.'

'She is a good deal older,' said Mrs. Patty.

'Oh! but she was always the same from a baby; she never was like others. Such clean frocks as she always had! And now, just look, isn't she sweet?'

Rosamond was standing with her arms round Catharine Verney's waist, upon the point apparently of setting off on a polka, as soon as the set of whirling couples should give them a good opportunity of joining them. Mr. Verney was on a sofa near, and whilst they were waiting, she was talking to him. He was remonstrating against ladies dancing together, and Rosamond was insisting that it was quite allowable and very pleasant. There was a pretty, patronising, protecting air about her, as she called upon Catharine to support her, and strenuously refused Mr. Verney's proposal to be her partner, saying that she was already engaged.

'She is so simple and good-natured,' said Miss Medley; 'that is what I admire in her.'

'But I should like to know what she is at now,' was Mrs. Patty's reply, spoken in a very absent tone. She waited for a few moments more, and then went up to her brother; 'Doctor, dear,'—the Doctor started—'we ordered the fly at half-past ten, and Miss Medley won't like to be late.'

'Oh! not for me; don't think about me, pray. I am fore-armed—protected; I wish you were the same. A little camo-milla does such wonders in quieting the system.'

'Those little girls won't have had enough of it till midnight,' said the Doctor, not moving his eyes from the dancers. 'But, Patty, I think I am tired.'

'To be sure you are, Doctor, dear; you ought to be in bed.'

'I should like to see Rosamond Cameron go round once more, though,' he continued.

'He is bewitched with her, like all the rest,' muttered Mrs. Patty to herself; and then she said aloud, 'Why, if you wait for that, Doctor, you may wait another hour. Don't you see she is talking to Mr. Verney?'

'Yes, certainly, but they are going off again. Only——Miss Medley, I beg your pardon,' and the Doctor seemed to wake up from a dream, and put up his hand and twisted his wig; 'It is a very strange thing—a very singular thing, that sense of rhythm. I should like to know Mr. Verney's opinion as to how far it is inherent in the Indian races; whether any similarity exists between them and the Greeks in this respect. Indo-European—there ought to be.'

'Doctor, dear, shall we ask for the carriage?'

'Certainly, Patty; I beg Miss Medley's pardon. No doubt Mr. Verney will give me the opportunity of discussing upon this topic. Do you think, Patty, they will ever stop?'

'You can make your way by the fire-place, Doctor; let me go before you.' Miss Medley placed herself as a guard between the dancers and the infirm Doctor, who, accompanied by Mrs. Patty, went round to every one, and wished a kindly and individual 'Good night.'

His move was the signal for a general dispersion. Mr. Cameron and Colonel Verney, who had been deep in controversy of some kind, were roused to the knowledge that it was growing late, and Mr. Baines had long before torn himself away.

'You will allow me, sir, to see you to your carriage, before I inquire for my own,' said Mr. Cameron, as Dr. Kingsbury came up to him.

'By no means, sir, would I give you that trouble, but I thank you heartily. Patty, where did I leave my stick?'

'In the hall, Doctor; we shall find it when we go downstairs. Good night, Mr. Cameron. I hope you and the Colonel have been having a pleasant friendly talk; you have been long at it.'

Mr. Cameron shrunk into himself and bowed; whilst the Colonel exclaimed—'Not one whit friendly, I am afraid, Mrs. Patty; Mr. Cameron is on the opposition bench, and likely to remain there, unless your influence can bring him round. We were discussing the Idiot Asylum, and the new regulations.'

'Oh! the Idiot Asylum. Dear me, I quite forgot! Mr. Cameron, I must, please, have your votes; you will promise me?'

'Pardon me, I never promise without investigation; but Miss Kingsbury's protégés will always have a claim to consideration. Good night!' and there was another polite bow, and Mrs. Patty and the Doctor moved on and at length escaped, not only from Mr. Cameron, but Mr. Verney, who was apparently too weary to do more than smile at the proposal made by the old man to discuss the characteristics of the Indian and Greek races on the earliest occasion.

Mr. Verney was not, however, too weary to offer his arm to Rosamond when she went downstairs; and not too absent to remind her of the topics which she had said she was always willing to discuss with persons who sympathised with her, and about which he begged for some information. Rosamond's reply was an appeal to Mrs. Cameron, who was close by her side.

'Mamma, what should you say was my favourite pursuit — the thing which most interested me? Is it drawing or music?'

'You have a taste for both, my dear; but what a strange question just now!'

'Only Mr. Verney wished to know what were the things I most cared for, and I felt doubtful how to reply; and one does not wish to be conceited,' she added, with child-like frankness.

'That was not an answer to my question,' said Mr. Verney, in a low voice, as he handed her into the carriage.

And Rosamond laughed lightly, and answered, 'I think the history of India is more in your way.'

DR. KINGSBURY was busy in his study, in the morning of the next day, looking over some school accounts, when Mrs. Patty appeared, dragging rather than ushering in Myra, who looked pale, weary, and uncommonly shy.

'I have brought a young visitor to see you, Doctor; one you will be very glad to say "How d'ye do" to. Sit down, dear child, and Faith shall bring you a glass of wine and a bit of cake—nice plain seedcake.'

'Oh no, thank you!' exclaimed Myra; 'I could not eat anything; but it is so hot, and I am afraid—Mrs. Patty said she was sure I might come, sir; but I knew I should disturb you.'

The Doctor had been slowly preparing for the meeting, putting aside his pen and paper, and rising with some difficulty from his chair. As Myra came close to him he put his hand upon her head and said, 'God bless you, child! Patty tells me you have been very ill.' And then he bent down and kissed her forehead, and looking intently into her face, added kindly, 'Patty must look after you, and not let you be tired.'

'It was her own will to come,' said Mrs. Patty. 'I thought it might be almost too long a walk; but she did so want to see you.'

'An old man's study can have nothing very attractive to a young thing like you,' said the Doctor, reseating himself, and turning his chair so as to give Myra his full attention.

'I like it,' said Myra; 'and it seemed so long since I was here.'

'And you have been ill,' observed the Doctor; 'illness makes time seem long to us.'

'You see, Myra, that the notes to St. Augustine are going on still,' said Mrs. Patty.

'And are not much nearer the end, I am afraid,' observed the Doctor.

'I should like to understand it,' said Myra; 'if it was in English, might I read it?'

'Surely, my child; that is, some portions. But you would do better to read it in Latin—and you understand Latin?'

'Oh no!' exclaimed Myra; 'I learnt the declensions, and I read the second chapter of St. Matthew in a Latin Bible once, but'—and she blushed—'I think I cried when Mr. Cole, the schoolmaster, began giving me lessons, and so I was allowed to leave off. But I would learn now, if I might, if any one would teach me.'

'You may have other—better things to do now,' observed the Doctor, and he adjusted his spectacles, and moved so as to face the folio volume on his desk. 'St. Augustine is a most valuable writer, and the notes, I hope, may be useful; but they take time, and writing is a labour.'

'If I knew Latin, perhaps I might be able to help you in that,' said Myra, in a disappointed, almost fretful, tone.

'The notes are English, my dear, for the most part; but you would find it troublesome work to make out my crabbed writing; and my hand has grown very shaky lately—rheumatic gout, I am afraid.'

'Might I try?' said Myra; 'I like making out strange writing.'

Dr. Kingsbury laid two or three bits of paper before her, scrawled over with what might as well have been Egyptian hieroglyphics, so far as regarded legibility.

'If I might take them home,' said Myra, 'I could make them out in time.'

The Doctor caught up the papers in terror. 'Patty, where is my note-case?' He thrust the papers into it, and tried to turn the conversation; but Myra was not to be daunted.

'I should like to copy something for you, if I might; would you only just let me try? Mrs. Patty, couldn't I do something? You know I have nothing in the world to do that is useful to any one.'

'Except to get well, my little woman,' said the Doctor.

Myra looked distressed; but it was more from physical

weakness than anything else. She was just in that state when the least contradiction seems unkindness.

' Doctor, dear, if you have a bit of writing that you don't care about, you might just let her try,' said Mrs. Patty.

Myra was proud and perverse then, and observed, ' that she did not want to try for amusement ; she wished to be of use.'

The Doctor had been looking at his school accounts, as though he would fain return to them ; but now he glanced at Myra with a look very unlike that absent, wandering inspection which was usual with him, and said, shortly, ' Patty, if the little girl likes to copy a letter for me, I should be glad for her to do it ; and you can leave her here, and come for her presently.

Myra could have found it in her heart to refuse, but she had no option. Mrs. Patty made her take off her bonnet, and cleared a space for her at the writing-table ; and in a few seconds, Myra, whose request had been little more than the impulse of wayward weariness, found herself with a sheet of paper before her, engaged in deciphering an interlined letter to an inspector of schools, and afraid to ask for explanations of the Doctor, who was apparently unconscious of her presence.

Mrs. Patty left them to themselves, promising to return again in a quarter of an hour, but Myra had only succeeded in getting through the first sentence of the letter when she appeared in the door-way again, ' Doctor, it really is too bad ; here is Mr. Verney ; he ought to have known better. Shall I tell him you can't see him before luncheon ? Shall I ask him to luncheon ? '

The Doctor finished a calculation before he spoke, and the delay was unfortunate. The dull servant girl, who had been sent from the kitchen dinner-table to answer the bell, had admitted Mr. Verney, and answered him that the Doctor was at home, and would be very glad to see him. Nothing was to be done but to admit him. The Doctor's wig was pushed and pulled in various ways, and some quick little coughs, approaching to grunts, escaped him. Myra thought she must go, but he put his hand upon her, and said, ' Won't you finish what you are doing, my child ? ' and then nodding his head to Mrs. Patty, he added, 'Very good, Patty, I will see Mr. Verney,' and almost at the same moment Mr. Verney came in.

He was a better-looking man by the morning light; or rather, perhaps he was feeling better, and so there was more animation in his face. But he was tall and stiff; and Myra, who, on being introduced, glanced at him for a moment, very earnestly wished herself with Mrs. Patty.

A few mutual inquiries about health began the conversation. Mr. Verney spoke of his own ailments with the nonchalant air of one who submits to an evil which he is too indolent to attempt to remedy. Dr. Kingsbury talked of his as though he had faced them and meant to do battle with them; all the while feeling that they were only the necessary attendants of his age.

'One learns to be ill in India as one learns to eat curry,' said Mr. Verney. 'It is all habit; I shouldn't know myself if I were to feel well again.'

'Good health is a great treasure, sir, not to be lightly thrown away; we are responsible for our health, as we are for all other blessings.'

'The responsibility is too heavy for me,' was the reply; 'I leave it all to my doctors; one being as good as another. I have no faith in any of them.'

Dr. Kingsbury was antagonistic to indifferentism in any form, and the gauntlet being thrown down he took it up. The medical science, indeed, had not perhaps advanced as rapidly as other sciences, yet it had made great progress of late years. He thought want of faith in medicine might be considered want of faith in the Providence which directed its use. Mr. Verney persisted in his incredulity, and the Doctor reiterated his assertion; and then came instances of ignorance of the treatment of maladies common in India; and in a few minutes Mr. Verney was in the full flow of eager conversation and anecdote, often paradoxical, always amusing, and from time to time bringing out some dry remark, which showed deep thought as well as quick observation, and which led the Doctor, even whilst he opposed him, to say, 'That is true, sir; I wish not to overlook the force of that observation; but on the other hand, I maintain, as I before said,' &c.; and so they went on, neither of them apparently thinking of Myra, except that Mr. Verney's eyes travelled round the room whenever he was not speaking, and seemed always to be employed in some office quite distinct from his ears.

The conversation would have given a remarkably different impression of the two men; Mr. Verney apparently not putting his heart into anything he said, yet with a tone of melancholy about him, even when he was most absurd in his perception of the ludicrous; and Dr. Kingsbury, wonderfully earnest even upon the lightest matter—but from the conviction of reason rather than the impulse of feeling—and never sad though always grave. Myra at last laid down her pen and listened; she could not help it. Mr. Verney noticed it, and remarked, with a laugh, 'We must be careful what we say, sir; we have an auditor. What is Miss Myra Cameron's opinion upon the vexed subject we have been discussing?' he added, turning to her with a satirical smile.

Myra blushed a colour deeper than crimson, and without answering went on writing.

'Is the letter finished, my little girl?' said the Doctor; 'I did not think it was such a long one.'

He meant the question kindly; but Myra thought it was a reproof. The blush became almost tears; but she struggled hard against such folly. 'It will be finished soon, sir; but there are three words I can't make out.'

The Doctor took the paper from her, and was going to put on his spectacles, but they were not to be found; he hunted for them in vain.

Myra would have knelt to search under the table, but Mr. Verney's gentlemanly feeling interposed; he begged her not to trouble herself, he would look for them; but Myra was only too glad to be under the table—anywhere—so that she might be hidden; and she disappeared so quickly that both Dr. Kingsbury and Mr. Verney began to laugh. Myra recovered herself then, and bringing up the spectacles in triumph from the floor, stood by the Doctor's chair and pointed out the illegible words.

'You are fortunate in having such an amanuensis, sir,' observed Mr. Verney. 'May I ask if the young lady's services are engaged for long ? I should like to enter into a negotiation on my own account.'

Myra looked him full in the face. 'I wrote this to help Dr. Kingsbury,' she said; 'I have no time to write anything else. If you please, sir,' and she addressed the Doctor, 'may I go to Mrs. Patty now?'

'Surely, my dear, if you like it ; and thank you very much. It seems all correct; and perhaps some day you will try another letter ; I should be glad if you would.'

Myra could not bring herself to express any satisfaction, and walked out of the room with a painfully self-conscious air. As she closed the door, she heard Mr. Verney say : 'What a strange little being; and what a contradiction between manner and words!' She could almost have stamped, she was so provoked with herself.

They met again at luncheon. Myra ensconced herself in silence, except when she said a few words in answer to Mrs. Patty's simple questions. Mr. Verney tried to draw her out, but it was evident that he only did it for his own amusement ; and when he found himself unsuccessful, he was too indolent to continue the attempt. And Myra tried to think she disliked him ; but she could not help listening to him, neither could she avoid showing that she was interested. Her countenance always expressed what was passing in her mind, in a way which she was not in the least aware of herself.

Even Mrs. Patty saw it ; and when they rose from table, said, laughingly : 'Now, Myra, if you can bear to leave this pleasant talk, I think I ought to be taking you home.'

'Oh yes, directly ! I am quite ready, Mrs. Patty—quite,' repeated Myra. 'I shall like to go home ; I think I am a little tired.'

'Only think,' said Mr. Verney ; 'that must be but a very small amount of fatigue ; but you don't look strong. Perhaps you will let me drive you home in my uncle's phaeton, which will be here presently ?'

Myra looked absolutely frightened at the suggestion, and

Mrs. Patty negatived it instantly : 'A little walking,' she said, 'was good for Myra ; and she had a message to send by her to Mrs. Cameron.'

The two assertions had no very obvious connection, but Myra seemed to understand and connect them in her own mind ; and Dr. Kingsbury having invited Mr. Verney to return with him to his study to look at some choice books, Myra and Mrs. Patty were left together.

Then Myra burst forth, seizing her friend's hand. 'O Mrs. Patty ! I am so glad ; I like it so much better when we are alone. Will he be here often ? '

'Who ? Mr. Verney ? I don't know, my dear. Why should you dislike him ? And you seemed to listen.'

'Oh yes ! listen ; I like to listen. But, Mrs. Patty, do you always remember yourself when people are near you ? '

Mrs. Patty looked amazed. 'Remember myself, my dear ? Remember others, I suppose you mean. How can one remember oneself ? '

'Oh ! you don't understand. I never met with any one yet who could help me. Mrs. Patty, will you make me as good as you are ? '

Another look of surprise mingled with as much disapprobation as Mrs. Patty's kindly nature admitted of. 'Dear little Myra ! I make you good ! What are you thinking of ? '

'Nothing,' said Myra, abruptly, and she hurried upstairs before Mrs. Patty ; but when they reached the landing-place she stopped, and said, 'I was rude ; you will forgive me, won't you ? '

It was impossible to resist that apology. Mrs. Patty, who had been just a little ruffled by Myra's awkwardness, forgave in a moment, and they went out together, happy and at ease ; not the less so because Myra's thoughts had been diverted from Mr. Verney.

CHAPTER XI

MRS. PATTY led the way through the Rectory garden, and by the pond, to the lane leading to the village. Then she and Myra crossed a few fields, and at length reached a little cottage standing alone on a rising ground. They had said but little during their walk; Myra was at times very silent, and Mrs. Patty was thinking over the arguments by which she might persuade the mother of the idiot boy to consent that her son should go to the Asylum. 'It I could only make her see things sensibly!' she exclaimed, at length, speaking her own thoughts rather than addressing Myra; 'but she never will believe that he will be taken care of.'

'Mrs. Ford, do you mean?' asked Myra. 'But she must be very glad to get rid of him.'

'Not at all, my dear. He is her child.'

'I daresay it is very hard-hearted,' continued Myra, 'but I should think it very dreadful to have him always about me. He can't speak plainly.'

'No; nor even feed himself, and he is eleven years old.'

'And they will teach him all kind of things at the Asylum, won't they?' inquired Myra. 'Papa said the other day, that it was quite wonderful how they brought the poor children forward.'

'Very true, my dear; but Mrs. Ford will be terribly put out with me for suggesting his going.'

'Then Mrs. Ford is an idiot herself,' said Myra bluntly.

'Hush! my dear, hush! Here she comes, and Johnny with her.'

The mother and the boy came down the centre walk in the little cottage garden together; Johnny dragging himself along with an uncertain step, and stopping every instant, against his mother's wish, to gather a leaf from a gooseberry-bush, or a cabbage. Even before his features could be distinguished, his gait showed his infirmity.

Mrs. Ford vainly tried to hasten; it was clear she could not trust him out of her sight for an instant.

'He has one of his troublesome fits on him to-day, ma'am,' was her greeting, as she allowed Mrs. Patty to approach without advancing herself to meet her. 'I shouldn't have a leaf left on the bushes, if I wasn't after him.'

Mrs. Patty seized the opening afforded by the observation, and went straight to the point. 'If Johnny was so troublesome, and took up so much of Mrs. Ford's time, the natural deduction was that it would be a great comfort to have him placed elsewhere. And she was come to talk the matter over.'

Myra looked eagerly at the woman's face. It had not quite the expression which Mrs. Patty had prognosticated. Mrs. Ford was at that moment suffering too much from Johnny's misdeeds, not to be alive to the advantage to be derived from having him taken care of elsewhere. But she had a good deal of the Anglo-Saxon independence of character, and was not at all satisfied that it was well for any one else to complain of her boy as a burden, however she might do so herself. 'To be sure,' she said, 'Johnny was a trouble; she hadn't a moment's rest with him. Even at night he was often up and about, when he ought to be fast asleep; but it was only for a time; he was a good lad within whiles, and very fond of her; and he would play with the kitten for hours. He was always good when he had the kitten; just now the kitten had gone off; they did not know where to find it, and she and Johnny were going out to look for it. As to the asylum, she had never heard about it; she didn't know. Would not Mrs. Patty come in and sit down?'

Mrs. Patty was relieved. She had expected a storm of abuse, for Mrs. Ford's reputation for good temper was not of the highest. In her benevolence she made an effort to conciliate the boy also, but Johnny's fits were far from amiable; and when Mrs. Ford interfered, hoping to draw him into the house by entreaties and force mingled, a decided struggle ensued between the mother and the child.

Myra stood by, watching all that went on; not caring, as it would seem, for the result, but observing and thinking.

Her thoughts could not have been pleasant, for her brow grew more and more contracted ; and at length she turned suddenly and walked away by herself.

In the field adjoining the cottage lay the branch of a fallen tree, and she sat down, leaning her head upon her hands, trying, it might have appeared, to shade herself from the low-glancing rays of the afternoon sun ; or perhaps wishing to shut out the sounds of altercation which were still to be heard in the cottage garden. She was so motionless that she might have been thought to be asleep, and probably the idea did suggest itself to Mrs. Patty, when, the interview with Mrs. Ford being over, she drew near the spot, and stood by Myra for a few seconds without speaking.

Myra looked up then. She was no longer perplexed and irritated. The tone of her voice was only sorrowful, as she asked, ' May we go now ? '

' To be sure, my dear ; I would not have kept you if I could have helped it ; but I hope the little rest may have done you good. And Mrs. Ford was much better behaved than I expected. She is to bring Johnny to the Rectory to-morrow, that the Doctor may see him.'

' Where is the good ? ' exclaimed Myra ; whilst again the look of perplexed irritability crossed her face.

' The good, my dear ? Why, the Doctor will talk her over, and settle the whole matter, and have the card printed, and then we shall begin collecting votes ; and that is what you are to tell your mamma.'

' But the good ? ' persisted Myra. ' There is no good in it ; Johnny Ford is an idiot ; he never will be anything else—never.'

' He may be a good deal better than he is now,' said Mrs. Patty.

' But that will be nothing ; there is no place for him anywhere.'

' A place ! Service, do you mean, my dear ? Certainly, I don't think Johnny Ford would ever be able to go to service.'

' Oh no, not that ; but a place—a use. What was he made for ? Mrs. Patty, what are we, any of us, made for ? '

F

Mrs. Patty paused; then she said, ' May be, my dear, we can't know till we get to Heaven.'

' But I must know ! ' exclaimed Myra. ' Mrs. Patty, I can't live without knowing. Johnny Ford is like me—he has no place; but I am not an idiot. There ought to be a place for me. Why is there not ? '

Mrs. Patty slackened her steps, and there was some perturbation in her countenance, but she was not wholly unused to Myra's singularities, and she answered quietly, ' My dear, you are so young now, you will find your place as you grow older.'

' No,' persisted Myra, ' I shall not. There are some people born to have no place. No one wants them, or makes use of them, or leans upon them; and they can do nothing. They are not pleasant, or clever; they are not like Mr. Verney. Mrs. Patty, how will Mr. Verney and Johnny Ford live in Heaven, if they are there together ? '

' Pretty much as they do on earth, I should think, my dear,' said Mrs. Patty.

' But so different as they are ! Mr. Verney knowing everything, and Johnny knowing nothing ! '

' As to that, my dear, it is not to be doubted that Johnny will be a great deal wiser in Heaven than he is now.'

' Then why isn't he wise now ? Why should Mr. Verney have all the cleverness, and he have none ? And why should I like to listen to Mr. Verney, as I like to listen to music, while Johnny's noises make me shudder? Mrs. Patty, if Johnny gets to Heaven, it will be no good to him to have been an idiot on earth. He might just as well have been taken there at once; and so might I, and a great many others. There is no place for us here; that is what I mean. You have a place, and Dr. Kingsbury, and papa, and mamma;—and Mr. Verney must make himself one always, because he forces people to listen to him, and he knows so much; but all the rest of us—Oh ! if I could only understand ! '

' Perhaps you would if you did not puzzle yourself with thinking so much,' said Mrs. Patty.

' But I can't help it ! ' exclaimed Myra. ' I must think, for the thoughts come whether I will or not. Mrs. Patty, did you never think when you were a girl?'

'Yes, my dear, a good deal in my way; but it was never a clever way.'

'And you always were of use; you always had a place,' continued Myra.

'Not always, my dear; but that did not trouble me as it seems to do you, because somehow I had learnt to look at things differently.'

'But how? O Mrs. Patty! do tell me; I can't bear to feel as I do now.'

Myra's face, which the moment before had been pale from recent illness, flushed with excitement as she spoke, and then the colour faded away again, and she looked quite ill.

Mrs. Patty hurried on to a stile, which separated the Hall fields from the Rectory garden. Making Myra seat herself upon the step, she said, 'Just rest a minute, my dear; you have walked too far. And don't flurry yourself; we will finish our talk another day.'

Myra only repeated, 'What made you think differently from me? What do you mean by thinking differently?'

'Thinking differently about this world and the next, my dear.'

'I do think about the next world,' said Myra gravely; 'but it will be so unlike this.'

'No doubt, my dear, in some ways; but shall I tell you a little how I came to think as I do? It was when I was about thirteen years old. I don't fancy I was what people would call a naughty child then, but I can't say I was particularly good; and I had a beautiful sister, much older and cleverer than myself. She was going to be married, and she really was very good, and every one said she would be useful and kind, and teach others, and set a right example; but the day before the wedding, she went out riding, and was thrown from her horse, and killed.' The last word was uttered in a lower tone, and there was the pause of an instant; then Mrs. Patty went on. 'They brought her home, and laid her on her bed, and I saw her. I had never seen any one dead before. They talked of it as her end, and I cried bitterly, and was very frightened ; for I knew that such must be my end too.'

' But she was good, and you knew she was gone to happiness,' interrupted Myra.

' Oh yes, I knew it ; at least I said it, and so did every one else, but no one seemed to believe it ; and I could not understand it, and wondered what she had lived for, and why she had learnt what she did, and why I should learn anything. It was all a puzzle to me, my dear, just as it might be to you. But the day came for her funeral, and I asked to go, and they let me go. The churchyard was quite close to the house, so we all walked. It was a beautiful calm day, the fifth of June ; I don't think there was a single cloud in the sky, and I remember the only sound I heard, in the pauses of the clergyman's voice, was the singing of a lark. We all knelt by the open grave, and the coffin was lowered, and the earth cast upon it. I could have thrown myself down into the grave and been buried too, for it seemed as though the end of all things had come before me.'

' And it was the end of earth,' said Myra, and she seized Mrs. Patty's hand.

' Not quite so, my dear. I listened to the clergyman's words. They had no meaning to me, but they stayed with me. I walked home with the rest, and then I went away by myself into a walled garden which we had, with straight walks, and fruit trees, and borders of flowers, and very quiet. And there I walked up and down, and thought. I said over to myself again the verse in the burial service, " Blessed are the dead which die in the Lord," and the words which complete the text came to my mind, " Their works do follow them." A kind of new meaning seemed given to them. I thought of my sister's works. They had followed her. Therefore she must have carried away with her all she had done and learnt, and would have to use it in the world to which she had gone.'

' And was that true ? ' said Myra.

' Surely so it must be,' said Mrs. Patty ; ' for, Myra, I went back to the churchyard after a while, and I stood by my sister's grave again. It had been filled in, and even her coffin was

hid from me, and there was nothing left—no end, or object—
no work done, or remaining. That could not be what God,
who is so wise, intended. But I looked up, and God's sky was
above me, the sun shining bright around, whilst the moon and
stars were waiting to come out, and I knew that her spirit
was gone to dwell amongst them. If her works were to follow
her, then they could not be lost—they must have something to
do with the life she was to lead there. I was like a blind person wakened to sight, my dear; for I saw for the first time
that death was no end, but only a beginning.'

'Yet still the works ended with earth,' said Myra.

'No, my dear, no,' and Mrs. Patty's voice grew eager; 'do
you not see they were not meant for earth, they were the
preparation for Heaven. She had taken them with her.'

'But where, and how? What good can they be there?'
asked Myra doubtfully.

'God knows, my dear; I don't. I shall know hereafter.
But, Myra, after that day I did my duties with a lighter heart
and brighter spirit, for I felt that God had work for me to do
in Heaven, and that now I was fitting myself for it, and for
the place which He had made ready for me.'

'And Johnny Ford?' said Myra; 'he has no work here;
he cannot be preparing for Heaven.'

'Perhaps, my dear, his work is to make other people thoughtful, and pitiful, and kind-hearted; and in Heaven he will have
his duty and his place too; who is to doubt it? His poor brain
will be clear then, and God will set him to that for which he
is most suited. Easy work, no doubt.'

'And Mr. Verney?' continued Myra.

Mrs. Patty hesitated. 'The work that is to tell in Heaven,
my dear, must be that which is done on purpose for Heaven.
The work that is done for earth, you see, goes down with
us to our graves. I don't know enough of Mr. Verney yet,
to say what kind of work his may be; and if I did, I might
not be the judge; so, please, I would rather not talk of him.
Now, let me help you over the stile, and then you will be
close at home; and I must go back, for the Doctor will be
wanting me.'

CHAPTER XII

WHETHER Mrs. Patty's comment upon the particular text she
had chosen was strictly according to the interpretation of
divines, is certainly open to question ; but the idea which she
had suggested was destined to work upon Myra's wayward
unsettled mind to a degree for which Mrs. Patty in her simplicity was quite unprepared. Not all at once, however ;
Myra had not arrived at that state of mental energy in which,
when a new idea is presented to us, we examine into, and
ponder upon it, and discuss objections, and finally reach a
definite conclusion. Her opinions were as yet held in solution ; they had not crystallised themselves into shape ; but the
process was constantly going on, though unknown to herself,
and probably all the more surely, and with a better prospect of
becoming permanently fixed, because they were not received
in a settled form from others, but were worked out by her
own experience. Such opinions become principles, and principles become influential motives.

Yet Myra was certainly changed since her illness ; every one
noticed it, and she was aware of it herself. That she was
God's child, that He could be pleased with her, was a thought
too pleasant to be put aside ; and there were moments when,
after some effort at self-control, some little kindness shown to
her sisters, or some act of obedience to her mother, the consciousness of that loving approbation seemed to thrill through
her, and bring a glow of happiness, as new as it was delightful.
With that happiness came also the sense of her Saviour's
presence ; the feeling, and not merely the acknowledgment,
that He was her Friend,—that she might go to Him at any
moment : and then came the longing to take advantage of
that permission, the yearning for prayer and its rest. It was
all very quiet and hidden. Myra was even more sensitive as
to notice when religion was concerned, than she was when her
studies were in question. And she was full of faults, and the

old traditions clung to her. In the circle of Yare Hall she was still 'That odd, uncomfortable girl, whom no one can understand;' only it so happened that, in spite of her oddity and uncomfortableness, Juliet and Annette were beginning to turn to her in a difficulty; and Rosamond was learning to make use of her, by sending her to attend upon her mother, whenever she wished to be free herself.

And this was not seldom. It was rather a gay time at the Hall. Godfrey and Edmund were paying a longer visit than usual. And this brought Mr. Verney to the house, sometimes accompanied by his cousin Elise, but very often alone. And with Mr. Verney came a great deal that could not strictly be called dissipation, or waste of time, though it certainly was of that nature.

He had left off talking upon India now, except to Mr. Cameron, and had adopted the musical and artistic line, which he found more suited to the general tastes. Godfrey's tastes, indeed, were universal; he would have discoursed as readily upon Blackstone's Commentaries, as upon the styles of the early painters, or the merits of great composers; but Edmund had a real passion for music, and sang glees with a stentorian voice, and an energy which never flagged. They were a very well-suited party, and very natural and right it was that Rosamond should make herself agreeable to her brothers, and her brothers' friend; and whilst Mrs. Cameron reclined on her sofa in the boudoir, within the drawing-room, and Myra sat at the writing-table to attend to her many needs, there could be no possible objection to the young people's spending pleasant mornings together, more especially as Mr. Verney was really not young, but rather worn out and hypochondriacal, and so very indolent and peculiar, that no one would ever think of him, except as a specimen of Indian curiosities. If he liked any one, it was Myra; he always talked more rationally to her than to the others. This was Mrs. Cameron's reply to a remark made by Mrs. Patty, who, in the innocence of her heart, ventured one day the very natural observation, 'That if persons were thrown together, results would follow; and she should not be surprised if Mr.

Verney were to lose his heart to Rosamond.' Mrs. Patty saw
no objection to such a possibility, and therefore did not
hesitate to suggest it; but the very decided negative which
was put upon it, proved that the consummation was by no
means devoutly wished, though Mrs. Cameron took no steps
to prevent it.

And perhaps she was right. There were as yet no symptoms
that Mr. Verney was falling in love with any one, and to put
an unexpected stop to such intercourse is, in the generality of
cases, very like telling the mob not to cut off the constable's
ears ! The prohibition excites the wish. So Mr. Verney
came, morning after morning, and sometimes brought sketches
and photographs to be looked over and criticised, and sometimes professed to have a great wish for a little music; whilst
at other times he was not inclined to do anything but sit on a
low seat in the bay window, talking nonsense to the dog, interspersed with a little good-natured satire addressed to Myra, if
she happened to come into the room—satire which always had
for its object her supposed learned tastes, and which Myra bore
with tolerable equanimity, because it was quite evident that in
his heart Mr. Verney sympathised with them.

He came one morning, bringing with him a collection of
engravings, etchings, and photographs, which were to form a
series of specimens of the works of the Pre-Raphaelite masters.
They were heaped together in a portfolio, with no attempt at
order. 'He had had no time to arrange them,' he said, 'when
he was travelling in Italy; and since his arrival in England—
he did not know how it happened—perhaps the cause was
indolence—he hoped it might be attributed to invalidism—
but anyhow, he had done nothing with them. There they
were, a complete chaos ; but if Miss Cameron would take pity
on them, and put them into a book, his cousin Elise would
lend her aid ; they both had so much taste, and ladies' fingers
were so well calculated for work of this kind. He should be
under a weight of infinite obligation, but it would be less heavy
to bear than the present burden upon his conscience of a resolution unfulfilled.' All this was said in rather an irritating tone of
taking it for granted that the young ladies would be more than

willing to gratify him, a tone which Mr. Verney every now and
then adopted when he was physically out of order, and did not
choose to exert himself to be agreeable. The book was laid
upon the table by the servant who had brought it from Stormont, whilst Elise Verney, really taking pleasure in the prospect of the work, entreated Rosamond to join her in looking
them over, and to give her opinion as to what should be done
with them.

•Rosamond was copying music at a table in the recess of a
distant window. She merely looked up in answer, and said,
that 'she should have thought some good printseller in London
might give an opinion upon the subject more worth having than
hers.'

'More worth as to the fashion of the day,' said Mr. Verney
indifferently; 'but these are just the things which one would
desire to see treated without regard to fashion.'

'A printseller would be much perplexed by a good many
of them, I suspect,' said Godfrey, as he drew near the table.
'Have you many of the Siennese School here? They are
the only things worth looking at in early art. Cimabue, you
know, is a modern compared with Guido da Siena. Of course
you saw that picture of his in the S. Domenico;' and without
waiting for an answer he went on, as he turned over the contents of the portfolio : 'Ah! I see you have Duccio di Buonin-
segna and Simone Memmi, and here are Sano di Pietro, and
Matteo da Siena, but there are a good many between Maestro
Gilio, Dietisalvi, Ambrogio, Lorenzetti, all that goodly list of
which specimens are to be seen in the *Istituto delle belle Arti.*
You will have some trouble in making your collection perfect.'

'I am not obliged to follow precisely the guidance of
Murray,' said Mr. Verney in a dry tone; 'I am not so well
up in him as you are,'—and turning to Myra, who had been
attracted by hearing of a portfolio, and after looking at it shyly,
was returning to her post at the writing-table, he asked her if
she had ever seen any of the works of the very early masters,
and if she knew their characteristics. Myra had listened to
her brother's catalogue of names with some alarm. She had
been two or three times to the National Gallery, and knew how

to distinguish Raphael from Paul Veronese; but more than
this she had never thought of attempting. Such an intimate
acquaintance with long buried painters was much more astound-
ing than Greek and Latin quotations. The latter she might
be permitted to disown any knowledge of, but painting was
an art which, of course, women ought to be acquainted with.
Myra was not simple, at least not by nature ; she was always
alive to what people would say and think of her ; and she withdrew, though very unwillingly, that she might be out of the
reach of awkward questions, and it was just then that Mr.
Verney seized upon her.

A glance of relief and pleasure brightened up her face ; she
was almost pretty as she came forward and said directly,
' That she knew nothing about the early masters, and should
like very much to learn.' But the words were scarcely out of
her lips before Rosamond appeared at the table, and insisted
upon being a pupil also ; ' She was so very dreadfully ignorant,' she said, ' it would be quite charity to teach her.' And
Elise added in her little plaintive voice, ' That it must be so
charming to be so clever, and know so much about art as her
cousin and Mr. Godfrey ; but then her cousin had travelled,
and every one knew that Mr. Godfrey was wonderful.'

' Quite !' said Mr. Verney ; ' we will have our lecture, Myra,
another time.' He called her Myra, on the strength of his
forty years, but he had taken care to apologise for the liberty
in the presence of Mrs. Cameron.

' I don't like favouritism,' said Rosamond, laughing. ' You
and I, Elise, are considered too old and too dull to be Mr.
Verney's pupils.'

' Nay,' was the rejoinder, ' but I had already proposed to
burden you with work, and I was unwilling to occupy more of
your attention, as you seemed so deeply engaged.'

' I am only copying a duet,' replied Rosamond. ' Elise, will
you come and try it over with me ? '

Edmund, who had been sitting apart reading the newspaper,
started up at this proposal, and went to open the piano ; but
Rosamond, though the suggestion for music had been her own,
did not appear at all inclined to act upon it. She lingered by

the table. Godfrey was looking at the photographs with an air of sulky criticism, and she leaned over his shoulder and interspersed her remarks with his. 'That is a good one; and so is that; and, oh! Mr. Verney, is this a Sano di Pietro? or,' she added, as an aside, 'Give me another unknown name, Godfrey.'

Mr. Verney was still talking to Myra, but he turned abruptly to Rosamond before the sentence was finished. She held in her hand a little *carte de visite;* as his eye fell upon it, a slight tinge of colour, scarcely to be perceived, except by some one who was closely watching him, reddened his sallow cheeks.

'That,' he said carelessly—'Oh! that must be—let me remember. I have collected several things of the kind merely as specimens of photography.'

Rosamond pointed to the initials, C.S., in the corner, and said: 'It must be an acquaintance, at least.'

'Yes, I recollect now, a kind of cousin; at least, a lady who claimed relationship, though she never managed to prove it. I don't know how she happened to find a place amongst my treasures. I must put her elsewhere.' Mr. Verney held out his hand, so that Rosamond could find no excuse for retaining the photograph. It was placed in a pocket letter-case; and then, instead of resuming his conversation with Myra, Mr. Verney devoted himself to his portfolio, looking over its contents with the greatest care, whilst he urged Godfrey to give him the benefit of his knowledge of art, as it appeared he was not likely to obtain much aid from the young ladies.

They were soon engaged in a discussion which was worth listening to, and Myra became so interested that she forgot her mother and the letters, as, leaning over the table, under pretence of looking at some etchings, she eagerly drank in all that was being said; Godfrey's quick captious negatives and objections only bringing out more clearly Mr. Verney's real taste and information. Rosamond, in the meantime, had engaged Elise Verney in a subject which had reference to the proposed work, and in which Elise was a first-rate authority. A neat illuminated border might, she thought, be an advantage to the prints and etchings; could Elise suggest any pattern

that would be appropriate? So they were both occupied, and
apparently both engrossed, except that Rosamond every now
and then asked for a specimen lying close to Mr. Verney, and
then apologised for interrupting him, excusing herself at the
same time on the plea of wishing to judge what space it would
occupy in a book. Her voice was so very soft and sweet on
these occasions, it was quite singular to observe how at the
moment her brother Edmund would start up from a reverie
over the newspaper, and give a push to a chair or a footstool,
and utter a slight exclamation, as if he was annoyed. No one
noticed it except Myra, and she looked up at him with less of
wonder than of sympathy ; and at last she left Mr. Verney
and Godfrey in the middle of their conversation, and went
back to her letter-writing in the boudoir.

The result of that morning's conversation was that Rosamond
and Elise undertook, not only to arrange the contents of Mr.
Verney's portfolio, but to ornament the book in which they
were to be placed ; whilst Myra, at Mr. Verney's suggestion,
agreed, with her mother's permission, to spend a little time
each day in looking at the specimens of the different masters,
Mr. Verney sitting by and pointing out their merits and
peculiarities. As Mrs. Verney said when she heard of the proposition, ' It was delightful to watch the rapid blossoming of a
young and ardent mind, under the invigorating influence of a
very cultivated intellect :' a remark to which Mrs. Cameron
thoroughly assented, adding that ' It was singular to observe
how much Myra had improved since she had spent more time
with persons older than herself. She really was growing quite
companionable.'

MYRA certainly was growing much more companionable, and not only that, but much more useful; so useful, indeed, that Miss Greaves was often tempted to occupy more of her time in the schoolroom than was quite compatible with other claims; whilst Mrs. Patty—her latent affection for Myra fostered by the circumstances which had thrown them together—was constant in her suggestions of parish duties,—the poor, and the schools, about the latter of which Dr. Kingsbury was particularly anxious.

It was difficult at times to balance these separate claims, and Myra had no one to help her—no one to whom she could go and open her heart, and from whom she might seek advice. Dr. Kingsbury, good and excellent though he was, was not at all at home in the little intricacies of a young girl's life. He could suggest principles, but he believed that the working of them must be left to the conscience of each individual. Perhaps he carried this system of non-interference a little too far; it certainly had the effect of throwing Myra back upon herself, and making her shy with him. He had noticed that, although confirmed, she was never seen at the Holy Communion, and one day he spoke to her about it, but rather drily, and without appearing to suppose that she could have any difficulties; and Myra, self-distrusting, often wayward, and always inclined to be exacting, fancied he took no interest in her, and had mentioned the subject only from duty, and brooded over her vexation till she made it a grievance which became almost a reason for delay. She had, as she said to herself, so many faults;—if Dr. Kingsbury were aware of them he would never urge such an act upon her; but he knew nothing about her, and she could never find courage to talk to him, and so she must wait and think about it. This morbidness was very dangerous. It might have been fatal to Myra's newly awakened principles but for one characteristic, which, humanly speaking, was her safe-guard.   She was thoroughly true—true, not only in word and act, but in her secret heart, in her desire to understand and acknowledge without disguise or extenuation all that was wrong in herself.   When Myra erred in self-knowledge it was from ignorance, not wilfulness, and therefore the view which she took of her own character and of the claims of duty, was free from that great and most ruinous defect of one-sidedness.   As she had no pet faults, so she had no pet virtues—the latter being quite as destructive of the balance of moral principles as the former.   And it was this which was the root of her rapid improvement.   There are many whose feelings have, like hers, been touched by some particular exhibition of Christian truth, and who have in consequence made stricter resolutions to lead a Christian life ; but the resolution, in so far as it has assumed any definite form, has, in general, had reference to some particular fault, supposed to be the great stumblingblock in the way of goodness.   Myra's resolution—and it was not made in her own strength—was that she would try in *everything*, that she would look out for duty, and not wait till it came to her ; and then the truthfulness of her nature, through God's mercy, came to her aid, and day by day her eyes were more open to see what was incumbent upon her, and wherein she failed.

And so with regard to the solemn act which Dr. Kingsbury had urged upon her, Myra in no way turned from it, or shut her eyes to the fact that it was a duty.   Her morbidness and shyness operated only to defer it till she could find some means of resolving certain doubts and difficulties which troubled her conscience, and which she would at once have placed before Dr. Kingsbury if he had given her encouragement.

Most innocent he was of any idea of discouraging or alarm-ing her.   In the simplicity of his heart he believed that he had said all that was necessary to invite confidence, if it was needed ; and accustomed to the sight of his own clever face and quaint brown wig, unaware of the effect of his old-fashioned politeness, and so intimate with St. Augustine and the Fathers, that he could not understand why learning, so easy of acquisi-tion, should inspire the slightest awe, it was a matter of daily wonder to him why the little girl, as he often called Myra, should be so evidently afraid of him, creeping into his study like a mouse, and speaking in a tone which often he could scarcely hear. The only explanation of the mystery was that shyness belonged to the nature of girls, and he, being a man, must make up his mind that he could not understand it.

It was about a week after the art mania, as Edmund called it, had seized upon the family. Myra had spent a pleasant half-hour with Mr. Verney—pleasanter even than usual, for she was becoming more and more at ease with him—and they had on this day wandered away from the styles of the early masters to the subjects which they chose; and some things he had said had given her what she fancied was a glimpse into his mind, and awakened a suspicion that he had deeper and more serious thoughts than he would allow to appear on the surface. Such a discovery, made as it seemed by herself alone, awakened an interest which, when added to her admiration of his talents, greatly increased her pleasure in his society. And now, as she walked with Juliet and Annette in the direction of Miss Medley's cottage, it was quite an effort to withdraw her thoughts from speculating upon what he had said, and what he meant, and keep up the conversation which Juliet endeavoured to force upon her.

'You are growing so grand and learned,' said the latter, as Myra made some rather ill-timed observation about the delights of travelling and picture galleries, 'that there is no bearing you. I wish Mr. Verney would take himself back to India again; the house is quite changed since he came.'

'Yes, indeed it is; Miss Greaves says so,' added Annette, 'and she must know.'

'Neither you nor Rosamond care in the least about Mr. Brownlow's sketches now,' continued Juliet. 'Rosamond said yesterday that landscape sketches were not worth looking at; and there is no chance of Annette's having the drawing prize, for she has no one to finish up her drawings for her now that Rosamond spends her time over Mr. Verney's book of engravings.'

Annette began to disclaim the imputation of needing such aid, but she was instantly stopped by her provoking sister.

'Truth will out, Annette. You know you have been in a perfect fume the whole morning because Rosamond has not been near you.'

'I know I have failed,' said Annette fretfully. 'It was stupid in me to say I would try.'

'Yes, till you had quite secured Rosamond's assistance,' persisted Juliet.

'How can you be so tiresome, Juliet?' exclaimed Myra.

'Tiresome, but true. You were ill, Myra, when the business begun, so you can know nothing about it.'

Annette took up the injured tone. 'Juliet,' she said, 'was always so ill-natured ; and now that Myra was so little in the schoolroom, there was no one to be her friend.'

Myra always felt very irritable when Annette was mournful about nothing ; but her voice only slightly betrayed it on the present occasion as she said, with an endeavour to be candid, that she was afraid she had not been any one's friend in the schoolroom.

'Quite true,' exclaimed Juliet ; 'Annette and I do much better when we are left alone, except when she has a fit of the glooms upon her. I think, Myra, she caught them from you.'

Myra bit her lip. Juliet certainly was in a most provoking mood that morning, and Myra's only hope of keeping her temper was by being silent. Even that remedy, however, nearly failed ; for thought will be busy when the lips are closed, and Myra found herself saying all kinds of bitter things to Juliet in her own heart, till a sudden consciousness of what she was doing came across her with a pang. It was a very great effort then to make a little good-natured remark about the probability of rain and of their being unprovided with umbrellas ; but it was made, and when the words were uttered the impending storm of temper had passed away.

Just then they found themselves in front of Miss Medley's cottage. It was at the entrance of the village, and a little discussion took place as to whether it would be wise to stop there and borrow an umbrella. Myra thought it did not signify,

Juliet thought it did, and Juliet gained the day; for she insisted upon it that Myra should run no risk of getting wet, and was so really anxious about her that Myra was at length persuaded to wait at Miss Medley's, and send her sisters to do what was to be done in the village.

They knocked at Miss Medley's door, and whilst waiting for the servant to come, Juliet, who had been looking down the village street, turned abruptly to Myra, and exclaimed—

'Myra, I was wrong about the glooms ; I ought not to have said it.'

Myra only smiled ; there was no time to say anything else, for the front-door was opened by Miss Medley, whilst at the same instant the parlour door was rather violently closed by some one in the room.

Miss Medley looked a little unlike her usual self ; she spoke in a flurried tone, and was very slow at comprehending what was wanted.

'An umbrella, my dears? yes ; but there are three of you. One for each, do you want ? I will ask Mrs. Haynes, but I don't think she has two. And then how can you manage?— dear me ! very unfortunate it is.' She gently pushed them all before her into Mrs. Haynes's room, disturbing the good woman just as she was sitting down to mend her husband's shirts.

Myra was too shy to explain what was needed, but Juliet never knew what it was to be shy, and at once enlightened Miss Medley's mind.

'They would borrow one umbrella, or two as it might be convenient ; but Myra wished to know if she might wait and see if the rain would pass over.'

'Certainly, my dear ; no doubt, colds are very dangerous, and frequently brought on by getting wet. Yes, wait, my dear Myra ; pray wait. Mrs. Haynes'——

Miss Medley seemed brought to a stand-still, and Mrs. Haynes looked and listened.

'An umbrella, Mrs. Haynes, if you please ; mine, if you would be good enough to fetch it. In the left hand corner of my room, my bedroom, Mrs. Haynes ; the left hand corner, near the window;—no, not the parlour.' Miss Medley followed Mrs. Haynes out of the room, and contrived to close the door behind her. They heard her go into the parlour, and she did not come back till Mrs. Haynes returned with the umbrella.

Juliet and Annette would then have departed, but Miss Medley kept them talking, asking them a series of questions, which she scarcely gave them time to answer. Myra was impatient, for they were expected home at a certain hour. She was watching for a pause, which might enable her to suggest to her sisters that they should go, when she heard some one open the front door and go out. Almost directly afterwards Miss Medley was seized with a sudden perception of the fact, that if they wished to do what they had to do, before the rain came on, they would be wise not to delay. She ushered them out of the house even more quickly than she had ushered them in, and then took Myra into the parlour.

'You will find things rather in confusion, my dear, I am afraid. I have been looking over letters and papers. Long past they are. You know nothing about such things now; you will if you live long enough. They bring many thoughts, my dear; sad ones for the most part; experience of men, saddest of all.'

'O Miss Medley!' exclaimed Myra. She stopped—thunderstruck at such an avowal. Reverence for men was not only part of her womanly nature, but the result of her education. Who that lived in the daily sunlight of Mr. Cameron's excellences, could doubt the superiority of the masculine character in all things?

'You are surprised, my dear; shocked perhaps. I have known many who feel with you; few indeed who feel with me. But I always say wait; wait and see; try them; prove them; watch them. Ah, Myra!—but it does no good to talk. I will just put up my papers, and if you like to take a book, you won't interrupt me; I know you are fond of reading.'

Myra was thankful for the permission. She never knew what to say to Miss Medley, and she felt a certain mistrust of her now, such as a person might be conscious of who had heard another give utterance to some heretical Christian doctrine. She took up a pamphlet; it was the Report of the Homœopathic Hospital, and not tempting. A dusky book by its side proved to be a volume of Blair's Sermons, which was still less inviting; and at last she had recourse to the book-case, and as usual seized upon the first author whose name she knew, and tried to solace herself with Burton's 'Anatomy of Melancholy;' but it was not till Miss Medley, having finished reading some letters, apologised for leaving her, and went upstairs, that Myra really breathed freely. She looked round the little room then, and fell into a reverie. Everything she saw was familiar to her eye, for she had known Miss Medley as long as she could remember; but neither furniture nor books conveyed any idea to her mind as to their owner's history. Miss Medley had lived in Yare for more than five-and-twenty years. That was like going back to the date of the Deluge with Myra, and she looked upon Miss Medley, in consequence, as we might be supposed to look upon an antediluvian; a specimen of an age and a state of society to which there could be no counterpart in the present day. And it was not till lately that Myra had formed distinct ideas of individuals, except as they affected herself, and so had become in a measure a part of herself. The blending of things essentially distinct would seem to be the infant state of the human mind, as it is of the human sight. As the child only learns by degrees and by experience that the chair and the wall are not one and the same flat surface, but separate objects with distinct uses, so, in like manner, it is taught gradually that the beings who form a part of its little world are not necessarily part and parcel of that world, but have feelings and wishes, hopes and fears, apart from and superior to it.

Myra was awakening to the romance of reality—that romance which is far higher and deeper than any fiction; and she indulged herself now in a speculative and imaginative retrospect of Miss Medley's life, based upon that one remarkable expression, 'Experience of men, saddest of all.' A gust from the half-open door blew some papers from the table to

the floor; Myra started up to prevent others from following
their fate, and whilst looking for a weight to lay upon them,
she saw a glove which had been hidden by them—a large
man's glove, one which she could not help recognising, because of its peculiar colour—Mr. Verney's glove. It did not
strike her as singular; very few incidents do so strike us at
the moment that they occur. She supposed Mr. Verney must
have been paying a visit to Miss Medley, and very probably it
was he who had left the house whilst they were talking about
the umbrella. So natural indeed it all was to Myra, that
when Miss Medley came back again she said to her, most
innocently, 'O Miss Medley! I have picked up Mr. Verney's
glove. I know it by the strange colour; he must have left it
just now.'

Myra could not help noticing the change in Miss Medley.
She grew pale and very nervous, and her reply was incoherent.

'Mr. Verney's glove, my dear! Oh no! it must be mine
—or Mrs. Haynes's, or—I don't know how things come here.
Just give it to me; I may have brought it away by mistake;
I was calling at Stormont last week.'

'But I saw him with both gloves on yesterday,' said Myra,
curiosity leading her to an absence of tact and consideration,
for which conscience the next moment reproached her.

'He may have a good many pairs; I don't know—I can't
understand!' Poor Miss Medley was perplexed to the very
verge of untruthfulness. She paused, and then, with the
impulse to relieve herself, said: 'Myra! I know you are to
be trusted; Mrs. Patty always tells me so. You won't say to
any one that Mr. Verney was here just now?'

'Oh no! certainly not; if you wish it to be a secret.'

'But I don't wish it to be a secret! I don't care! O
Myra! never have anything to do with men—never, never!'
Miss Medley's voice was pathetic in its earnestness.

Myra was not a child when she saw another person failing
in self-control. The sight roused her latent powers of judgment, and now, quietly and with some dignity, she said, 'I
should never repeat anything which I was asked not to repeat.
You may be quite sure I shall say nothing about Mr. Verney.'

'Not at home—to your father or your mother—not to any one ; you are quite sure?'

'Quite,' replied Myra rather shortly.

'Then, my dear, just sit down and don't trouble yourself about me ; don't think anything about it at all, but just forget it. Mr. Verney came to see me on a little business—a little private business, nothing of consequence, and— But here are Juliet and Annette.'

Miss Medley hurried to the door with most unmistakable satisfaction, yet, before opening it, she returned to repeat, 'I may quite trust you ; I know I may?' To which Myra could only answer, 'Yes, of course.' And being certain that Miss Medley would not be thoroughly happy till she was out of the house, she followed her, and met her sisters in the passage.

Miss Medley's hospitable temper struggled with her nervousness as she entreated them all to wait a little longer with her ; but Myra was decided ; and Juliet added her assurance that 'the threatening of rain had passed away for the present ; indeed, Mr. Verney, whom they had met, had assured them it was likely to be fine all the afternoon. He felt so sure of it himself that he was going up to the Hall to ask if Rosamond and Godfrey, or Edmund, would go out riding.'

'I don't believe it is going to be fine. Tell her not to go ; she will be sure to get wet,' said Miss Medley. Juliet laughed and turned away. 'Tell her I said so ; beg her not to go,' called out Miss Medley in her shrillest tones ; but her warning fell on very heedless ears ; and only Myra looked back and said, 'Yes, we will tell her. Good-bye, Miss Medley ; and thank you very much for the shelter.'

CHAPTER XIV.

'AND Rosamond is going to London with the Verneys?' said Mrs. Patty, taking her seat by Mrs. Cameron's sofa, about ten days after Myra's visit to Miss Medley.

'So I hear,' was the reply; and as Mrs. Patty looked surprised, Mrs. Cameron added, ' Young people in these days order things very much as they choose, my dear Miss Kingsbury; and Rosamond is of an age to judge for herself as to her own movements.'

Mrs. Patty's face expressed dissent, which she refrained from uttering. Mrs. Cameron continued: 'The Verneys are very kind, and press it; and really I don't know what objection to make. This place is dull; and my health prevents my going out, and indeed interferes with my doing half that I wish for Rosamond. She ought to see the world; she ought to have opportunities '——

'Of marrying?' asked Mrs. Patty simply.

'Well! yes; I suppose there is no harm in acknowledging it. Rosamond is, of course, a charge to me, different from one of my own children. I should never think as much about Myra's marrying; I can't tell why.'

'Perhaps because she is less likely to think about it herself,' said Mrs. Patty.

'Perhaps so. Myra is much improved lately, and is becoming a pleasant companion; and she waits upon me a good deal. I feel no inclination to part with her just yet; and happily there is no necessity. But Mrs. Verney has talked to me a good deal about Rosamond. She says—and I am afraid it is true—that I have failed to develop her properly; that she has the germs of genius, but that they are likely to be dwarfed for want of culture; and she thinks that London society may do a good deal for her.'

'Then she is to go out, and to have what people call a season in London?' said Mrs. Patty.

'Not exactly that. Rosamond's position scarcely entitles her to mix in very fashionable life.'

'What a blessing!' ejaculated Mrs. Patty.

'I daresay it is. Mrs. Verney disapproves of such society quite as much as you or I should; but literary and intellectual society must be good for a young girl; and wherever Mr. Verney is, there will be society of that kind.'

'But,' and Mrs. Patty's eyes opened widely, 'I don't quite understand. Is Rosamond going to London for the sake of being with Mr. Verney? because—perhaps I ought not to say it—but that strikes me as just a little odd.'

'Dear Mrs. Patty, you are so matter of fact. Mr. Verney is nothing to Rosamond, and Rosamond is nothing to him. He is a worn-out Indian invalid; and she is a young girl just entering life. He is quite a tutor to her.'

'But tutors fall in love,' persisted Mrs. Patty.

'Oh yes, at times, under certain circumstances; but you need not trouble yourself now. It is all quite safe; they have not the slightest thought of each other; and, in fact, if they had, nothing would be more desirable than to put Rosamond in the way of seeing some one else. Here they are necessarily thrown together continually.'

There was just enough truth in this statement to satisfy Mrs. Cameron's conscience that she was not making a mistake in sending Rosamond away from her; but it failed to satisfy Mrs. Patty.

'If there is no objection to the marriage, supposing they should happen to like each other,' she continued, 'then, of course, it is all right.'

'But I did not say that; there would be great objection; it could not be; Mr. Cameron would not hear of it,' exclaimed Mrs Cameron, growing excited; 'and, in fact— But we are troubling ourselves quite unnecessarily, for Mr. Verney will only be in London occasionally while Rosamond is there. He has visits to pay; Mrs. Verney told me that. I could not refuse Rosamond's going when every one wished it so much. *I* could not put Mr. Verney as an objection, when she sees him here every day; and when—But, dear Mrs. Patty, there is nothing in it—nothing; if you only would not talk of it.'

'Certainly I won't, if you wish me not to do it,' was the reply; 'and you must forgive me if I said anything which may have seemed interfering. The Doctor tells me I am too apt to speak what is in my mind, without proper consideration.'

'No forgiveness is required, dear Mrs. Patty. I am quite sure it is only the interest you have in my children. And now, shall we talk about the Idiot Asylum?'

Mrs. Patty was but little given to satirical remarks generally; but a question did arise in her mind then—which must occur to many of us as we go on in life—whether there were not as many idiots without the walls of the asylum as within it; whether common sense—the ordinary sense given to rational beings—might not have proved to Mrs. Cameron, that if there were strong objections against Rosamond's marrying Mr. Verney, it was unwise to throw her constantly in his society.

But Mrs. Patty was conscious of prejudice. She disliked Mr. Verney, and could give no particular reason for her dislike. That was a very disagreeable consciousness for a person naturally so charitable, and with the strict self-discipline which was habitual to her, she was inclined to take herself to task for the feeling, and strive hard against it. It was not softened, however, by the sight of Mr. Verney pacing the gravel terrace in front of the house, in earnest conversation with Myra. Falling in love was out of the question there. Myra was only a child, and by no means attractive; but what business had he to take any notice of her? What good could his society do her? Her eyes followed them as they passed the window; and Mrs. Cameron seized upon the incident as a kind of apology for the weakness of which, in her heart, she was fully conscious.

'You see, dear Mrs. Patty, I was right; Mr. Verney is quite the old man, quite paternal; it is Myra in whom he interests himself. I daresay they are talking upon some deep subject now. Myra is so strange, and reads such curious old books;

he is immensely amused with her. He told me the other day that her mind was a complete study to him.'

But that might not be good for her,' observed Mrs. Patty; 'it would be a pity for Myra to learn to think much of herself.'

'She is not likely to do that. He is so wonderfully clever; she looks up to him as to a superior being.'

'To Mr. Verney!' exclaimed Mrs. Patty, in a tone of unfeigned surprise.

'Yes, intellectually—only intellectually. Of course, not morally or religiously; Dr. Kingsbury has no rival with Myra there.'

'I wish I could understand better,' exclaimed Mrs. Patty, speaking rather to herself than to Mrs. Cameron; 'I don't know what superior beings without morals or religion can be like.'

Mrs. Cameron laughed: 'You do manage to accept one's words so literally, dear Mrs. Patty. I had no intention of taking away our good friend's character, and saying he has no morals or religion; I only meant that they are not his strong points; at least not to the same extent as they are Dr. Kingsbury's.'

At that moment Mr. Verney and Myra happened to pass the window again. Mrs. Patty rose from her seat. 'I must go, Mrs. Cameron; I never meant to stay so long.'

'But the Idiot Asylum—is the canvass to begin at once? Will you send me the cards?'

'Yes, thank you, directly; this afternoon. Good-bye!'

Just as the door closed, Mrs. Cameron called out: 'If you should see Myra, will you tell her to come in and write some canvassing notes for me?'

Myra had been walking up and down the terrace for nearly half an hour. The time had seemed to her not more than five minutes. She had been reading Dante with Mr. Verney; and the reading had naturally led to conversation—poetical, historical, and then religious. Myra had read the 'Inferno' by herself, with difficulty, and she had been unable to appreciate it. When Mr. Verney discussed it with her, it became a revelation of the great poet's mind—his principles, prejudices, aims; his hopes, and his despair.   There was great pleasure in this; but a more present interest—one to which it was impossible to be insensible—lay in the allusions, passing yet betraying deep feeling, which from time to time the speaker made to himself.

'*Lasciate ogni speranza voi ch' entrate,*' he repeated, as he closed the canto in which the words occur; and pushing the book aside, he added abruptly : ' One needs fresh air and clear skies after that.   Won't you come out with me ? '

So they went out upon the terrace; Myra feeling very timid, not at all understanding her companion's mind, but longing intensely to be able to do so.

' Those words were written from the heart, if any ever were,' continued Mr. Verney.   ' They are associated with the Inferno, but in Dante's own mind they belong to earth.'

' To give up hope ! ' said Myra ; ' but we must hope whilst we live ! '

' So young things fancy,' was the reply ; ' and I daresay there are some who can do so.   I believe I was born without hope.   Do you know anything of phrenology, Myra ? '

' Nothing, but what I have learnt from hearing people talk about it.   I know where the bump of self-esteem lies, because ' —— She paused and blushed.

' Well, why?   I like to know how you pick up your knowledge.'

' Because,' said Myra, ' it was pointed out to me one day.'

' On the head of some particular person who was set down immediately as a conceited booby.'

' Oh no, not that ! ' exclaimed Myra eagerly.   ' It was a very clever person—a person whom we all ' —— Again there was a sudden pause.

' ' Whom you all admired ? '

' Yes, a little, in a way ; that is, I don't think he is conceited.'

' That is right,' said Mr. Verney.   ' Don't let yourself be drawn away by such folly, Myra.   Self-esteem, as it is the fashion to call it, is as good as any other quality in its time and place. A man is worth nothing without it.'

'So I thought,' replied Myra, 'and I said it, but they laughed at me.'

'They—meaning whom?'

'Oh! a good many people. Elise, and Rosamond, and Juliet, and every one.'

'Hold your own ground, my child, and learn to judge and think for yourself; and especially, don't condemn other people because they are not exactly formed after your own model.'

'I have no model,' said Myra, 'except—we must all know what we ought to be.'

Mr. Verney laughed. 'Must we? That is precisely what I should doubt. Do you think your notions of goodness and Dante's would have agreed?'

'Yes,' replied Myra decidedly.

'You will have to do penance for conceit, after all. So you are the great poet's equal in moral philosophy.'

'I think Dante was religious,' said Myra timidly.

'Oh yes! religious. But I am not talking of religion now ; we will put that aside.'

'I don't comprehend,' said Myra. 'Is there any goodness without religion ?'

'Socrates, Plato, Seneca ; a host of others. What do you say to them?'

'They were religious as far as they knew.'

'That is to say, they were philosophers, but they were not Christians.'

Myra looked puzzled. Mr. Verney watched her compassionately. 'My dear little girl, I don't want to upset your pretty nursery notions. They are very good and useful; keep them as long as you can. Perhaps,' and he sighed, 'it might be better for many of us if we could keep them longer ; but don't let them render you narrow-minded. You think one thing good, I think another good. Don't condemn me, and I won't condemn you.'

'But there is something good, something apart by itself, true,' said Myra.

Mr. Verney shrugged his shoulders. '*Chi sa?* That is,' and he spoke more cautiously as he noticed Myra's look of distress, 'no doubt there does exist something good, as you say, apart by itself; but whether we are able to understand it is quite another question. And there your idol Dante would be as much at variance with you as I am.'

'Are you at variance with me?' asked Myra.

Mr. Verney was tenderly kind in the tone of his reply. 'No, not at variance, dear child. I used a wrong word. But a worn disappointed man, who has learnt from experience to disbelieve in abstract goodness, can scarcely be expected to look at his fellow-creatures as a young thing like yourself naturally does. Dante placed his great sinners in Inferno, and his great saints in Paradiso. I am much more inclined to put them all in Purgatorio.'

'And not to believe in anything absolutely great and good?' exclaimed Myra.

'On the other hand, not to believe in anything absolutely bad—what you would call sinful,' replied Mr. Verney. 'You see, it comes to the same thing in the end.'

Myra was silent, and it was just then that Mrs. Patty appeared at the end of the terrace.

'An excellent old lady, but marvellously quaint,' was Mr. Verney's comment. 'I wish she would have done us the favour to leave us alone.'

'I wish so too,' replied Myra; though as she said the words a feeling of relief came over her, as if she was escaping from something unreal. Yet she could not help saying to Mr. Verney, 'Thank you very much for reading with me and talking. It is very pleasant.'

'Pleasant to me too,' he replied. 'I don't like talking with every one.'

Myra went back to her mother to write the canvassing letters for the Idiot Asylum. Then it was luncheon-time. And after luncheon she was to go for a drive, and pay some morning visits. She had but very few moments for thought until she escaped to her own room after the late dinner, and before tea was brought in. Yet all that time the same sense of something unreal had oppressed her. It had made her feel irritable, and very much inclined to be discontented. Little duties seemed so very little, and great duties not much more important. But for that plodding, habitual temperament, which made her always anxious to do what she had been accustomed to do, or what she had resolved upon, she might have been much more unsettled. And Myra was also by degrees learning to discipline herself; not indeed upon any recognised principle, or because she was told or taught that she ought to do so; but from that impulse of conscientiousness which doubtless is, however we may fail to perceive it, the working of God's Spirit. The higher principles which had been awakened in her heart by Mrs. Patty's conversation during her short illness, had not been suffered to evaporate in mere sentiment. Action was a necessity of Myra's nature, and thus the feeling of religion embodied itself in prayer, and prayer settled itself into a regular habit at stated times. Myra had not learnt to be afraid of forms. She had never felt that there could be any danger in them. What she needed was something definite to mark her day—and so to satisfy her conscience that she was dedicating it to God. It might not have been the highest motive for prayer, and the petition when offered might have been less earnest than the spontaneous outpouring of a heart touched by some sudden emotion; but the habit was a support, a reminder; it recalled her when she had been going wrong, it spurred her on when she desired to do right; and who could venture to doubt that God's blessing would be vouchsafed upon such an effort to realise His presence, and live in constant remembrance of His laws? These noon-day prayers, as Myra called them, though in fact they were often from circumstances delayed to a later hour, were gradually becoming a necessary part of her inward life. She felt their blessing especially on this day; indeed, she was always especially soothed by them after a morning spent with Mr. Verney. For she could not help being influenced by him, still less could she avoid being excited by the interest which he so evidently took in her. The readings and conversations with him were looked forward to as the greatest pleasures which just then were granted her, but when they were over Myra was never thoroughly satisfied either with herself or with him. He roused her vanity. She found herself singled out by one whom every one was admiring; petted and brought forward in a way which, though at times it jarred upon her morbid sensitiveness, was still very soothing to her self-love, and to that latent consciousness of mental power which had been her perplexity from childhood. And, in consequence, she was always trying to please him. He sometimes joined in the laugh at her untidiness, or was gently satirical upon her efforts after fashion; and Myra, who before had scoffed at him, now spent many half hours before the looking-glass, trying to arrange her hair neatly, and to twist into shape a collar which was never made to fit; and the unsuccessful effort (for it almost always was unsuccessful) left her in a state of despairing self-consciousness which was not to be endured. An easy mode of escaping from it, indeed, was by remembering some of Mr. Verney's pleasant little speeches,—the remarks which proved that he did think her worth more than his cousin Elise; but that was a very petty satisfaction, utterly destructive of simplicity, and if ever Myra gave way to it, she hated herself more than ever.

It was a relief not to be told in words to turn from all this introspection, this imagination of a human eye, controlling and criticising, and lose the thought of self in the presence of Him to whom all hearts are known. Very simple minds would scarcely understand the fulness of such a rest. To Myra, the mere attitude of kneeling brought quietness and reality. After those few moments of prayer, and the clear unshrinking view of duty which accompanied them, the little world in which she lived appeared in a new light. Mr. Verney's opinion ceased to be of consequence, and praise or blame were alike indifferent. With one aim before her, one hope to cheer her, one joy to sustain her, Myra's eye became single; and the complex, bewildered, self-conscious mind grasped, for the instant, that priceless treasure of simplicity which is so often supposed to be unattainable, save on those by whom God has been pleased to bestow it at their birth.

And it was then that Myra fancied herself better able to understand Mr. Verney's character. Respect him thoroughly she did not. He was far removed from any standard of goodness which she had ever set up. He agreed with no hero of her imagination, either ancient or modern ; and Myra was too much of a child in all her feelings and thoughts to idealise and fall in love with him. She only desired to see him truly, and to explain to her own satisfaction what there was in him which puzzled her. She could not call him a careless man of the world, without principle, because he had such an appreciation of all things high and noble. Still less could she look upon him as an earnestly religious man. He ignored the duty of going to church, except on very rare occasions, and seemed to consider Christians, Mahometans, and Hindoos, as very much upon an equality, except as regarded civilisation. Yet he shared Myra's delight in the poetical passages of Jeremy Taylor, expressed all due reverence for Hooker, and what was still more astonishing, raved about the beauty of Isaiah's prophecies, sighed over the book of Ecclesiastes, and acknowledged that the sublimity of simple pathos had been attained in the Gospels. What did it all mean ?

Myra was so true herself that she could with difficulty believe in untruthfulness or unreality in others. People must be either good or bad, in earnest or not in earnest ; such was her theory, though it was perpetually meeting with exceptions which startled her. Certainly she had inconsistency enough in her own character, but then she looked upon herself only as a child, and failed to perceive that in this respect the majority of the world are children all their days. As to Mr. Verney, he was a man, a very clever man, extremely kind to her, and sympathising more than any one she had yet seen with her peculiar tastes. It was impossible to put him into the category of the false-hearted and careless ; and Myra at length, after much thought, found a place for him apart.

He was, she felt sure, a disappointed man, one who had endured great trials, but was very reserved in talking about them. He felt much more than he expressed, because he detested anything like show. His admiration of the Bible proved he was religious, and his singular neglect of outward forms must be the result of his long residence in India, in a very trying climate, and at a distance from a church. But he would soon come round after he had lived some time in England; and in the meantime it was much more really true and right not to make any pretence, not to do things for mere show.

And so Myra indulged her dreams of Mr. Verney, and if she could not quite put him on a level with Dr. Kingsbury, found a place for him in the prayers which she offered for those who were her best friends.

——

CHAPTER XV.

ROSAMOND'S visit to London was fixed for the twelfth of May. The Verneys had gone up on the fourth, and were impatient for her to join them. Myra felt that the prospect before her was a blank one. She was scarcely aware how much Mr. Verney would be missed until she looked forward to his absence. But as yet he lingered at Stormont, though left in the house alone, and without the society of gentlemen at the Hall; for Godfrey Cameron had returned to his work in London, and Edmund avoided rather than sought his company. Something in the two minds was antagonistic, and this was a vexation to Myra, who was very fond of her youngest brother, and always liked him to approve her choice of friends. His evident distaste to Mr. Verney would have seemed like a reproach to her own judgment, if she had not been upheld in her opinion by the rest of her family. But Mrs. Cameron was really mournful over the breaking up of their pleasant mornings; and Mr. Cameron, provokingly cautious though he generally was, gave it out as an oracular decision that Charles Verney might be a leading man in India or in any country if he would only take the trouble to exert himself.

The day previous to Rosamond's departure was naturally

an unsettled one. The schoolroom was in confusion, undergoing the ordeal of a search for all articles missing or possibly to be wanted. Rosamond in her very quiet way upset every ordinary arrangement at her will, and though poor Miss Greaves, when she found history, French, German, and geography alike disregarded, looked despair, she never ventured to utter it. Myra was conscious of great irritability, as Rosamond dragged her from drawer to drawer, or sent her from room to room, to look for things which common sense would have told must be of very little use even if found. She would have rebelled, but Rosamond was accustomed to be waited upon, and was so prettily and pleasantly grateful for the trouble she gave that there was no excuse for being out of humour, or disobedient to her gentle tyranny. She and Myra were looking over a portfolio of drawings; some were to be taken to London to be mounted and framed, and others—Rosamond did not exactly state why she thought it necessary to burden herself with them, but Juliet said for her that it was satisfactory to have something with which to make a show.

'You have put aside this one by mistake, Rosamond,' said Myra, pointing to the drawing of the Bridge of St. Martin, which had been begun by Annette.

'Oh no! I accept it as mine now,' replied Rosamond carelessly: 'it makes up the set, and it has done its duty in the schoolroom.'

'I beg your pardon,' observed Juliet sharply; 'it has done no duty; it made Mr. Brownlow think Annette could draw much better than she could, and it gained her a great scolding the other day.'

'My dear child, how you exaggerate! Gained Annette a scolding; how could that be?'

'But it did, Rosamond,' exclaimed Annette, coming forward, and speaking in an injured tone. 'You know you have been so busy lately you have not been able to help me at all, and so Mr. Brownlow is quite disappointed, and there is no hope of my having his sketch for a prize now.'

'Poor darling! that is grievous,' said Rosamond, still turning over the drawings.

II

'There would have been no disappointment if you had told the truth at first, Annette,' said Myra gravely.

Annette's face flushed.   'Told truth, Myra ! do you mean that I told a falsehood ?   I declare, it is the most unjust—it is cruel—dreadful—so very unkind !'

Rosamond laid her hand on her sister's shoulder, 'Hush ! hush ! my dear !   It shall all come right, and you shall have a much prettier drawing than Mr. Brownlow's when I come back from London.   Myra, why do you always make "Much ado about nothing ?"'

'I said what I thought,' replied Myra.

'And that is just what you ought not to do.   What would become of us all if we said what we thought—if we were compelled to live in the Palace of Truth ?'

'I wish with all my heart we could live there,' exclaimed Juliet.   'There is nothing I should like better than to put some people I know there.'

'But it has been tried, dear child, and failed,' said Rosamond.   'You remember Madame de Genlis' tale ?   Annette, will you be so very kind as to run up to my room and bring me down the green portfolio.   You will find it behind the arm-chair.   I can put up the drawings then, and we shall have finished the business.'

Annette obeyed.   Myra remained deep in thought.   Presently she said earnestly, 'I should like to have my mind set right about truth.   There seems to me a difference between saying all one thinks, and saying what one does not think.   Perhaps I was wrong about Annette and the drawing.'

'Perhaps you were, my dear ; very likely—I may say ; but we won't talk any more about it.'

'We can't,' said Juliet, 'here is Mr. Verney ; ' and just then Mr. Verney appeared at the half-open window.   He began with an apology.   'Am I very intrusive ?   I could find no one in the drawing-room, and Mrs. Cameron is not in the boudoir, and I thought I might just be allowed to leave a message in the schoolroom ; but I had no idea of interrupting so much business.'

'Pray, come in.'   Rosamond threw up the window, which

opened from the ground, and Mr. Verney entered. The drawings, which the moment before were about to be shut up in the portfolio, were now left open, and Mr. Verney was required to give his opinion as to the best mode of packing them. This led to an inspection of them, and the view from the Bridge of St. Martin was particularly admired. Rosamond had never been abroad, and Mr. Verney became interested, and as much excited as was possible for him, as he described the scenery of Chamouni and Mont Blanc.

Myra sat by, silent, and evidently not listening, as was her wont. Mr. Verney's quick eye remarked this, and he turned to her and asked what was the matter.

The short answer, 'Nothing, thank you, only I was wishing to understand something,' made every one laugh; and then poor Myra blushed, and felt that she had been very foolish, and not quite simple. When persons are thinking of anything which is really interesting to them, they are not so willing to let those about them know it. She was punished now, for no inquiry was made as to the subject of her cogitations, and Mr. Verney continued to give his attention to Rosamond and the drawings. Perhaps it was a little latent ill-humour which induced Myra to watch them so much and so critically. When we are vexed with ourselves, it is a relief to vent our vexation upon others. Mr. Verney was very agreeable in his information, and Rosamond very sensible in her questions, but Myra would have liked better to listen if they had talked as they generally did—lightly. It seemed unnatural to hear them say anything really in earnest, and she could have almost accused them of pretence, until suddenly a thought struck her, which as it flashed across her mind, cleared away a whole mist of perplexity : Mr. Verney and Rosamond were falling, or had fallen in love with each other. That was the reason why Mr. Verney lingered at the Hall, and why Rosamond was so charmed to go to London.

In one moment Myra was in the very centre of a romance, almost as exciting as if she had been the heroine herself. Yes, it was all true. All that she had heard and read of, and only half-believed in, was being acted before her. There could be no mistake. Rosamond was so much more shy with Mr. Verney than with any one else, and he was always watching her, though he talked but little to her. That was quite the right way of falling in love, and now Rosamond was showing herself to the best advantage, and Mr. Verney was drawing her out as he would draw any one out, and so they must understand each other better and better.

Mr. Verney was rather old, to be sure; but then he was infinitely more clever and pleasant than any young man she had ever seen, and Rosamond was quite of an age to be married. Myra did not exactly feel that she should like to marry Mr. Verney herself, she should be so much afraid of him, but as a brother he would be delightful.

In the excitement of her satisfaction at this, the first discovery she had ever made, or supposed she had made, in the great romance of life, Myra found herself compelled to rush away and calm herself by a solitary walk on the terrace, and on the way she encountered Mrs. Patty.

A rather hurried step and a quick utterance betokened some mental disturbance, as the question was suddenly put : 'My dear, are you sure your papa will be at home this evening?'

'Oh yes, quite sure; at least I think so. No one has heard the contrary that I know of : shall I go and ask mamma?'

'No, my dear, thank you ; I can ask myself, if you are in doubt.'

'I don't think I am in doubt. I am nearly sure I am not.' Myra spoke as though certainty upon any point was at that instant unattainable, and so, in her preoccupied state of mind, it was. Her manner tried Mrs. Patty's patience, and she said rather sharply, 'My dear, you will never get through the world if you can't tell "yes" from "no" better than that. What has happened to you this morning?'

'Nothing—nothing at all. I was only going to walk up and down the terrace. Indeed, Mrs. Patty,' and Myra's brain became rather more clear, and her manner more collected, as she saw her friend's eyes fixed upon her inquiringly, 'Indeed, there is nothing the matter ; it is all quite natural.'

'I don't understand what you mean by quite natural, my dear. Is Miss Greaves in the schoolroom?'

'No. She went home early, because lessons were rather irregular to-day. You know Rosamond is packing; at least, she was packing till Mr. Verney came.' Myra, as she said this, looked painfully conscious, for she felt as if she was betraying a secret. And perhaps she was awakening a suspicion, for Mrs. Patty said, shortly, 'Has Mr. Verney been here all the morning, then?'

'Oh no; only a little while. He came to leave a message, and then he stayed.'

'As he always stays,' murmured Mrs. Patty.

Myra read in Mrs. Patty's open face a confirmation of her own thoughts. The temptation to speak freely was too great to be resisted, and she exclaimed, 'O Mrs. Patty! do you think they will be married?'

'Married!' and there was a pause. 'My dear, don't trouble yourself about such things. If they come into your head, turn them out. They are not your affair.'

'But may I talk to you? will you come out on the terrace with me? I should just like to say what I think to some one,' said Myra.

Mrs. Patty assented in action, though she was silent, till they reached the terrace; then she said, 'Myra, who put that fancy into your head?'

'No one,' replied Myra. 'It came of its own accord, but I am sure it is true.'

'Then, my dear, you will do well to talk it out to your mamma, but to no one else. I would rather not hear about it.'

'But, dear Mrs. Patty, you know I can't say anything to mamma; she might be angry: and there may be nothing in it; only I am sure of it, and so would you be if I might only talk to you about it.'

Mrs. Patty was sorely perplexed. She had very strict notions upon many subjects, more especially upon the confidence which ought to exist between mothers and daughters, and the idea of discussing with Myra, unknown to Mrs.

Cameron, the probability of such an event as Rosamond's marriage, was opposed both to her lady-like sense of fitness, and her Christian sense of duty. The reply to Myra's remark was discouraging : 'My dear, I don't like gossip, and the Doctor doesn't approve of it.'

'But is it gossip to talk about one's family? I thought gossip only concerned other persons!'

'I never looked for the meaning in the dictionary,' replied Mrs. Patty ; 'but it strikes me that any such talk about things which don't concern one must be gossip.'

'And must I never be free—never say anything? Must I be shut up all my life?' exclaimed Myra fretfully.

'My dear, I am not quite the person to give an opinion, because I often say things myself which I ought not. But the Doctor declares that the first thing we should all learn, men and women both, is to hold our tongues ; especially about this little matter of falling in love.'

'But it is not a little matter. It is the great thing in life,' said Myra.

'All the more reason for being careful what we say about it.'

'Only we must talk of it,' persisted Myra, 'because it comes before us, and we can't help seeing it.'

'We can't help fancying we see it. But, my dear, when you have lived as long as I have, you will understand that it is one of those matters about which lookers-on are very apt to blunder. Half the people whom I thought were going to marry, have turned round at last and taken to somebody else.'

'So people don't marry those they fall in love with,' said Myra. 'But'—and she thought for an instant—'they do generally in books.'

'That is, I suppose, my dear, because the book would not be liked if they did not. But books and life are different.'

'Then Rosamond won't marry Mr. Verney, and it will be what is called a hopeless attachment,' said Myra, in a tone of sorrowful satisfaction.

'It will be what God chooses it to be, my dear ; what is best fitted for them both for their trial; since, anyhow, you know, Myra, marriage must be a trial.'

'Must it?' said Myra; 'I thought it was a blessing.'

'Surely, a blessing, but a trial too. All blessings are trials. They show what we are by the way in which we take them.'

'Yes, trials in that way,' observed Myra. 'But when a woman is married she is less responsible than when she is not married, because she has only to obey her husband; and, Mrs. Patty, that was what I thought about Rosamond, that she would have nothing to do but to follow Mr. Verney's advice, and that then she would be quite sure always to do right.'

'I am not so clear upon that point, my dear. I should like to know more of Mr. Verney before I quite decided that his advice would always be right. It might be; but then again, it might not. And, after all, though a woman is a wife, she has a soul of her own, and will be judged according to her own knowledge and conscience. No one can get rid of that responsibility.'

'At all events, Rosamond would find it easy to obey,' said Myra, 'for every one must feel obliged to obey Mr. Verney. That is what I should like, Mrs. Patty. I should hate to have a husband who was not determined to have his own way.'

'Very good, my dear. But first take care that his way is a right way.'

'I should find that out before I was married,' said Myra. 'I could never marry any man whom I did not respect more than any one else in all the world.'

'Quite right, my dear, but that is not the way of the world; at least, if one may judge by the way the young ladies go on in the present day. They can't respect the men they flirt with.'

'I don't think I quite understand what flirting is,' said Myra. 'I mean, I couldn't describe it.'

'But you can feel it fast enough, my dear,' said Mrs. Patty. 'It is a thing much better felt than described. When you see a young lady chattering and smiling in a way which makes you long to take hold of her and shut her up in a dark closet, you may be quite sure that is flirting.'

'But gentlemen flirt too, don't they?' said Myra.

'Certainly. But they can't unless women encourage them. Remember, Myra, if you ever find even the tone of a man's voice freer than is pleasant to you, you may be tolerably sure you have yourself to thank for it.'

'But it must be very difficult to keep such a watch over oneself,' said Myra, 'when one is in high spirits, and pretty, and admired, like Rosamond.'

'No doubt it is, my dear. And as I never was pretty and admired, I never had the temptations which many have, and so I have no right to condemn them. Indeed, I very often take myself to task for feeling as I do about flirting, but I can't be patient with it. It is something which gives me a kind of creeping shudder of distaste. I don't say it is right to feel it. We are all human, and very vain and weak, and it is a long time since I was a girl. I daresay I flirted in my way then, only I have forgotten.'

'But people need not flirt when they fall in love,' said Myra.

'Certainly not, my dear. Falling in love is the reality, and flirting is the sham; that is why it is so hateful.'

'Perhaps Rosamond is flirting,' said Myra thoughtfully; 'but then'—she paused for a moment—'Mr. Verney would not flirt.'

'Time will show, my dear. Anyhow, I don't want you to trouble your little head about it.'

And that was all the interest or sympathy which Myra could get from Mrs. Patty, and rather hard it seemed, especially as the few observations which had been made tended considerably to withdraw the veil of romance which she had been prepared to throw over her sister and Mr. Verney. Flirting could under no circumstances be romantic or exciting. Little as Myra knew about it, her womanly instinct told her that it was a low, selfish, cold-hearted amusement, utterly destructive of every high and noble feeling. The suspicion of blame, however, rested entirely on Rosamond. Mr. Verney was, in Myra's eyes, far removed as a saint from any such possibility. Perhaps he was really attached to Rosamond, and perhaps she was trifling with him. That was another phase of the romance of love of which she had read. One thing was clear—for Mrs.

Patty had betrayed it in spite of her caution—Myra had a foundation for her suspicions, and she felt herself suddenly grown older, as she saw herself thus brought face to face with a possibility which up to this time she had been taught to consider lying in the distant future.

CHAPTER XVI.

MR. CAMERON believed himself very exact in keeping his engagements. He had his chambers in London, and often slept there ; but he always took care to give his wife notice when he intended to do so. He rejoiced in telegraphic despatches ; there was an importance about them, and a freedom from any plebeian regard for money, which suited his dignity. But they kept his family in a continual ferment. Mrs. Cameron never knew till the last London train had arrived whether the alarming official document, containing the laconic announcement ' I sleep in London,' might not be put into her hands, bringing to her, in spite of long habit, visions of sudden illness, and railway accidents, and all their train of horrors.

It was in vain, therefore, for Mrs. Patty to ask for any certain intelligence of Mr. Cameron's movements, and to confess the truth, she knew this quite well ; but the peculiar habit of mind, which made her always look forward, and settle what was to be done, so, as she said, not to neglect anything, was too strong for her mental conviction, and like many overscrupulous persons, she often wasted valuable moments in endeavouring to make that assurance ' doubly sure,' which in reality could not be sure at all. Twice that day she stopped at the Hall, on her way to and from the village, to inquire whether any message had been received from Mr. Cameron— whether it was quite certain that he would be at home to dinner ; and each time, being told that he was expected, left a message that she would come up in the evening to talk to him about a little business. Probably Mr. Cameron was not particularly well pleased with the announcement, when he thought that his day's toil was over, but he made no comment upon it when it was communicated to him by his wife. His face had a preoccupied expression, and after a moment's silence, he said, 'You have arranged, I believe, for Rosamond's visit to-morrow ? '

' Yes ; that is, if you quite approve. I believe I did right ; you said that she might go up with you.'

' She can't ; I have an engagement out of town to-morrow. I shall not be there till evening ; then I shall sleep there.'

' Oh ! that changes everything. What would you wish to have done ? '

' What would you wish, my dear ? These are matters for a lady's arrangement.'

' Conyers might go up with her ; or— I think Mr. Verney is going ; he might take care of her for such a short way.'

Mr. Cameron's face darkened. ' Cordelia ! you forget the opinion of the world. I will not have my daughter travelling about with Mr. Verney.'

' Certainly not, my dear Mr. Cameron. (Mrs. Cameron had never reached the familiarity of a Christian name.) Anything you wish ; but it is such a very little distance, I thought '——

' My dear Cordelia, you think in the wrong place. When thinking would be of some use, you act without it ; when it can be of no use, you perplex yourself with it. I do not choose that Rosamond should go up to London with Mr. Verney.'

' Of course, it will be just as you wish,' was the reply.

' It must be just as I wish for the future, though it has not been for the past. Rosamond ought never to have been allowed to go to the Verneys.'

Poor Mrs. Cameron ! It was as if a thunderbolt had fallen at her feet. Why, the visit had been proposed, and discussed, and settled, all with her husband's consent. She would never have thought of it if he had objected. But some error had been committed, it was evident, and the masculine character was not to be called upon to bear the burden of that imputation.

'It ought never to have been,' continued Mr. Cameron ; ' Rosamond is too young to go into society without some one to watch her.'

' But I am so unwell, my dear Mr. Cameron, I can't bear late hours ; and Mr. Verney is such an old friend, and so very fond of Rosamond. Indeed, if you remember '——

' My dear, I can remember nothing, except that you have been guilty of a blunder, and that all we can do is to make the best of it. Why don't they send up dinner ? '

Mr. Cameron rang the bell ; desired that the cook should be told that dinner was ten minutes behind time ; declined to hear any explanation as to the difference of clocks, and walked out of the room. His wife was left in a state of nervous worry, which exhibited itself in a tone of voice so plaintive that Mr. Cameron, after bearing with it as well as he could until dessert was placed on the table, put an end to it, when the servants were gone, by saying, patronisingly, ' My dear Cordelia, you have good intentions—most women have ; I give you every credit for them.' And Mrs. Cameron sighed, and smiled, and sighed, and was ' herself again.'

But not so Mr. Cameron. Mrs. Patty perceived this when, on her arrival at the Hall after dinner, she was ushered into the library, and found him ready for the proposed business interview—ready, at least, so far as a seat in an arm-chair, and a paper-knife held in his hand, to be rapped gently when he grew impatient, could make him so. But not at all ready if any judgment could be formed from his face, for his cold grey eyes looked out from under their dark eyelashes with a glance which was all the more alarming to Mrs. Patty, because the irritability it betrayed was otherwise so outwardly controlled.

But Mrs. Patty was bold as a lion when she had to ask for another ; and she began without apology or preface : ' Mr. Cameron, I promised Miss Medley I would come and talk to you about a little business. She is too nervous to come herself; and I said—indeed, I was sure you would feel for her as a neighbour. As the Doctor says, it is a great bond, living in one parish.'

'The good Doctor says what is very true; may I ask what the business is?'

'It is a puzzling business. I don't know that I can make it quite clear. I am not so young as I was, Mr. Cameron; and my memory is not like yours.'

Mr. Cameron bowed, and merely repeated in a questioning tone: 'And the business?'

'Yes, the business; let me see. You know, Mr. Cameron, that Miss Medley has a nephew in India?'

'I believe I have heard so.'

'Oh! but you must know. Her nephew; the one she brought up; the last of her sister's family, for whom she sacrificed so much. He went to India just when she came to live at Yare.'

'Yes, I recall the circumstances now,' said Mr. Cameron.

'He has had more than half her money spent upon him, in one way and another,' continued Mrs. Patty. 'She spoilt him, no doubt; and '——

'He has been in India ever since, I believe,' politely interrupted Mr. Cameron.

'Yes, for five-and-twenty years. He is a widower, and has one daughter, who was educated in England; but he always kept her away from his aunt, because she was not grand enough for him. He is ungrateful, Mr. Cameron; he cares for nothing but himself.'

'And he is coming home?' inquired Mr. Cameron.

'Not yet; nothing is fixed. In fact, my belief is that he can't afford it; he has lived in such style. His daughter, Charlotte, has been indulged like a princess. They say she is very beautiful.'

'And you wish to have my advice about this young lady?' inquired Mr. Cameron, as he gently tapped the paper-knife.

'No, not about the young lady, but about her papa. Gentlemen are more difficult to deal with than young ladies, Mr. Cameron; at least, poor Miss Medley finds it so. Mr. Stuart, I fear, may be an extravagant man.'

'Perhaps what the gentleman is, will be found to be of more consequence on the present occasion, than what Mrs. Patty

Kingsbury fears he may be,' observed Mr Cameron in a tone which passed like a cold blast over Mrs. Patty's nerves, but which had the desired effect of bringing her to the point.

'You want me to ask my question at once, Mr. Cameron; but if I do, I shall have to go back afterwards. Mr. Stuart wants Miss Medley to lend him some more money.'

'Precisely.'

'But that is not the whole. I shall have a difficulty in explaining, because I don't know everything myself.'

Mr. Cameron stood up : 'Excuse me, my good Mrs. Patty, but if I am to give an opinion, do me the favour to refer me to some one who does know everything.'

'But I can't, Mr. Cameron ; Miss Medley will not tell me. But the question of security is what I wish to know about— what the Doctor wishes, rather. I told him what Miss Medley told me, and he could not understand '——

'Indeed !'

'But he said you might ; and so I came. This is what the Doctor wrote down about it. He is not at all well to-day ; but he took a great deal of trouble to make it clear, for he is very anxious that Miss Medley should not be led into difficulties.'

Mr. Cameron took the paper which Mrs. Patty held out to him with an inclination of the head, all the more courteous, because he allowed himself, at the same moment, to toss the paper-knife on the table.

In the solemn silence which ensued, Mrs. Patty might have heard the beating of her own heart, but for the ticking of Mr. Cameron's admirable time-piece, never known—or, which did just as well, never acknowledged—to lose or gain in the course of the year.

Mr. Cameron read through the paper carefully twice ; then, laying it on the table, said : 'Dr. Kingsbury asks a difficult question, requiring a careful legal answer.'

'No doubt,' replied Mrs. Patty ; 'because, you see, Mr. Cameron, if the question was not about law, he would most likely have been able to answer it himself.'

'Exactly so ; I think it may be better for me to reply to it in writing. Messages, Mrs. Patty, are apt to create, rather than to lessen a difficulty.'

'Very true ; especially when they are sent by a person who has a bad memory.'

'May I venture, then, to detain you whilst I write a note ?'

'Oh ! I can wait just as long as you like ; but the Doctor said I might ask you one more favour, in order to carry back a little comfort to poor Miss Medley.   She is very anxious to see some one who understands law matters ; and she thinks, that if you would kindly undertake to hear all she has to say, you might not only give an opinion as to the security, but help her to see her way as to some other points.   The fact is, Mr. Cameron—I don't wish it to go farther—but the Doctor thinks, from what I tell him, that the poor thing is being worried out of any sense she ever possessed ; and I never could think that much since I found her so bewitched with the globules.   Still, talking is a comfort to her ; and, if you could see her, you might get more out of her than any one else.'

'Dr. Kingsbury refers to this wish in his note,' said Mr. Cameron.

'Yes, he told me he should ask you.   The Doctor would see her himself if he were able, but he has symptoms of gout again, and even if he could go, he says he should not have the same influence.   The doctor is very good at a sermon, as every one knows' (Mr. Cameron bowed assent), 'but there is a difference, at least so he thinks, between that and law—though as I tell him, if people would listen to sermons, they would not go to law.'

'Most true ; and if people would listen to law, they would not talk so much nonsense in sermons, Mrs. Patty ;' and Mr. Cameron relaxed into a smile.   'But that is beside the point. If you and Dr. Kingsbury really believe that a visit from me would be any comfort to the unhappy lady, it would of course be my duty to go to her.'

Mrs. Patty looked and felt as though she had gained a triumph, and she was right.   Her simple kind-heartedness had without any direct intention touched Mr. Cameron upon a vulnerabe point.   He liked to be consulted ; he desired especially to be the general referee in his own parish; and he was by no means insensible to the wants of his fellow-creatures, whether moral or physical. The old nursery rhyme—

> 'Of all my mother's children I love myself the best,
> And when I am provided for, I care not for the rest'—

was true of him, as it is of a vast majority of persons, only so far as regarded the statement in the first line.

He wrote his note to Dr. Kingsbury, and then wished Mrs. Patty a really cordial good-bye, feeling that for once she had assisted him to recover the stately equanimity which alone befitted him. In the contemplation of his importance and usefulness, he was able to forget the stupid piece of gossip, overheard accidentally at the railway station, which had coupled Rosamond's name with Mr. Verney's, and asserted that she must be engaged to him, because she was going to stay with the Verneys in London. Mr. Cameron despised such reports; he knew there was nothing in them; they were but the rumour of a day, and would be forgotten to-morrow; and the idea was an absurdity. But still it irritated him. What business had people to talk of him or his family? It was so impertinent!

CHAPTER XVII.

IT was the same evening. The church-clock had just struck half-past seven, and the chilliness which lingers in the air, even in the month of May, was enough to serve as an excuse to fidgety invalids to light a little fire, and make a comfortable semblance of winter. Mrs. Haynes had persuaded Miss Medley to have a fire. 'It was good for company,' she said, 'as well as for warmth.' And the advice was taken, though not without evident compunctions of conscience on Miss Medley's part, and many expressions of self-reproach for such extravagance, 'Especially now, when it was right—when it was necessary—when indeed, if Mrs. Haynes did but know, she might say very differently. But it was cold, no doubt; people could not live without warmth; it was part of the principle of life, so Dr. Medley had often said. Caloric was a vital necessity,' &c. Mrs. Haynes cut short the scientific disquisition by putting a lighted match to the scraps of brown paper and fragments of damp sticks with which little Miss Haynes had filled the grate that morning, and in a few seconds after Miss Medley was in the middle of smoke, and its accompaniments—an open window, breeze-blown curtains, and flickering candles: and kneeling before the fire, forgot for the time her anxieties and her sorrows, in the eager desire to fan dying sparks and make green twigs *catch*. But that little excitement was over now. The fire was burning well if not brightly, and Miss Medley, seated in the leathern arm-chair, was listening to the footsteps which passed down the village street, whilst feeling too nervously expectant to be able to attend to the piece of knitting which, as a matter of course, had been made ready for the evening's employment.

There came a quick rap at the street-door, and Miss Medley seized her knitting, and as she tremblingly held the needles, succeeded in letting down two stitches, and so preparing for herself occupation both for mind and fingers in the work of taking them up again. That was a little help in the effort made to overcome nervousness; and in the slight delay which occurred before the door was opened, and Mr. Verney announced, Miss Medley was able so far to recover herself as to receive her visitor with the politeness and somewhat of the cordiality due to an intimate acquaintance.

Mr. Verney, on his part, was evidently quite at home; at least, so far as regarded making himself comfortable. He merely said, ' Your fire is pleasant, though it is the month of May;' and then he sat down in a low chair calling itself easy, and stretched himself out in a languid self-indulgent posture, only permissible in the presence of a friend.

' Yes, it is cold to-night,' was the reply; ' that is, chilly; that is, for an invalid. I have been sadly good-for-nothing to-day. Writing that long letter, yesterday, tired me a good deal.'

' And you have sent it ? ' he inquired.

' No,'—there was some hesitation—' I waited, and I thought I might have something to add at the last moment, but I wished to be ready for the mail. I have a great objection to being hurried, Mr. Verney.'

' So have a good many people,' replied Mr. Verney ; ' but if you are like me, Miss Medley, you will feel satisfied now that the thing is done, and not vex yourself any further. Vexation and worry try the nerves far more than hard work. May I be permitted to stir your fire ? I know it is taking a liberty, for we have not known each other seven years.'

' It must be two years since George wrote me home word that he had found a friend, who was likely to join him in a successful speculation,' said Miss Medley. ' I little thought you were that friend when we met the other night at the Colonel's. George keeps his business very secret always.'

' He was mistaken as to success,' said Mr. Verney, in a tone of indifference. ' I suppose I have no right to complain, but George Stuart is not a fortunate man. If I had known that at the time, the wisdom of the serpent would have taught me to avoid him.'

' It might have been well if you had mutually avoided each other, Mr. Verney,' said Miss Medley shortly ; and as she spoke she had recourse to her knitting-needles, and worked them so diligently that it would have appeared there was no desire to continue the subject. Mr. Verney, however, was proof against any such feminine mode of testifying disapprobation. He sat silent for a few seconds, perhaps to humour his companion's whim, and presently taking up a book, said, as he turned over the pages—

' I will put that letter into the post for you, if you like. There may be some mistake, otherwise, about the postage.'

No reply, but the knitting was evidently in inextricable confusion.

' Shall I take it for you ? ' was repeated.

' Thank you, no ; I can send it myself.' And then Miss Medley's candour got the better of her nervousness, and she looked up at Mr. Verney—her little grey eyes glittering with

I

excitement, and said : 'I don't think—I don't mean—that is, I feel it will be better—indeed, Mr. Verney, I have made up my mind to consult Mr. Cameron.'

'Mr. Cameron!' an exclamation escaped Mr. Verney's lips, which the next instant he repented. 'Excuse me, Miss Medley but really this is too senseless. Consult that stiff buckram fool! I must call him a fool, let him be never so much your friend. A man who knows no more about India than I do about Kamtschatka! Why, it is monstrous!' He started up, and paced up and down the room.

Miss Medley sat silent, but trembling all over.

'You have done it!' he exclaimed, stopping as if an idea had struck him. 'This is only an excuse for telling me that you have put my private affairs into the hands of a man with whom I have no concern, and who, for aught I know, may do me the greatest injury.'

'Injury! Oh no ; Mr. Cameron is incapable of that. And your private affairs! Mr. Verney, I should never mention your name. I have given my word : you could never believe me capable of such meanness.'

'I believe what I see, and what I know, madam,' replied Mr. Verney haughtily ; 'and since it is necessary, I must again warn you that your young niece's happiness, your nephew's prosperity—I say nothing of my own prospects—all depend upon your keeping these family arrangements strictly within our own knowledge.'

'But the security?' said Miss Medley. 'Dr. Kingsbury could give me no advice, but he warned me '——

'Madam! Dr. Kingsbury!—ask his opinion! Then let the whole thing go. Good evening! I beg pardon for having intruded upon you.' He turned to the door, bent, as Miss Medley supposed, upon taking his departure. But no one else would have been so deceived. Mr. Verney had not the slightest intention of going ; and when Miss Medley, in a feeble voice of remonstrance and apology, entreated that he would allow her to explain, he reseated himself, with a patronising and forgiving air, which had the desired effect of entirely confirming the poor lady's previous suspicions as to her own misdeeds.

'I would only wish to say, Mr. Verney,' she began—

'Say anything you please, dear madam. I shall be only too glad to find that I have been mistaken.'

'But you are not mistaken, Mr. Verney. Oh dear! it makes me very nervous; and I have forgotten to take my camomilla to-day; and Mrs. Haynes broke a bottle—but never mind.' Mr. Verney had thrown himself back in his chair with a slight groan. 'I have not mentioned you, Mr. Verney; I only spoke of George. I should never have done that, but Mrs. Patty came in, and found me crying. I had been thinking much of our last conversation; you had been very pressing.'

'Pressing, solely with a view to your niece's happiness,' interrupted Mr. Verney.

'Yes, poor Charlotte! Though I have seen so little of her, I am deeply attached to her. My poor misguided nephew's only daughter. It would be grievous to have the engagement broken off.'

'As it must be, unless her father's affairs are soon satisfactorily settled,' observed Mr. Verney. 'I have already explained how much I have done to save him from ruin; and now, if he should fail, I must all but fail too. At least, it would be impossible for me to think of marriage. If the catastrophe should come, it will be shipwreck for all. But so let it be, if so it is ordered.' The tone might have been that of a humble saint. It completely subdued Miss Medley's heart, and her tears flowed fast.

'Indeed, Mr. Verney, you do me injustice. Of course I would help. Of course I would do everything in my power. Relations have great claims, and George was quite like my own child. But supposing your plan for setting things right should fail?'

'My dear madam, it cannot. I feel for your anxiety, but you must place confidence in me, and I tell you that it cannot; a little ready money is all that is needed. However, if you choose to doubt my word, you must. I have nothing more to say, and I am not responsible for the consequences,'— which evidently implied that Miss Medley was; and as is the case with many nervous middle-aged ladies, responsibility was her bugbear.

'Poor Charlotte!' she murmured to herself.

'Poor Charlotte, indeed!' echoed Mr. Verney; 'but your pity for her will not be long needed, Miss Medley; she was a mere shadow when I left India'—a deep sigh accompanied the words.

'I am very sorry for you, Mr. Verney. I assure you I am, though you won't believe it.'

'I am bound to believe what a lady tells me,' was the sarcastic answer; 'but your pity is even more wasted upon me than upon your niece, Miss Medley. I have faced the future as a man should face it, boldly. I am prepared for my desolate life. And for her'—and his voice slightly faltered—'sorrow will soon take her to her rest.'

'It is very sad, very dreadful; if I only knew what to do; if I could only have another opinion about the security. But you know, Mr. Verney, I have spent such sums upon my nephew already.'

'I know you have, my dear madam. I don't say a word in his defence, only he is Charlotte's father.'

'And you are quite certain it is safe?'

'I am placing my own fortune in the same risk,' was the reply.

'And you don't think Mr. Cameron could give me a good opinion?'

'You may as well ask him about the affairs of the inhabitants of the moon, if there are any. Mr. Cameron is an English lawyer. India is a myth to him.'

'And Charlotte and you would marry directly if the affairs were put straight?' inquired Miss Medley.

'We parted with that understanding.'

'Oh dear!' Miss Medley's sigh came from the very depths of her heart. At that moment a knock was heard at the front-door, and she started up.

'James, from the Hall, ma'am, has brought a note, and waits for an answer,' said Mrs. Haynes, allowing only her head to be seen in the doorway.

'Come in. Tell James to wait.'

Mr. Verney took the note from Mrs. Haynes, and retained it till she had retired. As he laid it before Miss Medley, he remarked, carelessly, 'That stiff fool! How like the writing is to himself.'

The few lines were very easily deciphered.

'Mr. Cameron will come and see me to-morrow,' exclaimed Miss Medley.

'As you will;' and Mr. Verney drew near the table. 'The letters must go to-night if they are to be in time for the Indian mail, and the post closes at half-past eight.'

'But indeed you are mistaken. I always reckoned upon sending the letter to-morrow.'

'Then you must excuse me for saying you reckoned wrongly. Just calculate, and you will see I am right.'

Mr. Verney had suggested an impossibility. Miss Medley was far too nervous and confused to calculate anything. She could but lean back in her chair, with Mr. Cameron's note held in her trembling fingers, and say, 'Oh dear! oh dear!'

'Is the answer ready, ma'am?' asked impatient Mrs. Haynes, appearing again at the door.

'In a moment—just wait a moment; or say I will send an answer the first thing in the morning. O Mr. Verney! is it quite necessary the letter should go to-night?'

'A quarter-past eight.' Mr. Verney took out his watch, and held it in his hand.

'Oh dear! oh dear! You say it won't do to wait? Not if I pay extra?'

'Sixteen minutes past eight, and it will take ten minutes to walk to the post-office.'

Miss Medley opened her desk, and took out a letter, directed but not closed. 'I am afraid I have promised too decidedly. I might have given him hope enough to keep up his spirits, and nothing more.'

'Hope and ruin,' was the quiet reply; and Miss Medley closed the letter and put it into Mr. Verney's hands.

He paused one moment at the door. 'Let me remind you, secrecy is as necessary as help. Even now one incautious word about Charlotte, about myself, about anything, in short, and you may ruin us all.'

CHAPTER XVIII.

MYRA CAMERON'S life had sunk back into dulness greater than ordinary, in contrast to her recent excitement. She missed Godfrey and Edmund and Rosamond, but more than all she missed the stimulant of Mr. Verney's society. It was a difficult task to be cheerful, still more difficult to be obedient.

Mrs. Cameron took up Myra's time by giving her a number of petty employments—dressing flowers, writing notes, carrying messages backwards and forwards from the boudoir to the schoolroom, with an occasional interlude of novel reading. The good of such occupations was not clear, and Myra attended to them listlessly, and was, in consequence, found fault with. Then came the old evil of temper, and sometimes disrespectful words. Myra was scolded as a child, and, in consequence, retired in disgust to her own room to dream over past pleasures, and contrast Mr. Verney's unobtrusive flattery of her highest tastes with the wearisome complaints to which she was now subject.

It was a very dangerous state of mind, for vanity was at the root of it, and just that kind of vanity which was likely to disguise itself under the form of high aspirations, longings after the true, the real, the useful, such as often take the place of obedience to that matter-of-fact piece of advice, heard by so many English girls, and appreciated by so few, to 'do their duty in that state of life to which God has called them.'

Myra's safeguard was her truth; the instinct which made her see actions in their true light, and call them by their true names. And now when she unexpectedly made the discovery that she was constantly thinking of what Mr. Verney would say or had said of her, how he would advise her and talk to her, and regret the interruption of her studies—instead of believing that she was thirsting for intellectual companionship, and longing for guidance and direction, she simply faced the fact that she was very vain, and that vanity was a degrading fault, and ought to be struggled with and conquered. How? was the question; and it was one which sounded Myra's conscience to its very depth. For it is a great sacrifice which we are required to make when we are called upon to subdue vanity. No half measures will succeed. The root lies so deep and spreads so wide that the evil which to-day we believe to be dead, will to-morrow exhibit itself in a form and place for which we were wholly unprepared. And the fault is one with which the world deals very gently. It calls it by soft names. It talks of love of approbation, and says that no character is perfect without such love. Myra had heard this often, for it was a favourite axiom with Mr. Verney, who was indeed always as lenient towards principles as he was severe upon actions. Now and then she had ventured upon arguments with him on the subject, and as was naturally to be expected, had always been conquered. But only for the time. The instinct of her young honest heart was stronger than his phrenology and metaphysics; and Myra felt, though she could never have told why, that although love of approbation might be innocent, vanity certainly was not. Where the one ended and the other began there was no necessity for her to inquire. She was not called upon to write a book of moral philosophy for the enlightenment of the world, but to undertake the work of self-discipline. And now, in the solitude of her own room, out of the reach of Mr. Verney's sophisms, she was able to look at herself as in the sight of God, and in the consciousness of that Presence, to judge herself by the only true standard.

Strong faults of natural disposition are generally considered great evils. Yet, paradoxical though it may sound, it would probably be found upon inquiry that in very many instances they are great blessings. Certainly they were so in Myra's case. It was quite impossible for her to shut her eyes to her own moral deformity, especially since she had really, from religious feelings, striven to improve. The temper, selfishness, vanity, of which she had been accused from childhood, were quite evident to herself now. It might be very humiliating to acknowledge them, but Myra could not act a lie upon herself; and about a week after Mr. Verney's departure, the result of a display of temper caused by wounded vanity, which had brought upon her a lecture from her father, was the determination to take out her faults, as it were, one by one, to set them before herself as a whole, and see what was to be done with them.

There was a kind of stern satisfaction in the resolve, such as one might imagine Brutus to have had when he sat in judgment upon his son. Myra liked anything strong and determined, even if it were self-condemnation. It was not in her nature to tamper either with good or evil; and a few months before there might have been somewhat of the spirit of stoicism in this craving for self-discipline; but she had learnt to think very differently since her illness. If she longed for goodness now, it was not as it once might have been, because goodness was strength and sin weakness; but because there was the yearning, longing desire to love even as she had been loved —to obey because obedience was the test of love.

And this evening, as she sat lonely and unhappy in the evening twilight, struggling with the remains of her lately-roused temper, there was no wounded pride in her self-examination. She had prayed for guidance with as sincere a desire to be guided, as to act, when guidance should be granted; and it is this sincerity of purpose upon which the blessing of God will always rest.

Myra thought, and prayed, and thought again, and called her faults by hard names, and began to make special little schemes for circumventing each in particular, until it suddenly struck her, that the sacrifice she was to make was not the uprooting of any one, or two, or three faults, but of the root of all faults—the sacrifice of self. Temper, vanity, self-indulgence, were but different symptoms of the same disease; and hitherto, as one had died away another had sprung up. The consequence of this failure had been a want of fixedness of purpose. What was required was the renunciation of self in every form—in thought, in word, and in deed. Myra did not deceive herself as to what this renunciation implied. Pleasant memories of past praise; pleasant dreams of future flattery; pleasant schemes of self-gratification; pleasant visions of self-aggrandisement—all to be crushed, trampled upon, kept down, by a tread, firm and merciless; and in their stead a life to be lived for others—to be lost, as it were, in the happiness of others—with a spirit of self-sacrifice which should find its example in nothing short of the sacrifice of Him who had given Himself for her.

No marvel that the frail human heart should sink at such a prospect. Myra's heart did sink, but her resolve did not therefore waver. There were some minutes of grave thought, and then she knelt, and with an intensity of desire, before which all former resolutions melted into nothingness, commended her weakness to God's strength, praying Him to accept her will, and give her grace to fulfil that most earnest purpose of her soul.

Such seasons are, to the inward life, seasons of growth. Myra felt it to be so. From that evening she was conscious of having made a start into something more than womanhood—of having gained a strength of principle, which was something more powerful than any human stimulus. And yet the days which followed were marked by nothing except greater quietness, and a more evenly-balanced temperament. Only one thing struck Mrs. Cameron. Myra, rather timidly, said to her in the course of conversation, that she thought she was old enough now to stay at church on Sunday. This was her way of expressing her wish to attend to a hitherto omitted and sacred duty. Mrs. Cameron made no objection; only she warned Myra that young people who professed to be religious should not give way to temper and be perverse—a remark in which Myra acquiesced; and that was all the outward help she had in preparation for her first Communion. Dr. Kingsbury took his part in the service on the Sunday, and shook hands with her very kindly when they met afterwards; but the young, earnest, striving spirit was an enigma to him. He prayed for it, but he did not know how to aid it. It was ordered in God's Providence that its hopes and disappointments, its struggles and its victories, should alike be endured alone. A trial came on the following day.

'Myra, my dear, I want to talk to you.' This was Mrs. Cameron's usual mode of beginning a conversation about nothing ; and Myra sat down by her mother's sofa.

'Shut the door, my love. Are you sure that Juliet and Annette are in the schoolroom ? '

No, Myra was not sure, and was sent to make certain of the fact. She returned, and again took her seat.

' Is it anything of consequence you have to say, mamma ? '

' Of consequence ! Yes, my dear ; all things which concern my children are of consequence.'

Mrs. Cameron spoke more earnestly than usual, and Myra asked anxiously if anything was the matter.

' Nothing the matter, my dear ; only I do so dislike change. But your father thinks it necessary, and Mrs. Verney agrees with him.'

Myra started from her seat. ' Mrs. Verney, mamma ! Why does she interfere ? Am I to be sent to school ? '

' My love, you are so impetuous. I said nothing about your going to school. Pray, sit down again. I consider your education finished. But the two younger ones have had few advantages, and Mrs. Verney says very justly, that Miss Greaves is not sufficient for them. She believes, and I feel she is right, that with proper instruction Annette would be equal to Rosamond ; and Juliet, though so clever, would be much improved if she could be somewhat softened.'

Disliking Mrs. Verney, Myra's first impulse was to suggest every possible objection to the plan.

' I can't think school will be good for Juliet, mamma. Mrs. Verney can't know much about her. It will make her conceited. And Annette is, you know, not always truthful ; and if she should be placed with bad companions, she will be much worse. Every one says that schools are dangerous for girls who have not high principles. And then, what will poor Miss Greaves do ? She has nothing else to look to.' This last assertion brought Myra to the consciousness that she was exaggerating. Miss Greaves was by no means likely to want pupils, even if Annette and Juliet were taken from her. After the pause of a second, she added, 'At least, I don't think Miss Greaves will ever have any pupils she likes as well.'

'Myra, you are so tiresome. As your father says, you were born with a "no" in your mouth. Why will you always see difficulties?'

'I can't help it, mamma. That is, I know I see difficulties when I don't like a thing.'

'It is all selfishness, Myra. You are so very selfish. You never can think of what is good for any one but yourself. You must try and get over the feeling, my dear. It is a great fault.'

If Myra had been selfish before, she was tempted to give way to a fit of unrestrained ill-temper now. But all she said was, 'I suppose I am afraid of being lonely.'

'My love, I thought of that; but you must learn to be Rosamond's companion, and being with her more will be of use to you. As Mrs. Verney says, it will get you out of your awkward ways, and you won't be so affected in society.'

Poor Myra! This was the most trying of all accusations. 'Mamma!' she exclaimed, 'I don't care what Mrs. Verney thinks, but if you will only tell me yourself what you mean by being affected, I should be so very much obliged. Is it any one thing—walking or talking—or what is it? I don't mean to be affected, but I know I am, because people tell me so, and then I think about it, and try not to be, and that makes it worse. If I could only forget myself—if any one could only teach me what to do, that I might forget myself!'

'How silly, my love! To forget yourself, means not to think about yourself; there is nothing mysterious in it. When you go into company, or when you are introduced to any one, just put all thought of yourself aside, and be natural.'

'But, mamma, please listen—please try and understand. You know I can't dress myself properly; I can't make my hair smooth, or put on my things straight—I never could; and when I am dressing for company, Conyers, and Juliet, and you yourself, and even Miss Greaves, if she happens to be here, all come into my room and pull me about. I don't mean to be disrespectful, but I am pulled about just as if I was a doll; and then I am told that I have an awkward stoop, and that nothing ever sits properly upon me. And perhaps I hear you sigh quite loudly; and I see Rosamond so pretty— I don't envy her in the least, except that she has no trouble in making herself look nice; but after all this I am sent to the drawing-room, and perhaps at the very last moment stopped again to be set to rights, and told to look natural and forget myself. Mamma, if my life depended upon it, I couldn't do it.'

Mrs. Cameron looked thunderstruck at the bold avowal. 'My dear Myra, I don't understand you. But you are so nervous and sensitive, it may be better not to talk about yourself. Your father comforts me sometimes by saying, that when you have seen more of the world there is a hope you may be different; and so he and I are both agreed that you shall go with us to London for a couple of months.'

'Anything you like, mamma.'

Myra was natural even to indifference then.

'My dear, your father and I do everything we can to please you, and I should have hoped you would have accepted the idea in a different spirit. But I can see you are put out this morning, so we will just turn to a different subject. Did Rosamond say anything in her note to you about how long Mrs. Verney would wish her to stay?'

'Nothing, mamma, except that they all seem very glad to have her, and that they have engagements for the week after next, when Mr. Verney will be with them again.'

'Oh! He is away now, I believe.'

'He goes away on Friday for three days, Rosamond says.'

'Only for three days? Your father won't like that.'

'But I thought every one knew Mr. Verney was to be there all the time Rosamond was,' observed Myra; 'I heard him make the arrangements.' She looked in her mother's face to see if there was any mystery to be read there.'

Yes, there was some mystery, for Mrs. Cameron inquired in a disturbed tone : 'When did you hear it, Myra?'

'Just as Mr. Verney was saying good-bye ; the very day before he went away,' was the answer.

'But Rosamond told me he would be in Yorkshire.'

'Yes, afterwards, when her visit is over, but not now.'

'My love, ring the bell and ask if my coffee is ready.'

This was a signal that the conversation was to be at an end.

CHAPTER XIX.

MYRA wandered out into the shrubbery, seeking the most solitary and hidden path. A short conversation it had been, and yet how it had ruffled her. Myra was accustomed to her mother's mode of alluding to her temper and affectation, and could bear it better than many girls of her age would have done, especially now with the purpose which lay so deep in her heart, to make, in every form, the sacrifice of self. But human nature is human nature still, and struggle, even though it end in victory, must be felt. Myra paced the straight walk, by the side of the field opposite the Rectory garden, and tried to think of everything which might enable her to view her annoyances in the light in which they could be best borne, and as she uttered the few words of prayer which were becoming habitual to her whenever her mind was disturbed, felt herself recalled to a calmer, clearer atmosphere, in which everything could be viewed without distortion.

This sudden plan for her sisters might or might not be good, but the fact that it had been suggested by Mrs. Verney was sufficient to make it unpalatable. To think, act, blunder, and suffer their own way is in most cases the great desire of the young. As a general rule, they prefer to starve after their own fashion, rather than to live in luxury after the fashion of their elders. An influence external to the family is, for this reason, peculiarly obnoxious in their eyes. Let it be exerted never so sincerely for their benefit, it is still resented as an interference, and Myra certainly had no cause to look with favour upon any of Mrs. Verney's suggestions as they regarded herself. Very useful they often were, and very necessary; but the spirit in which they were offered was cold, criticising, and worldly. It was the latter element which made the two characters antagonistic.

Yet the suggestions of the world are not always to be set aside as valueless. Myra had too much common sense to think this, and being aware of her prejudice against Mrs. Verney, she tried all the more to view the proposed plan impartially. Juliet and Annette at school! It might be very desirable for them in many ways; it might give them regularity, and a stimulus which would make them work. And the unknown evils—she knew nothing about them, and had expressed all her fears when she said to her mother that Annette was untruthful, and that bad companions might make her worse. Perhaps, after all—it was the conclusion arrived at after the meditation of a quarter of an hour—it might not be her business to trouble herself about the matter; perhaps this habit of objecting, this perpetual 'no' of which her mother complained, and of which Myra herself was aware, was only another form of the self to be kept under. It might be that, at sixteen, she was not the best judge as to how her sisters' education should be conducted. It might even be more important to her to consider how she should conduct her own in the new phase of domestic affairs which had just presented itself. If they went to London, she would be obliged to see more people, and there would be no time for reading or drawing; it would be a perpetual round of sight-seeing and visitors —visitors involving dress, dress bringing up again the dread of awkwardness and affectation. The only comfort would be in having Mr. Verney there. If she could go to some of the exhibitions with him, it would be very pleasant; and perhaps he would persuade her father to let her have some drawing lessons; and she might find a little time for reading before the very late dinners which they were sure to have. After all, it might not be disagreeable.

It was self again—innocent, simple-minded, but neverthe-

less undoubtedly self; and again Myra's truth, and sense, and
honesty of conscience whispered to her that there was something higher than this reference to her own enjoyment—even
the thought of what she might do for others; how she might
accept her London life as a type of all life, and seek to fulfil
the claims which each day brought;—being useful to her
father, giving sympathy and attention to her mother, trying
to share Rosamond's pursuits, overcoming her shyness in
society, endeavouring to be pleasant in conversation; and
putting aside the care for herself, sacrifice the hermit life
which was her taste, whilst living the life of the world, if need
be, because it was in the world that God had placed her, and
there that He willed her to serve Him.

Myra could bear the prospect of London with more than
equanimity when she looked at it in this light. It roused her
energy—the energy of self-discipline and self-sacrifice; and
without this energy the most varied existence will become
vapid—with it, the most monotonous must be interesting.

Myra was really very happy when she knocked at the door
of the Rectory parlour, hoping to find Mrs. Patty, and talk to
her about some books for the Parish Library, which she had
undertaken to cover and catalogue. She had formed a little
plan for persuading her mother to ask the old Doctor and his
sister to stay with them for a few days in London, and consult
a London physician about the Rector's ailments; but this, of
course, was only a scheme in her own head at present. She
might, however, just say there was an idea of going to London,
and see what remarks Mrs. Patty would make upon the subject.
But she was disappointed; no reply was made to her knock—
Mrs. Patty was out, and the Doctor might very probably be
tired and resting. Afraid of disturbing him, she found her
way to the kitchen, where sat Faith, close by the window, with
a screen between her and the fire, employed in mending the
Doctor's stockings.

'Such a great hole!' Myra heard her say to Betsey, as the
latter stood by, gazing with a kind of alarmed satisfaction at
the heap of clothes to be mended, which were piled up in the
basket by Faith's chair. 'To think, now, of his not having had

any new stockings for three years. Would any one believe it ? Why a regiment might march through !' and her large thumb appeared filling up the delinquent hole.

'He would dress in rags, and be none the wiser, if it wasn't for Mrs. Patty,' replied Betsey. 'But—Why, here's Miss Myra, to be sure ! Beg your pardon, Miss. Do you want anything ? '

'Only to know where Mrs. Patty is,' replied Myra. 'Is she gone out ? '

'About half-an-hour ago; down to Miss Medley's,' said Faith, not thinking it necessary to raise her eyes from her work, seeing she had known Myra, as she always said, 'from a babby.'

'If you please to leave a message, Miss, we can give it,' observed Betsey more respectfully.

'No, thank you ; I can go to Miss Medley's after her.'

'Which you'd better not do, if you'll take my word, Miss Myra,' said Faith. 'She's not to be seen by every one to-day, is Miss Medley.'

'Is she ill, then ? What is the matter ? '

'Can't say, Miss Myra ; who can when people takes to pins' heads ? But she's been very bad all night.'

'Bad ? Ill ? Has Mr. Harrison been to her ? '

'No one has been ; not a Christian soul except Mrs. Patty, and she forgets everything when there's good to be done. But it's here,' and Faith pointed to her forehead ; 'we know it, don't we, Betsey ? We've seen it coming this many months.'

'It will be better not to go to Miss Medley's, then,' said Myra, perplexed and alarmed at these vague hints.

'Not unless you wish to find yourself very much in the way, Miss Myra,' replied Faith.

'But here is Mrs. Patty,' exclaimed Betsey, looking out into the court. 'Dear me ! how troubled she does seem ! '

Mrs. Patty was at the kitchen door before Myra could run out to meet her. She just put her head in, and said, 'Faith!' and Faith laid down her work silently and mysteriously, and obeyed the summons. She came back again after a conference of a few seconds. 'You had better just go and say your say now, Miss Myra; you mayn't have another opportunity.'

Myra hesitated. 'It was nothing of consequence,' she said; 'only about some parish books.'

'Mrs. Patty can attend to you. I told her you were here,' repeated Faith, as she opened the door of a corner cupboard, and began to search amongst a large collection of keys.

'If it's the medicine key you are wanting,' said Betsey, 'you will find it in the cupboard upstairs; I left it there this morning. Is Mrs. Patty going to doctor her?'

'She says she must if Mr. Harrison doesn't come. She's quite light-headed.'

Myra caught the words as she was leaving the kitchen. They startled her so that she forgot her little matter of business, and rushing up to Mrs. Patty, exclaimed: 'Is poor Miss Medley so very ill? Can't anything be done for her?'

'We must try what we can, my dear; but we can't make her take medicine like a Christian, and she is very strange. O Myra! never take to it, my dear, never. It is cruelty to your friends, and death to yourself.'

'How? What?' exclaimed Myra.

'The globules, my dear. But never mind now. She has quite lost her senses, poor thing. No wonder! And that man!' The last words were uttered in an undertone.

'Has Mr. Harrison neglected her? can we send for him? Dear Mrs. Patty, mamma would be so glad to help.'

'Not at all, my dear. Mr. Harrison will come when he can. But just go up to the Doctor, Myra, and cheer him a little. Poor dear, he is a good deal troubled. He always thinks he ought to go where there is illness, and he can't. He never could get up and down Mrs. Haynes's stairs. Just go and talk to him, Myra.'

'And will he be able to tell me about the books?' inquired Myra.

'Yes, about anything you want, my dear. Only turn his thoughts if you can, and tell him that if Mr. Harrison doesn't come soon, I shall put a blister on poor Miss Medley myself. There can't be any harm in that—can there, Faith?'

K

' None at all, ma'am.   Blisters are blessings, whatever folks may say to the contrary.'

' Very true, Faith,' observed Mrs. Patty mournfully.   ' I confess it almost sounds profane to me to hear people talk against them as they do.'

' Indeed it does, ma'am.   A well-risen blister is a beautiful sight and a comforting, and I hope with all my heart this one will do the poor lady good.   Shall I go and fetch anything for you, or would you like to go to the medicine chest yourself?'

' I will go myself, thank you, Faith ; and on the way I can just look in upon the Doctor, and see how he is getting on.'

' And your dinner, Mrs. Patty?   You haven't had a morsel to-day !' exclaimed Betsey.

' I forgot the dinner,' was Mrs. Patty's simple reply ; ' but now you remind me of it, you shall just put me up a sandwich, and I will eat it as I walk back—never mind what it is ; and Miss Myra will stay to keep the Doctor company, I hope.   Remember to have the lamb thoroughly roasted for him, Betsey —rather over-roasted than not—and some asparagus ; he ate a few yesterday and seemed to enjoy them.'

' There is no cold meat, I am sorry to say, for a sandwich, ma'am,' said Betsey.

' Then a little bread and cheese—it will do quite as well. Get it ready, and I will manage to eat it somehow.   Now, Myra.'   Mrs. Patty led the way to the Doctor's study, and was followed by Myra, a little alarmed at the new duties which she saw were to be thrust upon her.

CHAPTER XX

THAT the old Doctor required comfort was evident. Mrs. Patty and Myra found him seated by the fire, for he always had a fire in his study even on the hottest day, and leaning back in his arm-chair, with St. Augustine pushed to one side as if he had not the heart to study.

Mrs. Patty went up to him and touched him on the shoulder. 'Doctor, dear, I have brought you a little companion. She means to look after you whilst I am away. You do mean it, don't you, Myra? And you can write a note up to your mamma, and tell her where you are. She will be glad to know you can be of use. And, Doctor, Mr. Harrison is gone out; he has been called away for the day, and if he doesn't come back in an hour—for we have sent a messenger for him—I mean to try a blister myself, which is a thing, you know, that won't hurt a baby.'

'Does she know any one?' asked the old man eagerly.

'She didn't when I came away, so, you see, you could have been of no use. Don't think about it, Doctor, dear. Now, good-bye! Myra, be sure you take care of him.'

'Might I read to you, sir?' said Myra timidly, as the door closed behind Mrs. Patty. It seemed a most presumptuous proposition, but it was her only idea of being of use.

The Doctor took her hand kindly. 'My little girl, I shall tire you. Patty should have left me to myself.'

'Oh no, sir! I would do anything in the world I could, but I am so sorry you are ill.'

'Not ill, child; only troubled. The poor lady, good Miss Medley, is ill.'

'If she is good, her illness doesn't so much signify, does it?' said Myra.

'Ah! not for her; but, Myra, we should do our duty whilst we can. "The night cometh when no man can work," and that is the case with me now. I cannot go to her though I would.'

'But if you would, sir, is not that enough?'

The Doctor repeated the word 'enough,' and then rested his head against the side of his great arm-chair, and what to Myra seemed a long pause followed.

What was passing in the old man's mind she could not guess; perhaps if she had known she would scarcely have understood it. Such a single-hearted, earnest, and outwardly innocent life he had led; so much respect he had gained, so much good done, she could little have imagined with what self-reproach the spirit trembling on the brink of the grave looked back upon those bygone years. The world saw nothing to condemn in them. Dr. Kingsbury had been early noted as a scholar, a man of classical research, a good theologian. If he had entered upon his living late, and in consequence pursued his studies somewhat in preference to his parochial duties, it was only what was to be expected. And no one could say that he neglected his parish; the worst complaint that was ever laid against him was that he understood books better than men. He had always sought for good curates, and given them a large stipend; his charities had been profuse; his sermons full of thought and earnestness; his supervision of his schools careful and continuous. The one only point in which he failed was in gaining the personal confidence of his people. In years past, with his thoughts given to St. Augustine and the Fathers, Dr. Kingsbury had not seen and felt this. He visited the sick when they sent for him, and trusted to his sister to tell him of their needs when they did not send, and so his conscience was satisfied. But it was different now. The souls entrusted to him came before him in more distinct individuality; it was a more separate responsibility for each which weighed upon him. He would fain seek rather than be sought. He longed to change places with his sister; to know the needs of his poor by visiting them in their own cottages; to know the temptations of the young by the confidence they might be led to place in him. He thought less of sermons and more of conversation. But he was helpless; confined for the most part to his study, rarely

preaching, and indeed taking very little part in the public
service beyond assisting in the administration of the Holy
Communion. And not only helpless, but from habit and tone
of mind, incompetent—that was the most painful consciousness. If all his energies had been restored to him, he would
still have felt the personal individual knowledge of his parishioners unattainable. Myra little knew, as she sat, leaning
her elbow on the arm of her old friend's chair, how soothing
to the sensitiveness of his almost morbid conscience was the
fact that any young thing could thus come to him, and be in a
measure free with him. He did not know how to lead her on
to be more free; but he felt grateful to her, and in the simplicity of his heart, his gratitude showed itself by unreserve.

'The good lady, Miss Medley, has been failing for some
time, so Patty tells me,' he said, 'and Patty thinks she is wrong
in having taken to homœopathy; but there is a principle in
homœopathy—a very remarkable one—not to be put aside.
We must not reject without inquiry. The Jews rejected our
Lord because they would not inquire.'

'But some of them did inquire,' said Myra, 'and still they
did not believe in Him.'

'That was because they inquired in a wrong spirit, having
formed a previous judgment. All inquiry, to be honest, must
be unbiassed. My little girl, keep your heart right with God,
and then your judgment will be right with man.'

'I thought judgment depended upon cleverness,' said
Myra.

'Not so, child, judgment implies weighing one thing against
another; it is the science of proportion. Clever people are
very often wanting in this knowledge of proportion; they are
quicker upon one point than upon another, and so their judgment is defective.'

'But will doing right help one to decide about homœopathy?' said Myra. There was a little sharpness in her
tone, which the Doctor's grave answer instantly made her
aware of.

'My little Myra, you think that clever, but it is only superficial. Whatever helps to enlarge the moral powers, strengthens

the intellectual. If you accustom yourself to weigh evidence as a duty, and to save yourself from uncharitableness, you will also learn to weigh evidence to save yourself from being a fool.'

'But I am not able to weigh the evidence for homœopathy or against it,' said Myra.

'Then do not form a judgment about it till you can.'

'Only I hate doubting,' persisted Myra. She made the remark more for the purpose of carrying on the conversation, which she saw was rather drawing the old man's thoughts away from himself, than with any other object; and it had the desired effect. Dr. Kingsbury never knew whether he was talking to a child or a philosopher, and this was a charm to those who understood him, though it often proved a perplexity to his poor people.

'If you hate doubt,' he said, 'you hate the condition in which God has placed you. What is there which is not open to doubt? And if it was not, where would be the trial of faith?'

'But faith is the reverse of doubt,' said Myra.

'You are mistaken, child. Faith is the certainty of the spiritual faculties, opposed to the doubt of the material senses; but without doubt there could be no faith. Faith will not exist in Heaven, because it will there be swallowed up in sight.'

'Then doubt is not a sin,' said Myra.

'Not in itself; it is a necessity of our condition.'

'But heretics, sceptics, infidels, are all guilty,' said Myra.

'More or less, unquestionably, though God only knows what amount of guilt is to be laid to the charge of each.'

'And yet you say they were born to doubt?' said Myra.

'Not so; they were born to believe. There is the strange fact—the startling evidence against them, that let the evidence of the material senses be never so strong, the evidence of the spiritual senses is yet stronger. What demonstration can be more convincing to the senses than that of death? yet where is the nation, I might almost say where is the man, to be found who doubts of immortality? But I forgot—you asked to read to me '—and the Doctor turned in his chair, and twisted his wig, waking up to a sudden sense of having been carried away by his own earnestness.

' I like talking, sir, if you like it,' said Myra.

' Ah! child, yes, I like it. Perhaps I have been too fond of it in my day.'

' But you must always have liked reading better,' said Myra, ' you have read so much.'

' Yes, a good deal. But much study is a weariness to the flesh.'

' Not study of St. Augustine,' said Myra, smiling, as she pointed to the great book.

' The study of the living might have been better than the study of the dead,' murmured the old man. ' Myra, my little girl, if you put your heart into God's duties, your whole heart, you will never be tempted to carve out duties for yourself.'

' If I could put my heart into them!' said Myra; and she drew her chair nearer as she added, ' But I can never be as good as you, sir.'

' God, for Christ's sake, grant you to be ten thousand times better!' and the trembling withered hand rested tenderly upon Myra's head. ' I would say a prayer for good Miss Medley, Myra. It will seem as if I was with her; so open the Prayer Book at the service for the Visitation of the Sick.' The book was laid upon the table, and Myra was going away, but the Doctor motioned to her to remain. ' When two or three join together,' he said, ' the prayer is surely heard. It will be well for you, my child, to learn early to pray for others.'

Myra knelt down, partly shy, partly awed; but the earnestness of the old man's voice, and the solemnity of the words, heard now for the first time as one of the appointed services of the Church, and mingled with others more particularly suited to the invalid's case, soon carried her away from every thought connected with herself. She felt that the prayers were only too soon ended, and when she stood up again, said, in her quiet but rather abrupt way, ' Thank you, sir; I liked that very much. I hope Miss Medley will be better now.'

' That will be according as God may see best,' was the

answer. ' I think, Myra, now I could work a little at St. Augustine. If you would ring for Faith, she would wheel my chair round.'

It was late before Mrs. Patty came back, with the information that Miss Medley was quiet. Mr. Harrison had been to see her, and Mrs. Haynes was going to sit up with her. She found Myra gone, the Doctor having insisted that she should return home when it grew late.

'The little girl was very good to me, Patty,' he said, when his sister began lamenting that he had been left without a companion ; ' but I had had her with me a long time, and she read to me an essay out of that volume which Mr. Verney lent me, and we talked about it. She is very understanding and companionable.'

'So she ought to be,' observed Mrs. Patty, 'seeing she is more than sixteen ; but, Doctor, dear, could you find nothing better for her to read than a book of Mr. Verney's ? '

'Not his own, Patty. Mr. Verney is not an author ; but if he were, he would write well. He has much to say that is worth listening to upon all subjects.'

'He would write better than he acts, then,' exclaimed Mrs. Patty. 'I have learnt one thing this afternoon—that somehow or other, I can't tell how or why, but Mr. Verney is at the bottom of poor Miss Medley's trouble. She does nothing but talk about him.'

'Very likely, Patty. The brain is in a diseased state ; but its aberrations can be no foundation upon which to form a judgment, much less one that is uncharitable.'

'I don't know about foundation,' replied Mrs. Patty ; 'but I felt a distrust of Mr. Verney the very first time I saw him, when he was talking to Rosamond Cameron the night of Colonel Verney's party ; and Mrs. Haynes declares that every time he has been to see poor Miss Medley, she has shaken like an aspen leaf afterwards.'

'But Mr. Verney cannot have gone to see her so many times,' said the Doctor ; ' he was only a common acquaintance, except that I think he told me he had known something of her nephew.'

'Never mind what he says, Doctor; what he does is the question; and he was at Miss Medley's house every other day the week before last, and he has actually been down from London to see her once this week, though no one but Mrs. Haynes knows it; and the result is, the poor thing has a brain fever.'

'I do not see so plainly the working of cause and effect as you do, Patty,' replied the Doctor, 'and it is a peculiarity of the feminine intellect to put them together illogically. Mr. Verney has been to see Miss Medley—Miss Medley has brain fever; the two facts do not appear to me to have a necessary connection.'

'Not to you, Doctor, dear, but to me. I don't say that I should have brain fever if Mr. Verney came to talk to me three times a week, but I know I should not be far off from it; I can't believe him to be sincere.'

'I think, Patty, we will read the thirteenth chapter of the First Epistle to the Corinthians to-night, at family prayers,' said the Doctor gravely; 'it will do us both good.'

'Certainly, if you like it, Doctor, dear; and no doubt it may do me good, for I need it. But as to you, you are good enough already; and, in the matter of judgment of your fellow-creatures, it can't be doubted you are like most men, and have all the reason on your side; but still I can't trust Mr. Verney.'

'O Patty, Patty!' The Doctor looked really distressed.

'But, Doctor, dear, what can one do? How can one help judging from what one sees and hears? I only tell you what Mrs Haynes told me, when I was wondering what had brought poor Miss Medley to such a pass. Globules alone would not have done it, though, no doubt, they are a sign of something wrong. It is worry of mind—else why should she have talked to you, and wished to consult Mr. Cameron?'

'Yes, money anxieties,' observed the Doctor; 'the cause of much physical as well as moral suffering.'

'But who makes the money anxieties?' persisted Mrs. Patty. 'They are not human beings; they don't walk into a house of themselves.

'Very true, Patty; very true.'

'Then, if they don't come of themselves, and if they always appear just after Mr. Verney's visits, no one else could have brought them,' said Mrs. Patty, rather triumphantly. 'Not but what you may be quite right, Doctor,' she added, correcting herself the next instant; 'and if you say Mr. Verney is a good man, it is not for me to say he is a bad one.'

'I say nothing about him, Patty; I judge him only by what I see.'

'And I am afraid I judge him by what I feel,' said Mrs. Patty. 'That is not charity, I know; but, somehow, I can't help thinking that in this case it may be truth.'

'Patty, I should like the servants to be called in, and for us to have prayers,' said the Doctor.

'They won't be quite ready,' said Mrs. Patty; 'it wants five minutes to half-past nine. Did Myra talk to you at all about Mr. Verney, Doctor?'

'I think she said she should like to see him in London.'

'In London! But are they going there?' inquired Mrs Patty.

'Surely, if I understood Myra rightly. She would have persuaded me, Patty, to consult a London physician; but I told her that old age was a disease for which there was only one remedy, and that was sure to come sooner or later.'

'You would never bear the noise,' replied Mrs. Patty; 'yet it might do you good. But are they all going? it seems a very sudden move.'

'I was selfish, and wished them all to stay,' said the Doctor; 'but Myra has set her little heart upon many pleasant things.'

'Seeing Mr. Verney amongst them,' observed Mrs. Patty.

'Which will be a very safe pleasure,' replied the Doctor, 'for she is but a child.'

'Safe enough, as far as that goes,' replied Mrs. Patty; 'but it was not of her so much that I was thinking. I should like to find out what made Mr. Verney leave India—whether it was anything besides his health.'

'Patty, my dear, we should remember the ninth commandment.'

'Ah, yes, Doctor dear! You are quite right; but the ninth

or the tenth, they are all alike as to the difficulty of keeping them. I went through them this morning, with a prayer after each, but I forgot to put in anything about Mr. Verney—I must remember to do it to-morrow. There is the half-hour striking; so we can ring for Faith and Betsey.'

CHAPTER XXI.

MR. CAMERON'S family took possession for two months of a house in Chester Square. Colonel Verney was in Eaton Place. They were near neighbours, and Mrs. Cameron and Mrs. Verney could meet and talk over plans for pleasure or business just as if they were in the country. This was Mrs. Cameron's unfailing topic of congratulation. Just at that time, indeed, she particularly required all the support which Mrs. Verney's advice could give. She was left almost for the first time to decide an important point for herself. Mr. Cameron had agreed that Juliet and Annette should be sent to school; he only required to have a vote upon the subject. He would not have a large school, and he desired that it should be in a healthy situation; on all other points he begged Mrs. Cameron to consult Mrs. Verney.

'That is just like himself,' said Mrs. Verney, as she took her seat by Mrs. Cameron's sofa, spreading out her rich silk dress so as to preclude any approach within the distance of a yard. 'It is the peculiarity of Mr. Cameron's mind that, although able to embrace the smallest minutiæ, it soars so high as apparently to be indifferent to them; apparently only; great minds—and Mr. Cameron's certainly verges upon greatness—are really cognisant of all matters within the range of their influence or duty. His confidence, however, increases our responsibility. Of course the great object to be attained is the growth, moral and intellectual, of those dear children's minds.'

'They are backward now,' said Mrs. Cameron, 'owing, I suspect, in a great measure, to my ill-health ; and they neither of them take to study naturally, as Myra does.'

'Myra is remarkable.   There is an inconsistency about her which, I confess, perplexes me.   As my dear nephew says, she is very interesting, but I confess I begin to fear that she will not easily find her sphere in life ; and there will lie the difficulty of making her powers useful to the utmost.   I must watch her more narrowly before I can determine what her career is likely to be ; but the other dear girls have less complex natures.'

'You take such a kind interest in my children,' murmured Mrs. Cameron ; ' it is really a great comfort, for lately I have been feeling so unwell.   I sometimes think I may never live to see their entrance into the world.'

'You must banish those fancies, my dear friend ; they are mere depressions, arising, no doubt, from weakness.'

'And not being able to employ myself much,' added Mrs. Cameron ; ' my eyes are so weak that I cannot see to read as I used to do, and I am obliged to make Myra read to me a good deal.'

'An excellent occupation for her ; comfort yourself with that thought.   Myra's soaring and far-spreading mind may sometimes be the better for restraint.   It does not require the impetus which your little Annette's does.   It has an innate power of growth.'

'In which Annette you think is deficient ? '

'Scarcely deficient—that is not the exact term.   She and Juliet are both sweet girls, but the soil in which their individual capabilities have been planted is not perhaps of so rich a quality, and will therefore require more cultivation than Myra's ; and it is this cultivation which I hope and believe will be attained by the new plan of education proposed for them.'

'They will have excellent opportunities for improvement, with all the advantages of masters which their father is prepared to give them,' said Mrs. Cameron.   'He really is very good, and willing to make any sacrifices for them.'

'A pattern parent !' sighed Mrs. Verney ; ' I trust they will repay his care. I have not yet examined carefully the claims of the different establishments which have been brought before my notice, but I will inquire and give you the result of my observations. We shall, I think, be agreed in the wish to mature Juliet's rapid intuitions into ripe judgment, without checking those electric sparkles of wit which act with such magical attraction. Your dear Annette will require a more invigorating moral atmosphere. The stimulus of excitement may, I think, be judiciously applied to her, yet not to the marring of that graceful gentleness of demeanour which enhances every natural gift.'

' And in which she is very like Rosamond,' said Mrs. Cameron. ' Speaking of Rosamond, I may mention to you, in confidence, a circumstance which is likely to be of great importance to her. Her aunt, Mrs. Fitzgerald, who has been out of health a long time, is pronounced hopelessly ill, and if she should die the whole of her property will come to Rosamond. I have never said anything about such a possibility to Rosamond, neither has Mr. Cameron. Until lately, we have both felt that Mrs. Fitzgerald might recover, and marry again ; and, in fact, there are so many chances against an event of the kind, that it was very undesirable. Rosamond has a share of her mother's fortune, which would be sufficient for her under any circumstances, but if Mrs. Fitzgerald's should come to her she will really be an heiress in a moderate way. The fortune can be scarcely less than two thousand a year.'

'A very pleasant income for a single lady,' observed Mrs. Verney ; 'and a very pleasant addition for a married one.'

' But you won't say anything about it,' said Mrs. Cameron anxiously ; ' I should not have mentioned it, only that we were talking about the girls and their prospects. It seems a little hard to me, that my own children should have so much more of a struggle before them than Rosamond—but no doubt it is all right.'

' No doubt !' echoed Mrs. Verney abstractedly. 'Two thousand a year, did you say?'

'About that; I can't be certain exactly; but pray, pray don't talk of it. Mr. Cameron would be so very much annoyed with me for mentioning the subject. He would be so afraid of being thought grasping. Perhaps, upon the whole, it will be better for Rosamond to come back to us now, because she might hear things in conversation which would put the idea into her head.'

'I should have thought that more likely to happen at home;' said Mrs. Verney decidedly.

'Why, no; she might hear of her aunt's illness—of course, indeed, she would; but no one would think of talking about the fortune.'

'Dear Rosamond's thoughts are not bent upon that kind of worldly advancement,' observed Mrs. Verney. 'She is devoting herself to art, and Elise is sharing her pleasure. I should grieve to interrupt their enjoyment. They are spending this morning at the Royal Academy.'

'By themselves?' inquired Mrs. Cameron, in some surprise.

'Oh no! Charles is taking care of them. He came up from Northamptonshire last night.'

'I told Mr. Cameron that Mr. Verney was gone out of town,' said Mrs. Cameron.

'So he was; and he intended to remain away, but London has great attractions at this season. I daresay you will see him some time in the course of the afternoon.'

'I wish Rosamond would come back,' was Mrs. Cameron's reply.

'She shall if you wish it; only not to-day. Elise and she do so enjoy this picture-hunting. You must not urge the matter just for the few days that Charles is with us; he will be going back again into the country almost immediately.'

'Are you quite sure?'

'Quite—so far as that London makes him ill; and if he should not go of his own accord, the physicians will send him there. Poor fellow! He is a martyr to his exertions in that Indian climate.'

'He must have a great deal of energy of mind,' said Mrs. Cameron, 'in spite of his ill-health.'

'Immense! and such high aims; such a sense of the responsibility of the European nations—of England in particular—with regard to the advancement of universal civilisation! I wish you could have heard him talk last night about the separate vocation of each nation; it was better than any lecture. Being so clever, I feel that his society is the greatest possible advantage to my girls; and I am sure you will feel the same about your Rosamond, and be content to leave her with us.'

'I might be, if I could be quite sure that Mr. Cameron would approve.'

'Oh! leave Mr. Cameron to me. I shall soon persuade him. I mean him to dine with us to-morrow, and then we will talk about it. In the meantime you may be quite sure that Rosamond is safe. Now, good-bye, my dear; I have spent a great deal more time here than I can afford, with my whirl of engagements; but you know that your children's interests are always near my heart.'

Mrs. Verney kissed Mrs. Cameron on both cheeks, and turned towards the door, but came back again. 'I forgot the dressmaker; shall I send her here? She will effect a complete metamorphose in Myra's appearance.'

'I suppose it is necessary,' said Mrs. Cameron; 'but I really begin to despair about making Myra presentable.'

'But I do not. Madame Laget has a most wonderful genius, and she really is not at all expensive. I have such faith in her that I believe she could even convert Mrs. Patty Kingsbury into a first-rate specimen of fashion. And she has such a power of suiting the dress to the wearer; it is an absolute gift.'

'Poor Mrs. Patty!' observed Mrs. Cameron. 'Speaking of her reminds me that Myra had a letter from her this morning, full of lamentation over Miss Medley's condition. There seems really a doubt whether the poor thing will ever recover mentally. Mrs. Patty says that the fever is diminishing, but that she is as confused as ever, and Mr. Harrison thinks unfavourably of her.'

'Alas! alas! The poor human intellect! So soon ren-

dered useless!' sighed Mrs. Verney.   'It is a lesson for us all;
though I delight in talent—I can't help doing so.   I wish you
could be with us to-morrow.   We shall have some first-rate men,
and I quite look forward to hearing the conversation.   Now,
really, good-bye.   I am so sorry for poor Miss Medley, and
for Mrs. Patty, too; do tell her so; good-bye;' and Mrs. Verney
sailed out of the room, steering her way carefully amongst
the light chairs and fancy tables, and when arrived safely at
the door, turning round once more to smile, and whisper a
French '*Adieu, au revoir.*'

CHAPTER XXII.

MRS. PATTY'S letter was brought to Myra at rather an un-
propitious moment for sympathy.   London was very exciting,
and though Myra had thought beforehand that she should dislike it, she was beginning to feel the influence of the engagements and amusements in one way or other provided for her.
On leaving home it had seemed that nothing could be so important as the village, the school, Miss Medley's illness, and
Johnnie Ford's admission into the Idiot Asylum, which was
still in process of attainment, but not yet secured; but a morning
concert, a visit to the Water-Colour Gallery, a little shopping,
and a panorama, had given quite a new turn to her thoughts,
and Mrs. Patty's letter seemed to belong to a period of life,
and a state of existence, connected with years rather than weeks
gone by.

It was very useful to Myra to be recalled, though but for a
few minutes, to the quiet study at the Rectory, and the presence
of the good old man who, busy with his books, was steadfastly
preparing himself, day by day, for the hour which should end
all learning in one world, and open to him all knowledge in
another.   Still better, perhaps, was it for her to be told of
weariness, and watching, and the attendant trials of an illness

so serious that, even if life were spared, it could scarcely be expected to end favourably. The letter, in its quaint simplicity, took her back into a more natural and healthy moral atmosphere than that in which she was living, but it could not entirely counteract the influences which surrounded her.

Myra had already discovered that the world contains many inner worlds, each with its peculiar laws, and customs, and standard of propriety ; and she knew that all these lesser worlds could not be equally right in the sight of God ; but she was unable to separate the evil which they contained from the good, or to decide how much that was valuable in each might be accepted and enjoyed, whilst the rest was rejected ; and so for the time being she lived in her London world without criticising it, though with the uncomfortable sensation that it did not harmonise with that which she had lately inhabited, and which she still deemed better and happier.

Mrs. Patty's letter was read through twice, but though the facts made an impression upon Myra, the little pieces of kindly advice with which it was interspersed were thrown away. She failed to understand what Mrs. Patty had greatly desired she should understand, the warnings against admiring clever people who had strange religious notions, and neglected going to church.

Myra, dining with strangers nearly every day, was in the habit of hearing so many strange opinions broached, that the sense of novelty and falsity in them was wearing away ; and as for going to church—there were evidently, in London households, so many obstacles in the way of such a duty, that it was only charitable to believe some of them to be real. At Yare, Mr. Cameron was regular at church, both in the morning and afternoon—he felt it necessary to set an example to the parish : in London he never could manage more than the morning service, whilst Mrs. Cameron required a drive, and liked to have one of her children with her, and this often stood in the way of their going more than once a-day. Besides, it was considered a necessity to hear every celebrated preacher, and in consequence there was a great deal of planning with the Verneys as to who was to go with whom ; and a large portion

L

of the day was often spent in driving to some distant church, and then waiting in the aisles during half the service, unable to sit or kneel, and with the thoughts necessarily engaged with the desire to find a seat which would make seeing and hearing as possible as resting.

Dress, too, was an important matter in London on a Sunday, and dress was still Myra's bugbear.   The moments which she would have spent in quiet reading, before or after the service, were devoted as a matter of duty to fastening all the ribbons, and buttons, and cuffs, without which she could not possibly appear before Mrs. Verney, and then running from room to room to entreat that some one would tell her that she was all right, so that she might escape being grasped in the carriage with an ' Allow me, my dear Myra ; ' or ' Who did dress you, my dear?' or, what was still more trying—a quiet, sarcastic smile, whilst her bonnet-strings were gently untied, and tied again, just so tight, or so slack, as to make her uncomfortable for the whole morning.

A late dinner, with a few stray gentlemen friends, though never a regular party, closed the day.   Sacred music was occasionally proposed, but as Rosamond was away it was not very successful, and Myra generally spent the evening with a volume of French sermons before her, for, with her usual diversity of taste and occupation, she had lately taken to a diligent perusal of Masillon and Bourdaloue, whilst she kept a certain portion of her attention for conversation ; not joining in it, but listening whenever a word or a sentence struck her as indicating anything new or entertaining.

This kind of life was certainly little likely to foster any religious feeling.   Much might be said in its excuse, but there was undoubtedly no high tone about it, whilst there was a good deal of dangerous excitement.   Myra had no safeguard externally—no one advised, or attempted to guide her; and no one found fault with her, except when she dressed herself badly.   She was left apparently to herself— but it was only apparently.   We none of us know how our characters are being moulded, until after they have been worked into shape.   Those few strong resolutions—the result, as it might have seemed, of temporary feeling—were not to Myra herself as evidently influential now as they were when she first experienced them. But they were genuine, and they had been acted upon, and, as a result, they were becoming habits—habits of action, habits of thought—the latter the less obvious, but the more important of the two. When Myra found herself in a strange, uncongenial atmosphere, called upon to do things which, if not absolutely wrong, were still unsatisfactory to her scrupulous conscience—whilst so disturbed by the pressure of engagements, that feeling was almost dead within her, she was, through God's help, kept in the right path by duty. A very cold, dead guide that may seem to some—but it has one inestimable advantage, that it is wholly independent of outward circumstances. Myra read the Bible, kept to her times of prayer, checked her temper, and sternly battled with the self against which she had inwardly vowed such a deadly warfare, because—she scarcely could have told why at the moment, but she felt that she must do it, that obedience was necessary to her, and the sense of disobedience—the consciousness of being out of God's favour—so oppressive, that at any sacrifice it must be avoided. An observant person would have been struck by the effect which this unobtrusive but rigid adherence to a law of right insensibly produced. 'Myra is certain to do this or that'—'Myra will stay at home, or Myra will go'—or 'Myra has undertaken to write such a note, or to pay such a visit,' were the expressions commonly heard, and yet no one in the family was aware why Myra should be so depended upon. It was certainly not because she was entirely changed. Her peculiarities were still observable, but they were diminishing. She was every day gaining a respect from others which reacted upon her own mind, by giving her confidence. Knowing that she meant rightly, and with that singular sincerity of character which enabled her to look her virtues in the face, as well as her faults, she was becoming less and less sensitive to the opinion of others, and, as a consequence, more natural and unaffected. And thus Myra's difficulties were converted into blessings. Under more favourable circumstances, she might have leaned upon others (for the bent of her mind was to lean and be guided), and have lost both power and originality. But left alone, without sympathy, in the midst of temptation, and with her own strong natural faults struggling incessantly to regain their former dominion, the whole energy of her will was roused; and the will of man, when it is one with the Will of God, has a strength which none on earth, or under the earth, can withstand.

'Rosamond and Elise want you to go to the Royal Academy this morning, Myra,' said Mrs. Cameron, when they met at a late breakfast the day after Mrs. Verney's visit; 'you must be in Eaton Place by twelve o'clock. Conyers can walk there with you.'

'And Annette and I, mamma?' said Juliet.

'My dear, you must stay at home, and attend to your lessons. If you have so many holidays you will disgrace yourselves when you go to school.'

'Is it decided about school?' asked Annette mournfully.

'I am sure it is,' exclaimed Juliet, without waiting for her mother's reply. 'I was certain when Mrs. Verney went away yesterday. She had just the look of a person who has settled the world to her satisfaction. Where is the school, mamma?'

'Juliet,' said Mr. Cameron, raising his eyes from a sheet of the 'Times,' 'you will ask no questions until your mamma chooses to give you permission.'

'I only wanted to know in order to be prepared,' muttered Juliet.

'Do you want to go to any particular school, my dear?' asked Mrs. Cameron, desirous of averting a storm.

'I should like to go to that one at which Miss Greaves was teacher, and where Catharine Verney went for a short time,' said Juliet, considerably emboldened by her mother's inquiry; 'Mrs. de Lancey's, in St. John's Wood. Catharine only left it because it was too expensive; she was very happy there. And I wrote to ask her about it; and, mamma, here is the answer.'

Mrs. Cameron received the note, and laid it on the table

she was by no means inclined to take an active part in a task which had been placed in Mrs. Verney's hands. 'We will see about it, my dear,' was all the answer Juliet could obtain ; and a few minutes afterwards breakfast was declared ended, and the party dispersed.

Juliet followed Myra into the hall. 'Now, Myra, this is so provoking of mamma, just when I wanted to talk to her ; but you will say something, won't you ? You are going to Mrs. Verney's to-day. Catharine was so very happy at Mrs. de Lancey's ; and Miss Greaves told me that they have capital masters there, and French and German teachers ; and they go out to concerts, and have parties at home ; and, in fact, it is quite delightful. Miss Greaves says that she and Charlotte Stuart were never happier in their lives.'

'And who is Charlotte Stuart ? ' inquired Myra.

'Oh ! the daughter of a Mr. Stuart in India, who is immensely rich. I don't exactly know what position he holds ; I think he must be a merchant ; and I believe he is a relation of Miss Medley's, but I never asked much about him. I only cared to know what Miss Greaves did. She was a kind of half pupil, half teacher ; and Charlotte Stuart was only a year or two younger than herself, and they were great friends.'

'And Miss Greaves liked Mrs. de Lancey, did she ? '

'Oh yes ! extremely ; and Annette and I have made up our minds that we must go there. It will be such fun ! and we can write to Catharine all about it. Just talk to mamma and Mrs. Verney, won't you ? '

'I will if I can ; if I see my way to it.'

'But make a way ; it is only the will that you want.'

'I am not sure that I have the will,' replied Myra. 'Anyhow, Juliet,' she added, observing her sister's face of disappointment, 'I won't forget it ; but I may not see Mrs. Verney alone.'

'You will be sure to do that, if you go out in a party. Mr. Verney and Rosamond will be together ; and you, and Mrs. Verney and Elise will walk behind ; and Elise is nobody.'

'Mr. Verney ! ' exclaimed Myra ; 'he is not come back ? '

'Yes, he is. Conyers saw him yesterday ; and Myra '—

Juliet drew quite close to her sister, and spoke nearly in a whisper—'Conyers says every one at Colonel Verney's is talking about Rosamond's being married to Mr. Verney. Do you think she will be?'

Myra could have laughed at the suggestion, so like her own, and made almost in her own words; but Mrs. Patty's reserve had given her a lesson which she had profited by, and she answered, with grave propriety, that 'such gossip ought not to be listened to;' and then turned away, with a feeling of greatly increased satisfaction at the prospect of the morning's engagement.

CHAPTER XXIII.

THE drawing-room in Eaton Place was much more attractive than the drawing-room in Chester Square. It was a peculiar gift of Mrs. Verney's to throw an air of refined mystery over things as well as persons. When she spoke of her furniture, it was always in terms which idealised the several articles. Her curtains were not curtains, but draperies; they did not conceal windows, but they veiled recesses. Her sofas were couches; her ornaments, bijouterie; her books, the breathings of talent; her pictures, the efforts of artistic genius; and, to a certain extent, it was quite true that the everyday articles of comfort or luxury which Mrs. Verney collected together did, by some peculiar arrangement, produce a different effect in her drawing-room from that which they would have done elsewhere. Soft pink was the prevailing colour, and it seemed to pervade the atmosphere. The sunlight never glared upon it, and the clouds scarcely seemed to darken it. There were all appliances for reading, writing, and needlework, but no one would have thought of study or active employment in Mrs. Verney's drawing-room. Poetry might, indeed, be read, but it must be from a beautifully bound edition; and notes might be written, but the pen must be gold, and the paper must be embossed and scented ; and for needlework, Mrs. Verney's exquisite ivory workbox always lay open, but the implements it contained were fit for nothing but some very delicate piece of embroidery. The room was, in fact, as Mrs. Verney declared, devoted to the interchange of thought, stimulated and refined by the charms of elegance and art.

Rosamond Cameron was a fitting goddess for such a temple, and it was to be supposed that Mr. Verney thought so, for he had seated himself in the best position for admiring her, and though pretending to read a review, was really carrying on a bantering conversation, not one sentence of which could bear repetition, but which yet served to keep them mutually engrossed with each other. Myra's appearance was an interruption, and evidently not, to Rosamond, a very agreeable one. Mr. Verney, on the contrary, actually roused himself to go forward several steps to meet her, and ask how she was, and what she had been doing with herself ; and that in a very natural, hearty manner, which, in spite of his rather drawling tone, showed that he was really pleased to see her.

'I was coming to you this afternoon,' he said, 'if my aunt had not arranged our all going out together this morning. I suppose Mrs. Cameron would admit me.'

'Mamma drives out generally about four,' said Myra, 'and I very often go with her.'

'Then I shall come before four, and we will talk over the things to be seen and heard in London ; not mere sight-seeing, but lectures and curiosities.'

'Things to suit Myra's learned tastes,' said Rosamond, laughing, though a little sarcastically.

'I don't call her learned,' replied Mr. Verney. 'I hate learned women, be they old or young.'

'All gentlemen do,' said Rosamond. 'They are afraid of the discovery of their own ignorance.'

'Possibly,' was the languid reply, as Mr. Verney threw himself back in an arm-chair. 'I never took the trouble to inquire into the origin of the feeling. It is an instinct—born with us.'

'But do you think that women can ever be as learned as men?' asked Myra.

'Oh! spare us that discussion, my dear child,' exclaimed Rosamond; 'one might as well have a social science meeting at once.'

'Can a rose ever be an oak?' asked Mr. Verney. 'Yet who does not prefer the rose?'

'Except in a storm, when one wants shelter,' said Myra lightly. 'I confess I should like to be more useful than a rose. I doubt if it might not even be better to be a potato.'

'Eaten, digested, and giving nourishment,' said Mr. Verney. 'Well! it strikes me that you may very possibly obtain that amount of value, but I wish, for my sake, you would add a little grace and beauty to it. Be a potato in blossom at any rate.'

'If I could,' said Myra. 'But I must be contented to be what I am;' and then—as a reply, containing a little of that unmeaning flattery which even the most sensible men are apt to think women can enjoy, rose to Mr. Verney's lips—he was stopped by Myra's suddenly turning to a totally different subject, and saying to Rosamond: 'I have had a letter from Mrs. Patty, should you like to see it?'

'*Ça dépend*,' was Rosamond's answer. 'Is it legible?'

'Yes, quite.'

'Is it interesting?'

'Yes, to me.'

'That implies a doubt; what do you say, Mr. Verney?'

Mr. Verney's attention had been wandering rather uncivilly, for he required an explanation. 'Mrs. Patty Kingsbury, were you talking of? Any communication from her must be worthy of a place in the archives of the British Museum.'

'I don't wish any one to read her letter who would laugh at it,' said Myra.

'Laugh! who could laugh at Mrs. Patty?' exclaimed Mr. Verney. 'I have the profoundest reverence for her.'

'And so have I,' said Rosamond. 'She taught me to walk in pattens, and I have never lost the accomplishment.'

Myra was silent.

'We have touched a sensitive nerve,' said Rosamond ironically, as she turned to Mr. Verney.

But he answered in a different tone: 'I do reverence her really.'

'Every one must who knows her,' observed Myra, 'she is so very good.'

'Too good,' said Rosamond.

'But no one can be that,' answered Myra.

'Too good for this work-a-day existence, though,' said Rosamond. 'What would this world be if we were all like her? Fancy a continent, a kingdom, even an island, peopled with Mrs. Patty Kingsburys.'

'There is a place which will be peopled with beings very like them, I suspect,' said Myra, as the colour mounted to her cheeks.

'I was not aware that Myra could be so enthusiastic in her attachments,' said Rosamond; 'were you, Mr. Verney?'

'I guessed it,' was his reply; and Myra looked at him gratefully and said—

'Thank you. I should not mind showing you Mrs. Patty's letter.' He held out his hand for it, but Myra, when taken at her word, felt as though she might be about to commit a breach of confidence. Rosamond playfully caught the letter from her. 'It was offered to me first,' she said, 'so I will read it out for the benefit of the company, omitting all portions which should be omitted. Trust me, Myra,' she added, seeing her sister's look of caution. 'Now, Mr. Verney, attend.'

The preamble of the letter contained all Mrs. Patty's reasons, social and domestic, for not having written before; but the first was conclusive. She had not had a moment of time, for she had been waiting night and day upon Miss Medley, who was very ill indeed. Mr. Verney was holding a pencil-case in his hand. When Rosamond came to these words, he dropped it on the floor suddenly. Myra, who was looking at him, thought that he started; but it could only have been a fancy—he sat so still during the remainder of the letter, with his eyes fixed upon the ground, and listening.

When Rosamond had finished, he said quietly, 'Poor Mrs. Patty seems anxious about her friend.'

'And she has reason to be,' said Myra. 'Papa heard from some one else that it is feared Miss Medley's mind will never be right again.'

'I though it never was right before,' said Rosamond lightly. 'She was always half mad about homœopathy.'

'Yes, she was very strange,' said Myra, with a sudden recollection of the day when she had borrowed the umbrella, and Miss Medley had been so nervous at Mr. Verney's visit. She looked at Mr. Verney with a kind of vague expectation that he would make some allusion to his acquaintance, but, on the contrary, he began—as if Miss Medley was almost a stranger to him—asking where she came from, how long she had lived at Yare, who her relations were, &c.

Myra was puzzled. She said presently, 'But you do know Miss Medley, Mr. Verney.' Her decided tone seemed to strike him, for he looked up, and their eyes met. 'Yes,' he answered; 'that is, I have seen her, as I have every one in Yare, but seeing and knowing are very different. One thing, indeed, I did know—that she was a homœopathist.'

He spoke so naturally that Myra could not suspect any mystery. Perhaps Miss Medley's strange manner on that particular day might have been the forerunner of disease. She was almost tempted to make some remark which might bring an explanation, but she was bound by her promise; and in reply she merely said, 'It is not homœopathy which has brought on her sudden illness now; but some worry about money, so Mrs. Patty says in a note written to mamma.'

'To Mrs. Cameron?' inquired Mr. Verney. 'Does Mrs. Patty keep up such a very vigorous correspondence?'

'Oh! no. She only wrote a few lines about Johnnie Ford'——

'And the Idiot Asylum,' said Rosamond; 'I am tired of hearing about it. That good little Mr. Baines has been working so hard for it merely because I asked him. But Mr. Verney, you seem quite subdued by Mrs. Patty's mournful intelligence. Don't you think your spirits would be revived by the Royal Academy? It wants only five minutes to twelve, and the carriage will be here directly; I think I shall go and put my bonnet on.'

Rosamond glided gently out of the room, watched by Mr. Verney till the door was closed behind her, whilst Myra studied Mrs. Patty's letter again.

When Rosamond was gone, Mr. Verney said, ' I don't want my visits to Miss Medley to be talked about, Myra. You are to be trusted, I know.'

' I hope so,' said Myra, taken quite by surprise.

' Yes, you are to be trusted. I trust you.'

' I am glad you do.'

' And I mean to show it. You must let me know when you have news of that poor thing.'

' Of Miss Medley !' Myra could not conceal her astonishment.

' Yes ; never mind why ; only bring me news of her. Let me know as often as possible how she is, and if she wants for anything.'

It struck Myra as a very odd request, but she did not exactly see why she was to refuse, and she said, ' Yes, if I can.'

' Of course this is between ourselves,' added Mr. Verney.

And Myra again could say nothing but ' Yes.' Yet a little weight fell upon her heart.

CHAPTER XXIV.

THEY went to the Royal Academy, and Mr. Verney was particularly kind to Myra. He took her to the best pictures, and
pointed out their beauties and their defects. She had quite
an artist's lesson from him, and it was very enjoyable. But
when they parted afterwards, in Chester Square, he said, in a
low voice, ' I shall call to-morrow, to know if you have heard
anything more ; ' and then the weight became rather heavier,
and Myra ran upstairs to her own room without going to her
mother, because she wanted just to be alone, and think what
it was that was making her uncomfortable.

Secresy ! It was that which she disliked, though she could
not feel herself responsible for it. Myra had been often a
very tiresome playmate in her childhood, because she never
could be made to understand the pleasure of concealment.
Juliet liked it for what she called the fun of it, and Annette
had a natural taste for it, fostered by Rosamond's influence ;
but Myra was provokingly transparent. Plots and plans,
except in fiction, were odious to her, and, with her small
experience of the world, she was inclined to condemn all
mystery, without distinction. Now, however, she was brought to
feel that mystery might possibly be necessary. If it were not,
Mr. Verney would never have imposed the annoyance upon
her, for he must know that it was annoying. It was one thing
to be told not to talk of his visits to Miss Medley—they were
not her concern ; but to give private messages was very
different. Myra said to herself, that if any one else had made
the request she would have refused ; but Mr. Verney would
never ask her to do anything that was wrong, and if it was
not wrong then she need not worry herself about it ; and so
she went downstairs to read to her mother.

The next day brought Mr. Verney and his aunt, early—at
least before luncheon time. Mrs. Verney came to talk over

schools; Mr. Verney to arrange a party for a morning concert
the next week. Myra was uncomfortable the whole time, because she knew he was watching to speak to her alone, and
she had to manœuvre a little to give him the opportunity.
After all, there was little enough to be said, except that Mr.
Cameron had heard from Dr. Kingsbury, who mentioned in
a postscript that Mrs. Patty was still in attendance upon poor
Miss Medley, and that change of air was recommended for
her; but there seemed a difficulty about the financial arrangements.

Myra had a momentary doubt how far she was justified in
repeating this latter sentence; but then she had promised to
tell Mr. Verney what she knew, and if she told him only half,
she would not be keeping her word. He was so grateful to
her, so evidently and kindly interested in Miss Medley's condition, that she liked him more than ever. And there was the
flattered vanity also. Truthful, earnest, and watchful as Myra
was becoming, she was not quite aware yet of the power of
that most insidious of all influences. Mr. Verney's confidence
was very pleasant to her, and, if it was purchased at the price
of a little mystery, there was nothing, surely, required of her at
which any right conscience could fairly take alarm.

So matters went on for nearly a fortnight, whilst Rosamond
still showed no signs of intending to return home, and Mrs.
Cameron always talked as if she must and would, but never
issued her commands upon the subject; for Mrs. Verney was
bent upon keeping her, and Mrs. Verney governed both households. Not, however, with Mr. Cameron's knowledge; no
man ever more fully believed himself to be lord and master in
his own family. And had he not been put upon his guard
with respect to Rosamond? Had he not declared that the
report was an absurdity, that the difference of age was an insurmountable objection, that he detested the Stormont politics,
and would have nothing to do with them, and if people talked
so foolishly, he would never let his daughter go near the Verneys again?

Yes, Mr. Cameron had said all this, and a great deal like it
besides, on the day when he insisted to his wife that Rosamond

should not go up to London under Mr. Verney's escort, and
so he continued to say ; but not one whit the more did he act
upon his saying.

'My dear Mr. Cameron, your deep penetrativeness fathoms
my nephew's character,' said Mrs. Verney. 'His mind is
given to schemes of philanthropy.   He feels his broken health,
and under such a trial sympathy is a necessity.   So the society
of your dear family is soothing to him, and to us all.   Your
sweet Rosamond is a sunbeam in our household ; she and my
two girls make such a charming trio, I really cannot part with
them.   And separate action is so good for Myra ; you must see
how she is expanding, in her sister's absence.   I see traits which
remind me of your own noble independence, and self-reliant
energy.   Myra will gain strength daily by the freedom thus
given her.   I feel for your parental tenderness, but you are the
last person to allow feeling, even the strongest and purest, to
predominate over considerations which are material to your
children's best interests.

Certainly, Mr. Cameron had not the slightest intention of
allowing feeling to predominate under any circumstances; and,
moreover, he could not possibly contradict a lady who so
thoroughly understood him.   Generally speaking, whenever he
heard what was said of himself, it proved to be something
disagreeable—either that he was stiff, or unapproachable, or
obstinate, or selfish.   Most unpleasant remarks of this kind
had at times been made, especially after elections and public
meetings ; but such testimony to his virtues from the wife of his
political adversary was incontrovertible.   And as Mrs. Verney
could thus appreciate him, she would naturally appreciate his
children, and be a good judge of what was desirable for them.
The world's gossip was, no doubt, very disagreeable, but, after
all, it might be well to rise superior to it ; and so Mr. Cameron
did not interfere.

The school question was progressing to Juliet's satisfaction.
Mrs. Verney had collected reports and prospectuses of the
chief schools in and near London.   She had carefully balanced
their merits and demerits ; weighed the advantage of having
Mr. A. for drawing against the disadvantage of losing Signor

B. for singing, and collected the names of the young ladies who were considered the best specimens of the various systems; and, after thorough inquiry, Mrs. de Lancey's establishment in St. John's Wood was fixed upon, as being upon the whole pre-eminent in principle, accomplishments, and style. And it was style which Juliet and Annette decidedly needed—Annette perhaps the least; but Juliet, though she could not be said to dress badly, was unmistakably a country girl—abrupt in manner, loud in tone, dictatorial, and interfering. Quiet self-discipline might, perhaps, have been effectual in softening these disagreeable characteristics. It was singular to remark how much more gentle and pleasing Myra had become since she had learnt to watch herself, and prefer the wishes of others to her own; but then, as Mrs. Verney said, it was so excessively difficult to give girls of thirteen and fourteen any idea of self-discipline. They could not understand it, and it was such a very tedious process! Give them the habits and manners of refined society first, and by and by self-discipline would follow as a thing of course.

'The world teaches it, my dear,' she observed, when Mrs. Cameron one day remarked upon Myra's increasing self-control, and expressed a wish that her two younger girls might imitate it. 'The world teaches it, and school is a little world. Girls quiz one another, and governesses are strict and sharp; and where there is a tone of good society—call it fashionable society if you will—young people learn very quickly what they may, and what they may not do. Awkwardness makes them feel awkward, and so they strive against it. There is no discipline like it.'

'But Juliet is just one of those girls who might become what is called fast,' said Mrs. Cameron, 'and I detest fast girls, and it would drive her father frantic if she were to be one.'

'You need have no fear, my dear,' was the reply. 'The young people at Mrs. de Lancey's are just the class to despise vulgar fastness, they are above it. If there are little eccentricities and freedoms, they all are of a safe kind. As far as I can learn, and I really have inquired very narrowly, there is nothing in the school in the least approaching to bad taste. Mrs. de Lancey's young people are never noisy. I have never heard of one who had become an objectionable flirt. Of course, all girls will carry on a little innocent flirting in a quiet way, but that one must shut one's eyes to.'

' I suppose so,' said Mrs. Cameron, with a smile. ' I have heard Rosamond called a flirt.'

' It is very hard upon her,' replied Mrs. Verney, 'when she is so remarkably subdued and sweet in all her ways—so prettily unconscious of her own fascination. But I can understand what people mean. She does manage to attract men without appearing to make any effort. Even old Dr. Kingsbury is bewitched with her; and as for my husband, he says he really cannot give up the pleasure of looking at her and watching her.'

' It is curious how tastes differ,' said Mrs. Cameron. ' Rosamond is a much greater favourite with gentlemen than she is with ladies.'

' Yes, she is so bright and graceful, and makes such a pretty picture, and that is all that most gentlemen care for, unless they happen to be philosophers like my nephew, or have grave notions about marriage, and compatibility of taste. I don't mean that dear Rosamond is not a great deal more than pretty to look at, but only that it is that which is valuable in society, and which must, of course, therefore be aimed at. Will you allow me to enter into negotiations with Mrs. de Lancey?'

' I must speak to Mr. Cameron first, but I should think he could have no objection. I can't help wishing that the children could have been sent to her at once. It would be so much more convenient; for Mr. Cameron has been talking of going abroad, and I don't think we could take them with us.'

' Oh! don't trouble yourself about that for an instant; they should be under my charge till the school re-opens in August. I should be charmed to have them with me.'

' How kind you are, you obviate all difficulties; and really I am feeling so very unwell, that I don't feel at all equal to thought about anything.'

Mrs. Verney had heard this said so often that the words alone would have had no effect upon her, but she happened to look at Mrs. Cameron at the same instant, and it did certainly strike her that there might be some meaning in them. Mrs. Cameron was very thin, and just now appeared much older than her age, and there was a dimness about her eyes which was the more noticeable because her only claim to anything like beauty lay in the upper part of her face.

'I am afraid you are very unwell, my dear,' she said; 'you have had so much harass in coming to London, and so much to think of about the children. But change will, I trust, restore your too sensitive nature to its vigour. Where do you think of going?'

'We have not quite made up our minds yet. Godfrey has undertaken to mark out a route for us. I rather dread it; but Mr. Cameron seems bent upon it, and I suppose it may be as well. The doctors say that if I get my strength up my eyes will come right again, but really sometimes I begin to doubt. I don't know what I should do without Myra.'

'So useful, is she? I feared her intellectual faculties were so constantly exercised, that she might scarcely be able to understand the minutiæ of life, and I should have thought that Juliet would have had greater capacity for the attendance required by an invalid.'

'Juliet is very capable,' said Mrs. Cameron, 'but she wants the will. What I find in Myra is, that when she tells me she will do a thing she does it. You can't think what a help that is, in this London life especially. And then Myra reads to me, and I think she likes it; at least she makes pleasant bright remarks about the book, and never yawns as Juliet does. I should be glad if Mrs. de Lancey could do anything in the way of making Juliet more thoughtful for others.'

Mrs. Verney smiled. 'We must take one lesson at a time. Poor Juliet will have enough to do to think of herself at first. She will find herself so unable to meet the requirements of the masters, that she will be compelled to devote herself to the

M

one object of keeping on a level with her young companions. Competition will be her stimulus, and for the present I fear you must be prepared to sacrifice everything to this. Afterwards, no doubt, there will be other lessons to learn. Life in the world, as you and I know full well, is by no means easy; and young people are taught amiability by discovering how disagreeable they are without it. Your dear little Juliet will come all right by and by; only have patience with her.'

CHAPTER XXV.

MR. VERNEY dined in Chester Square the next day, but he seemed very unwell, and was thoroughly out of spirits. He had been invited to meet Godfrey, and talk over the projected tour, and his cousins Henrietta and Elise were to accompany him. It was to be quite a free, sociable party, without any strangers; and as Rosamond was really at last obliged to return to her own home, in order to prepare for going abroad, it would be a pleasant way of breaking off her visit.

But sociable parties require that every one should be in good-humour, from the very fact that they are so sociable as to require less self-restraint. Mr. Verney was sufficiently at home with the Camerons to feel himself released from the necessity of making himself agreeable. Rosamond, in her own home, and having only Henrietta and Elise Verney to trouble her, might be as indifferent to the general comfort as she chose; and Godfrey—always dissatisfied when he could not shine, and finding his efforts at wit and cleverness thrown back, like a gutta-percha ball, by Mr. Verney's sarcastic remarks—became more pretentious and dogmatic, and struck all the harder because he felt that he made no impression. They were an ill-assorted company, and no one felt it more than Myra. The same sensitiveness which made her so alive to her own failures in society, gave her an insight into those of others. Any want of congeniality, or any cloud of temper or depression, affected her like an east wind; she could not forget it. The very instant Mr. Verney entered the room she was quite sure that he was what is termed 'out of sorts;' and the tone of Rosamond's voice as she said, 'So you see, mamma, I am come back at last,' showed that no help was to be ex- pected from her in making the dinner and the evening pass off pleasantly. Myra secretly attributed the moodiness of both to the same cause. They were about to be separated, and, naturally enough, they were unhappy; for Myra had now established their mutual attachment as a fact in her own mind. She very much wished to be sympathetic, and she felt very sorry for Mr. Verney, and would have given a great deal to be allowed to tell him so; but Rosamond was selfish when she was unhappy, and to sympathise with selfishness is a serious difficulty, if not an impossibility. The dinner passed stupidly. There was a little commonplace conversation, carried on chiefly by Godfrey and Henrietta Verney, but Mr. Verney scarcely spoke. Mrs. Cameron was weary, and retired very soon after dessert; and then, when they went upstairs, Juliet carried off Henrietta and Elise to show them some illumination which she and Annette had been attempting for the first time, whilst Rosamond lounged in an easy-chair with a novel, and Myra was left to attend to her mother.

'I think, mamma, you would do better to lie down in the inner drawing-room just till the gentlemen come up: don't you think so?' she said.

'I should like to stay here for the present, my dear, and Rosamond will tell me what she has been doing.'

'I, mamma?' Rosamond looked up from her book. 'Oh, I have nothing to tell. My life has been just like every other person's life in London.'

'Except mine,' said Mrs. Cameron querulously. 'You have gone out to parties, which I have not.'

'Oh yes, parties,' replied Rosamond, returning to her novel, 'but they are all alike.'

'You and Mr. Verney were laughing about one yesterday, when I was in Eaton Place,' said Myra, 'and I thought I

would leave it to you to tell mamma about it for fear of making
mistakes. That party, I mean, where there were so many
foreigners.'

'Oh yes, that one !   It was very amusing.'

'Were they French?' asked Mrs. Cameron, in a tone of
interest.

'French, and Germans, and all sorts; they were very absurd.'

'Do tell mamma some of their blunders in speaking English,' said Myra.

'I can't remember them exactly. Do you know, Myra,
where the second volume of this book is ? '

'It may be in mamma's room,' said Myra.

'If you would be so good as to go and fetch it for me, I
should be so much obliged.   When one is once settled in an
easy-chair it is next to impossible to move.'

Myra could not but go, though her unwillingness was evident.

'It is a pity Myra is so disobliging,' was Rosamond's remark
to Mrs. Cameron in her absence.   'It really makes one quite
hesitate to ask her to do anything.'

'Myra is very good to me,' said Mrs. Cameron.   'What a
long visit you have paid, Rosamond ! '

'Yes, longer a great deal than I anticipated, but we have
had such endless engagements.   Do you know, mamma, Mr.
Verney says he thinks, after all, he may go back to India in
the autumn ? '

'Does he ?   We shall be all sorry for that.   But I hope his
health will stand it.   Did he go with you to all your parties,
Rosamond ? '

'Not to all.'

'Your dinners were on a grand scale, I hear,' said Mrs.
Cameron.   'The Verneys are certainly extravagant.'

'They give handsome dinners,' replied Rosamond.   'I
don't know whether they can be called extravagant.   Mrs.
Verney thinks them necessary.'

'And did you meet many celebrities ? ' asked Mrs. Cameron.

'One or two; at least they were pointed out to me.   I
seldom talked to them.'

Mrs. Cameron asked no more questions, but retired to the inner drawing-room, lay down on the sofa, and closed her eyes. Myra returned with the novel, for which Rosamond was graciously grateful, and then she also took a book and seated herself near her mother.

Presently she heard Mr. Verney enter the outer room, and say to Rosamond, 'Your father and Godfrey are looking over maps, so I came upstairs.

'And you would not stay to help them?' said Rosamond.

'Why should I? It is all the same to me, as I am to be left lonely.'

'But you will follow us as you have promised?'

'If I am able. You know how willingly I would say more.'

Myra coughed then, and Mr. Verney came into the inner room. Myra pointed to her mother, and he smiled and drew a chair near, and said in a tone of interest, 'I am so sorry to see her so tired. Do you think I ought to go away?'

'Not if you will talk low; she does not mind you.'

'Then I may have a little quiet conversation with you all by myself. It is not often I find the opportunity.'

'This is the last we shall have, I am afraid,' said Myra, 'we are going so soon. But, Mr. Verney, I shall never forget how kind you have been to me.'

'Not kind,' he said, 'if kind implies an effort or a sacrifice. It has been a pleasure to me to do anything for you.'

'And you have done a great deal,' continued Myra. 'You have given me so much to think about. I owe half my enjoyment in London to you.'

Mr. Verney sighed deeply. 'Ah, Myra,' he said, 'you don't know how I can reciprocate the thanks; how many times you have drawn me out of myself, and made me forget. There is the one longing of life—forgetfulness.'

'Is it?' asked Myra. · She fixed her eyes upon him wonderingly.

'Yes,' he continued. 'One might begin a new life if one could only forget that which is old. But, dear child, that is all a riddle to you. You will go abroad and enjoy yourself. You have no idea of the excitement of seeing a foreign country

for the first time. I am afraid though you will do what I cannot do, and at least forget me.'

'Excitement will not make me do so,' said Myra. 'When
any person has got into one's mind and helped one on, it is
impossible to forget.'

'You are attributing to me a good deed of which I was quite
unconscious. I have never helped any one in your sense of
the word.'

'You have me,' said Myra.

'But how?'

'By making me understand better how people may differ
and yet be good,' said Myra.

'I am thankful I have done that. It is a great thing to
learn.'

'Yet I can't think that differences are of no consequence,'
said Myra. 'Dr. Kingsbury always says they are.'

'So you pit me against the old Doctor. Well, he is a
worthy antagonist. But, Myra, when do you mean to think
for yourself?'

'When I have learnt and seen enough,' said Myra. 'One
can't think to any purpose without facts as a foundation.'

Mr. Verney seemed amused. 'I wish people would remember that,' he said. 'They confound the power of thought
with the exercise of thought. They draw their facts, as they
term them, from their own minds, and because they reason
cleverly about them suppose they have arrived at truth. You
are right, Myra. Study the world well before you arrive at
your conclusions.'

'Or, at least, before I confess them,' said Myra. 'I am
afraid I am tempted to arrive at them very rapidly.'

'You are a woman, and have intuitions. You may be thankful for them.'

'May I?'

'Yes. They save you trouble, and that is a great thing in
this weary world ; and they are just as likely to be right, as
our so-called reasonable judgments, which in nine cases out
of ten are worked out by prejudice that sees only one side.
Have you heard of that poor thing at Yare to-day?'

'Not to-day. We heard yesterday.'

'And she was going on well?'

'In some ways, but her mind is still confused, and Mrs. Patty thinks she must have some one to take care of her, only it will be very expensive.'

Mr. Verney began a sentence—stopped in the middle—and turned away abruptly, just as Mrs. Cameron languidly opening her eyes said, 'Myra, my dear, have the gentlemen come up?'

'Only Mr. Verney, mamma; I am so vexed we disturbed you,' and Myra drew near the sofa to arrange her mother's cushions.

Mr. Verney went to the outer room, and sat down near the folding-doors. Rosamond's attention was instantly disengaged from her book, and she said to him banteringly, 'You and Myra have been talking secrets so loudly, that you have disturbed poor mamma.'

'Yes, it was very wrong of us; I am extremely sorry.'

'I should like to guess what the secrets were,' continued Rosamond.

'Should you?' and he smiled; but the smile had no heart in it, and Rosamond could get nothing more from him till coffee was brought up, and the rest of the party reappeared. Then he joined in the conversation about the journey, and seemed himself again.

'My father and I have been looking at maps,' said Godfrey, 'and have settled everything admirably.'

'Taking in Paris, of course?' said Rosamond.

'Just not taking it in. It will be too much for my mother now; and you can spend a day or two there on your return if you like it. Besides, Rosamond, you have been to Paris.'

'Precisely the reason why I want to go there again. And there is Myra who has never seen it.'

'Don't think about me,' said Myra, who was making tea at a distant table, 'I shall like anything; and, in fact, there is no one to be thought about but mamma.'

'A consideration which at once simplifies the question,' observed Mr. Cameron. 'We will have no discussions, Rosamond; Paris is set aside.'

Rosamond did not look sulky or frown, but she went back to her novel.

'Then where are you going?' inquired Mr. Verney.

'To the Salzkammergut,' replied Godfrey. 'You know it, of course. The finest part of the Austrian Tyrol. Ischl is a charming place for headquarters.'

'Is it? I was never there.'

Godfrey's countenance brightened immediately. 'Indeed! But of course you don't know Europe thoroughly. A splendid country it is. The Dachstein is magnificent. We were seven hours in reaching the highest peak. Left at four in the morning, and were back at Gosau by eight.'

'But poor mamma can't ascend the Dachstein,' said Myra.

Godfrey smiled sarcastically. 'She can enjoy the scenery though, and she will. You will find the change work wonders for her, and it is quite within reach now. The railway is open nearly to Salzburg, so the journey is very simple. I don't think there is a doubt about the route we marked out being the best?' he added, turning to his father.

'Not if we decide upon going to Ischl,' said Mr. Cameron; 'but I should prefer consulting your mother's wishes.'

'If you will take my advice, sir,' said Godfrey, 'you won't think of consulting her. An invalid's fancies are endless. Just tell her where she is going, and she will bring her mind to it. There is not a greater mistake made than that of asking opinions unnecessarily.'

'Perfectly true in many cases,' replied Mr. Cameron, 'not in all.'

'Discussions do worry mamma,' said Myra. 'She told me so yesterday.'

'Myra is bewitched with the idea of the scenery,' observed Rosamond, looking up from her book. 'She forgets how dull mamma will be in that out-of-the-way part of the world.'

The colour rushed to Myra's cheeks. 'I hope I don't think of myself, Rosamond,' she began hastily; but she caught Mr. Verney's eye, and added in a different tone, 'Dr. Richardson recommended moving about.'

'In civilised places,' said Rosamond; 'not with the risk of wretched hotels and rough roads.'

'There is a capital hotel at Ischl,' said Godfrey.

'And what medical advice?' suggested Mr Verney.

That was a serious consideration; and for the time it put an end to the conversation as regarded Mrs. Cameron. But Godfrey was not willing to let his acquaintance with the Salzkammergut prove so utterly useless.

'You should go to Hallstadt,' he continued, addressing Mr. Verney. 'The salt mines are wonderful—immensely interesting to a geologist. You are a geologist, of course?'

'By no means of course,' was the reply. 'Are you one?'

'I don't profess to be so; one never likes to profess in these days; but I do just know the rudiments—what every one knows. I found some curious fossils at Hallstadt, and studied them a little, and when I came home I sketched out a theory which I put into the form of a pamphlet, and the Geological Society took it up, and made a laudatory fuss about it. But it was a mere outline—a suggestion—nothing to what I could have done if I had given myself to the subject. You know one can't do everything, and my time was really given to sketching. I should like to show you a little view of the Hallstadt Lake. Myra, I think I gave it to you?'

'No,' said Myra, 'it was to Rosamond. I have seen it in her portfolio since we came to London.'·

Myra went to fetch the portfolio from the inner room, and brought back another with it. 'O Mr. Verney!' she said, 'this is yours. You left it the day before yesterday, when you were showing mamma those views of Como.'

'I want to see Como,' said Mr. Cameron. 'I have an idea that, after all, the north of Italy may be better than anything else.'

'There are sketches of all kinds, taken by a friend of mine,' said Mr. Verney. 'We were a month or rather longer in the neighbourhood.'

He unfastened the portfolio, and Mr. Cameron looked at the sketches. He was pompous in his approval, but not personally

conceited, and Mr. Verney evidently turned to him as a relief
after Godfrey.

'This is not Italian, is it?' said Mr. Cameron, taking up a
drawing with the view of a bridge, a river, and a snow-moun-
tain in the distance. He examined it closely. 'Very pretty,
but a different style from the rest, not so decided.'

'Yes, it is different,' said Mr. Verney carelessly.

'It must be by a pupil of Mr. Brownlow's,' observed Godfrey,
laughing; 'I know that colouring so well.'

'Oh! that is Rosamond's,' exclaimed Myra, who happened
to draw near the table at that moment.

'Rosamond's!' repeated Mr. Cameron. His tone was
chilling.

'It is Annette's,' said Rosamond quietly. 'Mr. Verney
took a fancy to it at Yare, and so it was given him. That is
why it resembles Mr. Brownlow's style. Myra, you recollect,
it was Annette's prize drawing.'

Yes, Myra recollected that fact well enough; but she felt
very uncomfortable; almost as if she was sanctioning a
falsehood. She murmured an answer which was not very
intelligible.

'It is remarkably good,' said Mr. Cameron. 'Annette
should have had it framed if I had seen it. Not that I
grudge it you,' he added, addressing Mr. Verney, with a
stiff courtesy of manner. 'No doubt Annette was only too
proud to give it to you.'

'I could not part with it, at any rate,' said Mr. Verney; but
he turned it over quickly, and then shut up the portfolio.

Annette just then came in from the inner room, where she
had been listening to a conversation carried on between her
mother and Henrietta Verney upon school education. Mr.
Cameron was going to speak to her about the drawing, but
he lost the opportunity, for, before she approached the table,
Rosamond went up to her, and said something in a low voice,
and they left the room together. Myra was vexed with herself for the feeling of suspicion which lingered in her mind,
but the history of this particular drawing had from the first
been so associated with what seemed to her a want of open-

ness, that the sight of it, especially when it was so decidedly
pronounced to be Annette's, annoyed her. It was Rosamond's
drawing to all intents and purposes, and Mr. Verney evidently
considered it as such. He did not wish to conceal anything,
but Myra was quite sure that Rosamond did. To have
Annette drawn into and encouraged in anything underhand,
was an odious idea. Myra was almost inclined to talk to Mr.
Verney about the matter, but a dread of appearing impertinent kept her back.

She had great ideas of the privileges accorded to persons
in love, and believed that many little signs of private understanding were to be permitted to them, which were not admis-
sible in the case of ordinary mortals. Actual deception or
untruth could, however, under no circumstances, be placed in
this permitted category, and it would be impossible for Mr.
Verney to be a sharer in anything of that nature. Still, Myra
did not quite like to ask him who had really given him the
drawing, neither did she feel quite sure of having a sincere
answer from Annette. Like many other persons who are
doubtful of hearing truth, she preferred to remain in ignorance.

When Mr. Verney bade Myra good-night, he said, 'If you
hear anything more about expenses to be incurred for that
poor thing, let me know; I might be able to help.'

'Would you! Oh, thank you! Mrs. Patty will think it so
kind.'

A cloud came over his face. Myra fancied he did not like
to be thanked for his thoughtfulness.

CHAPTER XXVI.

WHOEVER has read Longfellow's ' Hyperion,' has heard of the lovely lake of St. Wolfgang, and the attractions of the little town of St. Gilgen. But the charm with which genius and poetry invest any particular locality, must always be, in a certain degree, dispelled by the stern experience of travelling. Fascinating as the village of St. Gilgen and its surrounding scenery would undoubtedly appear to a person strong both in physical and moral constitution, it was anything but fascinating to the two forlorn ladies who—ensconced in the interior of a shaky and dirty vehicle, capable of containing only two per sons, and closed as a protection from the deluges of July in a mountainous country—descended the road which leads to the shore of the lake, and, skirting its southern bank, conveys the traveller to the fashionable Austrian watering-place, Ischl.

The elder of the two ladies was plain in face, plain in dress, and middle-aged. She looked rather careworn ; and, if departed youth had left her any remnants of excitability, they were exhibited more in the form of anxiety than of pleasure. She was very anxious at that moment, no one could have doubted it ; and few who looked at the pale, though very beautiful, face of her young companion, would have deemed her uneasiness unreasonable. To be travelling with a half-fainting invalid, late in the evening, in an unknown country, seeing an indefinite distance before, and having traversed a weary length of way behind ; above all, finding no prospect of accommodation, but that which can be afforded by the most homely of what in England would be termed public-houses, is not exhilarating to the spirits.

Moreover, the lady in question was but a very indifferent German scholar, and up to this time had been dependent upon her young friend as a medium of communication with landlords, waiters, and peasants ; but there was no hope of such assistance now. The young lady's feeble voice could only just be heard, as she entreated that the carriage might be stopped; and when this was done, she leaned back as though unable to say more.

'Don't you think I might bring you something to eat, Charlotte, my dear? A little soup? You have had nothing all day.'

The question was put very hesitatingly, Mrs. Tracy being doubtful upon two points; first, how she should manage to ask for the soup; and, next, what it would be like when she obtained it.

'If you would, please. It might be as well.'

Mrs. Tracy left the rickety carriage, went a few steps forward, and then returned. 'The German for soup, Charlotte, my dear? I can't think of it.'

'*Zuppe*, Aunt Mary; but if I may have some water?'

'Certainly, my love. *Wasser—Zuppe*—that is right, is it not? You shall have some directly. *Wasser—Zuppe; ich will haben*'— and she proceeded on her way towards the little inn, repeating the words as she went, every now and then stopping to look back to the carriage, apparently with a faint hope that, after all, her niece would appear to help her, as she had often done before.

The open archway of the inn was crowded with peasants. They had placed a table in the centre, and were sitting round it, not exactly carousing, like Englishmen under similar circumstances, but imbibing beer and smoke, to the decided deadening of the few faculties they possessed by nature.

Mrs. Tracy threaded her way amongst them, gathering her garments closely together, and looking timidly from one side to the other, whilst she sought for some one to whom she might address herself. Gazing eyes met her; and laughs, by no means melodious or respectful, followed her; but she pressed forward undauntedly to the window of the little bar-room, opening into the court, where stood a stout German woman, dealing out portions of thick liquid, in which floated balls of unknown quality—possibly bread, possibly meat, possibly—it might be as well not to inquire.

' *Wasser, Zuppe, geben sie mir.*'   Mrs. Tracy felt quite in-
spirited when she found how much German she could, upon
an emergency, command; and something in her appearance
gained the attention of the bar-maid, who motioned to the
rough peasants to stand aside, and proceeded to ladle out, from
a huge receptacle in the background, a plateful of the thick
liquid, dipping into it a wide pewter spoon, and handing with
her fingers a piece of coarse brown bread.   With this, and the
glass of water, Mrs. Tracy hurried back to the carriage; and,
placing the plate of soup in her niece's lap, assured her that
it looked excellent, and she almost thought she must have some
herself.   ' Just try it, Charlotte, dear, if only one spoonful ;
remember, we have a long way to go even now.'

' The water, please, first, Aunt Mary.   I am so sorry you
should have so much trouble.'

' No trouble, my love, if you would only eat; and if I
understood German better.   It must be a long distance to
Ischl still ; so pray eat.'

' Aunt Mary '— and the young girl looked eagerly in her
aunt's face—' I have been thinking—wishing.   Can we not go
at once to St. Wolfgang ? '

' My dear child !   Impossible.   A country village ?   What
is to become of us ? and no doctor ! '

' But I long to go.   I want to see friends—those friends of
yours.   I shall hear something from them ; and I can rest by
the lake, and be still.   There will be no noise there—no people.
I dread Ischl, Aunt Mary.'

' My friends have long lived out of England, Charlotte ; they
will not be able to tell you anything you wish to know.   When
we have settled ourselves at Ischl, and you are better, you
shall drive over there.'

' But it will be quiet; and I want quiet.   They said, at
Salzburg, that Ischl was fashionable.   O Aunt Mary ! I am
so tired ; let me be quiet.'

The tone was that of a weary petted child, admitting of no
contradiction.   Mrs. Tracy again repeated that a good hotel,
and a doctor, were to be met with at Ischl; whilst at St.
Wolfgang they could expect only the kindness of friends, who

could not be expected to take them into their house, and who,
it was even possible, might not be there to greet them. The
invalid, with the wilfulness of illness, carried her point. And
Mrs. Tracy, taking the plate and the glass in her hand, went
back with them to the inn, leaving her niece to explain to the
driver the change in their plans.

The crowd in the archway had rather increased. Every one
was watching the strangers, and, as Mrs. Tracy approached,
a sturdy man placed himself in her way, and addressed her in
a German patois, to which, although unable to comprehend a
word, she listened with an air of polite attention, until the
countenances of the peasants round the table, and the tone of
the man himself, convinced her that the beer had been too
potent for him ; and that her ignorance of the German language was for once a blessing. The poor lady's equanimity
was completely upset by the discovery. She dared not attempt
to pass the man, so as to lay the plate and glass on the table ;
she could not appeal for assistance ; and she was upon the
point of turning back again to the carriage, when a gentleman
and two ladies, who had just landed from the lake, appeared
in front of the archway ; and the former, seeing her distress,
immediately came to her relief. He was English—a stranger,
apparently, like herself—stiff as English people always are ;
but he performed his little act of civility courteously, walked
back with her to the carriage, and made the remark that the
weather was very bad ; and he supposed she had come from
Salzburg.

'Yes, from Salzburg ; and we had thought of going to Ischl,
but my friend prefers St. Wolfgang.'

'You will have indifferent accommodation there, I am
afraid ; at least, if you are at all particular.'

'My young friend is a great invalid,' was the reply ; 'and
comfort is of the greatest importance.'

'Then by all means go to Ischl ; you will find Baur's Hotel
expensive, but good. Can I assist you farther ?'

'Thank you, no. I am greatly obliged.' And the gentleman took off his hat, and the lady made her curtsey ; and
though they had not said that they were mutually shy of new

acquaintances, the fact was as evident as though the words had been uttered.

'He looks like an English officer,' said Mrs. Tracy, as she related the little adventure to her niece. 'They came, I suppose, from the opposite side. That must be St. Wolfgang across the lake; I wonder whether we could find a boat to take us there instead of going round?'

The suggestion was delightful to the weary invalid; but the driver declared it impracticable. There was a boat to be had sometimes—he did not believe there was one now; he could not inquire about it, the weather was likely to be bad again; and it would make very little difference, the road was not long; and, in fact——

'He must have his own way, Aunt Mary,' said the poor girl in a languid voice; 'only tell him to go quickly. Perhaps it is as well not to run the risk of a storm. Just say "*'schnell*" to him; he will understand.'

But though '*'schnell*' might have produced an effect upon the driver, it had none upon his horses, who were taking their evening repast as deliberately as if they had been settled for the night in their stable, and of course a German driver could not hurry his animals.

'We shall never get there,' sighed Mrs. Tracy, as she looked out of the carriage window; 'and there are our friends setting off again in their boat. How I envy them! But there are two gentlemen now—I wonder where the other came from.'

Charlotte took no notice. Mrs. Tracy continued her remarks: 'He is very tall; very like——I can't see his face, and it is impossible '——

'Impossible! what, Aunt Mary?'

'Nothing, my love. They are waiting for the young lady who is gathering flowers.'

'Come, Myra,' called out the gentleman who had spoken to Mrs. Tracy, 'we shall be obliged to go without you; there will be another shower soon.'

The young girl ran forward, and, on her way, dropped her handkerchief. Mrs. Tracy saw it, and, leaving the carriage, followed her and restored it, at the same time gazing earnestly at the two gentlemen, but their faces were turned away, and she could not recognise them. A few seconds afterwards the boat put off from the shore, and glided across the lake in the direction of the white cottages and the tall spire of St. Wolf-gang.

If beauty of scenery could have diverted the thoughts of anxiety, or soothed the sense of illness, both care and suffering might soon have been forgotten in the loveliness of that evening drive along the shore of the still lake, shut in as it was by the mountains of Styria, which, though in one part terminating in precipitous cliffs, in another descended gradually to the shore, leaving space for the green alps, and woods, the rocks, and chalets which rose above the village of St. Wolfgang. The clouds were dispersing gradually, and the promise of the morrow was brighter than it had been for weeks. In the clear evening light St. Wolfgang looked quite close, but a few minutes' row across the lake. The strangers' boat could be seen, drawing nearer and nearer—not so the carriage. Along the rough road the horses soberly trotted, but no closer were they to the wished-for goal. The length of the lake, and not its breadth, lay between. The sick girl's face grew more pale, if that were possible. She could no longer attempt to sleep, the road was so bad. It left the immediate bank of the lake, and seemed to take a direction inland. That was quite hope-less. Mrs. Tracy suggested that the driver had lost his way; but it is not so easy to lose one's way where there is only one road to be taken. The driver knew quite well where he was going, seven long miles at least; any person might have been aware of that who had taken the trouble to calculate, but Mrs. Tracy had, till lately, left calculations to her niece.

They turned the head of the lake at last, and then once more hope dawned upon them, and a smile passed over the face of the weary girl. But the goal was still beyond; as far as they had gone beyond St. Wolfgang, so far, of course, they must go back. Mrs. Tracy rested her niece's head on her shoulder, and bathed her forehead with eau-de-cologne, and looked up to the mighty hills and the darkening sky; and if she had uttered her thoughts aloud, they would surely have been those

N

of regret for the task she had undertaken—the endeavour to give change and pleasure in a case in which the quiet and the comfort of home seemed the one imperative necessity.

St. Wolfgang at last! The carriage descended a steep though short hill, and they entered a scattered village—the houses of a tolerable size, but decayed, and fit only for a poor population. The little street through which they drove was irregular and dirty; there were gardens, and trees, and steep lanes leading to the green uplands on the mountain side, but it was decidedly not a resting-place for an invalid.

The driver stopped his horses in front of a moderate-sized hotel, which was situated in an open 'Place,' having the church and a flight of broad steps on one side. The landlord, a man of unprepossessing countenance, and with a disagreeably familiar manner, came out to receive them. Mrs. Tracy did not even ask if they could have comfortable rooms—her young companion was so entirely exhausted that accommodation of any kind must be accepted. They were taken up some dirty stairs, and through an ante-room with several apartments opening into it—one of them a kind of public salon, in which several men were drinking. The invalid was laid upon a bed in a cheerless room, with deal furniture and no carpet; the only attempt at comfort a rickety sofa; and such a noise from the salon! But there was no alternative; and the sick, lonely, and weary travellers were left to find what rest and comfort they could, under circumstances which, but for the hope of having friends near, would have been utterly disheartening.

CHAPTER XXVII.

IT was the hour for evening service at St. Wolfgang. The church was partially filled with kneeling peasants, and the organ was pealing through the building.

Myra Cameron crossed the open Place, and stopped for a moment to listen as she drew near the church ; then, ascending a flight of steps close to the entrance, she passed along a covered arcade overhanging the lake, and opened a door which led into a long vaulted passage, whitewashed, but decorated with twining creepers. At the end of this passage another flight of steps conducted her into a long corridor, at the extremity of which was a dining-room, large, but low, and hung with pictures. Within was a drawing-room, longer and narrower, and furnished with many English comforts. Still beyond were other rooms, some almost unfurnished. Myra hastened through them, till at length unlocking a small door, opening from a room evidently uninhabited, she entered a gallery from which she could look down into the grand old church dedicated to the memory and the miracles of St. Wolfgang.

Myra did not understand the service that was going on, it did but strike her as devotional. Pilgrims might indeed come to kiss the rock on which St. Wolfgang knelt, and hang effigies of arms and legs around his shrine in thankfulness for his miraculous cures ; but the absurd legends she had heard were at the moment forgotten, and, alive as she always was to external impressions, the splendid church—with its groined roof, its Gothic arches, and richly-carved altarpiece, seen in the dim light—was inexpressibly solemn to her. And at that moment Myra was alone—singularly alone in feeling—and the luxury of pouring out her heart to God was a relief in which she could not but indulge. So she knelt, and prayed long and earnestly, whilst the music rose, and swelled, and died away, and the

harsh voices of the peasants mingled with the deep tones of
the priest, as they offered their evening petition—it might be
indeed to the Blessed Virgin, and not to Christ, but of this
Myra did not think ; she felt only that she, like them, was
praying, and that God could understand and answer her.

Some one else softly entered the gallery whilst she was there.
Myra heard the step, and with the shyness of English feeling
instantly rose.   Mr. Verney was standing in the doorway.   He
made a sign to her not to move, and they remained for several
minutes listening to the conclusion of the service, and when it
was ended, watching the peasants as the greater number left
the church, whilst a few lingered still behind in silent prayer.
Myra would then have retired herself, but Mr. Verney prevented her.

' We shall not disturb them,' he said, in rather a low voice,
as Myra pointed to the kneeling figures below.   ' They can
say what they have to say without troubling themselves as to
the meaning.   That you see, Myra,' he added sarcastically,
' is one of the great advantages of Roman Catholic devotion.
But I came to say good-bye—I must go back to Ischl to-night.'

' Must you ? ' exclaimed Myra, in a tone of great disappointment.   ' I hoped you would stay till to-morrow.   Though
I know they will want you there.   Mamma has been better
ever since you have been with us, and you have managed
everything so nicely.   All has gone right since we met you
at Munich.   And having you here to-day has been delightful.'

' Yes.   That row on the lake was delicious.   But you will
be very happy here, Myra.   You have a most lovely country
to see, and your friends will be very kind to you.   You mean
to be with them about a week, don't you ? '

' Perhaps so.   I don't quite know how long mamma will be
able to stay at Ischl.   Shall we go now ? '   Myra spoke rather
abruptly ; she disliked this talking upon ordinary subjects when
looking down upon the church.

Mr. Verney changed his tone instantly.   ' No, we won't go
ust yet.   It is not often that we can have such quiet moments.
Should you like to be a Roman Catholic, Myra ? '

' No,' was Myra's decided answer.

'I think I should, if I could only believe. It would be a very resting faith.'

'I like truth,' said Myra. 'I like what I am not afraid to look into.'

Mr. Verney sighed, and answered rather ironically: 'I know you are inclined to Rationalism; so am I, unfortunately.'

'No,' exclaimed Myra, 'I am not a Rationalist, because Rationalists have no certain truth. O Mr. Verney! it would be miserable not to be believe something fixed and definite.'

'So people say,' he replied, and I daresay they are right : though when one has long ceased to know what happiness means, it is difficult to understand how any mere belief could give it.'

'I wish I knew how to make you happy,' said Myra earnestly; 'you have been so very kind to me.'

'One thing you may do for me,' was the reply. 'Try not to be led away by what the world may say of me.'

'But does the world speak ill of you?' inquired Myra. 'I never heard any one do so yet.'

Mr. Verney laughed. 'Then you are more fortunate than I am myself. But don't distress yourself; only, if people ever do abuse me, just try to take my part. And now I suppose I must go. What shall I say to your mother for you?'

'Tell her to keep well, and beg Rosamond to let me hear every day how she is. And please say I am enjoying myself here. Colonel and Mrs. Hensman are so kind, and I am to go up the Schaffberg one day. Are you sure you cannot come over again?'

Mr. Verney made no answer. He was bending over the gallery. A lady had just entered the church below, who was gazing about her with an air of mingled nervousness and curiosity. Two or three poor people, beggars and cripples, were still in the church, and one of them came up and asked for alms, and then the lady turned, and her face was clearly seen. Myra recognised her as the stranger at St. Gilgen, and pointed her out to Mr. Verney.

'Yes,' he said shortly, 'it is the same.'

'She looks frightened and unhappy,' whispered Myra, ' and see, she is praying.'

The lady knelt. She was no Roman Catholic, accustomed to devotion in public, for she looked round her, evidently fearing remark.

Myra instinctively drew back from the front of the gallery, but Mr. Verney remained there ; yet he might not have been watching the stranger, for his face was hidden by his hand. But when, after a few seconds, the lady rose and left the church, he also stood up and again said good-bye to Myra. His tone was then so strange, hurried, and faltering, that Myra was upon the point of asking him whether he was ill, but she hesitated for an instant, and before she had time to put the question he was gone.

Myra was very sorry, even more sorry than when they had last parted in England. He had been with them now for more than a fortnight, staying with them at Munich, and going through the galleries, and then travelling with them to the lovely König See and Berchtesgaden—from thence accompanying them to Salzburg, and seeing them fairly settled at Ischl, where Edmund was to join them, and they were to make excursions in the Salzkammergut. So far all had been well. Mrs. Cameron's health was improved, though her eyesight was still in an unsatisfactory state, and Mr. Cameron was pleased at being the manager of the party, and was glad to have Myra as a sensible companion. Mr. Verney had met them accidentally, at least so every one thought. He had remained in England long after them, and then, in taking a little summer excursion, had stumbled upon them, and arranged to join them just for two or three weeks. This was his own account, and there was, of course, no reason to doubt it. Myra was too pleased to see him to inquire particularly why, or from whence he came. Her own impressions about Rosamond would, indeed, have been a sufficient reason to account for his following them, but, strange to say, these impressions had lately been much shaken. Rosamond might flirt with Mr. Verney, and she did flirt with him, every day, and all day long, trying all kinds of wiles, and graces, and manœuvres to attract his attention ; but though he responded, as he always did, by a light *badinage* for the moment, he had long fits of grave abstraction, and even depression, from which no effort could raise him. Myra was very sorry for him ; she saw so plainly that he was an unhappy man, and often, in her earnestness and simplicity, she said things which seemed to touch him ; but if ever for one instant he alluded to any secret care, the next he was sure to turn off what he had said into something which, if not a joke, had a tone of irony in it. And he was so restless also, always advising that they should move from place to place—always finding some reason for a change of plans which had been carefully made, and then, after a discussion, returning to them again. It was as though he planned merely for the sake of planning. Myra did not exactly dislike all this. It excited her interest, and awakened a kind of romance in her own mind. She fancied that perhaps he was doubtful of Rosamond's feelings, and that this made him unhappy ; and she often tried to divert his thoughts, by talking to him about the things which interested him, art especially. Their stay in Munich had been a delightful lesson in this way. They had gone regularly every day to the gallery, and he had pointed out the pictures which she had so often heard him describe, and showed her where lay their beauties and defects. This seemed to be his chief enjoyment, and it was very flattering to Myra. She lived in the reflected light of Mr. Verney's talent, and the self-appreciation in which originally she had been almost painfully wanting, was fostered so as to give her ease and confidence in society, whilst Mr. Verney's remarks, with her own comments, enabled her to be agreeable in the family party. Myra was unconscious of the mode in which she was being educated, but she felt the results, and it was scarcely possible, under such circumstances, to look at Mr. Verney with unprejudiced eyes. And of late he had been careful to do nothing which could in any way shock her conscientiousness. Before they left London he had tried to make her of use to him, to employ her as a medium for gaining information which might be useful, but now he asked no question about Yare, he never referred to Miss Medley's illness, or made even common inquiries as to the news received from Mrs. Patty or Dr. Kingsbury. All that was gone by, and, as it seemed, forgotten, and whatever might be the subject of his preoccupied thought, Myra was in no way made a sharer in it.

And in one important respect Mr. Verney was an invaluable assistance. It is almost a proverb, that nothing brings out temper and disposition like travelling, and Myra had gained a considerable experience of the truth of the saying since she left England. Rosamond was no help to her in keeping up her father's spirits, or in waiting upon her mother; she was always either 'awfully tired,' or had a 'tremendous headache,' when they reached the end of a long journey, and it was absolutely necessary that she should have a quiet room, and go to bed soon. And then, in the morning she was so 'frightfully sleepy' that it was impossible to be up in time to assist any one ; in fact she required all the aid which could be spared for herself. If they were in a quiet place, Rosamond was 'bored to death,' and thought the Germans the most uninteresting people in the world, and wondered from morning till night why any one should take the trouble to come abroad. If they were in a gay place, she was equally 'bored' with sight-seeing, and thought every moment wasted which was not spent in the public promenades. Rosamond, in fact, was Myra's great care. Mrs. Cameron, feeling better in health, was willing to enjoy the novelty, and was much less fretful than she had been at home ; but, till Mr. Verney appeared, Rosamond's discontent had been a canker-worm to the pleasure of the party.

Now, however, all was sunshine. They had settled themselves at Ischl for a week, possibly a fortnight, for Godfrey had pertinaciously insisted upon the necessity of seeing the Salzkammergut; and Mr. Cameron, determined and self-dependent when brought in contact with ordinary people, always succumbed to the will of his elder son, as being the reflection of his own superiority. Ischl was likely to prove by no means a bad choice, or at least it would not be so if only the weather would be favourable. But the fate of travellers in mountainous countries seemed likely to follow them, and they were waiting now, day after day, in the hope that a clear sky would admit of an expedition to Aussee, Gosau, and Hallstadt. In the meantime Myra had been carried off by some old friends of Mr. Cameron's, who had taken a house for three months on the Lake of St. Wolfgang, and the novelty alone would have been delightful to her. But the house at St. Wolfgang had a charm peculiar to itself. It had once formed part of the convent, and was built upon the very edge of the lake, and the water washed the walls of the building. The garden extended along a steep ridge at the foot of the mountain, and in the short summer months was filled with the rarest and richest flowers and shrubs of a southern land ; the mighty walls, the rocks, forests, and alps of the Schaffberg, forming its background ; and the blue lake, the white hamlets, and the encircling mountains, with their deep glens and recesses— creating an ever-changing view around it. To Myra it was a Paradise, and for one day Mr. Verney had been there to enjoy it with her. For one day only. Rosamond's face when he accepted Colonel Hensman's invitation was sufficient, so Myra thought, to prevent him from staying longer. Probably Mr. Verney was flattered by it, at any rate he immediately assured Mrs. Cameron that he should go over only for one day, and Rosamond was bright and gracious as his reward.

Myra had watched this little scene as she watched many, making her own comments upon them, and drawing from them her own conclusions. But she had no one to show her whether those conclusions were right. She had read of love in books, and had formed an ideal of it in her own mind. What she now saw was very unlike what she had fancied, and at times it sorely perplexed her ; but it did not shake her conviction. Unless Rosamond cared for Mr. Verney she could not make such direct efforts to attract him. Unless Mr. Verney cared for Rosamond he would not be so marked in his attentions, and so desirous to meet her wishes. These were to Myra self-evident facts. She was herself so essentially sincere in every word and action, whether good or bad, that a mockery of feel-

ing was something utterly beyond her powers of comprehension ; whilst her vivid imagination intensified every indication
of interest, and deepened every expression of pleasure, till
Rosamond felt as she would have felt, and Mr. Verney loved
as she would wish to be loved. Why then should there be
any delay? Why any mystery or doubt? Above all, why
were her father and mother so blind to what was passing
before them?

CHAPTER XXVIII.

WHEN Mr. Verney left Myra, he crossed the open square by
the church, and lingered in front of the inn.

Part of the strangers' luggage was still in the entrance, and
he carelessly examined it, asking at the same time a few questions of the landlord, who, with a cigar in his mouth, was
standing by, giving orders for its removal.

They were very short questions, and put with a haughty
nonchalance, which had the effect of checking any familiarity
on the part of the landlord ; but Mr. Verney learnt from them
that the strangers were travelling alone, and were likely to
remain at St. Wolfgang for several days. They had ordered
dinner, and one of the ladies had been out, but was just returned ; the other was too ill to see any one.

Mr. Verney replied to this hint by taking out a card, writing
a few words upon the back, and desiring that it might be given
to Mrs. Tracy instantly, and as the man rather sulkily obeyed,
he followed him up the stairs to the ante-room.

The public salon was silent, for the party who had been
dining in it had betaken themselves to the open air, and their
noisy voices might be heard as they shouted and sang in the
garden at the back of the house. The room smelt of smoke ;
plates, dishes, and drinking cups were left upon the table.
There could have been no place less agreable for a private

interview, but it was Mr. Verney's only resource; and after hearing the answer brought back to his note—that the lady would see him as soon as possible—he sat down on a wooden bench waiting her arrival.

The dreamy, indifferent look was gone from his face now, and in its stead there was an expression of struggling feeling which seemed to make the delay even of those few moments almost intolerable to him. He rose at last, and went to the door, as if determined to go without having obtained the interview he had requested; but just then Mrs. Tracy appeared from the opposite side of the ante-room, and Mr. Verney, recovering himself, went forward to meet her, with the cool, easy, rather languid manner which never forsook him in the presence of others.

They met as old and intimate friends, or perhaps not really friends; Mrs. Tracy's face was much more expressive of her feelings than Mr. Verney's, and no one who looked at her could suppose that she was pleased to see him. Surprised and excited she evidently was, and her first words were those common to all persons under such circumstances : 'Where did you come from? How did you know we were here?'

Mr. Verney's reply was short and matter-of-fact. 'I have been travelling with some friends. I did not expect you here, but I thought I saw you at St. Gilgen.'

'Then you have not come purposely to meet us?' was Mrs. Tracy's disappointed question.

'Purposely? not exactly. But you say nothing of Charlotte.'

'She is very ill—worse.' They sat down, and there was a pause.

Mr. Verney bent his eyes upon the ground, and said, 'How long has she been worse?'

'For about a fortnight. The voyage did her good, and when we landed at Trieste I was hopeful about her. There we had your letter saying that it was better we should not go to England, and since then she has failed rapidly.'

'I said what was best for her,' he replied; and his voice

somewhat faltered. 'She needs amusement; in England she would only have care.'

'Charlotte does not dread care,' said Mrs. Tracy drily.

'Still it is better she should delay. You must travel during the summer months, and then go to Italy.'

'And you will be with us?'

Mr. Verney looked up suddenly. 'I thought I had explained everything in my letter. You heard from me at Vienna?'

'Our only letters have been those which we found at Trieste. I took Charlotte from thence to Venice. It was the only place in which she was interested; and we have travelled by Milan and Innsbruck.'

Mr. Verney looked excessively annoyed. 'I reckoned upon your going at once to Vienna,' he said; 'I wrote there and told you everything.'

'Everything! And what is everything, Mr. Verney?' exclaimed Mrs. Tracy indignantly. 'Be so good as to let me hear as quickly as possible; Charlotte is very ill, and does not know why I have left her, and I must return to her immediately.'

'My dear madam, calm yourself. It is a long story, but I will endeavour to shorten it. Whatever I may say, one thing you cannot doubt, that my affection is unaltered.'

'Mr. Verney, I do doubt it,' was the reply. 'No man with true love in his heart could trifle as you have trifled with that poor child for the last twelvemonths. I have said it to my brother-in-law again and again, and now I say it to you.'

'Then you do me a grievous injustice, Mrs. Tracy. As there is a God in heaven, I love your niece better than I have ever loved, or ever could love, any woman.'

'And why is she not your wife?'

'Answer the question for yourself,' he exclaimed. 'You know all the difficulties, the obstacles which have been put in our way. You know the condition of your brother-in-law's affairs—the risks I have run to help him, and the shattered condition of my health, which, independent of business, necessitated a return to England.'

'But you have been in England now several months, and my brother's affairs '——

'Are in a worse condition than ever,' interrupted Mr. Verney moodily.

'Be it so,' was the answer. 'Then see Charlotte yourself and tell her the truth.'

'I cannot,' he exclaimed; 'I should kill her.'

'You are killing her now; yes, Mr. Verney, killing her, as surely as ever man killed woman, by suspense and disappointment. You urged her leaving India, on the plea that when once in England together, and the health of both re-established, you might jointly consult and arrange for your marriage. That was the pretence—I repeat it, the pretence—it could have been no reality; your present conduct proves it. She obeyed, and now she is told to travel during the summer, and to spend the winter in Italy. Mr. Verney, what does it mean? As you are a man of honour, and a gentleman, I insist upon receiving an explanation.'

'As you will, dear Mrs. Tracy. This excitement distresses me; indeed, it is uncalled for. You will see it when I have explained myself.'

'God grant that I may!' was the muttered reply, and Mr. Verney continued—

'You know that I came to England partly for health, partly that I might look after your brother-in-law's affairs, in which my own were unfortunately involved. I made no mystery of the matter to you, but I did not wish it talked of to others; neither did I desire my engagement with Charlotte to be generally known. There were family reasons for this; the marriage would be uncongenial to my own relations. I told Charlotte so, and she understood it. They are proud; they would have put obstacles in my path. I hoped to see my way quickly and clearly, but I was disappointed. Stuart mismanaged his business grievously—that I need scarcely say to you. His affairs became more and more desperate. He wrote to me to raise money, and I knew no way of doing it, except as he himself had suggested, by applying to his aunt. It was entirely contrary to my wishes, but I had no alternative; I did apply to her; I suppose you know the result?'

'I know nothing,' replied Mrs. Tracy. 'We left India before we could have heard anything, even if my brother-in-law had chosen to be communicative, which he never does choose.'

'The poor old lady has become imbecile, or worse,' continued Mr. Verney. 'She had a severe illness, which fell on the brain. She may live for years, but she cannot recover. Thus the assistance which I thought would be forthcoming is unattainable. Stuart is by this time a ruined man.'

'He has long been so,' was Mrs. Tracy's quiet reply.

Mr. Verney looked at her in astonishment. Then he said as quietly : 'So you may have thought, and so I may have thought, but so the world has not thought—and that makes all the difference.'

'The difference as to your marriage with his daughter,' said Mrs. Tracy bitterly.

'You are hard upon me,' he replied. 'It is a question of possibility; our marriage at the present moment would be madness.'

'Mr. Verney, I am not hard upon you,' said Mrs. Tracy. 'I see your difficulties, and I feel for you—or, I could feel for you if you would be open. You say all this to me—why do you not say it to Charlotte?'

'In her state it would be cruel; but time will help us.'

'Time will not help us, and God will not help us, if we do not help ourselves,' exclaimed Mrs. Tracy indignantly. 'I tell you, Mr. Verney—and it is the result of a bitter experience —that if there is one wrong greater than another of which men are guilty towards the women whom they profess to love—be they mothers, sisters, or wives, it is that of shrinking from inflicting necessary pain. Tell us the worst, and we can bear it bravely; be true and open with us, and we will honour and obey you to the very last moment of existence ; but, keep back from us anything which we have a right to know, or, what is far worse, give us a half-confidence when we ought to have a whole, and we are paralysed ; we lose our trust, and with

it our strength. So you will surely find it to be with Charlotte.'

'Very possibly,' he replied; 'and yet it may not suit me to
tell the whole. Every man, Mrs. Tracy, is the best judge of
the necessities which guide his own conduct.'

'Then I am to understand that we are to go on as we have
been going on for the last year, in suspense—a suspense which
acts as a slow but most sure poison. Mr. Verney, are you a
Christian and a gentleman, and can you allow this?'

'I trust I have not lost all claim to either title, dear madam.
As a Christian and a gentleman, and, what is more, one who
most truly loves your niece, I believe that I am doing that
which is best, both for her and for myself.'

'Then you do not know her,' exclaimed Mrs. Tracy. 'Her
strongest support is the obligation of duty; and, ill as she is,
if you will plainly set before her the impossibility of her marriage at present, and the need that she should devote herself
to her father, she will at once face her position, and find a
stimulus in the effort she is compelled to make which will
strengthen her both physically and morally; only let me entreat you not to be afraid.'

'I am afraid,' was the reply.

And Mrs. Tracy murmured, in an accent of scarcely concealed scorn, 'Yes; I have known that from the beginning.'

'I am afraid,' he continued, 'because I know what a sudden
shock might do; and, moreover, I do not see the necessity.
You must forgive me for saying that, in such cases as these, a
woman's impetuous feeling can scarcely be considered a safe
guide.'

'The impetuous feeling has endured a long time,' replied
Mrs. Tracy sarcastically. 'I ask of you merely what Charlotte and I have been asking of my brother-in-law ever since it
first dawned upon us that his affairs were embarrassed. Month
after month we have begged to know everything, and been told
that we did know it, and then found that something was still
in the background. So we have both lost all trust and all
heart. It is this which has preyed upon Charlotte's health,
and brought her into her present condition: and this same

208 *A GLIMPSE OF THE WORLD.*

distrust has operated in your own case. You are indeed afraid of giving pain, Mr. Verney, but it is pain to yourself. You shrink from inflicting the stroke of the dagger, because you must witness the momentary suffering; but you have no hesitation in administering the slow poison, because you can hide your eyes from the lingering agony.'

Mr. Verney rose suddenly. His lip quivered, as he said, 'God forgive me for inflicting either! You must not tell her I have been here.'

'And are you going? You refuse to see her?'

'I cannot; I dare not. She shall hear from me.'

Mrs. Tracy seized his hand. 'Mr. Verney, you must see her! I will be no party to such conduct. She is dying— dying of hope deferred.'

'Which will be hope made hopeless when she has seen me. Take her to Vienna; give her change, comfort. Let her expect my letters—they shall not fail; and, believe me, I will prepare her.'

'For what? For the termination of her engagement?'

'I do not say so. I can tell nothing at present. Whatever I resolve upon, her happiness will be my first consideration.'

'And why have you come now?' exclaimed Mrs. Tracy.

'Because I acted, as you would act, upon impulse,' he replied bitterly. 'I would not have you remain here, and I came to say so.'

'Then we have wasted many unnecessary words,' was the cold reply. 'But your mind may be at rest upon that point. No place can be more unfit than this for a sick girl's resting-place. I find that the friends whom we expected to meet are away. They have let their house to strangers, and we have no inducement to remain. I would, indeed, that I could go this very night.'

'Let me know how you can be made more comfortable,' exclaimed Mr. Verney. 'Tell me in what I can help you. Let me arrange for your journey back to Vienna.'

'We do not go to Vienna; I shall take Charlotte to Ischl.'

Mr. Verney's countenance changed, as he answered hastily,

'But you must not! It is very undesirable. She ought to be where every comfort can be procured for her. I know nothing of the physicians at Ischl. Promise me that you will return to Vienna.'

'I promise nothing, Mr. Verney. I consider myself in no way bound to you.'

'But it is madness! I could not answer for the consequences. And you are travelling alone, without a servant!'

'We travel as we can afford. You forget that we are a ruined family, with nothing to depend upon but my own small income.'

'I must provide for that,' he exclaimed, and his sallow face flushed. 'I had no idea of such a state of things.'

'You need not distress yourself about us. Charlotte is independent in her habits, and the language is my only difficulty.'

'Mrs. Tracy,' exclaimed Mr. Verney, 'this is cruel on your part. You know how earnestly I desire that Charlotte should have every luxury—how gladly, how thankfully I would provide all '——

'That is fitted for a dying person. Rest of mind may, perhaps, be the one thing needful. Mr. Verney, good night, and good-bye. We are not likely to meet again. I thank you for having at length enlightened me.'

He detained the hand which was laid coldly in his, and said hesitatingly: 'Let me remind you, my own letters must tell my tale. I trust implicitly to your honour.'

Mrs. Tracy merely withdrew her hand, and without another word left the apartment.

———

CHAPTER XXIX.

'THE Doctor won't come downstairs to-day, Faith,' said Mrs. Patty, as she beckoned Faith into the study, and pointed to a pile of books heaped one upon another on the floor. 'I think if you and I were to set about it, we might do something towards putting things straight.'

'If the Doctor will allow it, ma'am ; but he scolded dreadful the last time Betsey and I touched his books.'

'The Doctor never scolds, Faith ; but he likes to have me present when his books are handled. Poor dear, he is as careful of them as if they were babies.'

'More careful a great deal,' was Faith's reply, 'seeing he would never let a drabby girl wheel his books about in a barrow, as babies are wheeled about in these days. It is a wonder to me that they are not half of them murdered. But, Mrs. Patty, if you will just leave the books to me, I will be special particular about them.'

'He won't be satisfied, Faith, and I can't bear to cross him. He thinks a good deal of his books now he is kept upstairs.'

'Ay, and to my mind he is likely to think a good deal more,' replied Faith. 'It will be a long day, Mrs. Patty, before we see him down again.'

'Mr. Harrison considers him better,' said Mrs. Patty, 'and he ate a whole mutton-chop yesterday.'

'A chop about the size of a five-shilling piece, ma'am,' answered Faith. 'As I said to Betsey, there is nothing differs more than chops, and it's no use to deceive oneself about it.'

Mrs. Patty sat herself down on a high leather-covered stool, rested her hands on her knees, and looked straight before her.

Faith bustled about the room, taking up papers and writing materials, and putting them down again, moving chairs, and brushing away dust with a duster, and every now and then glancing at her mistress. Not a word was spoken by either, till Faith approached the folio volume of St. Augustine, which lay near the Doctor's desk. Then one large tear rolled slowly down Mrs. Patty's cheek, and she rose and said, ' I will dust that myself, Faith,' and taking the cloth from Faith's hand, she moved it slowly over the book, wiping away every separate particle of dust, and rubbing the cover where it needed no rubbing, Faith all the while standing by waiting for her duster. Seeing at length that she was not likely to have it, she went out of the room to fetch another, and Mrs. Patty sat down again in the Doctor's arm-chair, and clasping her hands tightly together, murmured something which sounded like a prayer. When Faith returned Mrs. Patty was gone to her own room, but she was there only for a few minutes. When she came back she was cheerful again, and said that she had looked in upon the Doctor, and found him comfortable. He wanted to know if the post was come ; so she would take him the letters if there were any, and then return and settle what was to be done about cleaning the study.

' The postman ought to have been here ten minutes ago,' said Faith. ' I wonder why Betsey has not brought the letters in. Not but what master will be better without them, Mrs. Patty. They do but worry him since he has had so much to do for that poor daft Miss Medley.'

' It is all settled now,' said Mrs. Patty, ' or it will be soon. Mr. Cameron and the Doctor have found a person who will be kind to her, and look after her.'

' The Doctor has done it, you mean, ma'am,' said Faith. ' Mr. Cameron would have been of little use without him. Anyhow, it's a blessing that the poor lady has some friends. People say it was just a Providence that she lost her senses when she did, for she knew so little how to use them that she was always making away with her little money to help her relations out in India. So she would have been ruined if she had not been stopped in time. But there's always good comes out of evil.'

' Always, Faith,' said Mrs. Patty emphatically, ' but go and ask for the letters ; your master is waiting.'

Faith brought back a tolerably large packet, which Mrs. Patty looked through, putting aside those which she knew concerned domestic matters, and pondering over others as if doubtful whether or not to take them upstairs. Faith picked up one which had fallen on the ground. ' Here is the best of all, Mrs. Patty—a foreign letter. That will be sure to do you good, and the Doctor too.'

' From my little Myra,' said Mrs. Patty, in a tone of quiet satisfaction, and she examined the paper, the post-mark, the stamp, as persons do who have time to wonder at the fact that the letter they now hold in their hands has been only a few days before held in the hands of a person in a foreign land hundreds of miles off. ' She writes a good clear hand ; that is a comfort. Just take the other letters up, Faith, and let me stay here a minute, and look through this ; or stop, ,I will take them myself, and you go now ; never mind the books.'

Mrs. Patty was evidently not quite certain of her own mind, but Faith was, so she carried the Doctor's letters to him upon her own responsibility, and left Mrs. Patty to decipher Myra's communication.

' MY DEAREST MRS. PATTY,—I could make a great many excuses for not having written before, but they will take up my time and my paper, and I feel sure you will not require them. We have settled ourselves at Ischl, an out-of-the way fashionable place in Austria. I never heard of it till Godfrey talked of it, but every one in Austria thinks a great deal about it, and as the Emperor is often here, there are hotels, and good houses, and everything to make one comfortable.

' Mamma has been better ever since we left Munich, and we should all like Ischl extremely but for the bad weather. I think I told you that Mr. Verney joined us at Munich. He has been with us ever since, and it has been quite delightful having him. He knows everything, and amuses papa, and he is more kind to me than I can say ; and as for Rosamond, I cannot think what she will do without him, for indeed I am quite certain that they like each other extremely, though, perhaps, I ought

not to say it, as you told me one day it was better not to talk
about such things. Mr. Verney is a great assistance also in
enabling us to understand the particular beauty of this country.
He has travelled so much that he can compare it with others.
He says that it has not the grandeur of Switzerland, but that
no other scenery ever gave him such a sense of enchantment.
Berchtesgaden and the König See, to which we made an excursion from Salzburg, were quite perfect. We drove for miles
and miles, and every change in the position of the hills formed a
new view, which one felt as if one would fain carry away, stored
up as a treasure of beauty in one's memory. There were fore-
grounds of rocks and banks, covered with flowers and moss;
middle grounds of the most beautiful trees, planted as if they
had been especially laid out in a gentleman's park; and back-
grounds of cliff and mountain-tops, to say nothing of torrents
rushing down the mountains, and the König See, shut in by
walls of cliffs, rising so immediately from the water's edge
that there was not room even for a pathway. One walk I
shall never forget. We were stopping to rest the horses at
a little village called Insel; it had been raining all the morning, and we were rather out of spirits and disheartened because
of the weather, but at last it cleared up, and Mr. Verney proposed to Rosamond and me to go out with him, and in spite
of the mud we set off. Insel is a tiny village in a valley, with
great hills, woods, and gorges all round. Glorious effects
there were with the clouds clearing off the hills, but the
loveliest thing of all was the wood, to which we made our
way. It was all I have fancied a wood might be, when I
have been reading fairy tales and romances—glades and rocks,
most beautiful trees—beeches, sycamores, larches, firs,—and a
complete carpet of moss, and flowers, and wood strawberries,
which it was almost a sin to walk upon; whilst between the
branches of the trees and the openings in the wood there
were glimpses of the valley and the huge grim rocks towering
over it. We sat down on a rock to rest, and, oh! Mrs. Patty,
it really was Paradise.

'As Mr. Verney says, "What one especially feels here is
the lavishness of the beauty." It is not that one goes to see

a lovely *spot* but a lovely *country*, which is perfect even in its minutest detail. Rosamond declares that I am always sermonising about it, but I hope it is only that I feel thankful for it. Mr. Verney quoted that line from Keats the other day—

'A thing of beauty is a joy for ever;'

and, certainly, the sight of the Bavarian Alps will be a joy to me till the last day of my life.

'I am staying now at a lovely place near Ischl, a house which Colonel Hensman (you know Mrs. Hensman is a cousin of mamma's) has taken for some months on the lake of St. Wolfgang. It is about seven miles from Ischl. The house was part of a convent and joins the old church, and there is a gallery in it from which one can look down into the church. The grounds are exquisite; so beautiful that the Emperor of Austria and his friends often go over from Ischl to see them. They are close to the lake, and the mountains rise above them—real mountains, one (the Schaffberg) more than 5000 feet high; but it is very cold here in winter, and, indeed, for a great part of the year; and though there are all kinds of lovely rare shrubs and flowers they can only be left out a very little while. Colonel and Mrs. Hensman brought me over the day before yesterday, and I was to have stayed till Saturday. Mr. Verney came over yesterday for the day, and we were very happy rowing on the lake and walking about the beautiful grounds. He went back to Ischl in the evening, but he said nothing about leaving us, so you may imagine how disappointed I was when this morning, just as Mrs. Hensman was planning what we should do for the day, a messenger came from Ischl saying that I must go back directly, for that all the plans were altered because of Mr. Verney's being obliged to go away almost immediately, and that we were to drive over to Aussee to-morrow morning and sleep, and see some lakes in the neighbourhood, so that Mr. Verney might have the pleasure of being with us, and after that he would go, and Edmund would join us. I feel very ungrateful at not being pleased, but it entirely upsets all my own plans, and Mr. Verney's going is a terrible blank. I cannot help thinking that we shall leave

Ischl whenever he does, for papa really does not know how to
get on without him. I shall not much care where we go if this
should be arranged, for I enjoy everything, and much as I like
the idea of staying at St. Wolfgang, I do not like being away
from our own party. Ischl itself is very beautifully situated,
with mountains all round it, but it is too fashionable to please
me. There is an English service on Sundays, held in some
room hired by the landlord of the chief hotel, and fitted up
expressly for the purpose. This of course is very satisfactory,
though papa says it is only a speculation of the landlord's to
attract the English guests. The English clergyman sat near
us at the *table d'hôte* the first day we dined there, and told
us that the landlord gave him his rooms free of cost, and that
he considered it his business to entertain the English guests;
and then he began telling us who all the people were who were
present. We went to the service on Sunday. There was
Holy Communion, and before the offertory, notice was given
that the collection would be made to defray the expenses the
landlord had incurred in fitting up the room, and we were
told besides that the hour for the afternoon service would
be altered to suit the landlord's two *tables d'hôte.* I really felt
quite glad that Mr. Verney was not there to hear it, for he
cannot help turning such things into ridicule. I can't laugh
at them myself, they only give me pain, for they seem so irre-
verent. That is the one point upon which Mr. Verney and
I cannot agree. He never cares about going to these English
chapels and services; he says he can be much more devout
when he is wandering about amidst beautiful scenery, and I
daresay he may be right, only it seems strange. He likes
Roman Catholic services, though; at least, he likes to look on
and to hear the music; but then he says plainly that he only
goes to them as he does to the opera. Dear Mrs. Patty, these
things puzzle me very much, for Mr. Verney must be a good
man, he so entirely appreciates everything which is great and
noble, and he talks to papa by the hour about plans for doing
good in India.

'Tuesday afternoon.—I must finish this, and take it with me
to Ischl this evening. I am to go back after an early dinner,

which is not quite what mamma wishes ; for Rosamond wrote me word I was to return directly in the carriage that was sent for me, and Mr. Verney added a little line in her note, begging me not to delay ; but I really could not help it ; Mrs. Hensman entreated me so much to stay, and help her to take care of some poor English ladies, who are at a very indifferent hotel in the village, and whom she thinks it right to be kind to. They are an aunt and niece, and they are travelling for amusement, and have come here by a kind of accident, hoping to find some friends. Mrs. Tracy is the aunt, Miss Stuart the niece. The latter is very much out of health, but she is quite fascinating in look and manner. I have been sitting with her this morning in a lovely little pavilion in the grounds. It is fitted up most luxuriously, and has windows all round, which command enchanting views of the lake. Mrs. Hensman had Miss Stuart taken there this morning, carried in a chair, for she is too ill to walk, and then she asked me to go to her. You know how shy and awkward I am generally ; but that is when there is no exact reason for doing or saying things ; when I am obliged to put myself forward I can get on pretty well. Miss Stuart was very reserved in manner at first, and rather cold, till something was said about Mrs. Hensman's kindness, and then she was so grateful, her eyes quite sparkled as she spoke of it. They are such lovely eyes, very deep blue, with long eyelashes ; and the eyelids droop over them, and make them still deeper and darker. Their expression is very sad ; they seem to look out into the far distance as if expecting something which never comes. I could not help thinking, as I sat by her this morning, that if I were a painter, I should like to take her as a model for a picture of " Hope deferred, which maketh the heart sick." I really longed to kiss her and comfort her, but I did not dare to talk about anything but commonplace subjects, and these seemed an effort to her. She must have a history attached to her, I am sure ; but I am not likely to know it, for I shall scarcely see her again. They were going away from St. Wolfgang directly ; but I think now they know Mrs. Hensman, they may stay longer. It is such a comfort to them to be near kind people, and to have the use of the grounds. Mrs. Tracy looks rather bewildered, as if she had no plans and did not know what to do or where to go, and this makes it all the more sad and strange. They seem so very lonely and helpless. I have had an idea in my mind since I saw them, which seems unnatural, and almost impossible, but which I should like to be quite sure about. You know Miss Greaves had a dear friend whose name was Stuart, and who went to India ; and I have fancied whether this young lady could be the same. People turn up so very curiously in strange places. I would have asked Miss Stuart herself, only it might have seemed inquisitive. Please let Juliet and Annette see this letter. I will write to them next time. I send you a very great deal of love, dearest Mrs. Patty, and please give all kinds of respectful and most affectionate remembrances to dear Dr. Kingsbury. How I should like to see him, and talk to him ! When you write, pray let me hear all the Yare news. It seems an age since we went away.—Ever your very affectionate young friend, MYRA CAMERON.'

Mrs. Patty laid down the letter, took off her spectacles, sat for a few moments in thought, then put on her spectacles again, and re-read the portion of Myra's communication which referred to Mr. Verney, after which she walked very deliberately upstairs to the Doctor's room.

The old man was sitting in an arm-chair, propped up by cushions. There had been a gradual failing of strength lately, which no one could exactly account for. He felt but little pain, but he had lost his appetite and energy. The symptoms of a general break-up of the constitution were too obvious to be hidden from any eyes but those blinded by affection. Until this day Mrs. Patty had never realised to herself what a change might be at hand. Now, as she entered the room, it struck her how very worn he looked, how his cheeks had fallen in, and how dim his eyes were, and especially how thin and almost white his bony hands had become ; and for an instant forgetting the irritable feeling which had made her hasten to him with Myra's letter, she went up to him, and propped up his pillows, and drew his little table nearer to him, and cleared

away some papers which were lying upon it. But she could
not trust herself to speak to him, till he said—

'Thank you, Patty; I do very well. Have I had all the
letters?'

'All which were of any consequence, Doctor, dear. There
was one I saw from poor Miss Medley's nurse. What does
she say of her?'

'That she is afraid the poor lady grows worse. The change
has not been of any use. We must pray, Patty, that God would
please to take her home before long.'

'Ay! indeed we well may. It is a sore trial for herself
and her friends. And what has been settled about the money
matters?'

'Mr. Cameron has not written to say if he will subscribe, so
I must continue to advance what is necessary.'

'It is only doing what you have done all your life,' observed
Mrs. Patty, 'advancing for others, and waiting till they think it
proper to repay, but there will be the five pounds which Myra
told us Mr. Verney would give. I wonder why he wished his
name to be kept so secret.'

'There may be many good reasons for a man's not wishing
his charities to be known,' replied the Doctor. 'And as to
myself, Patty, I shall soon be where it will be no grief to me
to remember that I spent twenty pounds to provide a nurse for
the afflicted lady.'

'If you are doubtful about Mr. Cameron's directions,' continued Mrs. Patty, 'I can help you now; for I have a letter
from little Myra; shall I read it to you?'

'She is a good little girl, Patty, and I shall thank you very
much; but I think I will move to the sofa first. I don't wish
to be restless and troublesome, but I am. And lest I should
forget it, will you take charge of those clothing-club tickets,
and give them to Mr. Baines. I have signed them, but my hand
shakes greatly.'

So did Mrs. Patty's as she gathered up the cards on which
were traced the scarcely legible characters which had once
been written so firmly. She moved the Doctor to the sofa,
refusing to ring for Faith to help her, and then, when she had

made him, as he said, so comfortable that he desired to thank God for it, she sat down by him and read out Myra's letter, to which he listened with the fullest attention, interrupting Mrs. Patty's slow and emphatic reading, whenever he missed a word, with the request that she would be so good as to repeat that once more.

When she had ended, he said, 'Little Myra has a feeling heart, Patty, and she is much touched with that poor young lady's sorrow. May God keep her from much of her own, for I fear she would sink under it.'

'She is likely to have a good deal, I am afraid, Doctor,' replied Mrs. Patty, as she carefully refolded the letter, and placed it in the envelope. 'She gives her heart so soon to people who are kind to her, and I don't know what to say to her about it, because her parents don't see things as I do. I do wish she did not like Mr. Verney quite so much.'

'She is very grateful to him for his kindness, and she will be very fond of him if he marries her sister,' replied the Doctor. 'It all seems to me, Patty, quite natural, though I could wish that Mr. Verney was more settled in his religious views.'

'Ah, Doctor! you are a man, and never see anything but what lies straight before you, which, no doubt, is good and best, and the reason why men go through the world more quietly than women can. But what I should like to know, first of all, is whether Mr. Verney really does care for Rosamond Cameron, and if he does why he can't speak out at once.'

'Myra is discriminating, and appears to have no doubt of his feelings,' replied the Doctor.

'But she does not seem to me wise enough to take heed to her own,' replied Mrs. Patty.

'I do not understand you, Patty. Even if Rosamond Cameron and Mr. Verney were not attached to each other, as it appears they are, Myra would never care for a man so much older than herself.'

'Perhaps not care for him in the way of falling in love with him, though I would never answer for that, as time goes on, if they were thrown much together. But what would be worse than falling in love with him would be that she might take it into her head to marry him from pity and romance. There is a great deal of romance in this letter, Doctor, and I don't like it. Many a woman has sacrificed her happiness from no stronger feeling.'

'Patty, my dear, you trouble yourself about things which will never come to pass. Little Myra is pleased and happy, and I see no reason why she should not be.'

'But, Doctor, dear, answer me one question. Should you be satisfied if she were to marry Mr. Verney?'

'By no means. He has no fixed principles, and is much too old. I should consider it most undesirable.'

'Then,' exclaimed Mrs. Patty, 'I don't quite see how you or any one can wish her to be pleased, and happy, and full of romance about a man whom you could never bear to see her husband.'

'Because I am sure he never will be,' was the reply.

'Ah, Doctor! that is looking straight before you; but it strikes me there is something at the side. Suppose she never should marry him, which God grant she may not, and which I don't pretend to say is likely, seeing he appears to have set his heart on Rosamond; yet if she should go on romancing about him, and admiring him, surely she will become like him.'

'Not so, Patty. Little Myra has an honest heart, and a clear head, and God is her guide and protector. She will open her eyes as time goes on; she is a child now.'

'And that will be a grievous day,' said Mrs. Patty mournfully.'

'It is what we must all come to, Patty, as we travel through this disappointing world.'

'It is not what I ever came to,' exclaimed Mrs. Patty. 'I had my romance of respect when I was a child, Doctor, dear, and it was about you, and I have never seen cause to alter it, and it has kept me up and given me strength when things were so trying about me that if it had not been for that, I should have sunk quite. You must not measure women by men, Doctor. They were not made to stand alone, and when they lean and the reed breaks, ten to one but they fall to the ground; and that is my fear for Myra.'

'Nay, Patty. We must not doubt God's Providence over her.'

'Yet, Doctor, the old proverb says that God helps those who help themselves. Whereas it strikes me that in these days fathers and mothers fancy that God will do everything in the way of taking care of their children, and they are to do nothing. Neither Mr. nor Mrs. Cameron approve of Mr. Verney. Mrs. Cameron herself as good as told me she would not on any account have Rosamond marry him, and yet she allows them to be together just as much as if they were engaged. The world is a puzzle to me, Doctor, and it grows more so every day.'

'Because you do not understand inconsistency, Patty,' said the Doctor, and a smile passed over his kind face.

'It may be so,' said Mrs. Patty; 'yet God knows I can quite understand what the Prayer-Book makes one say. I am sure none do more things they ought not to do than I do, and no one oftener leaves undone things which ought to be done. I can't venture to find fault with any on that score.'

'Those are sins of infirmity, Patty.'

'Anyhow they are sins, and there are enough of them. They are not my puzzle, however, for you see they belong to myself. But what I don't comprehend is how persons can declare that they intend and desire to go one way, and then deliberately turn round and go the other. If Mr. Cameron wishes his daughter to marry Mr. Verney, well and good; but if not, let him keep his door shut against him.'

'It is the way of this fallen world in many other cases besides marriage, I am afraid,' said the Doctor. 'Men say they mean to walk towards heaven, but they do not the less turn their faces away from it.'

'Yes,' replied Mrs. Patty very earnestly, 'and so, surely, as the Bible says, they are fools, though no one ventures to call them so. But it is very perplexing, Doctor, when clever men are fools, whether in things of this world or the next. Little Myra would be much shocked if I said that I thought Mr. Verney was a fool, yet I can't help thinking so, and some day she will find it out.'

'You speak severely, Patty.'

'Do I ? Yet I would cut off my right hand to help him if he needed it. But truth is truth, and if this world is not to be ours always, as we know it can't be, then to live as if it were is just mad folly, and nothing less. And Mr. Verney may be the cleverest man that breathes as regards knowing about India, and government, and pictures, and music, and all those things which take poor little Myra's fancy, but if he neglects his religion, why, little Johnnie Ford in the Idiot Asylum is more rational ; for when he wants a thing he does go the shortest way to work to get it. Ah, Doctor ! you think so, don't you ? '

'Perhaps I do,' was the Doctor's answer. 'But, Patty, there is all the more reason we should pray for him.'

'Yes, and for Rosamond and little Myra, too,' added Mrs. Patty. 'And now, perhaps, I had better put up the letter for Annette and Juliet, or I may forget it.'

———

CHAPTER XXX.

THAT same day Colonel and Mrs. Verney, for the first time for many weeks, sat down to a *tête-à-tête* dinner in Eaton Place. Mrs. Verney was tired with her gaieties, and had entrusted her two girls to a friend who was to take them to a botanical *fête ;* and Colonel Verney had business which would occupy him all the evening, and which made a six o'clock dinner a necessity.

Mrs. Verney, as usual, threw a little romance over the matter-of-fact matrimonial reality. 'So pleasant it is, my dear Colonel,' she said, as the dessert was placed on the table, and she began to select the choicest raspberries from the dish before her. 'So quiet and soothing. Let me give you just these few raspberries, they really are splendid ; they were sent up from Stormont this morning. I almost wish we were going back there to-morrow.'

'Thank you, my dear; no more;' and the Colonel took the plate offered him. 'Stormont raspberries are always fine. Why don't you go back, if you wish it?'

'Ah! if I could only consult my wishes; but poor Netta and Elise, what would they say?'

'They are very good girls, and would do what you told them,' said the Colonel; 'and this having a house in town is an awful expense.'

'So it is, my dear Colonel; but one must be patient. It won't be needed always. The dear girls will marry, and then we can do as we choose.'

'I don't want them to marry,' said the Colonel bluntly; 'I like to have them about me. Now they are out of the schoolroom, and able to do as they like, why am I not to have a little pleasure from them?'

'Certainly; most natural and right; but we must not be selfish. Parents have great sacrifices to make, and you are the last man to stand in the way of your children's good. And that reminds me—have you heard from Charles to-day?'

'I don't see why it should remind you of him, my dear. What has Charles Verney to do with your children's good?'

'Nothing,' said Mrs. Verney, with a gentle smile, and a slight sigh, which were intended to have a great deal of meaning. 'Nothing, at least, apparently; but a mother will be anxious, and at one time, I confess, I was afraid that dear Elise's imaginative mind might have formed too vivid a picture of her cousin's talents and superiority. But that is over now. His attachment to Rosamond Cameron is too evident to admit of any mistake.'

'His attachment to whom?' exclaimed the Colonel, half starting from his chair.

'Rosamond Cameron, my love,' replied Mrs. Verney—she always said 'love,' when she was afraid of having an outburst of the reverse.

The Colonel sat down again. 'I don't understand this, Frances. What do you mean? Is Charles engaged to Rosa-

mond Cameron ?   Are they going to be married off at once ?
Why have not I been told of it before ?   It is very remarkable,
very strange, very unfitting '—the Colonel was growing redder
and redder, and his vocabulary of indignation was likely to
be lengthy.   Mrs. Verney bent forward, and pushed a biscuit
towards him, and put a few more raspberries upon his plate,
but she said nothing ; and the Colonel drew up in the middle
of his sentence, like a horse who, meeting with no opposition,
suddenly arrives at the conclusion that there is no need to run
away, and ended with, ' Well, my dear.'

' I have never heard that they are engaged,' was Mrs.
Verney's observation in reply ; ' but the world talks about it ;
and as he is gone abroad after them I suppose we must make
up our minds that there is something in it.'

' But there must not be anything.' exclaimed the Colonel ;
' Charles is not the man ; he is too old, and his health is
bad ; and those stories we heard against him have never been
cleared up, my dear.   Take my word for it, Cameron won't
allow it, and you had better write and tell Charles so at once.
I don't wish to have my nephew rejected, and he will be, as
sure as fate.'

' Are you not a little rapid, my dear Colonel?   It is for
Mr. Cameron to find out these objections—supposing they
exist—not for us to suggest them.'

' I don't desire that my nephew should run his head against
a post,' continued the Colonel.   ' When a man makes an offer
to a girl, all his antecedents and circumstances are inquired
into ; and I know Cameron well enough to be sure that he will
be sharp and shrewd in the matter, as all men of his stamp are.
We shall come to a split—we must.   I can't have my nephew
insulted and rejected, and people talking as they will talk.
Cameron and I have kept apart all our lives, and we must continue to do so ; we shall be very rough neighbours if we don't.'

' Well, it may never come to anything,' said Mrs. Verney
in a tone of indifference, as she leaned her white hand upon
the table and gazed at her diamond ring ; ' but where affections are engaged worldly obstacles soon melt away ; and
Rosamond Cameron is a very sweet girl.'

' She may have come straight from paradise for aught I care,' exclaimed the Colonel ; 'but I don't want her to be Charles Verney's wife.'

' Only if she should be so you will receive her kindly.'

' I won't receive her at all. I hate Cameron's politics. I hate being mixed up with them. Don't let me have the girl asked again to the house on any account. I won't have it, my dear ; remember now what I say—I won't have it.'

' Certainly, my love ; everything shall be as you wish. I only felt glad myself that Charles seemed to be attracted by Rosamond, because I had heard a rumour of a possible engagement in India, which would not be by any means as satisfactory.'

' He is always flirting,' exclaimed the Colonel. ' For a sensible man, there is no one has made more of a fool of himself in that way than Charles. The wonder is he has not been taken in by an Indian Begum before this ; ' and as the Colonel laughed at his own suggestion, the angry ruddiness of his cheeks subsided into a quieter and browner hue.

' I wish it may be nothing more serious than a flirtation,' said Mrs. Verney. ' I have only heard rumours, indeed, but they come from various quarters. Mrs. de Lancy told me when I took Juliet and Annette to school the other day that it was some niece of poor old Miss Medley's. I don't believe, though, it can be ; Charles never would mix himself up with any of her family.'

' Old Miss Medley ! My nephew marry a niece of old Miss Medley's ! The world is gone mad !' exclaimed the Colonel. ' Why, she is the daughter of a quack doctor !'

' Once a regular physician, I believe,' replied Mrs. Verney.

' Regular physician ! regular humbug! Hasn't she killed herself with swallowing his atrocious globules ? Charles marry her niece ! He should never put his foot in my house again if he did ; and you may tell him so.'

' And that Rosamond Cameron would be preferable,' said Mrs. Verney gently.

' I don't know—I won't say. Why should he marry at all ? What is the use of marrying ? It only brings trouble into a

P

family. If he must have a wife, let him go to Kamschatka
and settle there, and never let us hear any more of him. I
hate marrying ; it is the ruin of all peace—I hate it ! '

' Only, unfortunately, it must be. But, my love, we won't
think about it till it comes. Only let us be thankful that, at
any rate, we are more likely to have an English lady for our
niece than the descendant of a quack doctor.'

' Umph ! ' was all the Colonel's reply. But he did not
deny that he had cause for gratitude ; and Mrs. Verney was
satisfied.

She had reason to be so. By planting in her husband's
mind the thought of a possible connection with the family of
his political opponent, she had achieved an object which had
been weighing upon her mind for many weeks. Why such
a connection should have been a matter of importance, only
those who knew Mrs. Verney thoroughly could understand.
A watchful mother and a manœuvrer, the fear she had expressed lest Elise should become attached to her cousin
Charles was real. For Mrs. Verney could in her child's
case see clearly the objections which were deemed of no
consequence where the child of another was concerned. Age,
character, and fortune were all against Mr. Verney. It was
very well to idealise him to her friends, and set him upon a
pedestal, for a centre to a dinner-party ; but to accept him
for a son-in-law was quite a different matter ; and when the
possibility suggested itself to Mrs. Verney's mind, she at once
determined to take precautionary measures in time. Not,
indeed, that she said to herself that her nephew Charles was
a man of indifferent character, indifferent fortune, and indifferent health, and therefore it would be better to provide him
with a wife from her neighbour's family than from her own.
Mrs. Verney was as plausible to herself as she was to her
friends ; and she reasoned so sensibly, so philosophically—
at times even so religiously—that the inward eye and the
voice of conscience must indeed have been singularly clear
to have discovered wherein lay the self-deception in motive.
She said—and it was perfectly true—that the marriage of
cousins was very objectionable, and that, to prevent such a

catastrophe, it would be well to give her nephew some other object of interest. This was the ground-work of her course of action, and no fault could be found with it. With regard to Mr. Verney's character—'What the eye did not see the heart was not likely to grieve.' Report said that he had been wild and extravagant; but no doubt experience had done its work; and at his age, and with his good sense, he was likely to settle down into a very steady estimable man. Moreover—and this was a strong argument—Rosamond was not likely to know or care much about his antecedents. She had no particular principles; she was simply a very pretty, good-tempered, fashionable girl, who would be glad to be married, and might as well marry Charles Verney as any one else. Health, indeed, was one objection; for if Mr. Verney could not return to India, his income would be most materially diminished, and Mrs. Verney had been so far conscientious upon this point that, although she had passively encouraged the intimacy, she had never taken any very active steps to promote it, until the probability that Rosamond would inherit her aunt's fortune seemed likely to remove out of the way this—in her eyes—only important obstacle. Rosamond, with two thousand a year of her own, would really be a most desirable wife for a man thrown out of an Indian appointment; and then, too, all old associations would be broken off, and Mr. Verney's life might, as it were, be begun anew. With a natural delight in match-making, the temptation to interfere more definitely became too strong to be resisted; and before he went abroad Mr. Verney had received suggestions and hints and encouragements which— if only his affections had been engaged to the extent which his aunt chose to imagine—must long since have had the effect of bringing affairs to a climax. But—most unaccountable it appeared to Mrs. Verney—from some unknown cause the crisis never occurred. Mr. Verney flirted with Rosamond publicly, and expressed his admiration of her privately; he even went so far as to make her presents, and to receive drawings and guard-chains and purses in return; but he could never be brought to the point of proposal. Mrs.

Verney became uneasy. Like other manœuvrers, she cared less for the object than for the fact of success. Rosamond and Mr. Verney might or might not be likely to make each other happy; but if Mrs. Verney had determined they should marry, they must; and therefore she set herself sedulously to find out what hidden obstacles lay in the path. In the course of this inquiry—which was carried on with great skill and profound secrecy—the possibility of what she chose to call an Indian entanglement was suggested, and although no certain evidence was produced—for the information only came from friends' friends who had known Mr. Verney in India—it gave her a stimulus to exertion and a clue to her nephew's conduct that she was far too well practised in the work which she had undertaken not to use with skill for the attainment of her own purposes. Within the last fortnight a letter had been written to Mr. Verney, suggesting, in the most insinuating manner, the danger of his prolonging his foreign intercourse with the Camerons. The world, Mrs. Verney said, was beginning to talk. Rosamond Cameron was a most attractive girl, and was already looked upon as an heiress. She had been much admired in London; and Mr. Verney knew that on her return she would be likely to have many and most desirable offers if she were considered disengaged. But even before she left England, persons were held back by the reports of an attachment—even an engagement—between her and Mr. Verney. This was very unfair. Mrs. Verney put it to her nephew, as a man of honour, whether it was right that such a state of things should continue. If he had no serious intentions he had no right to feign them. He ought at once to leave the family. True, it might be too late. Mrs. Verney would on no account betray confidence; yet she could not but fear, from what she had seen and heard, that Rosamond's feelings had already been excited to a degree which might be very dangerous to her happiness. She was upon the surface a sweet, bright—some might even say a thoughtless—young girl; but such apparent buoyancy of spirits often concealed great capacities of suffering. Mrs. Verney entreated her nephew no longer to trifle in this matter. He might possibly have been influenced in his delay by the very advantages which a marriage with Rosamond Cameron offered. A wife, beautiful, accomplished, perfect in temper, fascinating in society, a member of a good family, and having the almost certainty of two thousand a year of her own, was certainly not to be met with every day ; and a man of very refined feeling might well hesitate before he ventured to ask for such a treasure. But morbid scruples would, in the end, be injurious to all parties. And it was due to Rosamond, and due also to her parents, and to Mr. Verney's own character—that attentions without meaning should no longer be suffered to stand in the way of her prospects for life. Mrs. Verney concluded with ardent wishes for her nephew's happiness, and an assurance that, whatever might be his decision, she should always be most affectionately interested in his welfare.

The letter was written and despatched ; but it lay rather heavy on Mrs. Verney's mind—perhaps it a little burdened her conscience. One thing was certain—she shrank from mentioning the subject to which it referred to her husband. Colonel Verney had great and very serious faults, but they were of a less insidious character than his wife's. He was more honest-hearted, more true and Christian in his principles. Mr. Verney not being a man whom he could approve of for his own daughter, he would have scorned the thought of encouraging his attentions to Rosamond ; and this his wife perfectly well knew. Again and again in life her schemes had been interfered with by her husband's blunt and sometimes very rough and awkward honesty. But, in this instance, his sense of the undesirableness of such a marriage for Rosamond would be strengthened by his own prejudices. He might bear with Mr. Cameron socially, but an actual connection would be entirely opposed to his views and interests. Yet he must be prepared for the contingency ; and this could only be done by accustoming him to the idea gradually. A sudden announcement of Mr. Verney's engagement (supposing it to exist) would almost inevitably produce an outbreak of incautious anger and surprise, the consequences of which it would be impossible to foresee. Mrs. Verney had pondered this matter well for several days ; and the result was the conversation which had just passed, and which had been much more favourable to her wishes than she could have ventured to anticipate. The Colonel was never a very reasonable or reasoning being. His one great weakness—violent temper—put him continually at a disadvantage with persons who could be cool and bide their time ; and Mrs. Verney knew full well that if she could excite his indignation at the prospect of being connected with the 'quack doctor,' he would accept whatever might be suggested in its stead, without pausing to weigh objections which, in calmer moments, might seriously interfere with her projects. She had calculated well and wisely. The Colonel sat in his arm-chair and drank his port wine and stormed mentally at 'Old Miss Medley ; ' and when he thought of Rosamond felt only—as his wife intended he should feel—that it would be a great gain for them all to have nothing worse than a Cameron instead.

CHAPTER XXXI.

WHEN Myra drove back to Ischl, in compliance with the order she had received, it was in a spirit of no very perfect submission or good temper. Principles sometimes change suddenly, but practice follows but slowly after them. Everything had gone wrong on that particular day. She disliked the upsetting of her plans; she was very sorry to leave St. Wolfgang; she was disappointed at not seeing more of Miss Stuart; and, more than all, she dreaded on every account travelling without Mr. Verney's help and companionship. As a climax, instead of having a pleasant drive in an open carriage with Colonel and Mrs. Hensman, she was told at the last minute that they were excessively sorry, but that most unexpectedly they were compelled to go in another direction to see a friend who was taken suddenly ill, and that the only mode of conveyance they could find for her would be a little country vehicle, half chaise, half cart, which would be driven by their servant. So Myra jolted over the rough road, and had scarcely heart to admire the scenery, even when after a drive of seven miles they came to the summit of a hill, at the foot of which lay the small town of Ischl, encircled by mountains and forests near and distant, a torrent-river rushing by it, and trees and cliffs breaking the outline of the foreground.

Sorrow may be soothed by the beauty of nature, for sorrow, like nature, comes from God, and is sacred; but temper is human, and refuses to submit to its influence. Myra suffered at that moment from a fit of discontent, which might have suited the days gone by; and, in order to indulge it, conjured up every possible form of disagreeableness which might be expected to await her at the Hotel Baur—her mother's complaining illness, her father's cold strictness, Rosamond's utter want of comprehension and sympathy, and Mr. Verney's moodiness. The first words she heard from Conyers, who met her at the entrance of the hotel, were by no means encouraging.

'Why, Miss Myra, how late you are! Master has been waiting dinner for you, and he is so angry. He thought you would have been here two hours ago.'

'It was very foolish to wait,' said Myra impatiently. 'I have dined.'

'How vexatious. And your mamma was to have had a drive somewhere this afternoon, but it has been put off because of dinner and your not being here; and now she has had one of her faints, and Miss Cameron and Mr. Verney are just gone out somewhere—I am sure I don't know where. Why didn't you come, Miss Myra, when you were sent for?'

'I came as soon as it was convenient, Conyers,' replied Myra haughtily. 'Will you be so good as to have my trunk taken to my room?'

Conyers moved sulkily away, and Myra went a few steps upstairs; then something seemed to strike her with self-reproach, and she came back.

'Is mamma ill from having been kept waiting, Conyers?'

'I believe it is worry more than anything else, Miss Myra. She thought something had happened as you did not come.'

Myra made no answer to Conyers, but went immediately to Mrs. Cameron's room. Her tone was humble and affectionate, as she said how sorry she was, how thoughtless she had been, how much she hoped that her mother was not seriously vexed.

'I have been nervous, my dear, but never mind; it is only for your father; he has been kept waiting for dinner.'

'I thought they would dine at the *table-d'hôte*, and so it would not signify,' said Myra.

'No; they had a fancy for a private dinner to-day. I think it was Mr. Verney's wish, or Rosamond's; but go and get ready, my love. Don't think about me; I shall do quite well. I hope you have enjoyed yourself.'

Myra could scarcely say she had. It was so chilling to be received as if the breaking up of her pleasant little visit was of no consequence. She turned away pettishly, went to her

room, and took off her bonnet and cloak, brooding all the
while over she scarcely knew what ; and then, as she looked
at her watch, recollected that in packing and departure the
morning had gone by without allowing time for the serious
reading and prayer to which she was accustomed. There was
no time now ; at least, none which would be sufficient : but
Myra's sensitive conscience was touched. She felt herself
thoroughly put out and wrong. She was thinking of nothing
and no one but herself ; she was prepared to take offence
before it was offered. A little more yielding to weakness and
perverseness, and the old uncontrollable ill temper would be
upon her. Conyers knocked at the door.

'Dinner is on the table, Miss Myra, and master won't wait
another instant.'

Prayers may take but one moment. Myra's was scarcely
longer, but after it came the struggling, earnest, almost physical effort to resist the self which was striving for the mastery ;
and Myra's smile of apology as she met her father on the
staircase was so sweet that Mr. Cameron's usual indifferent
sternness of manner melted before it, and instead of finding
fault, he stopped to kiss her, and said that ' he did not like her
being away. They were none of them comfortable without
her.' It was the first time that Myra had ever realised to
herself the place she was gaining in the esteem and the affections of her home.

The conversation at dinner turned upon the plans for the
next few days. Mr. Verney took part in it ; but his thoughts
were evidently elsewhere. This jarred upon Mr. Cameron, and
it was only by the exercise of his punctilious politeness that he
prevented himself from showing his annoyance. Myra found
herself obliged to take a prominent part in proposing and
settling what was to be done, if it were only to please her
father. She had studied Ischl and its vicinity in the guide-
book as a matter of information, and in spite of Rosamond's
ridicule and Mr. Verney's assurance that whenever he wanted
to go to sleep he always took a dose of ' Murray.' Her father
kept her with him after dinner was over, with a view to some
final discussions with the landlord, and the help of her German

knowledge; Mrs. Cameron had dined in her own room; and Rosamond and Mr. Verney left the saloon together.

At the head of the staircase Rosamond stopped, and said she must go to her mother. Yet she lingered; and as Mr. Verney opened the door into the private sitting-room she entered, whilst he followed. There was a balcony before the window overhanging the street. Rosamond went out, and still Mr. Verney accompanied her. Rosamond remarked lightly, 'One should sleep through last days; they are so weary.'

'Sleep and dream?' said Mr. Verney. 'That might be worse than waking.'

'No,' replied Rosamond, 'because anything that is disagreeable in a dream becomes a pleasure when we wake up from it.'

'And the memories of these last days may become a pleasure by and by then,' said Mr. Verney.

'Oh yes, they may; very likely they will. I have no doubt they will to you.'

'Why no doubt to me?'

'Because you like to view things poetically, and you will easily make a romance of them.'

'And what shall you make?' he inquired eagerly.

'I? oh nothing. I shall'—Rosamond paused—'I shall forget them.'

'That is not flattering.'

'But it may be wise;' and Rosamond turned away her head and gazed down into the street.

Mr. Verney drew nearer. 'When things are indifferent to one, there can neither be wisdom nor the reverse in forgetting them.'

Rosamond was silent.

'And these last days will be matters of indifference to you?' he continued.

'Did I say so?' and Rosamond looked up in his face and smiled.

That must have been a very prosaic and cold temperament which could resist such a smile. And Mr. Verney was lonely at heart—weary of the world—hopeless of the realisation of what had once been his day-dream of happiness with Charlotte Stuart; above all he had that morning received his aunt's suggestive letter, and the insidious words were indelibly impressed upon his memory. 'A wife, beautiful, accomplished, perfect in temper, fascinating in society, a member of a good family, and having the almost certainty of two thousand a year of her own, is not to be met with every day.'

The generality of men are not deliberately treacherous. It is opportunity which is their snare: and when Mr. Verney answered Rosamond's smile, by an eager outpouring of flattery and excited feeling, he no more thought whither he was tending than the man who on a sudden impulse has cast himself into the rapid current of a river meditates upon the ocean in which his course is to close.

It was Rosamond who thought—Rosamond who drew him on—Rosamond who smiled, and sighed, and pretended that she would not and must not hear—Rosamond who at length blushed, and in a subdued voice said, 'I did not think you so cared for me.'

What man could escape from such a snare? Mr. Verney's answer was a protestation of unwavering affection; and in ten minutes from the time he entered the room he was engaged.

CHAPTER XXXII.

RAIN still! It had rained almost without intermission from the time that Myra had left St. Wolfgang. Why then, as she asked herself, must they leave these comfortable quarters at Ischl, and establish themselves at a little country inn at Aussee? Why, especially, should Mrs. Cameron be subjected to such a risk? Simply because Rosamond and Mr. Verney insisted upon it. It was certain to clear, so said the latter, and he must leave Ischl—he must see Hallstadt and Gosau— he must part from his friends unless they could accompany him. And the 'must' was uttered so earnestly that every one was compelled to believe it.

They left Ischl in the interval between two storms, when the clouds were lifted from the hills sufficiently to satisfy Mr. Cameron that he was not acting quite madly. And at Aussee the rain poured down again, and all that could be attempted was a stroll in the evening along the banks of the Traun, undertaken by Mr. Verney, Rosamond, and Myra. They had often been thus together before, and to Myra it seemed quite natural that her sister and Mr. Verney should walk apart, and that she should be allowed to stray at will, gathering wet flowers, and joining them whenever she felt inclined.

She saw they were earnest in conversation, and Mr. Verney's manner occasionally seemed to her excited almost to irritability, but Myra was by nature unsuspicious. She took her evening walk, and spent the hour after tea in conversation and draw- ing, full of plans for the next day which was to bring a bright sun and an expedition to the lake of Hallstadt, without once thinking that any secret was kept back from her.

When she wished Mr. Verney good night, she said, with her usual openness of manner, 'One more day, and then it will be good-bye; and we shall be so sorry; but I know you will come back.'

He started, and said quickly, 'How do you know it?'

And Myra answered, 'Because we all care for you and you care for us.' And then there was an expression in his face which perplexed her. It was as if she had said something to displease him, and she went to bed wondering whether she had been wrong, because as the words were uttered, she had thought of Rosamond, and perhaps any such allusion was unfitting.

Sunshine greeted them the next morning; but it was a fitful sunshine, gleaming at intervals, and Mrs. Cameron was afraid to trust it. She proposed to go back to Ischl with Conyers, and leave the rest of the party to explore Hallstadt, and either sleep at Gosau, or return to Ischl in the evening, as they might think fit. The proposal was made in the tone of a martyr, as Mrs. Cameron's self-sacrifices generally were; and in consequence no one except Myra appreciated it. Whilst the horses were being ordered for herself and Rosamond, she stole quietly to her mother's side and whispered a wish that they could all remain together, and undertake some less fatiguing expedition; but she was cut short by Rosamond, who happening to overhear her, declared that the arrangements were quite made, and that it was much too late to think of any change. If they did not set off at once they should miss everything : a fact which Mrs. Cameron accepted without questioning, though she said mournfully : 'It does not signify much where I go, my dear, my eyes are so bad I can't see, and I daresay I shall have a headache before the day is over.'

'Mamma, I must go back with you,' was Myra's answer. 'You can't be left to Conyers.'

'It is but for the day,' said Rosamond. 'We shall only make papa angry if we alter the plan.'

Again Myra repeated, 'Dear mamma, they will do quite well without me.'

And Rosamond very gently pushed her towards the door, saying, 'You will be late as you always are.' Myra's heart was set on Hallstadt, and all the more resolutely she lingered. But there was no help from her mother, who could only say in a dreary tone; ' My love, go; they all wish it, and your father will be displeased, and I am accustomed to be left.'

The last words would, as Myra well knew, be a text for lamentation and complaint for many days to come, but she could do no more, and hurried away, followed by Rosamond, who with a good-humoured patronage insisted that she would keep them all waiting, and leave half her things behind her if she was not looked after; and upon this pretext contrived to remain with her till the horses were at the door, so as to leave no moment for thought and fresh suggestions which might interfere with her own wishes.

Myra, with her over-scrupulous conscience, was a little inclined to worry herself at first, lest she had not made all the effort for her mother which she ought, but her natural good sense suggested that self-accusations which interfere with present duty are always better put aside. So she devoted herself to her father, feeling a little penitential satisfaction in the fact that she would much have preferred riding by Rosamond's side and listening to Mr. Verney, who was full of excitement at the beauty of the pass between Aussee and Hallstadt, which they began to ascend almost immediately upon leaving the former village. Again and again he called out to Myra to stop and admire the points from which they could look far down the side of the mountain, and watch the effect of the sunlight gleaming through the trunks and branches of the dark pine forest; but Rosamond never allowed him to leave her, and even when he walked on a little way with Mr. Cameron, had always an excuse ready to bring him back—the saddle had slipped, or would slip, or the road was narrow, or the mule went too near the edge; something there always was to retain him near her; with or against his will it would have been impossible from his countenance to decide. He was imperturbable and impenetrable as ever.

They descended to Obertraun, a small village about half a mile from the lake of Hallstadt, and here clouds began to settle upon the tops of the mountains, sinking gradually lower and lower, with that occasional dispersion and swift gathering together again which is so trying and dispiriting to travellers in a mountainous district.

The lake of Hallstadt looked extremely gloomy. The snow was lingering on the summits of the precipitous pine clad mountains, which close it in at its southern extremity, and the nearer cliffs descended so abruptly to the shore as, in one part, to leave only sufficient space for a footpath. In winter the inhabitants of the village of Hallstadt never see the sun above the highest mountain tops, and even now in the middle of summer, the grey mists and the wall of jagged rocks cast a twilight shadow over the deep dark waters, disturbed by the ominous ripple of an approaching storm.

A boat was moored under a shed against the shore ; a short row would carry them across the lake to Hallstadt. There was no comfortable shelter where they were, and Mr. Verney urged that they should go. Mr. Cameron demurred, and a short argument arose, in the midst of which the heavy rain-drops began to fall, and all hurried towards the shed. Rosamond and Myra seated themselves in the boat, and had scarcely covered themselves with cloaks when a torrent of rain and hail pelted and dashed into the lake, and a gust of wind rushing through a gap in the hills, nearly broke the umbrellas with which they were trying to screen themselves from the streams which assailed them on all sides. The roll of thunder and the flash of lightning followed, and Rosamond looked round in terror. Mr. Cameron was arguing with the guides, who, he thought, were endeavouring to cheat him, and an earthquake would not have disturbed his attention. Myra was leaning forward over the boat, lost in admiration at the effects of the storm on the mountains. Another dazzling gleam lit up the lake, and a faint scream burst from Rosamond, and as she looked imploringly to Mr. Verney for protection, he put his arm round her, and some very endearing expression escaped him. At that instant Myra turned, her eyes met Mr. Verney's, and for once the colour rushed to his cheeks. The expression of surprise in Myra's face was unmistakable. She turned round, drew her cloak round her, and sat facing him, but per-fectly silent. He made a trifling remark, and Myra just answered him, but that was all. Rosamond was conscious of nothing but the thunderstorm. At each successive flash of lightning, she renewed her little screams, and at last entreated to leave the boat, and nothing but Mr. Cameron's stern command kept her in her place. Yet there was no real cause for terror. The lightning was merely sheet lightning at a distance, and the only danger was that of being wet. Mr. Verney insisted that Myra should come and sit between him and her father, that so she might be more protected; and Myra did as she was ordered, keeping, however, close to Mr. Cameron, and continuing so silent that the latter gave her credit for sharing Rosamond's alarm.

It was all over in a quarter of an hour. The clouds were lifted from the hills, the blue sky appeared overhead, and a line of brilliant light streamed over the lake. Rosamond's spirits rose as quickly as they had fallen, and as the boat pushed off from the shore, and cliff after cliff broke from the mist and stood forth in savage grandeur, she became enthusiastic in her admiration, and declared that it was quite worth while to have endured the storm and the terror for the contrast of the beauty which succeeded it—a remark to which Mr. Cameron gave the short answer : ' It may have been worth while for you, my dear, but it was certainly not worth while for us.' So silence fell upon the party, and even when they passed below Rudolph's tower—perched on a projecting rock—and the village of Hallstadt, nestling below it, came in sight, no one expressed satisfaction except Mr. Cameron, who remarked that it was a good thing that they had not been detained longer, as they should have time now to order dinner and take a walk whilst it was getting ready.

The village was straggling and dirty, as the generality of such secluded villages on the continent are ; the peasants who inhabited it had no standard with which to measure themselves, but the inn was of a superior stamp, thanks to the travellers who in the summer time frequented it.

Two gentlemen had already taken possession of the long low saloon, into which Mr. Cameron's party were ushered, and early though it was, were just sitting down to dinner. English exclusiveness suggested to Mr. Cameron the necessity of having another room to themselves, but the idea was negatived by Mr. Verney, who seemed relieved at the prospect of having any one to converse with besides his stiff and silent companions. Mr. Cameron left the room to try and find mules or donkeys, which would carry Rosamond and Myra to the Strub water-fall, and Mr. Verney hearing one of the strangers acciden-tally mention Gosau, went up to him, and began to make inquiries about the distance, the roads, and the accommoda-tion.

In a few minutes he returned to Rosamond and Myra, who were standing by the window, and said : 'I am afraid from what I hear we shall be obliged to alter our plans. The inn at Gosau will never do for you and your father. These gentle-men are just come from it, and say the accommodation is wretched.' Myra made no reply ; Rosamond declared that she did not in the least care for comfort, she could sleep any-where. 'But your father cannot,' continued Mr. Verney, 'and the clouds are gathering again ; we shall have more rain. I can't but think you will do better to see what you can here, and then drive back to Ischl.'

'And you?' exclaimed Rosamond.

'I must go to Gosau as I had settled ; and from thence I shall make my way to Golling. I have not fixed upon my route afterwards.'

Rosamond's face clouded with disappointment, as she an-swered rather pettishly, 'I see no must in the case, except your own will.'

Mr. Verney glanced warningly at the strangers, for Rosa-mond had spoken quite loudly enough to be heard, and Myra noticing this moved away. A rapid eager conversation ensued, in the midst of which Mr. Cameron came back with the in-formation that the mules were ready and dinner was ordered. They might go to the waterfall, and by the time they returned it would be ready.

The road led up one side of a deep wooded ravine. Mr. Cameron and Myra went first, Rosamond and Mr. Verney followed ; but as the little guide who attended Myra's mule

Q

stopped to point out the line in the stupendous cliff opposite to them, which, as he said, marked one of the paths by which the Dachstein could be ascended, Mr. Verney left Rosamond and came forward to question the boy about the mountain, and when they went on again Myra found herself the foremost of the party, and Mr. Verney beside her.   Her mule moved more quickly than Rosamond's, and though she several times proposed to stop, in order that the others might come up with them, Mr. Verney would not attend to her wishes.   He hurried her on till they were a considerable distance in advance, only pausing when they stood in front of the beautiful waterfall, which, tearing through a narrow ravine, falls boiling and tossing from a height of 240 feet into a hollow of the rock, rising again in foam and dashing on its impetuous course to the lake ; whilst another stream at its side descends continuously in a sheet of light vapoury spray.   It was the first fine waterfall that Myra had seen, and, breathless with awe and delight, she hung over the abyss, lost in the overwhelming perception of whirling movement, which it seemed had known no beginning, and could know no end.

Mr. Verney's voice recalled her from her abstraction. 'Myra, you are angry with me.'

Myra turned round, and as the colour mounted to her cheek, answered gravely and shyly, 'I have nothing to be angry about, Mr. Verney.'

'Yes,' he said, 'you have, or you would have, if you were not mistaken in what you think ; but, Myra, Rosamond and I are engaged.'

The smile on Myra's face was like the glitter of a sunbeam, and as she held out her hand to Mr. Verney in the fulness of her relief and satisfaction, she said, 'Oh ! thank you, thank you.   I am more happy than I can say.   I hoped,—I thought '——

'That I could not, under any circumstances, forget propriety,' he said, with a faint laugh.   'I am grateful to you for the doubt.   But, Myra, I must say a few more words.   Can you not move on with me ? ' and as Rosamond and Mr. Cameron came in sight, he went nearer to the waterfall, and placed himself so that the rush of the torrent effectually prevented their conversation from being overheard.

Myra followed him eagerly, but when she looked at him, it was evident to her that he was by no means as completely at ease as herself. 'We are engaged,' he repeated hesitatingly. 'But it won't do to talk about it.'

'Not to people generally, of course,' said Myra.

'Not to any one.'

'Except papa and mamma?'

'Not to any one.'

Myra glanced at him as if doubting that she had heard aright.'

'You must put faith in me,' he continued hurriedly. 'It is impossible for me now to explain the reasons of our secrecy, but I would not have burdened you with the knowledge of our engagement if I had not seen that you suspected it.'

'I wish you had not told me,' exclaimed Myra, 'except—no, I don't wish it. Mr. Verney, you must know best.' The words were uttered in the quick determined tone by which persons so often endeavour to hide from themselves a doubt.

'Of course I must know best,' was the reply, 'and what is more, Myra, I know what you will do to help your sister.'

'I! but if you are engaged you cannot want help.'

'You will write to me, I am sure, and tell me how you are getting on, and I shall write to you; and if I enclose a note for Rosamond, you will not object to give it to her quietly, without making any remark.'

Instead of replying, Myra moved some steps towards the spot where her father and Rosamond were standing. Mr. Verney followed and detained her.

'It would be unkind, Myra,' he said, 'to let scruples interfere with a little act of good-nature to Rosamond. You know quite well that your father always receives the letters, and knows my handwriting. It would be out of the question for me to write to her without his noticing it, and there are good and substantial reasons why, at the present moment, our engagement should be kept to ourselves. I hate asking such a favour. I am putting myself entirely in a false position by it;

but the fact is, that Rosamond would not do it. She declared you would never consent, and she had made up her mind to spend weeks, perhaps months, without hearing from me; but as I told her, such scruples were too absurd, and I would not hear of them. Of course if you don't choose to gratify her there is nothing more to be said, we must accept what cannot be avoided.'

It was the first time that Myra had ever seen him seriously annoyed, and she actually trembled at the proud gloom which overspread his face. The anger of a man, and that man Mr. Verney, was very terrible to her; and the sense of her weakness, her inferiority in age, judgment, knowledge of the world, in everything which can give the right of forming an independent opinion, pressed upon her overwhelmingly. She said falteringly, ' May I not think about it ? '

' Certainly, certainly ; if such a trifle requires thought,' and he turned contemptuously away.

That was worse to Myra than anything. She could have borne to argue the point with him, and perhaps she might have held her ground against him, but she could not bear his scorn. The romance of admiration which she had indulged turned, as it were, against her, and as she remounted her mule and rode slowly back towards the inn, all the powers of sophistry which she possessed,—and from the peculiarly metaphysical turn of her mind they were by no means slight,—were enlisted against the instinct of conscience. Mr. Verney must know best, he must be right ; that was the premiss from which Myra drew all her conclusions. No doubt there were cases in which concealment upon such subjects was a necessity ; she could not be the judge whether this was one of them, and to attempt to decide the point was taking upon herself a responsibility which did not belong to her. If her father and mother so evidently trusted Mr. Verney, and approved of him, there could be nothing wrong in following his guidance ; and there was not the slightest doubt that he would in the end be able to explain everything satisfactorily. If, on the other hand, she refused, Rosamond would be wretched and moody, and her temper would react upon Mrs. Cameron. The advantage which had been

derived from the journey would be neutralised, her father would
be disappointed, and every one would be miserable. And it
was not as if Mr. Verney was a young man. At his age he must
be able to judge what it was allowable and right to do. To
dispute his wishes would be like disputing the wishes of her
father. It was all very plausible; the only reason for doubt
arising from the fact that the case required so much argument
before Myra could make up her mind. She continued to weigh
the *pros* and *cons*, always putting her will into the balance
opposite to the side for which she happened at the moment to
be contending, until she really did not know what she desired,
or thought, or proposed to do, but left herself simply at the
mercy of circumstances. Very weak it was, very unlike Myra,
but Mr. Verney's influence was the magnet which controlled
both conscience and intellect.

They reached the Hallstadt inn, and found dinner waiting
—a good dinner, and well-dressed—a circumstance soothing
to Mr. Cameron, and rendering him less sensible to the annoyance of the weather, which had again so clouded over, that
Mr. Verney's suggestion as to giving up the expedition to
Gosau was acknowledged by all to be the only thing
practicable. Even Rosamond agreed, but her eyes glistened
with tears, perceived both by Myra and Mr. Verney, but
absolutely unnoticed by Mr. Cameron, who had betaken himself to a careful study of 'Murray,' in order to persuade Mr.
Verney that it was an absurdity to think of going, as he had
proposed, from Gosau to Golling, and that it would be much
better to return with them to Ischl. Mr. Verney had that
elastic indiarubber will which, by giving the impression of
yielding, serves to occupy time and attention, and in the end
is found precisely where it was in the beginning. He talked
to Mr. Cameron till the moment arrived when it was necessary
to start, and even when they seated themselves in the boat
which was to carry them to a spot called Gosau Mühl, where
they were to separate, no one could have undertaken to say
what he finally intended to do. To Myra he was very chilling,
and this appearance of indifference was so painful to her that
she could not resist placing herself near him, in the hope of

having an opportunity for asking him to forgive and understand her.   So, at least, she said to herself, though what
there was to forgive when she had by no means resolved
to refuse his wish, was more, perhaps, than she could have
told.

After a short row, they landed near a solitary house—the
mill—at which they had been told that conveyances would be
found to take them either to Ischl or Gosau, as they desired ;
and a carriage there certainly was, but neither horse nor mule
to draw it.

Travellers to Gosau had already carried off all that were to
be had, though Mr. Verney was told that a *char-à-banc* would
be returning to Gosau in two hours' time, in which he might
possibly find a seat.   As for Ischl, it seemed as impracticable
to get there as it was to procure accommodation at the mill.
Rosamond and Myra would gladly have changed their plans
again, and taken the risk of the wretched Gosau inn, but Mr.
Cameron's dignity was lowered by what he called the deception which had been practised upon him.   An animal of some
kind he was resolved to have, and after a lengthened discussion, the boatman who had brought them to the Mühl was
sent back to Hallstadt for a mule, whose ' local habitation '
he professed himself acquainted with ; the said mule having
to traverse the distance between Hallstadt and the mill by a
footpath along the shore of the lake.   As this was likely to be
a very slow proceeding, nothing remained but to rest in a little
wooden room at the landing-place, or walk up and down the level
green space which formed the shore at this extremity of the lake,
and watch the clouds hovering over the cliffs on the opposite side.
Myra had no heart to sketch—no heart to talk.   The cloud upon
her spirits was as heavy as the cloud gathering over her.   She
drew near Mr. Verney, but he took no notice of her ; if he did
speak, it was in a tone of matter-of-fact indifference which was
much worse to her than anger.   He did not even talk much to
Rosamond—perhaps he was afraid of attracting Mr. Cameron's
attention.   Full an hour passed in this wearisome way, and then
Mr. Verney came back from a short walk to the mill, with the
intelligence that a man and a mule were in sight.

'Joyful news!' said Mr. Cameron in a solemn voice; an exclamation which received no echo. 'And, of course, you will come with us now,' he added, addressing Mr. Verney. Both Rosamond and Myra looked up anxiously.

'Thank you, no; I don't think I can. The Gosau *char-à-banc* will be here directly. Can I collect anything for you? Are you certain everything was taken out of the boat?' This question was put to Myra, and Mr. Verney drew near to listen to the answer. Poor Myra really could not speak. Most heartily ashamed of herself she was, but tears were streaming down her cheeks, as she turned aside her head and bent down over her carriage-bag. Mr. Cameron left the wooden room and stalked along the shore, evidently supposing that his own hasty movements would quicken those of the mule. Rosamond was standing apart; and Mr. Verney said to Myra coldly, 'I am sorry to see you so distressed.'

'If you would only forgive me;' and Myra strove hard to recover her self-possession.

'There is nothing to forgive. I respect scruples, however weak I may think them.'

'If I were quite sure this was a scruple,' said Myra.

'Are you not sure? I can have no doubt of it. But don't let us talk any more about it.' Mr. Verney was going to move away.

'Please stay, please. Yet you want to talk to Rosamond, I know; and she is dreadfully unhappy.'

'No doubt; but it cannot be otherwise. I must find, however, some mode of communication.'

'Yes, some; only not through me.'

'So as to avoid bringing you into any difficulty.'

'O Mr. Verney! it is not that I care for.'

'Indeed! I fancied it was.'

'Difficulty? I would brave any difficulty to help you.'

'Would you?' He paused and looked at her steadily.

'It is a question of right and wrong,' said Myra.

'Oh!'

'Won't you believe me? Do you not give me credit for thinking it so.'

'I am bound to do so.'

'But bound or not, Mr. Verney, if you knew half the pain it is to say no—when you have been so kind to me.'

'My dear child,' he exclaimed suddenly, resuming his familiar half-paternal tone ; 'it is mere nonsense to go on in this way. I don't want you to do anything as a return for what you call my kindness. If you have your little particular theories of right and wrong, keep them as long as you can—only don't let them quite stand in the way of common sense, because that is a pity.'

'And you don't think this is common sense,' said Myra.

'Of course I don't. If I did I should feel with you.'

Myra remained silent, and thought. Then she said, 'I should not care if I were quite sure that papa and mamma would agree with you.'

'Mr. Cameron has not quite lost his intellect yet, I hope,' was the reply.

'And you could explain it all to him,' said Myra.

'Explain what will want no explanation, when everything comes out, as it must shortly,' he replied. 'You don't think, Myra, I intend to keep up this farce a moment longer than I can help. But don't worry yourself. I never thought of having all this fuss when I spoke ; I merely felt that Rosamond would like to have one line to tell her where I was, and that I could send it better through you than through any one else, because I have confidence in you.'

'I could not betray you,' said Myra.

'Betray !' and he laughed sarcastically ; 'Rosamond and I are obliged to you ; but we have nothing that we fear to have betrayed. We really are arrived at years of discretion, though your superior wisdom may not have discovered it.'

'Perhaps it is foolish in me,' said Myra, beginning to feel ashamed of her scruples.

'There is no perhaps in the case,' he said carelessly ; 'but here comes the mule, and I must say one word to Rosamond.

'Stay, just one second. If you could be quite sure that papa and mamma would understand it.'

'Dear child, don't trouble yourself any more about it. It is not worth while.'

'Except that I could not bear to see Rosamond miserable.'

'She will survive it ; so shall I.'

'But you won't think the same of me as you did before.'

'Never mind what I think ; but don't keep me now.'

'It shall be as you like,' said Myra hesitatingly.

'The question is not what I like, but what I must,' replied Mr. Verney, avoiding any direct thanks for the implied consent ; 'but make your mind easy, my dear child, it will not be for long. Trust me always,' he added, taking her hand in his old kind winning way.

Myra was at the moment too relieved at finding herself restored to her place in his regard to feel much compunction at the terms on which the restoration had been effected. She hurried away to help her father in his German conversation, and Rosamond and Mr. Verney were left to say their farewells alone.

Myra's romance of love would have been greatly lessened if she had heard and seen them. Feeling there was indeed on both sides, but vexation mingled with any sorrow which Rosamond might have experienced ; and she was almost pettish in her regrets and expostulations at his determination to leave them, whilst Mr. Verney was alternately soothing and impatient ; uttering hurried expressions of affection, and then turning to some observation about the journey, the lateness of the hour, or his own movements ; as if anxious to escape from the obligation of saying what he knew he ought to feel. It was only every now and then, when Rosamond showed real regret, that he became in the least earnest ; and when he did so, he made the most of his impulse—repeating in a colder tone the endearing term which had escaped him in an instant of excitement, and trying to cover the rapid cooling process which began as soon as the word was spoken by some little tenderness of manner. And so they parted.

CHAPTER XXXIII.

THAT parting was the beginning of a succession of provoking little *contretemps*. Mrs. Cameron had caught cold at Aussee, as every one might naturally have expected she would, and Edmund could not join them as soon as he had promised. Both these circumstances compelled the party to remain at Ischl longer than they had intended, and this necessitated giving up Vienna. The weather cleared a little, and Mr. Cameron and Rosamond made two or three day-excursions ; but Myra was generally left behind, because her mother really could not spare her. Mrs. Cameron's eyesight was so weak, that she found it difficult to amuse herself, and Rosamond had a feeble voice and could not read aloud, and as a matter of course Myra was sacrificed. Not that she felt it a sacrifice, or at least to the extent which many persons might have imagined. The effort of sacrifice lies in the will, and Myra's will was given already. To destroy self was her profession, and every occasion for exercising this profession roused her energy ; so much so that she was sometimes surprised at her own equanimity under vexations and disappointments which at one time would have fretted her beyond endurance.

But though Myra did not look upon herself as a victim, other persons did. Colonel and Mrs. Hensman came over from St. Wolfgang, and found Myra alone with her mother, and lamented that she was missing the beauties of the neighbourhood ; and Mrs. Cameron herself mourned over it in a lugubrious chanting tone, though she took no steps towards a different arrangement, her only hope apparently being that when Edmund arrived things would be different. Mrs. Hensman, a good-natured, sensible woman, who had taken a great fancy to Myra, seized upon this idea, and worked it judiciously : Mr. Cameron was obliged to be in England by a certain time ; as soon therefore as Edmund came they were all to move homewards. So, also, Colonel Hensman's destination was England ;

he would be there probably a few days later than Mr. Cameron, and if Myra could be allowed to remain behind with them at St. Wolfgang, and then—moving more rapidly than would be possible for Mrs. Cameron—meet her father and mother in Paris, it would give her the opportunity of seeing some of the places she had missed. Edmund's society would be a pleasure to Mr. Cameron, and Mrs. Cameron would not miss Myra's reading when they were travelling. It was a well-arranged little plan, which, being put into the right groove, ran very smoothly, and Myra was grateful and happy, and wondered that every one should be so considerate for her. She had indeed but one regret—for Rosamond, who she thought would miss not having some one to whom she could speak of Mr. Verney.

For beneath all this surface of matter-of-fact-ness the romance of life was still working, and Myra never forgot it, and, indeed, was not allowed to do so. How much or how little real feeling Rosamond possessed, was a question which it would have baffled even a keen scrutiniser of the human heart to discover. One thing was clear, that she believed she had a great deal; and by acting upon the belief, to a certain extent created the feeling. Being parted from Mr. Verney it was necessary to be melancholy; absent in manner, moody and uncertain in humour, the latter being indeed a necessity of nature rather than of circumstance. As a natural consequence remarks were made, and Mr. and Mrs. Cameron were somewhat uneasy, and a little suspicious, and thought that perhaps, they had not been quite wise in throwing the young people, as they were called, so much together; all this attracting a good deal of notice towards Rosamond, creating an interest in her, which was just what she liked, since there was not the slightest idea on the part of her parents of the extent to which things had gone. As for Myra, she at once accepted her sister's expression of feeling as reality, and treated her accordingly. Rosamond carried on long conversations at night, and gave way to sighs and secret allusions by day, not to Myra's satisfaction, very much indeed to the reverse; but it was all taken in perfect good faith, and Myra was becoming daily more and more convinced that Rosamond's affections were irrevocably engaged, and that it would have been cruel in her to have stood in the way of the one only comfort which could be afforded her in Mr. Verney's absence. As to conscience—when a person has once decided that it is better to yield to the guidance of another in any doubtful case, it is astonishing how soon conscience becomes silent, especially when its voice is obeyed in all other instances. Myra did not allow herself to question Mr. Verney's judgment, when she had resolved upon following it, but went on in happy unconsciousness of error, never disturbed except when she received a short note from Mr. Verney, enclosing a letter for Rosamond, and found herself obliged to resort to a little manœuvring in order to conceal the fact from her parents. Then, indeed, she did feel uncomfortable, but as she was not called upon to say what was untrue, and contrived to avoid deliberately acting it, she escaped any severe self-reproach. This first note was from Golling, and in it Mr. Verney announced his intention of making his way to Innsbruck, where he hoped to find letters. Beyond this his route was, as usual, uncertain. He might go to Meran and the Lago di Garda; he might take the Ampezzio Pass to Venice; or, on the other hand, he might give up any notion of Italy, and make his way into Switzerland. Myra tried to find out if Rosamond had received any more definite information as to his future movements, but Rosamond merely smiled sweetly, and said she supposed they were both equally wise, and then she put the letter away in her writing-case with an air which said more plainly than words, 'you are not to ask any more questions.' Whatever Mr. Verney had written had, however, the effect of making Rosamond very anxious to leave Ischl, and she was almost out of temper when Edmund arrived, and tried to persuade his father that the delay of a couple of days might, with good management and a different route, make no difference as to the time of their reaching England. For almost the first time since they had been abroad, Rosamond talked a great deal about Mrs. Cameron's health, and the danger of fatigue, and Myra in her simplicity was glad to think that as she herself was going to stay behind at St. Wolfgang, Rosamond, at least, would be thoughtful and watchful for her mother. The party broke up at last, with the understanding that Colonel and Mrs. Hensman were to bring Myra with them to Paris, and Myra bade her own family good-bye with a heart all the more open to enjoyment because she was not, as on a previous occasion, disturbed by a newly-awakened regret for the loss of Mr. Verney's society.

And thus once more Myra found herself in the pleasant *salon* of the old conventual house, with its windows opening above the blue lake ; and the jagged mountains—varied in colour by every golden gleam which lit up their sharp points, every purple shade which rested upon their deep recesses— set before her, like a wonderful panorama, which she might gaze upon and study, and imprint upon her memory to be a vision of delight for all future years. It was vexatious at first to find that she was not to enjoy her visit alone, but that Mrs. Tracy and Miss Stuart were staying at the *château*. Myra had a latent love of solitude and silence, which, though it was overruled by the buoyancy of spirit natural to her age, exhibited itself on all occasions when her feelings were touched. Nothing excited her like the beauty of nature, but the excitement could not be shared. When in travelling her heart beat quickly, and her eyes grew dim with sudden tears as the glorious mountain peaks and the fair valleys of the Bavarian Tyrol spread themselves before her, she instinctively turned aside from the rest of the party, half-surprised, half-ashamed of her own emotions. A light tone or a trivial remark jarred upon her at such moments like a false note in music, and even Mr. Verney's poetical admiration failed to touch the chord which could harmonise with her own feelings. She needed something deeper, more reverent, more nearly approaching to worship. If she had been alone she would have knelt in thankfulness and awe, for in no other way could she have given vent to the fulness of that deep and pure delight which at times overwhelmed her. And she had looked for such enjoyment at St. Wolfgang. She had pictured to herself a morning spent in the garden, revelling in the gor-

geous colours of the flowers and the delicately-pencilled foli-
age of the shrubs, watching the shadows on the hills, and the
silvery sparkle on the water, and dreaming—no, not dreaming, but feeling—forgetting care, perplexity, regret, forgetting
above all herself, in the sense of all-pervading and mysterious
beauty.

Mrs. Tracy's rather monotonous voice, and Mrs. Hensman's
sensible remarks, were but ill suited to such anticipations, and
Myra's first feeling of disappointment, when the latter proposed,
the morning after her arrival, that they should all take their
work and spend a pleasant sociable morning in the pavilion,
was very great. She could have found it in her heart to
complain that Mrs. Hensman had deceived her, and she said
to herself that if she had known there were to be other visitors
she would not have accepted the invitation. But Myra was
very unfair upon poor Mrs. Hensman. There had been no
deception in the case. When she invited Myra, she had not
known herself that Mrs. Tracy and Miss Stuart would be her
guests likewise. They had been stationary at the little inn,
detained day after day by illness. Mrs. Hensman had pre-
vided them with many necessary comforts, and shown them
great kindness, but her offer of rooms at the *château* had been
always declined till the very day of Myra's arrival, when some
impertinent behaviour on the part of the disagreeable landlord
had so distressed Mrs. Tracy, that from mere nervousness and
alarm she had taken refuge with her new friends, hoping, as
she said, to be able to remove to Ischl in a very few days.

Myra would have cared less, she would scarcely, indeed,
have cared at all, if Charlotte Stuart had formed one of the
sociable pavilion party, but she was not well enough to appear
at breakfast, and Myra found herself condemned to a morning
of needlework and conversation ; the former consisting on her
own part of some fancy knitting, which she had not once taken
up since she left home, and in which she had not the slightest
interest, whilst the latter was merely an interchange of remarks
upon the beauty of the view, varied by Mrs. Tracy's account
of her voyage from India, and the difficulties she had experienced in travelling through the Tyrol. Myra listened to

the latter for some time, in the hope of gaining some information as to the antecedents of her new acquaintances, but Mrs.
Tracy, though she talked freely upon other subjects, was
singularly reserved on all points which regarded herself or
her niece, and Myra at length, heartily tired, ventured to take
up a book and steal away to a little distance, where—half
hidden by a flowering shrub—she might occupy herself in
some degree, and at least for a short time, according to her
own ideas of enjoyment.

The book was a series of essays. It had been marked for
her by Mr. Verney, and Myra turned over the pages, reading
different portions as revelations of Mr. Verney's own character.
All that was noble, generous, unprejudiced, beautiful in expression, or pure in feeling, had touched him with sympathy
and admiration. And there were marks of reference to other
books, quotations, similes ; the volume seemed to Myra a mine
of poetry, wisdom, and valuable information. She felt proud
of his friendship for her, it seemed to ennoble whilst it humbled
her. She thought of her sister almost with envy. Rosamond
would have his companionship always. Would she appreciate
it, was a question which Myra did not think of asking. The
habit of her own mind was reverence, and Rosamond's outward
gifts had always somewhat dazzled her, and now, seen in the
light of Mr. Verney's admiration, she became actually idealised,
and Myra, indulging the romance which the knowledge of their
engagement awakened, laid aside her book, and lost herself in
a reverie of the perfection of such a marriage—beauty, refinement, amiability, intellect, poetry, and nobility of heart united—
and she herself—it was the one thought of self which entered
into the dream—the sharer and chosen confidante of their
happiness.

The reverie was interrupted by Miss Stuart. She came
into the garden walking with the slow step of illness, and
drawing a shawl round her. Since Myra's former visit her
complexion had become more transparent, and the hectic
colour on her cheeks was nearly gone, and now the searching, anxious eyes were almost too large—too full for beauty.
Whatever characteristics of temper and mind there might have

been in the small firm mouth, the short upper lip, the chiselled nose with its rounded nostril, and the square open brow, were all lost in the one expression of hopeless unrest.

And the voice with which she spoke to Myra told the same tale as those lovely piteous eyes.

'Have I disturbed you, Miss Cameron? I ought not to do so. It is so pleasant to be quiet on such a perfect day.'

'I like it,' said Myra, 'but I don't think all persons do. Won't you sit down?' and as she spoke she left her seat, and placed herself on the grass, leaning against the trunk of a tree.

'You should not sit there,' said Miss Stuart, still standing. 'You will take cold.'

'Oh! I never take cold. Please sit down, and I will fetch you a cushion from the house.'

'Don't on any account trouble yourself. The chair will do perfectly well, but indeed you ought to be careful. I said just as you say once.'

'Did your illness come on with a cold?' asked Myra.

'Yes—no,' and a slight blush overspread Miss Stuart's cheek. 'It came on gradually; it is a kind of complication; no one knows what is the matter with me.'

'You must try London physicians,' said Myra.

'Yes, when I go to England.'

'And you are not going now?'

'I don't know. I never do know anything till the time comes.'

'It must be very disagreeable to live in uncertainty,' said Myra.

'Yes, for some people.'

Myra was inclined to say, 'Is it so to you?' but the personal question would have seemed impertinent.

'How one ought to enjoy this day!' continued Miss Stuart, as she sat down in Myra's chair, and languidly gazed around her.

'One can't help enjoying it,' observed Myra.

The only answer was a sorrowful smile, and Myra added,

'At least when one is blessed with good health. I am afraid you are too ill to enjoy anything.'

'I am soothed,' was the reply; 'and that is in a measure enjoyment.'

'I suppose it may be, where people have suffered much,' replied Myra.

'Yes, there is a good deal of compensation in this world. People learn as they go on in life to be contented upon very little. But you are so young, you will scarcely understand that theory.'

'I am more than sixteen,' said Myra.

'I daresay that seems old to you. I know it did once to me.'

'It seems not like real age, but like drawing near to it,' said Myra.

And Miss Stuart slightly laughed as she inquired, 'And what do you call real age?'

'Being old enough to have sorrows and trials,' answered Myra.

'You are right; that is age, and there are some who never have known youth, but '——

'There is the servant with the post from Ischl,' exclaimed Myra, interrupting, and then apologising. She ran forward to meet him, and returned with two letters. 'I am so sorry there are none for you.'

Charlotte Stuart's hand, which had been stretched out to take the letters, dropped as if it had been paralysed.

One of Myra's envelopes fell on the ground; as she picked it up she said, 'I am surprised this has ever reached me, it is directed so illegibly—just look.' She held out the envelope for Miss Stuart to see it.

'Is it the handwriting of a friend of yours?' The question was put in a hard ringing tone, like the striking of metal.

'Yes, a very great friend, a Mr. Verney. He has been with us quite lately. He only left us the other day.' Myra was scarcely thinking of what she said, she was so engrossed in her letter; and when Miss Stuart repeated, 'The other day?

R

lately? do you mean at Ischl?' she replied in the same absent
way, 'Yes, last week,' and went on reading.

'I think I must go in,' was uttered in a faint voice, and
then Myra woke up to consciousness again. Miss Stuart
was standing, or rather leaning against the chair. She said
to Myra, 'Please ask my aunt to come to me,' and Myra
hastened to the pavilion with a feeling of self-reproach at
having been so absorbed, yet not without a sensation of relief
when Mrs. Tracy said, ' You had better leave my niece to me,
my dear Miss Cameron, I will take her into the house.' Mrs.
Hensman went away also, and Myra was left in the pavilion
alone.

And then she read her letters in peace. Mr. Verney's was
singularly interesting, giving a short account of his movements,
and a long account of what he had felt and thought. In this
respect it was the only unreserved communication Myra had
ever received from him, yet it contained no reference to his
engagement, though a note to Rosamond was enclosed. In
the postscript he said, 'I should not wonder if we were to
meet again before you reach England,' but he gave no clue
as to his route, and did not say where letters would reach
him. It was quite a downfall in feeling to turn from this
imaginative and poetical and almost confidential letter to
Annette's gossip about school. Myra had nearly forgotten
the existence of Mrs. de Lancey, and the remarks on the
French and German teachers, and the peculiarities of the
masters, were profoundly indifferent to her. Annette could
write and think of nothing else. Naturally enough, St. John's
Wood was her world, and quite as large and important to her
as the world of which Mr. Verney was the centre could be
to Myra; but romance is not generally sympathising. Myra
hurried through the crossed page—feeling extremely provoked
that any one should think of writing across on thin foreign
paper, and not understanding that Annette had but two or
three sheets in her possession and did not know how to get
at more—till she came to a sentence written at the side of
the page, and corrected and underlined. Myra could make
out the words Mrs. Patty, and Miss Greaves, and something

about a message, and India, and it was not till after much
careful examination that she could manage to read one
sentence. 'Mrs. de Lancey says, that the Charlotte Stuart
who was Miss Greaves's friend has left India in ill health.'
Then came something almost entirely illegible, the only
words which could be deciphered being—'engaged to Mr.
——' whom, it was impossible to say ; though, according to
Annette's usual style, there were two notes of admiration after
the name.

The 'whom' signified but little to Myra just then, but the
fact of the engagement was interesting and explanatory of
Miss Stuart's reserve. Still there was a little natural curiosity
awakened as to the illegible word. The first letter might be
a V, or a T, or a W, and Myra recalled all the names she had
heard which might fit what appeared to be the number of
letters ; all except that of Verney, which did not suggest itself,
until, holding the paper at a distance, and catching what might
be called the general effect, it flashed across her suddenly.
For a moment she felt thunderstruck, but looking at the name
again, she read it as Vernon, or, possibly, Varney, or—she
could not be sure what it was, only, it could not be Verney.
She hurried from the pavilion ; why, she did not know. It
never occurred to her that she was hurrying from her own
thoughts. On her way to the house she met Mrs. Tracy,
looking even more anxious than was her wont. Myra's impulse
was to join her, and inquire how Miss Stuart was ; and the
short nervous answer, 'Better, thank you,' was given ; and
then they walked slowly side by side without speaking, till
Mrs. Tracy said abruptly, 'I think you have a friend—Mr.
Verney ? '

'Yes,' answered Myra ; and as she spoke, her heart seemed
to stop beating.

'Should you mind telling me something about him ?' continued Mrs. Tracy.

'No, certainly not. I don't know much ; he is a great
friend. Would you mind sitting down for a minute ?' Myra
pointed to a garden seat.

'Oh! no, not at all. I am afraid you are not strong. Are you tired this morning?'

Myra waived the answer, and said, 'Mr. Verney is the nephew of a Colonel Verney who lives near us.'

'Yes; I know. A son of the elder brother, and just returned from India.'

'He came back some months ago. He talks of going back again, only his health is bad.'

'And I think—I imagine—he must have been with you abroad.'

'Yes.'

'And he has left you. Can you tell me where he is to be found?'

'He was at Innsbruck; I don't know where he is now.'

'And you cannot tell where a letter would be likely to reach him?'

'No; he does not say.'

'Thank you. Excuse my questions. I have a little business with him, that is all.'

Mrs. Tracy rose and moved away, and as she left the seat, Colonel Hensman came up to it.

'What! all alone? It is very rude of my wife; I must go and scold her.'

'I like being alone,' said Myra.

'Oh! poetical, are you? Well, I hope you have been enjoying yourself to your heart's content. There is nothing to disturb you here.'

'No,' replied Myra; 'it is deliciously quiet.'

'So that poor love-sick girl says; I have been telling Mrs. Tracy that she should not indulge her. If she were taken to Vienna, or any place where she could have something to distract her thoughts, there might be some hope for her; there will be none soon if they let her brood over things as she does now.'

'Is that what is the matter with her?' asked Myra; and her voice faltered.

Colonel Hensman laughed. 'How you young ladies catch at the least rumour of a love story! But you must ask Mrs. Hensman to tell you; she knows more than I do.'

' I should not like to ask her,' said Myra.

' But you don't mind asking me. Is that because I am more tender-hearted ? I shall disappoint you, though. I know nothing about it, except that some good-for-nothing fellow is playing fast and loose with her. I can't tell you the name, and a story is nothing without that.'

Colonel Hensman walked off, and Myra took up Mr. Verney's letter again. But with what a changed feeling ! This dull pain at her heart—this aching uneasiness—how was she to bear it. What was to be done to relieve it ? Did she really suspect, and if so, why did she not at once take some step to find out the truth ? She began to read, but something seemed to stop her ; the meaning of the words seemed altered, they gave her no pleasure ; and she went up to her own room, and brought out from her drawer a little box containing the few other letters which she had received from Mr. Verney. They were all laid before her ; but still she did not look at them more closely, and they remained on the table whilst Myra walked up and down her room, because she could not bear to sit quiet, trying at the same time to think how foolish it was, how like her own hasty judgment, to let an idea gain possession of her which could have no foundation ; then taking up a book, and after a few minutes wandering off from it to a repetition of the same arguments—the same reasons why she was not to think what she could not help thinking, to suspect what she could not help suspecting. The summons to luncheon obliged her to appear in the dining-room. Charlotte Stuart was not there ; she very seldom did appear at luncheon, so Mrs. Hensman said, and her aunt wished to remain upstairs with her. Colonel Hensman made some allusion to the cause of Miss Stuart's low spirits, which was instantly checked by his wife, and Myra saw from Mrs. Hensman's manner that there was no likelihood of obtaining any information from her. A drive was proposed for the afternoon. Myra did her best to appear pleased, and felt, indeed, that it was the only thing under present circumstances which could be in any way soothing to her ; but the slumbering pain awoke again when, as she was leaving the room to dress, Colonel Hensman called out—'If you have any letters for the post you must let me have them now, as I am going to send into Ischl.'

Mr. Verney's letter to Rosamond was to be forwarded, and for the first time for many days Myra's conscience was aroused to the question, 'Was her part in the correspondence justifiable?' Too late it was then to ask; too late to draw back. The letter was sent, but the weight upon Myra's spirits grew heavier; and the sensitive, self-reproaching heart, tortured by affection, and bewildered by sophistry, could find no repose but in a forced gaiety, which was a strain upon the powers both of body and mind.

CHAPTER XXXIV

IN four days' time they were to leave St. Wolfgang. Those four days were to be given up to excursions, and little else was spoken of but guides, mules, *char-à-bancs*, and provisions. Mrs. Tracy and Miss Stuart lived apart. Myra scarcely saw the former except at luncheon, and Miss Stuart was said to be too unwell to leave her room. She also was to move to Ischl, and from thence to Vienna, when the party broke up. This was all that Myra could learn of her plans. Several other persons were now staying at the *château*, but they were chiefly foreigners. Mrs. Hensman was much engaged with them, and though very kind to Myra, could give her but little personal attention; and so Myra carried her lonely burden about, finding no one with whom to share it, at times forgetting it, then having it brought back by some chance observation; and then again arguing against conviction, and even conscience—carrying on a vain struggle with the truthfulness which was the great and precious gift bestowed upon her by nature, and which up to this period she had so carefully cultivated and cherished.

The last day came, the day before they were to set out for Paris. Myra had that morning ascended the Schaffberg, in order to obtain the earliest and clearest view of the mountains and lakes of the Salzkammergut. She had returned very tired to rest in her chamber the early part of the day; and as she closed her eyes, all the wonderful scenes upon which she had been gazing floated before her, and the enchantment deadened the secret pain, and she fell asleep tranquil and almost happy. She was awakened, after a long rest, by a gentle tap at the door; and when she started up, Charlotte Stuart was standing before her. An open letter was in her hand, her look was haggard, and her breath came quick and faint. Sleep had scarcely left Myra, and but for the glorious sunlight streaming over the lake and flickering upon the walls of her apartment, she might have thought, as she looked upon that wan white figure, that she was still dreaming.

'Don't move; ' Miss Stuart drew near the sofa; 'only let me speak to you. They will miss me soon and search for me. Listen, while there is time.'

'But you are ill,' exclaimed Myra, scarce knowing what she said.

'Yes, very ill. Tell me—you know this handwriting?'

Myra looked at the envelope held before her. 'Yes, it is Mr. Verney's.'

'Your Mr. Verney—your friend—the same who wrote to you the other day—there is no doubt?'

'None, so far as I can tell.'

'But you must be sure. The Mr. Verney who—who is engaged to your sister Rosamond?'

The hollow laugh which accompanied the question sounded like the tones of insanity; and as Myra delayed to answer, Miss Stuart caught hold of her hand and grasped it tightly, whilst, looking at her fixedly, she said, 'Speak, I must know. I will—I do know.'

'If you do know, there is no need to speak,' was Myra's hesitating and evasive answer.

The grasp laid upon her hand relaxed, and Charlotte Stuart hid her face upon the couch, and a low wail of agony broke from her. Myra made a movement of sympathy, but the unhappy girl turned round almost fiercely. 'Don't pity me, I have no need of pity. He loves me; he does not love her. Pity her—warn her. He loves me—yes; he tells me he loves me. God forgive him my misery !'

Myra could not echo the prayer. A gulf seemed to have opened before her in which all trust in human honour, all confidence in human truth, were buried.

'Who told you of his engagement?' she asked in a trembling voice.

Instead of replying, Miss Stuart placed in Myra's hands another letter in Miss Greaves's handwriting, and pointed to the following passage :—'I cannot bring myself to believe a report which I have heard to-day, though it will account for all which has been so inexplicable to me in Mr. Verney's conduct to yourself. It has been told me, upon excellent authority, that after travelling with the Camerons for more than a month he has engaged himself to Rosamond. I need not say how anxiously I shall look for a contradiction of this rumour from you, and for an assurance that your relations with him remain unaltered.'

'I can contradict it. You know I can,' continued Charlotte, her large lustrous eyes gazing wildly upon Myra. 'He writes to me, and loves me. It is the world's talk. The cruel, cruel world.'

'If he loves you, you cannot be miserable,' said Myra ; but a pang of torturing self-reproach shot through her at the falsity of such comfort.

'If—there is no if. It is she who is false, she who has tried to win him from me. But he is mine still,—my all !'

Myra unconsciously repeated the words 'my all;' they sounded to her profane.

'Tell her he is my all; she cannot take him from me. Oh ! she cannot, she cannot.'

'It is Mr. Verney's own doing,' replied Myra.

'Then is it true ? Oh ! say it is not true ;' and again the long low wail echoed through the apartment.

'Stay,' said Myra, rousing herself from the sense of wretchedness which was so bewildering to her faculties ; 'what is true or what is not true, I am not at liberty to say. You must inquire of Mr. Verney himself; only remember that my sister is in no way to blame.'

'He tells me nothing. I cannot inquire. I do not know where to seek for him. But you know.'

'No,' replied Myra. 'I know no more of his movements than you do, except'——

'But your sister knows. He writes to her ?'

'Indeed, indeed you must not question me in this way,' said Myra ; 'but I may see him soon, and if you would trust me with a letter or a message '—— she stopped. It was treachery to Rosamond, but pity was too strong for her.

Miss Stuart answered eagerly, ' Yes, I trust you.   You will help me—yet you are her sister.'

'I will try to do what is right,' continued Myra; and she added, after a moment's pause, ' I shall, I must see Mr. Verney.'

'See him ! look,'—and Charlotte Stuart held out her transparent hand—'my life is wasting away; my days are numbered.   Yet of those precious days would I gladly give up all save one—if that one might be spent with him.'

Before Myra could reply, a knock was heard at the door, and Mrs. Tracy entered.

In one instant Miss Stuart had recovered her composure. The few words which she spoke in answer to her aunt's affectionate reprimand for having left her room were uttered quite calmly, and with the same air of reserve and self-command which on ordinary occasions was habitual to her.   Without making the least allusion to the subject of their conversation, she went back to her own room almost immediately, Mrs. Tracy accompanying her, and Myra was left to solitude and reflection.

Mrs. Patty Kingsbury was right.   There is no trial so overwhelming to the affections and principle of the young, as that which first destroys their confidence in one whom they have accustomed themselves to respect.   The shock of that moral earthquake is a shock which is felt for life.   Yet, better it may be that it should be experienced early—better that it should come with one great blow from which the elasticity of youth may partially recover, than that distrust should eat into the heart with the slow destructiveness of the canker-worm.   The pain, indeed, is greater, but the wound is not so deadly.   Myra had been to blame.   She had indeed been deceived, but the deception was of her own creation.   That, however, was a consciousness yet to come.   In the first moments of conviction, her chief thought was still to extenuate Mr. Verney's conduct, to seek for explanations in circumstances of which she knew nothing.

All possible and impossible motives suggested themselves, and were one by one rejected; and Myra's excitement of feel-

ing increased, her brain worked more restlessly, and a throb-
bing headache made her every moment less capable of thought,
whilst thought appeared to her more and more necessary.
For she must act, she must write or speak, she must in some
way communicate with Mr. Verney. To be made the instru-
ment of his treachery by being the medium of conveying his
letters, was no longer possible ; and her own weakness in ever
having consented to place herself in such a position stood out
still more clearly before her. She felt herself condemned in
her own sight, condemned also, as she assuredly would be, in
the sight of her parents ; a party to deceit with her sister, a
party to Mr. Verney's treachery,—because she had trusted
and believed in him, because she had wilfully put aside her own
knowledge of right, and turned from the instinct of her honest
conscientiousness, and feared his sneers.

Myra did not hate Mr. Verney. She was too generous—
too true and simple-minded, to seek any excuse for herself by
a burden laid upon another ; but a sense of unutterable help-
lessness, insecurity—an aching distrust for which there could
be no cure, made her heart turn faint, and her limbs tremble,
whilst she rested her head on the sofa pillow, unable to find
even the merciful relief of tears. She was in this state when
Mrs. Tracy once more knocked at the door, and asked for
a few moments' conversation. Myra had as yet but little
practice in self-command. A nervous, irritable, impetuous
temperament had been her torment from childhood. She
could never conceal when she was unhappy, though she could
not merely conceal, but subdue her temper. When Mrs.
Tracy came up to her kindly, and begged her not to disturb
herself, and then sat down and asked, with somewhat of a
mother's thoughtfulness, whether she was over-tired or ill, the
feeling of oppression which seemed to have dried up the fountain of her tears was melted, and her almost uncontrollable impulse was to tell everything, to ask advice, to throw herself once
more upon guidance, and so, if it might only be, to have rest—
rest for the conscience, rest for the heart.

But she had no opportunity for yielding to the temptation.
Mrs. Tracy began immediately in her very quiet rather slow

tone : ' I would not have disturbed you if I could have avoided it, but I am obliged to speak for Charlotte's sake. You know how we are situated with regard to Mr. Verney. I have seen the report in Miss Greaves's letter, but I cannot find out whether you confirm it; and, indeed, it is very important that I should know.'

' If you would not ask me ! ' exclaimed Myra, ' I told Miss Stuart that she should write to Mr. Verney. I cannot answer or say anything.

' In those few words you have said enough,' replied Mrs. Tracy somewhat haughtily. ' I can, of course, quite understand. Only, Miss Cameron, for your sister's sake, it is fair that you should know the character of the man to whom she is willing to give herself.'

Myra's face became rigid in the effort to keep down her struggling feelings.

Mrs. Tracy went on : ' Two years ago Mr. Verney became attached to my niece. Her father was then in possession of a good fortune, and he was likely to increase it. Mr. Verney knew this, and I do not think I do him any injustice when I say that money is a great consideration with him. He is a man of self-indulgent, extravagant habits. At one time he gambled considerably, though when he first became acquainted with Charlotte, he professed to have given up the practice. He won her affections slowly, by the most unremitting attentions. He flattered and sympathised with her, and they had literary pursuits in common. She disliked his principles at first, but by degrees she became accustomed to them, and '—Mrs. Tracy paused, and drew a long breath—' that is the saddest part—he calls himself a Christian ; for any definite faith he possesses he might as well call himself a Mahometan. They have been engaged now for nearly a year. At first the marriage was to have taken place at once, but my brother-in-law's affairs were rather embarrassed at the time, and there was a delay in consequence. It was thought that they would soon come right, and Mr. Verney exerted himself very much to set them right. He lent money, and mixed himself up with business, entirely, as he said, from love to Charlotte, and I believed him. I believe him now. I have no doubt of his love for her, but '——

'But what?' exclaimed Myra.

'I believe he wants moral courage, and there is nothing so cruel as cowardice. He knew from the first that his own income would not be sufficient to marry upon, because he had involved himself by his gambling debts and extravagance. He did not dare say what his real condition was, and so he speculated, hoping to retrieve what he had lost.

'Things became worse and worse. He was never open either with Charlotte or her father. It was always delay, excuse, and hope—hope which was never fulfilled. He left India partly because his health had suffered from the climate, partly with the idea of raising some money that was needed for my brother-in-law's business, which, in fact, had become in a great measure his own. When we parted, I entreated him to break off his engagement, or at least, to tell Charlotte exactly how he was circumstanced. I felt, and he felt, that it was excessively unlikely the marriage could ever take place. I saw that uncertainty was rapidly undermining Charlotte's health, and I was quite sure that she was brave enough to bear the truth ; but I could get nothing from him. If for one moment I brought him to the point of courage and sincerity, the next he slid from my grasp, and everything was as vague as before. In my heart I felt convinced that he would have been thankful to be free. He loved Charlotte unquestionably, but not well enough to make sacrifices for her. He is a man of the world, Miss Cameron, and no man of the world can ever make self second. He suggested that I should tell her everything, and should persuade her to take the first step towards breaking off the engagement. So mean it was in him ! so cowardly ! He wished to screen himself from any blame which the world might attach to him. When I declined to interfere, he strove to throw the responsibility of the consequences upon me. But I have seen enough of life, Miss Cameron, to know that it is the greatest of mistakes to undertake a duty which does not belong to you. Mr. Verney's affairs and Mr. Verney's marriage were in his own hands. Neither my brother-in-law nor my niece would have endured any interference from me. And, indeed, so unstable is Mr. Verney, and from his moral cowardice so little to be depended upon, that even if I had consented to open the question with my niece, I could not have reckoned upon his support. He would have allowed me to urge the breaking off of the engagement, and then, when he saw her distress, he would have turned round upon me with reproaches.'

Mrs. Tracy paused for an instant, but Myra made no observation. Except a nervous movement of her hands, there were no outward signs of feeling. Mrs. Tracy went on : 'Directly after Mr. Verney arrived in England he wrote, begging that Charlotte and myself would follow him. He spoke hopefully of his prospects, and appeared excessively anxious about Charlotte's health. My brother-in-law insisted upon our going. He is a man of essentially weak character; his whole life has been a failure, and he believes in every new plan which is suggested to him. Moreover, he had been from the first entirely under Mr. Verney's influence. What he expected from our visit to England, except the possible improvement of Charlotte's health, I cannot say. For myself, I had no hope of improvement in that respect from anything except certainty, it mattered not of what kind. It is suspense which has worn, and is still wearing away this poor child's life.

' As to Mr. Verney, I believe his love rose and fell with the condition of his pecuniary affairs. If he could marry Charlotte and live in ease and comfort, he would be glad to do so ; and when first he came home I have no doubt he persuaded himself it would be possible, and wrote to us accordingly. But his views were all dreamy. He did not really know what he expected, and before we reached Trieste everything was as unsettled as ever. We were met there by letters telling us that we should do better not to come to England ; that it would be more economical to be on the continent ; that he would join us.'

' But you have not seen him ?' exclaimed Myra.

' Yes,' replied Mrs. Tracy ; 'I have seen him for one half hour ; the first night of our arrival. He refused to see

Charlotte, he refused to be open with her. He said, as before, that he would write to her. So he left her, I believe, to die.'

Myra buried her face in her hands. It was at that very time that Mr. Verney had engaged himself to Rosamond !

'Now remember,' continued Mrs. Tracy, 'that when I tell you all this, I do not in the least accuse Mr. Verney of deliberate treachery. Even if, as I fully believe, he has engaged himself to your sister, and has thus most miserably deceived both her and Charlotte, I believe there has been no preconceited cruelty to either. Mr. Verney is not an unfeeling man; on the contrary, he is rather tender-hearted ; there is nothing he dislikes more than the sight of pain, and it is because of this dislike that he has shrunk from saying to my niece what he knew would distress her. Possibility also is everything with him. That which he can do easily he will do readily. And what I am now going to say I must beg you to believe is from no wish to make inquiries which may seem impertinent. But, as there is no doubt that the pecuniary difficulties which have stood in the way of his marriage with Charlotte have cooled rather than stimulated his love, so if a marriage with your sister has in any way been made practicable to him—the very fact of its practicability is likely to have excited what he may fancy an affection for her. He would fall in love, or imagine himself in love, with the heiress of twenty thousand pounds more readily than with the heiress of five—not from any deliberate calculation, but simply because in the one case he would see his way to the attainment of his end more quickly than in the other.'

Myra looked up shocked, and a faint smile passed over Mrs. Tracy's face. 'We must not be hard on human nature, my dear. Mr. Verney would not be a bad man because he unconsciously calculated consequences, but he will be a bad man if he is not open with your parents and your sister. I can talk to you without the slightest wish to bring Mr. Verney back to my niece. On the contrary, I have but one earnest desire—to have all connection and communication with him broken off. But it is due to you to say that the same difficulties which have prevented his carrying out his engagement with Charlotte not only exist still, to my certain knowledge, but are very greatly increased. His income, if he should return to India, would be claimed by his creditors, and he would be utterly unable to support a wife and family, for whatever private fortune he may at one time have had is now gone, swallowed up in the wreck of my brother-in-law's affairs. The latter fact is by no means generally known. There have been hopes of retrieving the business till within the last two months, but my brother-in-law himself now acknowledges that it is hopeless. You may make use of this information as you think best.'

'And may I say that I have received it from you?' asked Myra, her voice trembling with agitation.

'Certainly: your friends will, I hope, understand that I can have but one object in making such a communication. If they do not, still I must say what I feel to be right, and bear whatever imputation of a double motive may be laid upon me.'

'They could not distrust you, I would explain,—I would assure them '—— began Myra.

But Mrs. Tracy interrupted her. There was something almost bitter in her tone as she said: 'Dear Miss Cameron, do not trouble yourself with any explanation on my account. When you have had my experience you will learn to accept misconstruction and misrepresentation very quietly. There is a day coming when we shall all know each other truly. I am quite willing to wait for it. Only forgive me for taking up your time, and, I fear, giving you pain.'

Myra had no wish then to open her heart to Mrs. Tracy, and seek counsel and comfort. The stoicism and apparent indifference of her manner were repelling. She had never before seen the effect of long-continued disappointment and experience of deception. Sorrow would have seemed natural, but calm enduring contempt chilled and perplexed her. Even now she could not realise Mr. Verney's baseness; she only thought of him as having once been noble.

CHAPTER XXXV

BRILLIANT, noisy, and sunshiny were the splendid streets of Paris. Carriages thronged the Champs Elysées and the Bois de Boulogne, groups of idlers crowded the *cafés* and the restaurants, men of business rushed along the Boulevards; fashionable worshippers and curious sightseers ascended the steps of the Madeleine. There was no place so pleasant to Rosamond as Paris; whilst she could *flâner* through the streets in the morning, go to the theatre in the evening, eat an unlimited quantity of ices and bonbons, and spend a moderate sum in lace, ribbons, and little jewelleries, she could even be content for a while to exist without flirting. Under present circumstances Rosamond naturally attributed this possibility to her attachment to Mr. Verney. She was sentimental to herself about it, and found actual pleasure in contrasting her own pretty quiet, modest ways, with the forward independent style of the fast young ladies who presented themselves to the astonished Parisians as the *élite* of English society. For this was one great advantage possessed by Rosamond—when she found herself so placed that she could not attract admiration from others, she was always able to admire herself. Like the camel in the desert, she kept a supply of civil speeches and pleasant flatteries in her memory wherewith to refresh her thirsty spirit whenever she was inclined to grow weary of a matter-of-fact life. And now she had something still better to fall back upon. She was engaged—and that to a man whom every one allowed to be superior in taste and talent, and whose least words of approbation, therefore, carried weight. For the present, indeed, the engagement was secret, and so there was an absence of outward excitement; but the conceal-

S

ment was only temporary, and it certainly heightened the romance. And thus Rosamond was very happy in Paris, and quite contented to walk with her brother Edmund, and drive with her mother; and when she was not otherwise engaged, to write to Mr. Verney. She knew what no one else did —all his movements; and it had been one of her little inward triumphs to hear the complaints of his silence and indecision, whilst she knew exactly where he had been and where he meant to be. Rosamond's element was petty mystery, and up to this time she had never found sufficient to satisfy her.

But the correspondence had not been very frequent, on Mr. Verney's side especially. He had written once to Ischl, and the enclosed letter to Rosamond had been forwarded by Myra. Since then two other letters had been addressed to Myra at Paris. It was evident, therefore, that he did not yet know that she had been left behind at St. Wolfgang. Rosamond concluded that, as it so frequently happens when people are travelling, the particular letter in which she had mentioned this circumstance had not reached him. The arrangement, however, worked just as well as regarded herself. She opened Myra's letter, took out her own, and forwarded the few lines to St. Wolfgang; and then, in her kind pleasant way, expressed her satisfaction at Mr. Verney's being so fond of Myra. ‘It was such a good thing for poor little Myra, and had made her quite a different person,’ and stately Mr. Cameron eulogised Mr. Verney in a speech so well put together that it would have been quite an event if anything so good had been heard in Parliament, and innocent Mrs. Cameron said to herself, and repeated in a letter to Mrs. Verney, that the friendship of a man of Mr. Verney's age and character was quite a boon to her young people. So safe and so superior he was, she only longed for him to return to them!

Only Edmund was silent. He cordially disliked Mr. Verney, and for that reason said little about him. He had no suspicions, however, and nothing in Rosamond's manner awakened them. It was merely the instinct of a truthful nature, repelled by one that was false. Edmund and Myra were alike in this characteristic ; and Myra would long since have judged Mr. Verney as her brother did, but for the unconscious vanity which was flattered by his sympathy, and the womanly reverence and longing for guidance which made her submit to his intellect, whilst wilfully closing her eyes to everything that was deficient in his principles.

'He is a very good fellow, I don't doubt,' was Edmund's exclamation at breakfast the fourth morning of their stay in Paris, in reply to one of his mother's now frequent sighing wishes that they could hear something of dear Mr. Verney. 'But I am not bound to like him. I believe I inherit my father's prejudice against all Verneys.'

'Except the Colonel,' said Rosamond. 'You and he are immense friends.'

'Well, yes. He does give you a blow in your face and not behind your back ; which is more than can be said for his wife.'

'Edmund, my dear,' interrupted Mrs. Cameron, 'I must beg of you not to say anything against Mrs. Verney, it may be so awkward, for I have a note here, telling me that they are in Paris.'

'In Paris !' and Edmund uttered a hasty and not very complimentary ejaculation. 'What do they come here for ? '

'To see the world, I suppose,' observed Rosamond. 'That is what every one comes to Paris for. I think myself that it will be charming having them here. Mrs. Verney is so good-natured, and knows every one.'

'I wish you to understand, Rosamond,' said Mr. Cameron, looking up from the 'Galignani,' which, in default of the 'Times,' was his morning soporific—'I wish you to understand that I can allow no such constant intercourse with Colonel Verney's family in Paris as went on in London. It was too much. Politically opposed as we are, our social intercourse must necessarily be subject to certain restraints. Mrs. Verney's great good sense is indeed a very redeeming item in the aggregate of family qualities, and I do not hesitate to say that I very highly appreciate her; but, unfortunately, her excellence will not in the eye of the world atone for her husband's violence and party-spirit; and I heard remarks made before we left England, which proved to me that it would be unwise to allow any further demonstrations of great intimacy. I have thought fit to say this, and I desire you to remember it.'

Mr. Cameron laid down the paper, and stalked out of the room, Mrs. Cameron looking at him with a strained frightened glance of her weak eyes; whilst Edmund strolled to the window, and Rosamond, who had not quite finished her breakfast, remarked how difficult it was in Paris to get an egg properly boiled.

'Your father places me in a very awkward position,' murmured Mrs. Cameron, after carefully glancing round the room, to be certain that the door was closed; 'he shows such attentions to the Verneys whenever we are near each other; indeed, I often say he listens to Mrs. Verney much more than he does to me; and it was entirely his doing having Mr. Verney with us at Munich and Ischl. I should never have thought of asking him to stay; I should not have considered it proper —indeed, it was not; but I could not help it, and he made himself so helpful and agreeable, and is really so very charming.'

' I don't see the impropriety,' exclaimed Edmund, laughing. ' Rosamond and Myra are not likely to fall in love with him, considering his age. It would be of no use, indeed, if they did, for he is engaged.'

' Engaged! Mr. Verney engaged!' Mrs. Cameron almost screamed her surprise. Rosamond turned pale, spread some butter on a roll, and said, ' Engaged, is he? To whom?'

' Some Indian girl; so I hear.'

' Oh!' And Rosamond cut her roll into small pieces, but did not manage to eat it.

' But not to tell us!' exclaimed Mrs. Cameron in a soliloquising tone. ' I don't believe it; I can't think—Rosamond, my dear, he certainly did pay you great attentions; and he is fond of Myra, very fond of her—he told me so.'

'Platonic affection for young ladies in general,' said Edmund. 'Just like Verney's humbug.'

'But an Indian girl! Not a native, of course? that would be too shocking!'

'A Parsee!' exclaimed Edmund banteringly; 'a regular fire-worshipper; a Miss Something-jee—Something-hoy. A capital hit it will be for Verney. He will get up the Parsee philosophy, and talk down all the learned men at all the learned dinner-parties in London.'

'But may we know the lady's real name?' asked Rosamond.

'Certainly, when I know it myself. As it happens, I only heard it in an accidental way, and have quite forgotten it. Are you coming to the Louvre this morning, Rosamond?'

'I think so. What time are we likely to get our letters to-day?'

'I will go and inquire for them, and you can be ready by the time I return. I suppose you will call on Mrs. Verney to-day, in spite of my father's warnings?'

'Oh no, Rosamond! don't go, my love,' exclaimed Mrs. Cameron. 'Let Mrs. Verney call upon us; she says, indeed, that she will. I do hope your father will be out.'

'Nay,' said Edmund, 'you had better hope that he may be at home, for he will be certain to ask her to dinner. What will you bet me, Rosamond, that we don't find Colonel and Mrs. Verney established here, in the same hotel, by the time we come home?'

'I never bet,' was Rosamond's reply. 'Will you go for the letters?'

'Oh yes, at once; only I shall be back again before you have settled which bonnet to put on.'

Rosamond smiled her reply and walked out of the room, not in the least hurried or excited, leaving Edmund to place Mrs. Cameron's work by her side, and arrange her sofa cushions.

No letters !—a circumstance which Edmund considered worthy of congratulation, as they were able to go off to the Louvre without delay. He was enthusiastic about pictures in his own way, which was not in the least that of a connoisseur. Rosamond, on the contrary, always knew beforehand what she ought to admire, and stood before Murillo's 'Assumption of the Virgin,' murmuring, just loud enough to be heard, 'Exquisite—quite exquisite !' and then professing to be unable to leave it, begged Edmund to walk through the gallery and return to her, and stationed herself in a graceful attitude of admiration with her head turned from the door. A gentleman placed himself near to her, but rather behind her. Rosamond would on no account have turned her head directly to look at him, but she moved her position a little, and as she did so Mr. Verney's voice said, 'Rosamond, are you alone ?'

Rosamond did not start, though her face flushed. She merely put her glass to her eye, to be quite sure that her brother was not near, and then turning to him, answered, 'I am alone just for these few moments. If you have anything to say privately, say it quickly. When did you come ?'

'Late last night, or early this morning rather. I told you you might expect me in Paris this week, unless you heard to the contrary. Where is Myra ?'

'At St. Wolfgang ; or, at least, she was when she last wrote.'

Rosamond was not looking at Mr. Verney, or she might have been startled at the change in his countenance. When he paused to reply, she added, 'I mentioned that Mrs. Hensman took her back with her after you were gone. What is the matter ?' She noticed his expression now.

'Nothing, nothing ! She is at St. Wolfgang, you say ? Alone, I suppose, with the Hensmans !'

'No ; that Mrs. Tracy and Miss Stuart whom she so raved about are there, with several other people ; but indeed, I told you of it all in my letter.'

'Foreign posts !' he said carelessly ; 'but she will be here soon, no doubt.'

'I can't tell anything about her precise movements, only the Hensmans are most likely going to bring her here before we leave Paris. You look so distressed I protest I shall begin to be jealous.'

'Poor little Myra!' he exclaimed; 'yes, I am very fond of her. She is such a good little thing—only too good.'

'Just what she is—too good. Her conscience-crotchets are always coming in her way. But I won't find fault with her; I know you are devoted to her. By the by, a most absurd thing happened this morning; Edmund propounded at breakfast the fact of your engagement.'

'Mine! Ours?'

Yours—not necessarily mine. I hope the Indian young lady is quite well?' and Rosamond looked at him archly, but trustingly.

His sallow cheek was quite livid as he said, 'I don't like jokes upon such subjects.'

'You like them better than earnestness, I suppose,' replied Rosamond gaily. 'If I had believed it, what would you have said?'

'That you were not what I imagined you to be. Who has sent such a report abroad?'

'I never inquired; I did not dare, or I might have betrayed myself. It only shows how much we are to believe of the world's gossip.'

'It must be put a stop to soon.' He hesitated. 'Rosamond! in six weeks' time I must be on my way to India. Are you prepared to go with me?'

It was Rosamond's turn to look grave then. She repeated, 'Only six weeks?'

'Only six weeks; it may be even less. What will your father say?'

'Ask him.'

'And if he should refuse?'

'Ask him again.'

Mr. Verney was silent, and Rosamond continued: 'I don't foresee the objection; I don't see what there is to object to. My father knows I must marry.'

'It might be better to have an advocate,' said Mr. Verney; 'my aunt would take our part.'

'But you have insisted upon secrecy; you have urged it.'

'Up to this time; but things are changed. Rosamond, I must be married immediately, or not at all.'

'Immediately meaning in six weeks' time?' said Rosamond.

'Yes. The world is so absurd about these matters, otherwise one might just manage the matter one's own way, and ask permission when the deed was done.'

His tone was light, and Rosamond answered in the same style: 'Thank you. To be married privately, as if I was ashamed of what I was doing! No congratulations, no presents—only grave looks and reproaches. Where is the love that would be worth such a sacrifice?'

'Where, indeed?' he replied bitterly. 'But, Rosamond, if your father should refuse his consent?'

'A very large "if," and a very unlikely one, as I have always told you. I would have asked him long ago but for your mysterious reasons for delay, which I never could understand.'

'Still, if he should refuse, what would you do?'

'I will answer the question when he has refused; all I say now is, try him.'

'When?'

'To-day.'

Mr. Verney shook his head.

'Are you a coward?' exclaimed Rosamond rather indignantly. 'Then let me try him.'

'My poor darling! so ignorant, so imprudent!' Mr. Verney's caressing, patronising manner for the moment awed Rosamond with an idea of some unknown danger. He continued in the same tone: 'But leave it to me, Rosamond; leave it to me, trust me. And you may trust my aunt; that at least will be a comfort to you.'

'If I want comfort,' said Rosamond petulantly. 'But I see no occasion to trust any one except ourselves.'

'I do; and I must be the judge.'

'As you will,' was the light reply. 'If the end can be gained, I give up the question of means—here is Edmund.' And moving away with her quiet graceful step, Rosamond went up to her brother to express her surprise that Mr. Verney should so unexpectedly have returned to Paris.

CHAPTER XXXVI.

'My dear Charles, and you are really engaged to that sweet girl ! Indeed I congratulate you.' Mrs. Verney took her nephew's hand in both hers, and looked inexpressible satisfaction.

'I did as you bade me,' was the slightly sarcastic reply, and Mr. Verney withdrew his hands, and took care to place them so that they could not again be seized.

'She is indeed a charming creature, full of grace and animation ; and such a temper ! absolutely unruffled. The world will only go too smoothly with you both. My theory, I confess, is that the union of two dispositions, equally disposed to glide down the current of life rather than to battle with it, is not desirable for the wellbeing of either ; but in this instance I own I am in fault. Your noble manliness, my dear Charles, will be a support to her feminine weakness ; and when storms come, and of course they will come, you will naturally confide in and understand each other. It is indeed a refreshing prospect.'

'I wish I could think it so,' was the answer.

'Ah ! you are morbid. But that has to do with health. I know you always foresee difficulties.'

'I do not merely foresee them ; they are present,' he replied ; 'I must leave England in six weeks' time, and I must be married, if I am married at all, in a month. Mr. Cameron will never consent, and I believe I was a fool not to think twice before I committed myself.'

'Oh! fie, fie! A man in love to talk so! Faint heart never won fair lady. I am ashamed of you.'

'If Rosamond had the courage, or the love which she professes to have,' observed Mr. Verney, sinking languidly into a chair, 'we should avoid all scenes and all difficulties, by not troubling ourselves about consent. When the deed is done, consent is always ready. But she likes the fuss of a public wedding, which I detest.'

Mrs. Verney laughed. 'What a naughty man you are! The idea of suggesting a private wedding because you hate a public one. No wonder Rosamond is frightened at you. But what is all this terrible difficulty?'

'Merely that Mr. Cameron is a strait-laced prig,' said Mr. Verney; 'and will have his daughter wooed and won in regular order, for which I have neither time nor patience.'

'Very right in Mr. Cameron. Quite consistent with his sense of propriety and decorum; but I suppose you foresee no real objection?'

Do you?' Mr. Verney raised himself a little, and listened somewhat eagerly for the answer.

'Well! I will not absolutely undertake to say there will be none. Objections are fashionable. A marriage without them would be *hors de régle.* As Shakespeare says, "The course of true love never did run smooth," and the world is determined it never shall. But I see none which would be insuperable.'

'And those which are not insuperable, will be what?'

'My dear Charles, what a singular question! You can answer yourself much better than I can.'

'Money,' said Mr. Verney.

'Money, alas! the root of all evil.'

'And settlements.'

'And settlements, as you say. But with Rosamond's prospects, and your Indian income, there can be no ultimate difficulty on that score, though there may be a certain amount of hesitation. I should suppose that your health might be a matter of uneasiness. It might compel you again to leave India.'

'And in the meantime Mrs. Fitzgerald will die,' said Mr. Verney, 'and we shall be able to live comfortably in England.'

'Very true! quite unanswerable indeed; except that lawyers are not fond of contingencies. But you would be able to come forward with a settlement of your own, independent of your professional income.'

Mr. Verney was silent.

'I understand,' continued Mrs. Verney, with a meaning smile; 'slightly encumbered! most single men are. They want wives to teach them economy. But Mr. Cameron is not a grasping man. When he sees it is a case of real affection, a real union of hearts, he will not stand out upon the question of a few thousands, knowing, as he must know, what Rosamond has in store.'

'I should like to be certain of it,' said Mr. Verney.

'Then, my dear Charles, make up your mind to take the only step by which to obtain certainty. Communicate upon the subject at once with Mr. Cameron.'

'It will not be possible at once. He is so steeped in prejudice, so anti-Verney politically, that I shall have to fight a pitched battle upon the question of marriage at all, before we even approach the matter of settlements. And it might all be avoided,' he added in a lower tone. 'It is nothing but a woman's delight in the frippery of a public wedding.'

'Hush! hush! I can't have you talk so: you forget what the world would say.'

'The world would talk for a day, and then it would forget,' was his reply.

'But, my dear Charles, you are merely joking, and the thing is an absurdity, an impossibility. It would be out of the question for me to help you, if you had any idea of the kind. You must see at once I should be compelled to ignore the whole proceeding. So improper, so highly improper it would be!'

'Highly improper, but particularly satisfactory,' observed Mr. Verney, in a tone which left it uncertain whether he was in jest or earnest.

'You really alarm me, Charles. I feel quite afraid of mixing myself up with an affair which may have such a doubtful char-

acter,' exclaimed Mrs. Verney. 'I never knew you so disposed
to set the world at defiance before. But if you are in such
terror of Mr. Cameron's frown, why not leave the matter to
me? or at least let me sound him? I am not afraid.'

'You are not going to ask to marry his daughter,' said Mr.
Verney, throwing himself back in his chair, with the comfortable
sigh of a tired man, who has suddenly found out a position of
rest. 'I am not at all sure that you would not state the matter
much better than I should myself. You have but to convince
him that he need not turn liberal because his daughter marries
a Verney; and as to settlements'—— he paused.

'Ten thousand he will think very little,' said Mrs. Verney,
'but that, if I remember rightly, was all you originally had.'

'You must make him contented with less,' was the reply.

Mrs. Verney shook her head, and then murmured to herself,
'Certainly, there is the professional income, and a retiring pen-
sion after due service. He ought to be satisfied.'

'Afraid, like myself, I perceive,' said Mr. Verney, with a
languid and rather amused smile.

The suggestion touched Mrs. Verney's pride in her manœuvring powers. 'It would be for the first time in my life then,'
she exclaimed. 'If I might be permitted to give my experience,
I should say that what is commonly termed moral cowardice
is more frequently found in your sex than in mine.'

'And women rush in where angels fear to tread,' he replied.
'Forgive the false metre. But I grant you have the courage of
ignorance.'

'Ignorance or knowledge, it stands us in good stead; and I
find as a rule that you gentlemen are extremely glad to avail
yourselves of it. But, my dear Charles, in the present instance
you do not need to be assured that my best efforts will be
exerted in your behalf. To see you and that sweet girl united,
would be a repayment for any anxiety. You believe me?' and
again Mr. Verney's hand, which had been incautiously placed
in a position of danger, was seized, and a murmured 'God bless
you!' completed the interview.

CHAPTER XXXVII.

SADLY and monotonously day after day wore away in the sick-room of the good old rector of Yare. Sadly, at least, to all but to him, who was the one object of sorrow. It was such a quiet, painless sinking to rest after the work of life was done, that no one could with reason wish that circumstances should be altered. Dr. Kingsbury had outlived his generation : there were others more active and original, with feelings more in accordance with the spirit of the age, waiting to take his place ; and none could venture to say that a change might not be beneficial to the parish. The old Doctor himself felt it, and said it. In moments when he could be roused to conversation, he pointed out his own deficiencies with a clearness which was a new revelation to the single-hearted Mr. Baines, accustomed to regard his rector with a reverence that had scarcely allowed him to face the possibility even of a mistake in his judgment. But there was something about to be taken away which no talent, or zeal, or originality could supply; something which was embodied not in the quaintness of the old rector's dress, or the abstruseness of his sermons, but in the firmly-grounded quiet consistency of life and teaching, with which no peculiar opinions of his own had ever been permitted to interfere.

Whether our principles of action are to be governed by 'we,' or by 'I,'—by collective and traditional, or by individual judgment—is in fact a question which we must all, in one form or another, be called upon to debate at every step in life. At Yare, the 'we' was passing away with Dr. Kingsbury, and there were those who, although unconscious of the cause, grieved over the loss with a yearning regret, which seemed almost disproportioned to the termination of an earthly existence already unusually prolonged.

And there was one to whom the old man's death would prove not only the breaking up of hallowed ties, but, so far as human eyes could judge, the entire wreck of happiness. Every one spoke of, pitied, and felt for Mrs. Patty; yet Mrs. Patty was perhaps the only person, except the Doctor himself, who could allude to the approaching parting with perfect calmness.

After that first pang, kept to herself, or acknowledged only to God, Mrs. Patty never once shrank from the sorrow that lay in her path, never once tried to deceive either herself or others respecting it. It was strange to hear her mention it, strange, at least, to those who had been accustomed to put aside the thought of death—to look upon it as a fearful mystery, only to be hinted at.

'When you are gone, Doctor, dear,' she would say to her brother, 'so and so must be done;' and then the old man would smile, and answer; 'Yes, Patty, quite true,' and proceed to give his advice as calmly as though he had been speaking of things dependent upon a common journey. It was a great comfort to them both to be able to do so. They had been so dependent upon each other for happiness, that the idea of any separation of interests, even for a time, would have been more bitter far than the bodily parting. They had talked of where Mrs. Patty should live, and fixed upon a cottage in Yare, and calculated the expense, and even gone into details of arrangement, not at all with the idea of taking thought anxiously for the morrow, but merely from the habitual necessity of consulting and knowing each other's plans. And what would have been agony to many was soothing to the simple mind of Mrs. Patty. For, as she said, 'I shall feel I am doing right, Doctor, dear, if I have your sanction ; and if it should please God to interfere and prevent it, why then I shall feel right in giving it all up. And anyhow, doing right is all I shall have to think about for the few years, or maybe months, till we meet again.'

It seemed to those who looked on, more likely to be the latter than the former, for Mrs. Patty was much worn by her constant watching and nursing, and Faith and Betsey complained bitterly that she would fidget herself about the Doctor's dinner, and not take a mouthful herself. She was very energetic though, and kept her eye upon the parish, and knew perfectly well what was going on at the schools, and by no means lost

her interest in her neighbours ; for all these things, besides
being more or less duties, were interests to the rector, who
listened to her report of them with a pleased smile, even when
he could scarcely rouse himself to answer.

'Doctor, dear, the Camerons are coming home, you will be
glad to hear,' was the information given him one morning, as
Mrs. Patty, rather breathless, took possession of the arm-chair
opposite to that in which he was sitting propped up by pillows.

Only a smile in reply, and she went on : 'Mr. and Mrs.
Cameron, and Edmund and Rosamond, are to come first, so our
servants say ; but little Myra is left behind with some friends.'

'Then I shall not see her,' murmured the old man.

'Please God you will, Doctor, dear ; for Mr. Harrison says
you have a good deal of strength yet. The thing which
troubles me, though, is that it has got about, I can't make
out how, that Myra has been ill."

'Poor little girl ! that must be sad in a foreign land. She
has not my comforts, Patty.'

'She won't want them so much, I hope,' replied Mrs. Patty,
'for young things have a wonderful way of learning to do without what they can't have. But I should like to hear more.
The news came through Miss Greaves, and she heard it from
Mrs. De Lancey, but—isn't it time, Doctor, for you to take
your medicine ? '

'The globules will be best, Patty,' said the Doctor, and a
smile which had something almost arch in it lit up his face.

Tears started to Mrs. Patty's eyes.

' O Doctor ! and you a sane man and a good ! '

' They are least trouble, Patty.'

' And they are poison ! ' exclaimed Mrs. Patty.

' It is all a question of proportion, Patty. But I will not vex
you.'

' It is Mr. Harrison whom you will vex,' replied Mrs. Patty ;
'and I thought, Doctor, you had given up the globules since
poor Miss Medley lost her senses by them, and is never likely
to recover them.'

' So I had, Patty ; so I had. But I talked to Mr. Harrison
yesterday, and he quite agreed that his medicine did me no

good; and it has a very nauseous flavour. But I will take what you pour out. Did you say Mrs. De Lancey knew about little Myra ? I have forgotten who Mrs. De Lancey is.'

'The lady who has the school in St. John's Wood, where Juliet and Annette have been sent,' replied Mrs. Patty. 'Now' —and she handed him the medicine—'just take this. Mrs. De Lancey knows that Miss Stuart whom Myra wrote about; but you don't recollect. Ah me !'

Dr. Kingsbury leaned his head back in his chair, and his countenance showed that even this short conversation had been trying to him. Mrs. Patty took up her knitting, and they both sat silent for some time, till the Doctor looked up and said : 'Mr. Baines will be here presently for prayers.'

'At three o'clock,' replied Mrs. Patty, 'and it wants a quarter to three."

'I pray God to help little Myra, and to comfort her friends if she should be taken from them,' continued the Doctor.

'Surely we must all do that,' said Mrs. Patty; 'and it cheers me to think that little Myra loves her Saviour, and trusts Him, and so it must always be well with her, but I don't imagine though, from what I heard, that she .is so very ill. Mrs. De Lancey must have heard the news from Miss Stuart, because she is staying with Mrs. Hensman, at that odd place where Myra has been. You remember now, don't you?'

'My memory grows confused, Patty, but I think I recollect something. Was Miss Stuart a very pretty young lady?'

'Very pretty and very unhappy, from all I can hear; and what is more to me, and to you too, Doctor, they declare she is engaged to Mr. Verney. Now, what do you say to that?'

Mrs. Patty gave a triumphant glance at the rector, evidently hoping that she should excite and rouse him by the intelligence which she had with most resolute self-denial kept as a *bonne-bouche* for the last.

But the old man was too tired to be excited, and he merely answered quietly, 'Then you need not fear any more for Rosamond Cameron, Patty.'

Mrs. Patty's eyes twinkled a little impatiently. 'I should fear for her more than ever if I were her mother, for I should expect her to die of a broken heart. I never in my life heard of anything so double as Mr. Verney. Miss Greaves says that from her experience she has no faith in Indians, but I tell her that is uncharitable; and I know, Doctor, you wouldn't like me to say so.'

'Indeed not, Patty, and I am sorry that Miss Greaves should indulge so harsh a judgment. The foundation of prejudice against individuals is constantly to be found in prejudice against classes, and I beg you to tell her so from me. I wish Mr. Verney well, whomsoever he may think fit to marry.'

'Ah! Doctor, but in these days engagements don't seem to lead to marriage, and there is the difficulty of being charitable. Miss Greaves declares, and I can't help fearing she may be right, that Mr. Verney is playing false with them both; and I had it in my mind this morning to write to Mrs. Cameron and tell her what I had heard, only I did not quite know how to begin.'

'Perhaps,' said the Doctor drily, 'the young ladies may have been a little in fault, Patty. Young ladies are sometimes wrong, and as we are quite ignorant, it may be as well to divide the blame.'

Mrs. Patty shook her head, but she would not contest the point with one who, as a matter of course, always took up the side of the accused; and she merely said: 'I wish, at all events, Mr. Verney would make haste and marry some one, and then our minds might be at rest.' A remark to which the Doctor roused himself enough to answer, 'Which is more perhaps than his would be, Patty. I don't think, from what I have seen in life, that marriage is a very resting process.'

That was the conclusion of the conversation for the time, and it soon passed from Dr. Kingsbury's thoughts, but not so from Mrs. Patty's. She had so accustomed herself for years to look upon the affairs of the Cameron household as her own, that anything which affected, or was likely to affect them, was recognised at once as a personal interest, and again she pondered the possibility of addressing a warning letter to Mrs. Cameron; and being stopped as before by the insurmountable difficulty of the first sentence, satisfied herself at last by

T

anticipating a long conversation the very first day of their meeting.

'I must be patient with the poor thing, though,' said Mrs. Patty, uttering her self-admonitory thoughts aloud; 'she is quite ill, and nearly blind, and, I daresay, does not see half that goes on. Well, as poor Miss Medley used to say, men are strange—some men at least.'

Mrs. Patty's determination to postpone her letter did not interfere with the indulgence of a little natural curiosity ; and at the end of her morning's walk of inspection through the village, she turned up the road to the Hall, in order to make assurance doubly sure by inquiring the exact day when the family were expected, and whether any further tidings had been received of Myra.

The house looked—as most houses cursed even temporarily with absenteeism do look—the picture of desolation. Carpets had been taken up, curtains taken down ; whitewashers were in the kitchen, a charwoman in the scullery. Mrs. Patty nearly fell over a dust-pan in the hall, and upset a bucket on her way to the drawing-room ; and then, finding no one to give her information, made her way through a freshly-scoured passage to the housekeeper's room. But the only person to be found there was a little kitchen-maid, once a school-girl, busied in laying the cloth for Mrs. Pearson, the housekeeper's, dinner, the said Mrs. Pearson having gone out, and not being expected to return for half an hour.

'And are you left alone in the house, Fanny?" said Mrs. Patty kindly ; 'you must have enough to do.'

'Please, ma'am, the others are gone away for a holiday, but they are all coming back to-morrow.'

'So soon ! I suppose, though, you expect your master and mistress back.'

'Please, ma'am, they are to be here by the end of the week, Mrs. Pearson had a letter to-day ;' and Fanny looked up, proud of the extent of her information.

'And Miss Myra is not coming, I believe,' said Mrs. Patty.

'Mrs. Pearson did not tell me, ma'am ; she only said things were to be put right in a hurry, which is why we are so busy.

Conyers wrote to Mrs. Pearson too.' Fanny paused—it was evident she wished to be asked what Conyers had said ; and Mrs. Patty very innocently fell into the snare, and inquired if Conyers had mentioned anything more.

'Only about the wedding, please, ma'am.' Fanny simpered, and looked at Mrs. Patty's astonished face, and simpered again ; and unable to resist telling what she knew, added, 'Miss Cameron and Mr. Verney, ma'am.'

Not one word was obtained in answer from Mrs. Patty. She stood as if turned into stone, her eyes fixed upon the surprised and rather frightened girl—who, instantly conscious that she had betrayed what had been confided to her in secrecy, added, 'If you please, ma'am, I was not to say it to any one ; but Mrs. Pearson could not be angry about you. Only, if you please not to say I told it ;' and then, taking up some plates which she had just laid on the table, she hurried out of the room, not daring to trust any longer to her own prudence.

Bewilderment had been Mrs. Patty's first sensation, utter incredulity was the second. The very fact of the intelligence reaching her in such a form was conclusive against it. It was but the revival of the old report, and her own private information from Miss Greaves must be more trustworthy. But Mrs. Patty could not be satisfied with these convictions. She sat down to await the return of Mrs. Pearson, not intending to ask any questions which might betray her authority, and so cause mischief, but feeling quite sure that it would not be in the housekeeper's power to conceal the news if it really had been given her as anything more than rumour.

And so, to Mrs. Patty's dire amazement, almost the first words which were spoken by the portly Mrs. Pearson, as she came in tired from her walk and apologised for sitting down in her arm-chair, were, ' Of course, Mrs. Patty, you have heard, and I need make no secret—it has not, indeed, been told me officially, but I shall doubtless receive instructions by to-morrow's post—the wedding, Conyers assures me, must come off very soon, for Mr. Verney goes to India immediately. Poor Miss Cameron ! what a change for her, but there is no doubt she will be happy, and young ladies like to see the world ; only ne does seem rather old, Mrs. Patty, doesn't he? And then his health; I can't say I should have thought Mr. Cameron would have approved; but one never can say. We shall be so busy now. I have been down in the village trying to get help, and I can't say I have succeeded yet as I wish. The house is in terrible confusion, Mrs. Patty, as you see, and all to be ready by Friday; and the wedding to come off no one knows how soon!'

Mrs. Pearson giving an opening for an observation by a pause, Mrs. Patty asked: 'Has Mrs. Cameron written to you herself, Pearson?'

'No, ma'am, not exactly. That is to say, she sends a few lines, just to tell me what changes she wishes to have made in the boudoir; and to beg that the work-people may be hurried; for, indeed, they are terribly dilatory; but it is Conyers who gives most of the news, as might have been expected. I have no doubt, Mrs. Patty, that my mistress would have written to me herself, if she had not been coming so soon; but as they are to be here on Friday, it was to be expected that she would keep the news till then. There can be no doubt, however, of the fact—no doubt at all,' repeated Mrs. Pearson, perceiving Mrs. Patty's look of incredulity. 'I will just tell you what Conyers says, if you like to hear.' Without waiting for an answer, Mrs. Pearson dived into the depths of her pocket, and brought out the important document. 'Let me see; it is just at the beginning. "I told you in my last that I should have news for you before long. Mr. Verney and Miss Cameron have made up together at last; and we shall have a gay wedding at the Hall before many weeks are over. It is not yet publicly given out; but I don't doubt that it will be almost directly. The Colonel and Mrs. Verney are here, in the same hotel; and Mrs. Verney has had talks with my master by the hour; so I suppose there have been some difficulties. It is sad to think of poor Miss Myra being ill and away, when such things are going on; but they say she will do very well, if she is kept quite quiet; and, of course, she will be home before the wedding comes off." Then, at the postscript, there is something still more decided: "Miss Cameron has begun to talk of buying her things ; for it seems that they must sail for India next month." Was there ever anything so quick? There can be no doubt after that, you see, ma'am,' observed Mrs. Pearson, as she folded up the letter triumphantly.

Still Mrs. Patty made no reply, except to inquire if Conyers said anything more about Miss Myra?

'Only just a few words, ma'am. In the first page, I think it is. "Miss Myra was to have been here to-day ; but Mrs. Hensman has written to say that she has a kind of bilious attack, which will prevent her coming ; so she is to travel home with them all the way." '

'Thank you, Pearson,' said Mrs. Patty. 'We must hope all things will go well, both with Miss Cameron and Miss Myra.' And very greatly to the housekeeper's wonder and disappointment, Mrs. Patty wished her good morning, and left her.

CHAPTER XXXVIII.

ALONE, ill, weary at heart, troubled in conscience, Myra lay, tossing on her bed, in the least noisy room of the Baierischer Hof at Munich. One form was ever flitting before her nervous, tremulous vision—that of the wan girl who had bent over her at St. Wolfgang, and murmured : ' He is my all !' And now Myra kept close to her pillow a little box, which held a lock of dark hair and an enamelled ring ; and as she clasped it from time to time, to be certain that it was safe, the same sad voice sounded in her ears the farewell with which Charlotte Stuart had parted from her, when, in the midst of the confusion of a general departure, she had sought for one moment of privacy and confided the treasure to her care. 'Give it to him, Miss Cameron, alone. Tell him it contains his choice. He asked me for the hair ; if he should keep it, he will return to me. He gave me the ring ; if he should accept it again, he is gone for ever.' Hours had seemed days since Myra received that charge. It was in vain that Mrs. Tracy had equally urged her, in a last interview, to do and say nothing which should in the slightest degree influence Mr. Verney ; in vain she assured Myra, that for her niece's sake everything would be far better left as it was ; that a meeting would but bring pain ; that under present circumstances, a renewal of the engagement would be most unwise, if not actually wrong. The one idea pressing upon Myra's conscience was the duty of perfect openness upon all points. With her father, with Rosamond—above all, with Mr. Verney—to have no concealment or reservation. Rosamond's happiness, Mr. Verney's most dreaded anger, and the confession which she must herself make of having been in a degree party to the secret, were all put aside. She was, as it were, goaded forward by the bitterness of her disappointment in Mr. Verney, and the sting of her own self-reproach ; whilst the

tenderness and sympathy of her young heart made her feel
intuitively the mockery of her sister's professed affection compared with the passionate love of the unhappy girl, whose
misery was leading her to the verge of the grave.

Myra looked her last at St. Wolfgang—the grey mountains
and spreading forests, the white walls of the conventual house,
and the steep banks of the garden washed by the waters of the
silvery lake ; the old church, with its picturesque arcade and
tall bell-tower ; the cottages bordering the shore, and the boats
drawn up in front of them, under dark wooden sheds,—all
which she had first gazed upon as forming a scene so grand,
yet home-like, that it might make life on earth a paradise—and
felt but one wish—to be away from it, and, if possible, forget it.
But it was not to be forgotten. Myra was very young, very
inexperienced, and most lonely, and the thought now connected
with St. Wolfgang haunted her. It followed her in the long
weary journey to Salzburg ; it pressed upon her still more when
she found herself in the same hotel at which she had rested on
her journey to Ischl ; it urged her to an almost unendurable
eagerness and impatience when Mrs. Hensman proposed the
delay of two or three days, in order that they might see the
things most worthy of note in the neighbourhood ; and by the
time they had completed the railway journey to Munich, Myra
was suffering from something very like a nervous fever. Mrs.
Hensman was frightened ; the English physician perplexed.
It was said to be a bilious attack, because no one knew what
other name to give it. But one thing was clear, that excitement and fatigue were equally to be avoided ; and Mrs. Hensman, in her almost daily bulletins to Paris, entreated that the
letters in answer might contain nothing which should in the
least disturb Myra, or aggravate the feverish desire to be at
home, which it was so impossible to satisfy. Not that there
was any danger—the doctor assured them again and again that
there was not the slightest cause for alarm. Rest and quiet
were all that would be needed, and in a few days—a week,
probably, at the utmost—they might hope to move again.

Rest and quiet ! What prescription is more frequently given,
or more easily acquiesced in ? Mrs. Hensman, indeed, was

quite relieved to think that things were no worse ; but Myra turned her head aside, and felt too stony-hearted for tears, and too irritable and wretched for speech.

Griefs and trials are all matters of comparison ; we are apt to overlook this as we grow old. When we have faced the great battle of life, and learnt to stand alone in the conflict, looking but to Heaven for aid, we can scarcely recall the trembling, almost agonised hopelessness with which we gazed around, searching for human guidance, when, in the Providence of God, we were first brought into a position of difficulty and left to act according to our own discretion, with our faith in the judgment of others shaken, and our confidence in ourselves—nought. And this was Myra's trial, as it is the trial of hundreds who, like her, have within themselves the power and the will to act rightly and fearlessly, but whose faults have hidden from themselves the strength of their own characters.

God's system of education is very unlike man's. He does with us what we should never venture to do with ourselves. Man must guide, and check, and make definite rules, and map out the lines of duty ; God places us where there seems to be no guidance, no definite law—where rules are intricate, and the path of duty is vague : and when, in our weakness, we would fain find support in the wisdom of an idol of our own uprearing, He dashes it to the ground, and leaves us standing powerless and alone to work out our career for ourselves. So, at least, we say. Whether the complaint be true—whether we are really to be powerless and alone, is the question which must, for the most part, be determined for each of us by the spirit in which we meet that first trial. As the horses and chariots of fire, though hidden from mortal sight, guarded the prophet of old, so the strength and the wisdom of God are guarding the children of His love, though their eyes are blinded and they cannot know it. Alone, yet not alone ; perplexed, yet secretly guided ; weak, yet strong with a strength which the bravest of worldly hearts might envy ;—it needs but one prayer of steadfast faith, one fervent appeal to the boundless wisdom, the unwearying sympathy, which have been theirs long, long before

they have learnt to seek them—and discouragement has
loosened its chilling hold, and the young heart springs upwards
with a vigour of purpose, a noble consciousness of power, which
is worth all the aid and all the direction that the wisest of
earthly friends could bestow. True, indeed, it is a trial which
not all can stand. There are those who must be tended and
advised at each step, and for them God most mercifully provides
the outward helps which are essential. And there are others
also, who, reckless in their self-confidence, seeing no help from
their fellow-creatures, and not caring to seek it from God,
rush forward blindly to their destruction ; but it is not the
less true that the highest natures, those most fitted to exercise responsibility and be the leaders of thought and action,
whether in public or in private, are in most instances trained
apart by God, through the direct orderings of His Providence,
without the intervention of man. Little do they know at the
time of the aim and purpose of their lives. Whilst struggling
with difficulty, and disheartened by the sense of their own
infirmity, little can they feel of the steadfastness of purpose, the
clearness of judgment, which they are hourly gaining. It is
only when looking back—possibly after many years, possibly
at the very close of life, with the blessed assurance of victory
won, and the glorious crown already in sight,—that they can
venture to recall the difficulties of that season of peril. Then
indeed will they look up to God with humble thankfulness,—
acknowledging that He who hath done all things well is in this
most worthy of humblest gratitude, that, by leaving them
destitute of human support, He compelled them to cast themselves upon Him.

But those thoughts were far off from Myra in her sick-
chamber in a foreign land. As she lay restless upon her bed,
and so feverish that she was unable to collect her ideas, it
seemed an impossibility to settle what was to be done, or how.
At one moment she determined to write to Mr. Verney ; but
the inexperienced girl of sixteen writing to the man of forty—
and such a man, so clever, so sarcastic, so well versed in the
ways of the world!—it was a task for which she felt herself
buite unfitted ! And what could she say to him ? How could

she express herself? In what way could she appeal to him? Admiration, awe, even something like respect, still kept their hold upon her. The idol was not quite shattered, and in Myra's secret heart there lingered the hope, though scarcely the belief, that some undreamt-of explanation would restore it to its former perfection. No; she could not write to him and accuse him. Or again, she would write to her father, her mother; she would consult Dr. Kingsbury; she would speak to Mrs. Hensman. But it was a question of honour. Mr. Verney had confided his engagement, trusting to her secrecy. Charlotte Stuart had given her confidence in the tone and spirit of one who knew that it would not be betrayed. There was only one thing to be done—she must see Mr. Verney and talk to him. He was always so kind to her, so sympathising; he would understand the pain she suffered, he would forgive her; and he might—yes, she ought to believe and expect it—he might explain his conduct. And then Myra went through the interview in her own mind, feeling herself all the humiliation which she believed Mr. Verney would feel, and then imagining his answer, and being crushed with shame by the discovery that she had been guilty of a most unjustifiable accusation. Or else, —supposing it all true, and picturing to herself his anger and scorn, and Rosamond's distress, and in all probability the necessity of applying to her father, and confessing not only Mr. Verney's misdeeds, but her own share in the concealment. Myra trembled at the prospect, and at last remembered there was a third alternative—to let everything take its course. The engagement with Charlotte Stuart, as Mrs. Tracy acknowledged, was virtually at an end. Why, then, was she to trouble herself with it? The pecuniary affairs were in no way her concern. What could she know about them? No doubt her father would make due inquiries, and if he was satisfied, what right had she to suggest suspicions of Mr. Verney's integrity? She might write to Charlotte Stuart and say, that upon consideration she felt that it would be better not to interfere personally between her and Mr. Verney, and therefore, the ring and the hair should either be sent back, or else forwarded with a note from Miss Stuart herself, as soon as she reached England.

To adopt this alternative was a sore temptation, resisted, returning, resisted again, and even then not overcome, but only adding to Myra's physical and mental disturbance, though still the innate truth and strength of her character compelled her to see that the difficulty lay not in the conflicting claims of duty, but in the necessity of rousing her moral courage. If she had not feared Mr. Verney, she would have felt no perplexity ; whilst, however she might reason upon the various results of her possible decision, one thing was clear : that the consequences of human actions are uncertain, and therefore can never be a safe rule of right. It took a long time before Myra perceived the force of this axiom, self-evident though it is. It dawned upon her only by degrees ; it might have been the answer to her intensely earnest and perfectly sincere prayer, and even then the shrinking timidity of her woman's nature made her long to put it aside. It was too rigid ; it made too little allowance for circumstances or human infirmity ; and though at sixteen Myra could not reason upon its strictness, yet she felt it. Even when at length, after arguing and counter-arguing, it stood out clear, and she saw that there was no escape from it, and that it must lead her to speak openly to Mr. Verney at whatever cost of pain, she acquiesced in it with a hesitating submission, very unlike the assured satisfaction of mature age, when once it has arrived at a decision, and feels that that decision is right.

Strong in will, impulsive and passionate in feeling, alarmed at the consciousness of her own force of character, Myra could have thrown herself unreservedly upon any guidance which came before her with a claim of authority ; and at the moment when she most needed it, she had nothing to aid her but the still small voice which none can hear save the upright in heart.

God help those who stifle it, for it is a voice which, when once unheeded, grows fainter and fainter, until at length it fails to be distinguished from the subtleties of human reasoning.

CHAPTER XXXIX.

AND while all this conflict of thought was wearing away Myra's strength at Munich, what was the state of Mr. Cameron's household at Paris?

The news of Myra's illness had been received with very varied feelings. Mr. Cameron, annoyed at not being able precisely to carry out the plans formed, in his own opinion, with consummate wisdom, felt—as he often did feel when things went wrong—that somehow the world might be improved by being governed differently. Mrs. Cameron had from anxiety an attack of nerves, which made her more dependent upon Rosamond than usual, and therefore more inclined to miss and want Myra. Edmund, with a dawning suspicion that Rosamond was not quite open in all her actions, was vexed at not being able to talk out his uneasiness with the sister who, though so much younger than himself, had lately been peculiarly congenial to him. Rosamond, though expressing publicly a due amount of disappointment, was not sure whether she was glad to be freed from Myra's scruples, or sorry to lose her sympathy; and Mr. Verney felt as if an intolerable load had for the time been removed from his shoulders, and was only anxious to make use of the breathing space allowed him before Myra's presence—full as she would be of St. Wolfgang and its guests—should increase the awkwardness and the risk of his position.

So it was that Mrs. Verney, urged on by her own delight in the exercise of her manœuvring powers, and by her nephew's indolent impatience, determined at once to break the ice, and bring before Mr. Cameron's mind the first idea of the marriage. She had never been more careful or exercised more delicate tact. She was not, of course, to propose in Mr. Verney's name ; that would have been taking from him his man's privilege and position. She was only to insinuate, to sound, to suggest the idea, and then propound the difficulties herself, instead of allowing Mr. Cameron to do so ; and in that way to awaken a spirit of contradiction on the right side. By raising imaginary objections, she was to exercise his skill in knocking them down with the decisive blow which a man always delights to aim at a woman's weak argument. When by this means she had en- listed his temper and his pride on the side of her secret wishes, she was quietly to retire from the field, and leave it open to Mr. Verney to come forward and make the direct attack, which she prophesied must, after such a preparation, be immediately successful.

Poor Mr. Verney ! he had never felt more grateful to any one in his life. His was an unutterably mean position, and he was not mean by nature. To plan a deception, to carry it on con- sistently, was not a pleasure to him as it was to Rosamond. He had been a gentleman once, in the world's sense of the epithet, and he could not as yet realise the fact that he was not one still. He might break a heart—that was quite consistent with the most refined feelings—but he could not deliberately go and declare himself possessed of a good professional income and a tolerable private fortune, when he knew that in strict justice he had not at that moment a penny which he could call his own. It was a most happy suggestion for him that Mrs. Verney should first introduce these dangerous topics. She would do it in perfect good faith. She might utter unnumbered falsehoods, but they would to her own mind be truth ; and Mr. Verney's task would then for the most part be limited to a mere confirmation of her statements. A positive declaration is one thing, an assent is another, at least in the eyes of a moral coward ; and as Mr. Verney reposed upon the velvet couch in his aunt's *salon*, and listened to her report of the various con- versations which were held, and the progress which the affair was making, he became at length so fascinated by Mrs. Verney's description of his prospects, as she had placed them before Mr. Cameron, that the truth faded gradually more and more from his mind ; and before the day of trial arrived he was able to face the awkward demands of his false position with a boldness which, in a better cause, would have been quite exemplary.

All this was extremely hard upon Mr. Cameron, so very unsuspicious as he was, having his eyes so carefully blinded by the veil of his own supreme self-idolatry. How was such a man to suppose that he could possibly be taken in on the question of his daughter's marriage? Other persons might blunder, might act hastily, might be influenced by unworthy motives, or, what was yet more likely, might be such fools as to be weakly won over to consent to what their better wisdom disapproved. But Mr. Cameron!—why, he had no passions, no prejudices—he was absolutely untouched by the ordinary infirmities of human nature. Let the whole world be wrong, yet he must be right; and when he said 'yes,' the man would be an idiot who should venture to declare that he ought to have said 'no!'

The idea of woman's influence in such a case was an absurdity. Look at the way Mr. Cameron ruled his wife; look at her almost abject submission, her utter prostration of conscience and intellect before the shrine of his supreme authority. Listen to him when he spoke of women generally. Watch with what dignified courtesy he quietly put their opinions aside whenever they differed from him; how blandly sarcastic he was in manner; how politely compassionate to their physical weakness; how patronising to their intellectual powers. One might as well have imagined a man in full possession of his powers allowing himself to be directed by an infant in long clothes, as Mr. Cameron in any way directed by a woman!

Mr. Cameron had indeed begun his short residence in Paris with a strong determination to keep the two families apart, but when a man is conscious of his own strength of purpose inwardly, he can afford to be a little inconsistent outwardly. A most benevolent desire to give his friends the benefit of his infallible judgment induced him to listen complacently when Mrs. Verney complained of the noise of the hotel they had chosen, and asked his opinion as to the desirableness of taking rooms elsewhere. It would have been quite unkind to throw off a person who evidently trusted so much to his wisdom, especially as the

Colonel was worse than ignorant in all matters appertaining of foreign life, and uttered his few words of French with a vehemence of false accent quite excruciating to Mr. Cameron's most correct ear. Mr. Cameron had chosen the best apartments in the best situation for himself, and he could not possibly avoid stating the fact. It would have been unfair to himself not to have done so, for with his reserved, rather stiff style of conversation, which was not at all egotistical in small matters, the world might otherwise have remained ignorant of the perfection of his travelling arrangements.

It was quite natural for Mrs. Verney to exclaim in reply : ' The best in Paris ! then there can be no hope for us of anything but second-best ; but yours is such a charming situation. Is it absolutely impossible, do you think, to find apartments in the same hotel ? '

Doubtless Mr. Cameron might have thrown cold water upon the idea, and would have done so, if this had been all, but when Mrs. Verney added, ' To be under the same roof with you would be everything to us—your advice would be so invaluable ; ' the assertion was so entirely in accordance with Mr. Cameron's own views, that he really could not help admitting it, and as a necessary result felt himself bound in conscience to further the plan.

Thus Mrs. Verney established herself *au second*, and when the unhappy Colonel, oppressed by the weight of sixty years, and constantly threatening gout, toiled and panted up the endless stairs, and wondered why on earth she had brought him to such a tower of Babel, she sweetly smiled, and drew his easy chair to the window, and bade him rest and enjoy himself with the charming view, and the columns of the ' Times,' and then glided away to a few moments' enlivening chat with her ' dear Mrs. Cameron,' ending, as opportunity offered, with a request for a little advice from her ' excellent Mr. Cameron.'

The little advice became a lengthened conversation ; the lengthened conversation did its work, and at length the die was cast. After a short and somewhat embarrassed interview, in which Mr. Verney told no actual falsehood himself, and only implied that the statements Mrs. Verney had made were in the main correct, he was allowed to seek Rosamond, in order, as it was supposed, to communicate to her for the first time the state of his feelings.

Rosamond, when afterwards summoned to Mr. Cameron, played her part with the most perfect grace and simplicity. She was modestly shy, deeply touched by her father's kindness and generosity of feeling, and finally brought to the confession that he had made her supremely happy;—and so the engagement was acknowledged.

When the fact was announced to Mrs. Verney, she poured forth a torrent of congratulations and approval, quite sufficient to convince Mr. Cameron that he had acted—as indeed, how could he have done otherwise?—the part of a tender, watchful, wise, self-sacrificing parent.

'My dear Mr. Cameron, you have been only too good in this matter. I could not have expected as much in a similar case from the Colonel. He, you know, though most excellent, allows himself at times to be carried away by political feeling, until the claims of private life are unfortunately ignored. But you are so calm, so far-seeing, so raised above all petty rivalries. Your dear child's happiness is to you so superior to every other consideration. And my dear nephew ! you have raised him to the very summit of felicity.'

'Mr. Verney confesses himself deeply attached to my daughter, and expresses great satisfaction at the prospect of a union with my family,' said Mr. Cameron, raising his head so as to show the full height of his very stiff cravat. 'I could have wished, Mrs. Verney, that some things had been different, but I waive the objections. I have considered them, and I waive them.'

'Ah ! most kind ! most unworldly ! would that there were more like you ! We should not then so often see young people's happiness wrecked by considerations of mere interest.'

'My dear madam, understand me. I cannot look upon these questions as you ladies do. An *affaire du cœur* (Mr. Cameron was always pleased to bring in a French expression that he might give his hearers a lesson in pronunciation) is to you, I am well aware, one of primary importance, and, pardon me for saying that it sometimes engrosses your sympathies so as somewhat to warp your judgment. The reverse is the case with me. I wish to consider my daughter's feelings, but I should be wrong to act without reference to her material interests. If I were to do so, I should ultimately sacrifice both.'

'Most true,' replied Mrs. Verney. 'The old proverb, "When poverty comes in at the door, love flies out at the window," is I fear but too true.'

'Proverbs, my dear madam, contain the wisdom of ages. That which you have so aptly quoted is a remarkable example of this statement, and acting upon it, I could not of course listen to your nephew's proposal without fully weighing the position in which my daughter would be placed as his wife. Now, I freely own that this is not in all respects such as I have been in the habit of contemplating for her. Rosamond is singularly endowed ; she must command admiration. I might have anticipated for her a brilliant position,—rank, fortune, social, even political influence. But, my dear Mrs. Verney, I have lived to see the instability of human greatness ; I have learned to rise superior to it. When you so candidly pointed out to me the objections to the union, I saw them. I was indeed more alive to them than you could possibly have been yourself; but I reasoned thus. If, I said, I interpose to prevent this marriage, the responsibility of my daughter's happiness will for the future rest upon me. Am I prepared to accept it ? This was my question, a very important one, as you will no doubt admit ; and I answered it in the negative. Then again you suggested the awkwardness which might arise from the different views which the Colonel and myself are apt to take of political subjects. I could not deny your statements. I know that in the generality of cases political differences are likely to become private differences, but I felt—forgive me for saying so —I felt that yours were the fears of your sex, accustomed as they are to be governed by impulse. I have no fears for myself, my dear madam. I am confident—not, I hope and believe, too confident—of my own self-control ; and I may safely engage, that however vehemently Colonel Verney may think fit to ex-

U

press his dissent from my opinions, I shall always receive that dissent with calmness, and shall never permit it to interfere with the courtesies which the union of the two families may demand. There remained then only one point for consideration ; and here again I give you full credit for the openness with which you expressed your alarm lest the income which Mr. Verney could offer, might not be sufficient to provide my daughter with the luxuries to which she has been accustomed. I granted the correctness and the weight of your calculations, but I felt bound to place in the opposite scale the fact that these luxuries were not absolutely essential. I considered, and I believe I was justified in considering, that if Mr. Verney could offer but a comparatively small income for a few years, yet the experience of those few years might be ultimately beneficial to Rosamond by giving her habits of economy ; and I know that, should your nephew's health be spared, as I trust it may, the income of a civil appointment must increase, whilst my daughter (though she is not aware of the fact) is certain to receive a considerable increase of fortune by the death of her aunt. I confided this fact to you in secrecy, but it naturally held a foremost place in my deliberations. The result was as you know ; I sacrificed private feelings, and what might perhaps be called a justifiable ambition for my child, and have given her to the man of her choice. The world may disapprove ; perhaps it will, but I have acted considerately, prudently, conscientiously, and I am satisfied.'

'Indeed you have reason to be.' Mrs. Verney was so affected by Mr. Cameron's touching summing up of his own merits, that her voice actually faltered, and to spare the betrayal of her weakness, she had recourse to a tender pressure of the hand. And Mr. Cameron himself was for the moment almost unmanned. It was rarely he received such winning sympathy ; and when Mrs. Verney softly murmured, 'We understand each other ; now let us go to your dear wife,' he really did feel that to purchase such true appreciation of his virtues, he could admit to terms of brotherly intimacy, not only the passionate Colonel, but even the motley crew of Liberals, his political followers, upon whom, when the door of his chamber was closed, and the world was not near to listen, Mr. Cameron was apt to bestow epithets which it would be by no means seemly to repeat.

One great point was gained, but there were two others, almost equally important to be attempted. The first to induce Colonel Verney to recognise the proposed alliance graciously, so as not to offend Mr. Cameron's pride, and the second to hasten the marriage before any obstacles could arise to prevent it. The former was Mrs. Verney's task, and she felt now the full benefit of the conversation by which she had so prudently prepared her husband's mind for what was to come. The outburst of contradiction with which, as a rule, Colonel Verney considered it incumbent upon him to receive all propositions, had already in some degree had its vent. What remained could very well be borne by Mrs. Verney, certain as she was of ultimately bringing him round to her own views. With admirable discretion she carried him off to Versailles the very day of his nephew's proposal, and did not allow him to hear of what had taken place till they were comfortably settled in their hotel, with a quiet day before them. Having him then completely in her own power, she broke the intelligence gradually, agreed with him in seeing all the disagreeables, listened with exemplary patience to his recapitulation of everything Mr. Cameron had ever said or done to annoy him, and at length so soothed him, that by the following morning he was in a condition to take upon himself the part of forgiving and forgetting, which best suited his really generous disposition, and to write a cordial note to Mr. Cameron, accepting the marriage with a very good grace.

Mr. Verney's business, that of hastening the marriage, was more difficult.

The idea of India had not hitherto been a serious objection to the marriage in Mr. Cameron's mind, because he had looked forward to it in the distance. An event which might take place some time in the next year gave leisure for preparation, and Mr. Cameron could accept most changes with equanimity so long as his dignity was not disturbed by his being hurried. But to be told that Rosamond must be married, and ready to leave England in a month's time, would be an announcement the effect of which no one could calculate. He had so far accepted the new state of affairs as to acquiesce in the proposal that they should go home at once, but this was merely a concession to feminine weakness.

'Ladies,' as, with a patronising smile, he observed to Mrs. Verney, 'ladies are apt to be excited by the prospect of a wedding. They believe that it involves an amount of work which cannot be completed under many weeks. I see no cause for such haste myself. The marriage is as yet only an indefinite idea for the future. We shall have full time for a consideration of the details when the event is fixed. At present I should suggest that little might be said about it. It involves gossip, my dear Mrs Verney; and gossip, as you will agree with me, is objectionable. Still, as to our return, I give in. In Mrs. Cameron's state of health I should be sorry to disturb her, and she fancies that it is necessary to be at home; therefore I give in.'

These very vague notions of time were of most serious moment to Mr. Verney. He had made retreat impossible, and all that remained for him was to carry out his plans boldly and speedily, for always in the background was a vision of Myra returning from St. Wolfgang with remarks, suspicions, and questions, which he might not be able to parry, and which might risk the loss of all that he had sacrificed honour to obtain. And Mr. Verney's position as regarded Rosamond was by no means happy or satisfactory. Whilst he had been uncertain of obtaining his prize, there had been a little excitement in striving for it. Doubt as to whether she cared for him had roused his vanity, and served as an incentive to the efforts he made to please her; and when first secretly engaged, they were separated, and had no opportunity of trying each other's tastes, or testing the stability of their professed affection. But once acknowledged as Mr. Verney's affianced bride, and Rosamond was fully determined to enjoy all the privileges of her condition. They are privileges which a woman can never enjoy twice, for a second marriage must, of course, be quite matter-of-fact, compared with a first. To be idolised, and made the centre of attraction, though only for a few weeks, must be a most tempting pre-eminence for many. Rosamond delighted in worship, and worship she was resolved to have. She was the most sweet and gentle-mannered of tyrants, but she allowed her slave no rest. Mr. Verney, intensely indolent, devoted to self-gratification, roused only by the interest of literature or art, was called upon to accompany Rosamond in her walks and drives ; to wait for hours whilst she was making her little purchases, to take part in discussions upon dress, to pay visits to tiresome people, to give up everything which had a tendency to occupy his exclusive attention ; and if he showed the slightest symptoms of rebellion, to receive a shower of complaints, quiet, but sharp as the quills of a porcupine, which perhaps only feminine irritation could invent ; and which were all the more unendurable because, though aimed at random, they were sure to strike upon that one point—the sincerity of professed affection—in which Mr. Verney was defenceless.

He was to be pitied. He might have been open to contempt if the world had known the truth ; but he was much more to be pitied. He had never deliberately intended to sin against truth and honour ; he had drifted away from them—that was all. The currents of life had been too strong for him, and his very talents had hidden the fact from him. So keen and vivid in his perceptions when he chose to exert them ; so quick in seizing the negative on all subjects—in seeing what ought *not* to have been said or done ; so cleverly cynical ; so courteous, even when he withered with his censure, it had never once struck him that the least, the very least, practical effort after goodness, even let it be never so great a failure, is better and nobler than the most clear-sighted view of human imperfections, or the most eloquent criticism upon human plans. His words had been a veil to his deeds throughout his whole life ; but words have no power over feelings, and still, in the secrecy of his heart, Mr. Verney's thoughts reverted to the sorrow-stricken girl, brought face to face with the destiny of misery which he had himself prepared for her, and which, in his better moments, he would even now have averted from her, at any sacrifice short of the courage required to draw back instead of to go on. For Mr. Verney was no monster of wickedness and cruelty. There was much good about him—

not *in* him, but *about* him—hovering near, overshadowing his
faults, but not making its home in his heart.   Yet he did not do
the less evil; and now, because he felt that to stand still was a
greater danger than to advance, his very cowardice made him
bold; and four days after the engagement was first recognised,
he suddenly announced to Mr. Cameron that, from private information, he was led to expect a recall to India almost immediately,
and that, under these circumstances, he was compelled to press
the question of an immediate marriage.   If a delay could afterwards be obtained, Rosamond would be able to remain with
her own family until the last moment, but the marriage itself
was a necessity.   Mr. Verney blundered in using that word
'necessity.'   Mr. Cameron was far too elevated above the rest of
mankind to recognise any necessity but his own will, and the
inadvertence caused Mr. Verney a two hours' argument, ending
very nearly in a complete rupture.   It was only through the aid
of Mrs. Verney's flatteries that he again carried the day, and
left Mr. Cameron satisfied with the conviction, so dear to his
self-appreciation, that he was, as usual, acting the part of a
paternal martyr.

They started for England, and Rosamond was to be married
in three weeks.

CHAPTER XL

'A LETTER for you, Myra,' said Mrs. Hensman, coming into Myra's room at Munich before the latter was dressed, and laying before her a very English-looking document, directed in a large legible hand. Mrs. Hensman had no fear of the exciting contents of that letter; it certainly did not come from home; the handwriting belonged neither to Mrs. Cameron nor Rosamond, and they had been Myra's only correspondents for the last fortnight. Besides, if it were not so, Myra was better and stronger, and they were talking of leaving Munich, and it would be impossible then to keep from her the intelligence which had been conveyed to Mrs. Hensman, a few days previous, that Rosamond was engaged to Mr. Verney. And really it did not seem there could be any reason for making a mystery of it. Rosamond and Mrs. Cameron had indeed both written anxiously, entreating that Myra might not be informed of it until she was quite strong, as it was likely to excite her too much; but Mrs. Hensman did not understand the excitement of young ladies about anything except their own marriage, or some subject connected with it, and she gave the newly-arrived letter to Myra, in the full belief that, whatever might be its contents, it would do her good rather than harm. And certainly, to judge from Myra's exclamation and smile of delight, Mrs. Hensman had judged wisely.

'From Mrs. Patty! How very good of her! Please, dear Mrs. Hensman, open the blinds; I am so much obliged to you for bringing it.'

Myra was much altered, even from that short illness. Her features had a thin sharp look, and her eyes were almost painfully bright. And she was very nervous too;

her hand trembled so much that she could not open the letter herself.   If Mrs. Hensman had been a more diligent observer of human nature, she might have remarked these symptoms, and wondered at their cause ; but she had one explanation for all phases of illness—fatigue and biliousness, long journeys and foreign cookery !   And Myra had rested for a fortnight, and been fed on chicken and rice, and of course, therefore, she was recovering rapidly, and all that remained to make her uncomfortable would soon pass off.   This confidence in Myra's improvement was a little shaken, however, as Mrs. Hensman lingered in the room whilst the letter was being read.   Myra's face showed such unmistakable eagerness, surprise, and distress, as to create a very uneasy misgiving as to the wisdom exercised in giving it her.

'No bad news, my dear, I hope?' she ventured to say; and Myra looked up, and answered hurriedly, 'Oh no ! none, thank you,' and went on reading, and of course Mrs. Hensman left her.

This was Mrs. Patty's letter :—

'MY DEAR MYRA,—The Doctor and I have heard that you are not well, and we are troubled at the news, though I am not thinking that you are very ill for one or two reasons— first, because I know your mamma is coming home to-morrow, and next because Mrs. Pearson told me to-day about Rosamond's being about to be married so soon to Mr. Verney. Neither of these things would be thought of if your friends were anxious about you ; but the Doctor and I still think it must be very uncomfortable to be ill in a foreign land, where, as I have always heard, there is more show than comfort, and we wish you to know that we think about you.   As to Rosamond's marriage, I wish her more happiness than falls to the lot of most people ; and I hope she has chosen well, and will make a good nurse to her husband when he grows old, which he is likely to do many years before she does.   You are so fond of Mr. Verney, my dear Myra, that I dare say you are very glad to have him for a brother-in-law.   I wish he may prove a good as well as a pleasant connection, but if he will stay in India it will not so much signify. The Doctor sends you his best love, and would very much like to see you. When he heard you were ill, and kept behind at Munich, he began to think that he should not live to do so, for he grows very weak, and does less and less each day. But, as I tell him, God most times takes off the earthly garments of us old people slowly, in order, no doubt, not to hurry or frighten us. And I don't see myself all the bad symptoms which he sees. Mr. Harrison comes to him every day, and so does Mr. Baines, and he is able to talk to them both. Mr. Baines told him yesterday that Johnny Ford is quite a different boy since he has been at the Asylum, which was very pleasant hearing for the Doctor, and will be the same for you also, as you were so interested in him. I always remember the day you and I went to see Johnny—the day that Mr. Verney came to luncheon. How little I thought then how much he would have to do with your family ! Mr. Baines has asked for a little holiday, and is likely to be away at the wedding, if, as I hear, it is to come off soon. He is not looking very well ; I wish he did not want to go just now, but health must be attended to. Dear Myra, I shall be very pleased to see you again. The Doctor says you will be a comfort to me by and by, and he pleases himself with thinking that I shall be nearer to you in my little cottage than I am now. He made the landlord come and see him last week, and settled how they were to manage for me to have two little parlours and a bed-room for a friend. Poor dear ! it comforts him to look after everything for me, but my thoughts turn more to a resting-place in Paradise than to any rest on earth. And I shall soon follow the Doctor. He and I often talk of it, and he says he does not doubt that he shall be allowed to come and meet me. It would be very home-like and pleasant if it were so ; but anyhow I could never feel lonely or strange with my Blessed Saviour to take care of me, and so I tell the Doctor, and he and I are quite happy, and quite willing that things should be as they are ; and so must you be, dear Myra. We shall all shed sorrowful tears, no doubt, when the time comes to say good-bye; but I have learnt to feel that tears are of many kinds, and that there are some which God's love so sweetens that one should be loth to exchange them for smiles.

'And now I must say good-bye, for Faith is going to the post, and to do some errands in the village, and if I write any more I shall make her late in returning. I send my best love, and the Doctor bids me add his blessing. We shall both look anxiously for news of your being better.—Your very affectionate old friend,   MARTHA KINGSBURY.'

Myra read through the letter to the end. What impression she received from the latter part it would be difficult to say. There are times when the utter dissimilarity between those who are living for this world, and those who are living for the next, presents itself to us so vividly that they appear scarcely to belong to the same race of created beings. That simple trusting mind which could accept parting and grief, Death and Eternity so quietly, what connection could it have with the false, selfish, sceptical heart which seemed destined to work misery for all who were brought in contact with it? Myra read Mrs. Patty's words of confidence in God as if they were the words of the Bible, but it was impossible to feel that they could be an everyday reality. The one reality to her at that moment was cold-hearted deception and its consequences. Rosamond to be married to Mr. Verney immediately! Then it was all known, acknowledged, settled; and she had not been told of it. For an instant every other feeling was swallowed up in the bitterness of wounded pride, and the thought crossed her mind that, as she had been wilfully kept in ignorance, events must take their course, and she could not be responsible for them. But again, why had she not been told? What motive could there be for withholding the intelligence? Myra was too generous to indulge an angry feeling groundlessly, and she seized upon the doubt at once. Mrs. Patty did not say how, or from whom she had received the information; and surely, if the news were true, Mrs. Hensman would have heard it, but she evidently knew nothing. It would be better to wait quietly, not to say or do anything, at least for a few days, when there would doubtless be a confirmation, or a refutation of the report. And Myra strove to be patient, and exerted herself to dress, and then went into the *salon*, and tried to read, and talk, and be natural ; and failed so entirely to conceal her nervous uneasiness, that Mrs. Hensman secretly decided that she had made a mistake in giving her the letter, as it had so evidently done her harm, and that it would be a dangerous experiment to repeat. The one thing to be done was to keep her quiet, and get her to England as soon as possible. When once in the care of her own family they might treat her as they thought best. And with this idea Mrs. Hensman wrote by that day's post, quite agreeing that nothing should be said about the engagement at present, and suggesting that frequent letters were upon the whole rather to be avoided than encouraged ; Myra was so nervously excited with the least thing, and then the feverishness returned, and the weakness consequent upon it. Mrs. Hensman hoped to be in England with her in the course of a fortnight, and there everything might be broken to her prudently.

The days wore on lingeringly, anxiously, doubtfully, and Myra improved so little, if at all, that Mrs. Hensman at length moved in despair. They travelled slowly to Stuttgardt, Heidelberg, Frankfort, Coblentz, Cologne, Liège, Lille, resting often for a day, but always with such uncertainty in their movements that there was no opportunity of receiving letters, and still Myra did not even know decidedly where Mr. Verney was, still less had she time or power to write to him. But she was going home ; in a few days she would be in England. It was only to be patient ; to pray to be shown what to do ; to ask for courage that she might not fail in her duty ; that she might say the right thing in the right way. How often she went over in her mind the dreaded interview need not be told, nor how she pictured to herself Mr. Verney's withering smile and quiet sneer, and thought how he would hate, perhaps despise her—and marry Rosamond after all. Myra never believed that she should prevent the marriage. Her confidence in Mr. Verney's power was far too strong for that.

He would carry his point and put her aside, and she would be his sister, but not as he once might have been. He would never forgive her—never love her again ; and even now Myra's heart was so earnest, so true in its affection, that the thought drew bitter tears from her eyes.

The Hotel Dessin, at Calais, was not reached till late at night. The wind howled through the uncarpeted passages, and the rain beat against the imperfectly-fastened windows, and a distant roar of the angry sea was heard as the undertone to every burst of the tempestuous wind ! But it was for one night only,—anything may be borne for one night ; and there are very many worse shelters from a storm than the Hotel Dessin. When Myra was told, however, the next morning, that it was too rough for her to be allowed to cross the Channel, her heart absolutely failed her, and she burst into tears.

'Weakness of spirits, consequent on loss of strength,' said Mrs. Hensman ; and perhaps she was right. At any rate, she was more confirmed in her resolution not to run any risk ; and the faint hope which Myra had entertained of being able to gain her point, and be permitted to cross at all hazards, was extinguished. She sat down in the comfortless *salon*, not even attempting to read, but trying to amuse herself by watching the sturdy peasants, who, regardless of the rain, to which French people generally seem to be supremely indifferent, were trudging through the streets with their *sabots* clattering on the rough *pavé*. But a white cap and a wooden shoe were no longer novel sights, and Myra's eye was much more quickly caught by the black coat and white necktie of an English gentleman, a clergyman evidently, rather young, not very dignified in his appearance or walk, but surely, Myra thought she knew him—doubted, looked, doubted again ; then as he finally stopped before the entrance to the hotel, exclaimed, 'Mr. Baines !' and, absolutely forgetful of propriety, almost ran out of the room to meet him.

Mrs. Hensman was very glad to see an English face, though it might be that of a person nearly a stranger. Colonel Hensman laughed, and declared that his little friend Myra was so excited, he could not but fear the meeting would be dangerous; but still, in a foreign country, civility was a first duty; and he forthwith went downstairs to renew his acquaintance with Mr. Baines, and invite him to join them in their private *salon.*

Mr. Baines, struggling with the difficulties of a French sentence, and a first experience of *francs, sous* and *centimes,* received the invitation with a thankfulness which was quite touching; and confiding his purse to the Colonel, who promised to make all due payments, and engage his bed-room for him, was ushered upstairs by the waiter, and when the door of the *salon* was opened, found himself alone with Myra. His first exclamation was one of pleasure; his next of most perplexed surprise.

'Are you not intending to cross? Surely you are going?'

'Mrs. Hensman won't go,' said Myra; 'she is afraid of the storm.'

'But not going? You will be too late! Is it impossible?'

'Not at all impossible; but I am not allowed.'

'But you must go—surely you must. You will not be in time.'

'Not in time for to-day, but in time for to-morrow.'

'But a day will make so much difference. I don't understand.'

'Neither do I,' said Myra.

'You intend to be present, of course?'

'Present at what? Please to speak out, Mr. Baines. You look so strange. What is the matter?'

'But—surely, it can't have been kept from you. The day after to-morrow is '——

'What?'

'Your sister's wedding day.'

Myra turned very pale, sat perfectly still for about two seconds, and then rose and walked slowly out of the room. Almost immediately afterwards Mrs. Hensman entered. Mr. Baines stood up to explain, and attempted to apologise for having been abrupt, but Mrs. Hensman interrupted him: 'Excuse me; we will leave all that. Is this news true?'

'Quite true.'

'The day after to-morrow?'

'Undoubtedly. I understood that Miss Myra Cameron was expected at home yesterday.'

Mrs. Hensman thought for a moment. 'Is the packet gone?' she rang the bell. It was not answered for several minutes; Mr. Baines proposed to go in search of Colonel Hensman; Mrs. Hensman followed him, but the landlord of the hotel was met on the stairs, and the question was repeated.

'He did not know whether the packet was gone; he would inquire; he thought it possible—probable; he would return directly.' But ten minutes, which seemed an hour, went by, and still he did not come. At length the answer was brought—the packet was at that very moment leaving the harbour. Mrs. Hensman gave a sigh of relief, and led the way back to the *salon*.

'Now, Mr. Baines,' she said, as she sat down on the velvet but cushionless sofa, and begged him to take the arm-chair opposite, 'we have time before us; you must tell me all about it. It is a most inexplicable and unfortunate blunder. I knew, certainly, that Rosamond Cameron was engaged, but this marriage is a thunderbolt.'

It was placing the unhappy young curate on the rack, but he bore the ordeal with great outward composure. 'Mr. Cameron's family,' he said, 'had been in England, as doubtless Mrs. Hensman knew, for more than a fortnight. Miss Cameron's engagement had been announced directly they arrived, and he always understood that the marriage would be speedy, but he had heard nothing definite till ten days ago, when he was told that no time could be lost, as Mr. Verney was under the necessity of starting immediately for India, and that the wedding day was fixed. At the same time, he understood that Miss Myra Cameron was on her way home, and would probably arrive there three or four days before the wedding. Beyond this he knew nothing. As to why he had chosen that precise time for leaving Yare, and escaping the wedding festivities, Mr. Baines said nothing. He confined himself to a bare narration of facts, given in a dry tone, and with considerable rapidity of utterance.

Mrs. Hensman listened politely, but it was evident that she scarcely heard what he said; and when he ended, instead of making any direct reply, she merely remarked, ' I see how it is; they must have written to Munich after we left it. We went off earlier than we had intended, in order to have a day at Heidelberg. How very provoking ! '

' But you were prepared; you knew of the engagement,' said Mr. Baines.

' Oh yes, in a way; that is, Colonel Hensman and myself did. But it has been kept from Myra—she has been so unwell, and she is so easily excited. We wanted her to be at home, and be told of it by her own family quietly.'

' And I mentioned it so suddenly ! ' exclaimed poor Mr. Baines, looking alarmed at the thought of the possible mischief he had done.

Mrs. Hensman gave him no consolation; she did feel very unreasonably provoked with him, and she said coldly, ' It is too late to regret, and Myra must have been told before to-morrow. She will be at home now in time.'

' But it is so startling—it will all seem so hurried ; and she will lose a day with her sister,' said Mr. Baines, in the tone of one who thought the latter vexation too serious to be endured with anything like equanimity.

' Myra is too sensible to fret unnecessarily,' was the reply ; but Mrs. Hensman did not apparently feel as certain of this fact as her words implied, for, without any apology, she went immediately to look for Myra, and poor Mr. Baines was left to meditate upon his blunder and his disappointment, and console himself as best he might with Murray and a foreign Bradshaw, or, when they failed, to amuse himself with the novelties of the *sabots* and *blouses*, the torrents of rain, and the *pavé* streets, which had so entirely failed to interest Myra.

CHAPTER XLI.

'No news of Myra?' said Mrs. Cameron, watching her husband anxiously as he opened the post-bag at breakfast time.

'I do not see what news you are to expect, my dear; Myra will be here almost as soon as a letter could reach us. Rosamond, these documents are for you; a secretary will be required to answer them.'

Mr. Cameron handed Rosamond a collection of letters, some congratulatory, some from tradespeople and milliners. They were glanced at, and laid aside with an air of quiet importance, and Rosamond continued her breakfast.

'I shall be very glad when this turmoil is over,' observed Mrs. Cameron plaintively; 'and I don't understand about Myra. I thought she would certainly have written a few lines to her sister. And it is such a storm to-day! They cannot possibly cross, and Myra will not be able to try on her dress. Are you sure, Rosamond, that Conyers gave the right pattern? And then she has been ill, and perhaps she is thinner; it would be so very awkward if the dress did not fit. Don't you think it impossible for them to cross to-day, Mr. Cameron?'

'I think nothing impossible, my dear, that is necessary. Myra must come; I told Mrs. Hensman so. If they had done wisely, they would have taken the Ostend passage and have been here yesterday. It is very unwise to hasten things in this way.'

Mr. Cameron looked a dignified rebuke at Rosamond as he said this, for in his secret heart he was not quite easy as to Myra's silence; and whenever he was uncomfortable he solaced himself by blaming some one for some thing. Just now, everything disagreeable was laid to the charge of the hurry and business occasioned by the wedding.

' I can't help thinking it was foolish in us to keep her so much in ignorance,' continued Mrs. Cameron; 'she will be so very much startled, and she takes things to heart curiously sometimes. But then we did not know anything ourselves for certain till quite lately. It is a thousand pities Mr. Verney could not have waited a little longer.'

'Myra will do very well, mamma,' said Rosamond, in a tone of quiet assurance, which was like an opiate to Mrs. Cameron's nervous fidgetiness. ' She will have sufficient time to think and reconcile herself to everything on the journey, and she will have been spared a great deal of confusion and worry by not having been here the last fortnight.'

' Certainly, that is very true. I have never suffered so much in all my life from the whirl of things as I have since we came home. I have not been able to settle myself in the least, and Conyers seems to have no time to attend to anything. And now, to-day, how many people are coming ?'

' I have made a list, my dear,' said Mr. Cameron, ' I will read it to you.'

He drew a paper from his pocket-book, and went through the names of aunts, uncles, cousins, intimate friends, persons who were certain to come, persons who were doubtful, persons who had been asked and refused, persons who would like to come but could not, till poor Mrs. Cameron felt as if she had been looking at a merry-go-round, and the various individuals mentioned flitted past her bewildered brain, and became absolutely undistinguishable.

I desire to do everything with method,' said Mr. Cameron. ' There is nothing like method for the avoidance of confusion, more especially when time presses. You will understand now, my dear, all that you have to do, and I will leave a copy of this paper with you for your instruction. Juliet,' and he turned to the two younger children, who had been brought from school to be present at their sister's wedding—' you write a good and legible hand, let this list be copied for your mamma, and then return it to me.'

' And who did you say were coming to sleep ?' inquired Mrs. Cameron; ' I did not quite understand.'

'The paper, my dear! You will have nothing to do but to consult the paper. Rosamond, I shall require your attendance in my study this evening. The necessary legal documents will by that time be prepared.'

'And if Myra should not come?' inquired Mrs. Cameron.

'Myra will come, my dear. She must come, and she will. I beg that you will not distress yourself.'

Mr. Cameron begged in the tone of command, and his wife was silenced; but when he had left the breakfast table she again confided her misgivings to Rosamond.

'There was a storm, that was certain; and packets did not always cross in stormy weather, and what should they do if Myra did not come?'—observations which had all been made and answered before, and Rosamond's only resource was to divert Mrs. Cameron's mind for the present by talking of the crowd of visitors, whilst earnestly hoping in her own mind that Mrs. Verney would, as usual, drive over from Stormont early, and use her all-powerful influence for the quieting of Mrs. Cameron's nerves.

Rosamond really was to be admired that morning for the tact, patience, and self-possession which she displayed. Myra, under similar circumstances, would not have done half as well. Rosamond might have been the most unselfish of mortals, to judge by the care and thought which she bestowed upon all things and all people. Mrs. Cameron complained of hasty arrangements, and had more than once been heard to prophesy that nothing could by any possibility be properly managed when so little time was allowed for preparations; but Rosamond had from the first determined that whether much haste or little were to be used, she would not bate one iota of the essentials of a wedding ordered in the best style; and quietly and diligently she had worked, not only for the last fortnight, but even before they left Paris, with the view of being ready at the appointed time.

'Miss Cameron is so far-seeing about everything,' said Conyers to Mrs. Pearson, when the wedding was discussed that same day in the housekeeper's room. 'Would you believe it, she had ordered half her dresses before any one else would have thought about them, and now she takes everything as quietly as if she had been getting ready to be married for the last six months. Mr. Verney would not find many ladies with such thought. Just imagine what poor Miss Myra would have done in the same case ! Why, she would not have had a thing ready, even at the last moment. Well ! there are some people born with brains for common use, and some with brains for uncommon ; and for my part, I begin to think the common ones get through the world much the best.'

'Very true, Conyers,' was the reply, 'but, do you know, I can't help taking a greater fancy to Miss Myra of the two. I shouldn't like to be her lady's-maid, and no doubt you speak feelingly ; but Miss Cameron is never caught in the wrong in anything, and somehow that strikes me as being what my Scotch grandmother used to call " uncanny."'

Uncanny or not, Rosamond was most surprisingly useful on that day. Not even to Mr. Verney, on whom she had latterly vented any secret feelings of annoyance, did she show the slightest shade of impatience, fretfulness, or discontent. She was evidently basking in the sunshine of her position, supremely pleased with herself, and only one degree less pleased with every other person. As for Mr. Verney, he was the root and author of it all, and of necessity received his due share of appreciation. Rosamond was sweetly deferential to him now, at least whenever any one was present. It belonged to the part of a *fiancée*, and she would on no account have been otherwise. If she had no eyes to see that he was cold and irritable almost to nervousness, that his face looked haggard, that he started at sounds which were perfectly natural, examined the weather-glass as though some important event depended upon it, and was so abstracted that he often answered her questions in a way which was scarcely sensible—who was to blame her ? She had gained her object. She enjoyed the *éclat* of her engagement, and looked forward to the dignity of a wife. Mr. Verney was clever and exclusive, and she was proud of his admiration. She liked him, and, indeed, believed she loved him. He was too indolent to contradict her, and with him she thought that she should be more her own mistress

than she could be in her father's house.   In short, marriage
had presented itself as rather an agreeable and exciting possibility, and as there seemed no particular reason against it, it
appeared better to accept it.   Rosamond had taken care of
herself, and Mr. Verney had, no doubt, taken equal care of
himself.   It was only unfortunate that he did not show his
contentment to the world, or at least to that portion of it
which was prepared to criticise.   Mr. Cameron, indeed, was
absent as usual ; Mrs. Cameron was closeted with Mrs.
Verney, or engrossed in busy nothings ; and the guests who
arrived by instalments were at first too much occupied with
themselves, their journeys, and their requirements for comfort,
to scan his words or actions very closely.   But the servants
made their remarks freely, and by them it was decided that
Mr. Verney looked much more as though he was preparing
for his execution than for his wedding ; 'a thing not to be
wondered at,' as Conyers observed, 'seeing that the gentleman
was nothing on such occasions, and every one wished him out
of the way.   It was only when the wedding was over that he
would have things according to his own fashion.   If they
would just wait a little they would see quite a change, for she
knew from what she had heard at Stormont, that Mr. Verney
was not a gentleman to be put upon by any one.'

The early part of that day was occupied by Rosamond in
giving orders for Mrs. Cameron ; the afternoon was devoted
to farewell visits in the village, in order to leave the next day
absolutely free for packing and final arrangements, so that
there might be no confusion on the wedding morning.   Mr.
Verney offered to go with her, but Rosamond negatived the
proposal.   They might meet possibly at the Rectory, she said,
but parish visits she preferred paying alone ; they would be
managed more quickly.

The visit to the Rectory was Rosamond's last duty.   She
delayed it till she had only ten minutes to spare, if she hoped
to be at home in time to dress for dinner.   Mrs. Patty had
engaged that the Doctor would see her at any hour.   Weak
though he was, he would make every effort to say good-bye to
her ; a more solemn good-bye far than any which Rosamond

contemplated ; but she either could not or would not face the fact, and tripped as lightly up the stairs to the sick-room, as though she was about to enter a ball-room.

Yet even Rosamond was sobered when she approached her old friend. There is a vast difference between the aspect of illness, however serious, and of death—a difference which none can understand who have not witnessed it. We may watch by a sick-bed, week after week, month after month, and feel no hesitation in bringing to it the pursuits and amusements of common life. We smile, and the smile is without sadness ; we laugh, and the mirth gives us no shock. We even wish, as we say, to distract the invalid's thoughts ; we know that business and pleasure imply the existence of a hope of recovery, and we feel that by encouraging such a hope, we do in fact strengthen life. But there is a look, indescribable, but instantaneously felt, which acts upon us like the solemnity of a religious rite. As we gaze upon it, business becomes profanation, and mirth a mockery. Death has laid its grasp upon that mortal frame, and death, however gentle its approach, is the summons to a Presence before which every interest, thought, and enjoyment of earth must be tested for eternity.

Rosamond Cameron was the selfish, frivolous devotee of this world, when she crossed the threshold of Dr. Kingsbury's chamber ; but when she sat down beside the old man's bed, and caught the earnest expression of his glassy, deep-sunk eye, and the flickering of his heavily-drawn breath, she was the awed frightened worshipper of a power which for the moment touched her conscience to the quick, and withdrew the veil from the self-deception of her life. She was very silent, very still, and the old man held her hand, and looked at her steadily. 'You are kind in coming,' he said, with a tenderness of tone which Rosamond had rarely heard.

'I wished to say good-bye,' said Rosamond, 'and to-morrow I might not have time.'

'A long good-bye ; not a good-bye for ever. God grant it, my child.'

'Thank you, sir,' and a tear dimmed Rosamond's eyes ; 'but I hope—I think I may see you again before I sail.'

'As God wills. I have done little for you, my dear. I ought to have done much. May God forgive me.'

'Oh! sir, indeed, indeed '—and Rosamond looked perplexed and troubled—'I ought to be much better than I am.'

'I have done little for you,' he repeated; 'but I pray for you. Will Mr. Verney come and see me? I should like to see him.'

'He will be here almost directly, I expect,' replied Rosamond, feeling relieved at the introduction of an ordinary topic. 'But are you sure, sir, it will not tire you to see him?'

'Not at all, if he will forgive my talking much. My breath grows very short; I cannot enjoy his conversation as I did. I trust we may meet where there will be no such drawbacks.'

'Doctor, dear, don't tire yourself,' said Mrs. Patty, looking in at a doorway which opened into a dressing-room.

'I will take care, Patty, thank you. Will you bring me the book?'

Mrs. Patty entered with a heavy tread, to which, however, the old man seemed quite insensible; she placed a Bible upon the bed, and went away.

'I daresay you have several, my dear,' he said to Rosamond, as he pointed to it, 'but I give you what I value most. When you look at it'—he paused for breath, and at that moment a shadow darkened the doorway, and Mrs. Patty again came up to the bedside and said—

'Mr. Verney, Doctor; only for one instant. I have told him he must not stay longer.'

The old Rector's eyes lighted up with a gleam of their former interest, and when Mr. Verney approached, without waiting for any greeting, he took his hand, and joined it with Rosamond's, and murmured as he held them both, 'Grant that they may so live together in this world, that in the world to come they may have life everlasting.'

There was no response, but Mr. Verney's face was ashy in its paleness. Rosamond sat down trembling.

'Shall I move the book, Doctor?' said Mrs. Patty.

But he laid his hand upon it. 'I was saying—I wished to say—Mr. Verney, death is the truest of all tests.'

'It is not death with you yet, Doctor, I hope,' began Mr.
Verney.

'Yes, sir, it is death ; not perhaps to-day, or to-morrow, but
death inevitable, and very soon. My dear,' and he turned to
Rosamond, 'the Bible is for you both. Mr. Verney, a dying
man's words are for you both. Christianity is truth ; Christ
is everything. Live for Him ; for there is nothing else worth
living for.'

A sigh rose from the depths of Mr. Verney's breast, and he
said in a tone low and earnest, and in which there yet blended
somewhat of his natural sarcasm, 'I wish you could give me
the legacy of your faith, Doctor ; I should be a better man
than I have ever been yet.'

'Sir, it will not come by wishes ; it will come by prayer.
But we should have spoken of these things before.'

'Yes, indeed we should ; that is, if it would have done any
good ; but I am afraid it is too late now.'

'Too late, too late for so many things. Lord, I pray Thee
to pardon me ;' and the old man clasped his hands together,
whilst an expression intense in its sorrowful humility rested
upon his sharpened features.

Mrs. Patty came forward. 'That is enough, Doctor, dear.
Now Mr. Verney, if you please.'

Dr. Kingsbury looked at Mr. Verney intently, and murmured a solemn farewell ; and then, as Rosamond drew nearer,
he took her hand and pressed it to his lips with a half paternal, half courtly tenderness, and said, as he released it, ' My
child, I would give you my last blessing.'

She knelt, and laying his hand upon her head, the old
Doctor committed her to 'God's gracious mercy and protection, and prayed that the Lord would lift up His countenance
upon her, and give her peace, both at that time and ever-
more ;' and then Rosamond rose up and left the room
with Mr. Verney, feeling for the time a better Christian in
spirit than she had ever been before in the course of her
whole life.

CHAPTER XLII.

So gay they were that evening! Mr. Verney seemed quite to have rallied from any depression of spirits, and was really the life of the party. They were mostly relations who had arrived, and every one felt at liberty to be at home, and Rosamond enjoyed showing her presents, which gave topics for conversation; but better than anything, a telegraphic message had been received from Calais, stating that it was impossible to cross because of the gale, but that Myra might certainly be expected the next day. Mrs. Cameron therefore was no longer uneasy, and having again been assured by Conyers that Miss Myra's dress was certain to fit her, felt herself no longer burdened by responsibility, especially as Rosamond herself promised to take especial care of Myra's 'toilette,' so that she might not, according to her mother's fears, make herself remarkable by being quite a figure on the wedding morning. Mrs. Verney was more than ever amiable and agreeable under the burden of the preparations for the coming event. She quite undertook the duties of hostess at the Hall, when Mrs. Cameron was too tired to exert herself, and went through a series of pleasant flatteries to the elderly relations, whilst Rosamond played, and sang, and talked with the younger ones; Mr. Verney hovering near her, watching her as though she had been a pretty and petted child, and every now and then leading her out to some quick repartee, which, uttered in Rosamond's sweet voice and with her very quiet manner, never failed to be perfectly lady-like. In that respect Mr. Verney had certainly chosen well. His wife would never offend his taste. And Rosamond was more to be loved that evening. She was more real, more genuine in her good-nature, more earnest and simple in all she said. The better part of her nature had been touched by the old Doctor's farewell, and its influence still lingered with her. But it was only lingering; there was no depth in the feeling; it awoke no self-scrutiny, no penitence; it was accompanied by no resolutions. The blossom was fair to the eye, but the plant had no root, and in a few hours it would fade. By the next morning it had faded.

How, indeed, could it be otherwise? No leisure was there for thought or regret, for hope or fear, on that crowded, busy, most matter-of-fact day. We idealise important occasions. We look forward to them as we imagine they ought to be; as in fact they are in spirit; but we forget that the material forms in which they are presented to us will at the moment, in all probability, entirely prevent our realising this spirit. If we have not learnt to perceive the unseen and invisible under the veil of our ordinary life, we shall be unable to discover it when it is presented to us under circumstances which are extraordinary. They who live with falsehoods—fashion, vanity, worldly ambition, self-importance—as if they involved lasting interests, will be blind when brought in contact with the most impressive realities, because, in the ordering of God's Providence, the same forms invest both truth and deception, the things of Time and the things of Eternity; and only the eyes which have been opened by His grace can see the immeasurable difference between them.

Rosamond Cameron's last day of preparation for her wedding was, as such days always must be, distracted by orders, interruptions, trials of temper, little disappointments, cares of the most minute character. And as Rosamond had never trained herself to see in all such daily occurrences anything by which to elevate her mind by the exercise of self-discipline, or lead her above the world by the very turmoil and annoyance which beset her in it; so now they entirely overpowered the higher yearnings which the thought of death had awakened. The seed had been sown in the heart, but the cares and the pleasures of life were already springing up and choking it.

Mr. Verney was not like Rosamond; he was too indolent, too indifferent, to be engrossed by petty business. He gave his orders to his servants, and then left them to be executed. It was not in his way to trouble himself, except to find fault when anything was forgotten or done amiss. And it might be that he did see deeper into the meaning of all that was going on; that he did in one sense realise more of its importance. Boxes and packages, dresses and presents, were nothing to him, and he gave them no attention; but the prospect of relief from pecuniary care, and the attainment of luxury and worldly position, were a great deal; and all these were involved in his approaching marriage; and, therefore, whilst smiling patronisingly upon Rosamond, he kept himself as much as possible aloof from the business which gathered round her; as though marriage was too serious to admit of such lighter considerations; and looked, moved, and spoke with dignity and calmness, and in his secret heart was—miserable.

'Myra must be here soon,' said Mrs. Cameron, entering the schoolroom where Edmund, Juliet, and Annette were engaged, under Rosamond's superintendence, in packing a box of books and drawings, which were especially to be cared for. 'It is getting on for five o'clock, and your father said certainly she would be at home in time for dinner.'

'Godfrey says she can't come till after eight,' said Juliet, 'and he must know.'

'I don't see, my dear, why Godfrey is to know better than your father. I shall go and ask Mr. Verney. I know he is in the library, and really I am anxious.'

'Let me go,' said Edmund, 'though I don't suppose he can tell us more than Bradshaw.'

'Godfrey understands Bradshaw best,' persisted Juliet, 'and he and I looked at it last night, and settled it.'

'Then of course it will be so,' said Rosamond, laughing.

'Of course,' repeated Edmund. 'It is such a pity that Godfrey and Juliet can't undertake the government of the world; they would manage it admirably.'

'With Mr. Verney to help us,' said Juliet. 'I am sure he lays down the law more than any one.'

'Only he does it in a discreet way,' observed Rosamond.

'Yes,' said Juliet meaningly, 'he is very discreet. We all know that ; don't we, Annette ? '

'Juliet, the sooner you go back to school the better,' remarked Edmund sharply.

'I meant no harm,' replied Juliet in a tone of mock humility. 'I only repeated what Miss Greaves said.'

'Edmund, if you would just go and look for Mr. Verney, and bring him here,' said Mrs. Cameron. 'And, Juliet, you must learn not to be pert. What does it signify what Miss Greaves said ? '

'Nothing now, mamma, certainly,' replied Juliet. 'And Miss Greaves has never really known Mr. Verney ; though she has heard things said of him.'

Rosamond looked up quickly, but she did not ask what Miss Greaves had heard. Juliet, however, answered the glance.

'She heard of him, you know, from that young Indian lady, Miss Stuart, whom people said he was going to marry.'

'Oh ! ' was Rosamond's short reply.

'And you can't think how surprised she was, when Mrs. de Lancey told her of your engagement, Rosamond. She would not believe it at first, and I was so glad when I could prove it was true, though I heard Miss Greaves say to Mrs. de Lancey that Miss Stuart has been jilted.'

'Juliet, this gossip is wrong and unladylike,' observed Mrs. Cameron severely ; ' don't let me hear any more of it.'

But Rosamond only smiled, and said gently, 'Oh yes, mamma, if you please ; it is amusing to know the nonsense the world talks. Let me hear it all, Juliet.'

'Yes, let us hear it all ; ' and Juliet felt a hand laid lightly on her shoulder, and, turning round, saw Mr. Verney standing behind her. 'Young ladies' stories of their schools are a revelation of a new world.'

Juliet coloured crimson, shook off Mr. Verney's hand, and remained silent.

There was a most awkward pause. 'Mysteries!' said Mr. Verney. 'I won't inquire, but you might trust me.'

'No mystery,' observed Mrs. Cameron; 'but Juliet brings home schoolroom gossip, and I don't approve of it.'

'It was not gossip, it was truth,' murmured Juliet to Annette; but Annette was prudent, and took no notice.

Rosamond busied herself with the packing, but that she was uncomfortable was very evident. Mrs. Cameron had recourse to Bradshaw, and engaged both Mr. Verney and Edmund's attention in the endeavour to explain it, which, as her sight was so bad that she could not read the figures, was no easy task. Mr. Verney glanced at Rosamond more than once, and when at length Mrs. Cameron released him, he went up to her, and said: 'You are tiring yourself; you had better let me help you.'

'Thank you, no; I can manage for myself,' and Rosamond turned decidedly away from him.

'Isn't it so curious how days come over again?' exclaimed Juliet. 'Don't you remember, Mr. Verney, the day we were packing for Rosamond before she went up to London, how you came in just when she was looking over a portfolio as she is doing now, and how, you admired the "Bridge of St. Martin?"'

'Yes,' he said, 'I have reason to remember it;' and drawing nearer to Rosamond, he added, in a tone intended for no one but herself, 'It was the gift of that drawing which first gave me confidence.'

Juliet's quick ears had, however, caught the words, and with her usual utter want of tact, she exclaimed: 'It was only half Rosamond's after all. It did duty for Annette too, when it was wanted, so it was very convenient. It gained Annette a prize, and '——

Edmund interrupted her. 'Juliet, it strikes me that both you and Annette chatter much more than you work. You may just as well put on your bonnets and come for a walk with me. Perhaps, though, my mother wants you?'

'No.' Mrs. Cameron did not want them; 'she was going to lie down in her own room; she was very tired, and her eyes ached ; she wished Myra was at home to read to her, and then perhaps she might go to sleep.' Annette offered to take Myra's place, but Mrs. Cameron was fanciful about reading. She was accustomed to Myra, and could not reconcile herself to any one else; and Edmund, who seemed bent upon taking possession of his two younger sisters, and leaving Mr. Verney and Rosamond alone, repeated his proposal for a walk, and succeeded in dispersing the party.

Whether his thoughtfulness was appreciated, remained to be proved. Rosamond continued her occupation, Mr. Verney stood by her; neither spoke for some seconds. Then Mr. Verney said, ' And you won't let me help you ? '

' No, thank you.'

' There is something the matter, Rosamond.'

' Nothing, thank you.'

' That means something; I must know.'

' And if I do not choose to say ? '

' You are annoyed at some nonsense of Juliet's ? '

' I have not heard any nonsense that I am aware of.'

' Some sense then; something she has told you.'

' She has said nothing to annoy me.'

Mr. Verney bit his lip. ' Rosamond, I can't stand this.'

' Neither can I. Would you kindly move out of the light ? '

He made a gesture of impatience, and was going away. Then he stopped, and said : ' Are we to go on in this way all day ? '

' In what way? I shall soon have finished what I am doing.'

' You mean to drive me wild ! ' he exclaimed. ' How can I explain what is amiss if you won't tell me what it is ? '

' There is nothing amiss. I daresay your young Indian friend has recovered her disappointment by this time, and of course she is the only person to be pitied.'

Mr. Verney turned very pale.

' I see,' continued Rosamond bitterly, ' there is no need of explanation. It is all very natural. I don't find fault, only I think I might have been told.'

' Told ! what? That intolerable school gossip ! '

'Yes, it is quite intolerable.'

'But what is it? For pity's sake, Rosamond, don't go on with this absurd mystery.'

'I merely follow your example,' said Rosamond. 'If you had plainly told me, when I alluded to a similar report in Paris, that you had been engaged before, I should have understood it. I am not jealous.'

'But I was not engaged; I was—it is all nonsense. What do you mean?'

'Only that I should have felt it was treating me more honourably to be quite open, as I have been with you. I have never been engaged till now. I should have told you if I had been.'

'Engaged? folly! absurdity! Do you suppose, Rosamond, that a man of my age is bound to confess every passing fancy?'

'Certainly not. A passing fancy and an engagement are very different.'

'And if I had been engaged, where would have been the harm?'

'None at all. Though I don't know that it is pleasant to go about the world, as the person who has caused another to be jilted.'

'I don't allow that word, Rosamond.'

'I don't wish you to allow it. Tell me only that I may contradict it.'

'I will not answer the question; it is an insult. Rosamond, you can't doubt me.'

'I don't want to do so,' said Rosamond more gently, 'but I cannot have a child like Juliet sneering at me. And—I should like to know the truth.'

'Would you?' and he smiled a little sarcastically; 'it would be very easily told. You had better apply to the circulating library, and read how often foolish men have been caught by pretty faces, and then repented. Seriously, it is not worth your inquiring about; only I can't bear to see you unlike yourself. Was the young lady's name Stuart?'

He hesitated as he spoke the name, but Rosamond did not remark it, and before she could answer, he went on quietly, 'An Indian fancy! one must have something to amuse oneself with in such a wearisome life. And all men take to flirting more or less. I don't pretend to say that I was better than the rest, and I daresay the young lady—as most young ladies do—considered it a more serious occupation than I did. But it is not worth your troubling yourself about, love. Won't you believe me?'

Rosamond was touched by the tone. Her pride rather than her affection had been wounded, and to see Mr. Verney in the least humble, quite satisfied her.

She looked up and smiled, as she answered: 'I only wish you would take Juliet in hand. She is much worse than she used to be, and she was intolerable enough before. I wonder how it is that nothing can ever make her a lady.'

Mr. Verney shrugged his shoulders. 'Nature!' he said. 'It is always too strong for art. But leave her to me; she shall not torment you any more.'

'She has no reserve, no discretion,' continued Rosamond. 'And she piques herself upon it; she calls it truth.'

'Truth which is not always to be spoken,' said Mr. Verney.

'No; in this respect she is somewhat like Myra, who is also at times uncommonly awkward and disagreeable in what she says. Don't you think so?'

Mr. Verney made no answer.

'I forgot—Myra is such a pet of yours,' continued Rosamond, interpreting his silence; 'you won't be satisfied till you have seen her.'

'Perhaps not,' and Mr. Verney very quickly left the room.

CHAPTER XLIII

How he did despise himself! There is no feeling so utterly unendurable as that. And Mr. Verney was not a man to take out his actions, examine, and make excuses for them. He was too proud to own that he was wrong, too indolent to endeavour to prove that he was right. His effort for years had been to escape from himself, and he was an adept in the art. When, as a youth, he did what conscience condemned, he simply strove to forget it, and so he did now. And under the circumstances in which he was placed, he could have forgotten, he could have made himself fairly comfortable, if only he had not been haunted by an apparently unreasonable dread of Myra's return. How she could interfere with him, indeed, he did not see; and whatever she might say, he had but to adopt the same tone which had just succeeded so well with Rosamond, for there is nothing like acknowledging a report up to a certain point if one wishes to stop it. But, after all, Mr. Verney had not lost the feelings of a gentleman, however little he might retain those of a Christian; and when he was compelled to evade, equivocate, perhaps even to utter a direct falsehood, he despised himself, and then he was wretched. He wandered into the garden now, and finding Godfrey Cameron there, endured the penance of his society for nearly an hour, because he could not bear to be left alone. He strolled into Mrs. Cameron's boudoir, and again went through all the Bradshaw calculations, in order to occupy his thoughts; he almost determined to walk down to the Parsonage and inquire after the rector, but he was afraid of being asked to walk upstairs, and he could not face another interview with a dying man, and that man Dr. Kingsbury; and at length, as the dinner hour approached, he hurried back to Stormont, dreading, as he said to Rosamond, to be scrutinised before the appointed time by a fresh relay of guests; and, by the aid of a cigar, a novel, and his toilet, contrived to distract his mind until the carriage was announced which was to take him to dine at the Hall.

And then came the ordeal of the stiff circle before dinner, and the introductions and the attempts at conversation; but all that was an assistance to Mr. Verney. He was in his element when called upon to exert himself conversationally, and the sight of numbers awoke his spirit of criticism, and so his self-appreciation was restored. Whenever he could be satirical he felt himself superior, and then the ordinary laws which govern, or ought to govern, the common herd, became a matter of less importance to him; he could afford to overlook them. By the time dinner was on the table, ladies glanced at him timidly and admiringly, and gentlemen listened to him as a man whose opinions were worth having, and Mr. Verney was satisfied, and at ease.

'Was not that a ring at the bell?' asked Mrs. Cameron of the butler, just as the second course was placed on the table. Mr. Verney, who was seated near her, turned round as though he had been shot. The butler left the room to inquire.

'We are expecting Myra,' said Mrs. Cameron in explanation to the gentleman at her right hand. 'Mr. Verney is as anxious about her as any of us; she is such a favourite of his.'

Captain Stevens, who was a distant relation, laughed, and made some commonplace remark about its not being permitted to fall in love with two young ladies at once.

'I am afraid it is an offence rather frequently committed,' exclaimed Colonel Verney, joining in the conversation. 'I have heard of three cases of jilting this season.'

'If the first culprit could have been hung, it would have been a warning to the rest,' said Edmund Cameron, from the opposite side of the table. 'One dreadful example every season would save an infinity of trouble.'

'I hope you would not make an example of both sexes,' observed Mrs. Verney, 'for jilting, you know, is considered by some young ladies quite their privilege.'

Y

There was a general exclamation of disavowal of the doctrine from all the ladies present, and Godfrey, thrusting himself into the conversation, and taking their part for the sake of contradiction, undertook to prove from his own knowledge that in one or two instances, generally known, the fault had rested with the gentleman. Rosamond's taste went against the topic, and she tried to stop him; but whenever Godfrey was in the vein for anecdotes, it would have been as easy to do this as to arrest the current of a river. Story followed story, whilst, one by one, the attention of nearly every person at table was attracted, and Godfrey had, what of all things he most coveted—the command of the conversation.

'It was not Myra,' said Mrs. Cameron, leaning forward and addressing Mr. Verney in an undertone. He bowed and smiled, and said he did not expect her so soon; and then he went on quietly discussing a question of political reform with General Mainwaring, his next neighbour, apparently not hearing a syllable which Godfrey was saying, and only pausing to fill his glass whenever the wine came round. He drank but little generally, but that evening was an exception.

'I understand your nephew has first-rate powers of conversation,' remarked Captain Stevens to Mrs. Verney. 'It is a pity he does not give more people the benefit of them.'

'He has no morbid desire for social distinction,' replied Mrs. Verney. 'It is a mind sufficient for itself, requiring no support, and therefore not always ready to exert itself. But he can be drawn out by those who understand him;' and acting upon her own suggestions, Mrs. Verney dexterously insinuated herself into the political conversation, and compelled her nephew to give her his attention and his opinion.

But she failed in persuading him to display himself. He answered her, but it was with only that amount of interest which politeness required, and he shrank back into what Mrs. Verney called his shell, and, with a smile, she banteringly told him that he was so nervous and so pre-engrossed she would wait till after the next day to gain his attention.

The ladies left the dinner-table. Mrs. Verney persuaded Mrs. Cameron to go and rest in her boudoir. Rosamond also withdrew. Coffee was brought in, the ordinary circle was formed, the ordinary little nothings were said, and the spirit of *ennui* was stealing over the party. Juliet looked at the time-piece.

' Five minutes to the half hour ! Myra ought to be here. Hark ! '

The carriage was distinctly heard, the wheels crashing over the gravel. Juliet and Annette rushed down the stairs.

' How pleasant it is to see such sisterly affection !' murmured Mrs. Verney. ' Elise, my love, I wish you would just go and prepare Mrs. Cameron for dear Myra's arrival. Mrs. Cameron is so sadly nervous,' she continued, addressing the party generally, ' and she has been painfully excited by Myra's delay. But it is all over now. I felt sure myself that nothing could occur to mar the general happiness on an occasion so auspicious.'

There was a bustle on the staircase, a murmur of voices ; then Elise Verney came back, saying that Myra was gone to her mother. She was not looking at all well ; the journey had fatigued her a good deal, and they had had a bad crossing.

Every one was immediately very sorry, but thought it quite natural, and had no doubt she would soon recover ; and then each lady who had enjoyed the privilege of crossing the Channel felt anxious to relate her experience, and listened with polite impatience to her neighbour's details, till she could find an occasion to introduce her own. So the stiffness of the party wore off, and Mrs. Verney, perceiving that the conversation had become more general, took the opportunity of stealing out of the room, with a really good-natured wish to know something about Myra.

She met Annette in the corridor. ' Myra is with mamma. We have been sent away. Mrs. Verney, is there anything the matter ? ' and Annette, who was naturally timid, and really tender-hearted, crept up to Mrs. Verney's side, and looked up anxiously in her face.

'The matter, my dear, no. What should be the matter? Poor little Myra is tired. Just go and tell Rosamond that she must come down and make herself agreeable. I will go and speak to your mamma.'

'But Myra looked as if she was unhappy,' said Annette, 'and mamma exclaimed so when she saw her; and she is ill, I am sure.'

'My dear Annette, do not let your little head be disturbed with fancies. Go and fetch Rosamond, and stay quietly in the drawing-room. Tell Rosamond I shall return in a few minutes. When the gentlemen come up we must have some music.'

'The gentlemen are coming up now,' exclaimed Annette; 'I must go and tell Mr. Verney that Myra is come; he will be so glad.' But Mr. Verney was not there, he was still in the dining-room talking politics, Edmund said, and Annette must not trouble him about Myra; he would know about her quite as soon as he wished. Annette went back to the drawing-room discomfited, and Mrs. Verney, not without a slight feeling of curiosity, knocked at the door of Mrs. Cameron's boudoir.

'Come in,' was said in a weak voice, and Mrs. Verney opened the door just as Myra, who had been kneeling by her mother's sofa, started up, endeavouring to appear as if she had been standing.

'Charmed, most charmed to see you, love,' said Mrs. Verney, kissing her; 'you have had a wretched journey, I hear; a miserable crossing. Let me see how you are looking.' She gently laid her hand on Myra's shoulder, and turned her to the light, as she might have done when she was a child of ten years old.

Myra bore the touch bravely, but her answer was, in spite of herself, chilling. 'They had had rather a rough passage, but it was nothing like that of the previous day.'

'And you have been surprised, excited, your nerves are shaken —you were not prepared for this sudden and most interesting event? Dear Mrs. Cameron, she will do well to retire to rest immediately, after having eaten something. Don't you think so ? '

' I wish to go into the drawing-room,' said Myra decidedly ; ' mamma, if you don't object, I will go and dress at once.'

' It is a strange fancy, my dear,' was the reply; ' very unlike yourself.' And Mrs. Cameron appealed to Mrs. Verney, ' She does not look like herself, does she ? I was quite startled when I saw her at first.'

' Feverish,' said Mrs. Verney, with a smile ; ' feverish from excitement, but it will wear off. Are you quite certain, my love, that you will do wisely in attempting to see your friends to-night ? You will have such a very trying day to-morrow ; and you must be up early, so must we all.'

' And I want Conyers to try on your dress,' said Mrs. Cameron ; ' I should like to see it on myself. Indeed, it is so late, Myra, I think you will do much better not to think of appearing in the drawing-room ; no one will expect you.'

' You have seen Rosamond, of course,' said Mrs. Verney.

' She has seen no one but myself and the two children, I believe,' observed Mrs. Cameron. ' We were just having a little talk about the marriage when you came in, my dear Mrs. Verney. I was telling her that she must not put on a sad face, when her sister is going to be so happy.'

' Dear child ! She was always so sensitive,' murmured Mrs. Verney. ' But you will see Rosamond looking so bright, my love ; and Charles is supremely happy.'

Alas ! for Myra, and that unfortunate impossibility of concealing her feelings which entirely prevented her being a heroine. Her face expressed a mixture of impatience and misery, which the effort to subdue only served to intensify.

' Mamma, I think I should like to go to my own room,' was all the answer she could make.

' Do so, my dear. Make yourself comfortable, and tell Conyers what you would like to have—a little tea, I suppose ;

and perhaps some chicken, or a cutlet : order just what you fancy.'

'I can't eat,' said Myra, ' my head aches ; and I have not seen Rosamond, or '—her voice was scarcely audible, as she added—'Mr. Verney.'

Mrs. Verney laughed. 'Oh ! is that it ? The old fancy. Well ! I must say you are constant ; and you need not be at all jealous ; he is devoted to you still.'

'He has been looking forward to seeing you all day,' said Mrs. Cameron. 'Suppose,' and she turned to Mrs. Verney— 'Would it be troubling you very much to ask him to come and see Myra here ? The gentlemen must be out of the dining-room by this time.'

'O mamma ! no, not here ; ' Myra paused, conscious of the strangeness of her words ; then added, ' It will tire you ; and indeed, if I may, I should like to go into the drawing-room.'

'But with a headache, my dear, and having had nothing to eat ? '

'Poor child ! she won't be satisfied till she has had him all to herself,' said Mrs. Verney. 'I daresay she has something very important to say to him. They were always famed for having secrets, and I think under the circumstances we may trust them.'

Mrs. Cameron received the suggestion quite literally. 'I don't understand,' she said. 'Mr. Verney can come here very well, and then Myra can have something to eat and go to bed ; that seems to me the most sensible notion.'

'I have not seen papa, either,' persisted Myra.

'Homesick for every one, I perceive,' said Mrs. Verney. 'What do you say to indulging her, my dear Mrs. Cameron, and allowing her to go into the drawing-room just as she is ? The party are all relations or intimate friends, and they will quite understand that she has just come off a journey.'

'As you will,' said Mrs. Cameron languidly. 'I don't think I can appear again to-night myself ; I am quite exhausted. I should like to see Rosamond before she goes to bed ; and Myra, my dear, when you go up stairs remember you must put on your dress and let Conyers see that it fits.

I think I may depend upon her, don't you?' she added, speaking to Mrs. Verney.

'Without doubt; or Rosamond will look at it, I am sure. Now, Myra, love, just go and take off your bonnet, and make your hair smooth, and then I will introduce you, as you wish it so much.'

But Myra had just arrived at the conclusion that she did not wish it at all, that she had made a most foolish blunder, and in her intense dread of drawing upon herself unnecessary remark, had decided, as is so often the case, upon the very line of conduct which would be the most remarkable. All through the long journey she had been endeavouring to plan how she should meet Mr. Verney, and what excuse she could make for seeing him alone; and finding herself unable to determine a question which could only be settled by the circumstances of the moment, she had worked herself up into a state of nervous uncertainty, which was the sure precursor of a blunder. She had already drawn upon herself her mother's attention, and Mrs. Verney's, and now she was going to do what of all things she most dreaded, face a large party, who would look at and watch her; and perhaps, after all, she might fail in finding the moment which she desired for begging to speak with Mr. Verney alone. As she passed the drawing-room, on her way to her own room, she stopped; the door was half open, and she looked in. Mr. Verney was there, standing with his back to her, drinking coffee, and talking to some ladies. Myra forgot she could be seen, and stood riveted to the spot, her heart beating violently. Perhaps he would turn and see her; if so, he would surely come and speak to her; and once she was nearly certain that he did see her. But he walked to the other end of the room immediately afterwards, and Myra could then only follow her own much regretted idea, and prepare herself for the drawing-room ordeal.

Happily, other persons had considered her comfort more than she was inclined to do herself, and when she went to her room she found Annette there, and a very comfortable repast provided; the bridesmaid's white tarlatan dress, with

its pale blue ribbons, was spread upon the bed, and Conyers
was waiting to put it on, as soon as she was ready. Myra,
thankful for any delay, sent Annette to beg Mrs. Verney not
to wait for her, and poured herself out a cup of tea, but she
could eat nothing.

‘If you don't eat, Miss Myra, perhaps you would try on
your dress at once,’ said Conyers, ‘and then I could set about
altering it, if there should be anything to be altered.’

‘Oh no, Conyers! not to-night; I can't. Take it away,
please.’

‘But, indeed, Miss Myra, it will only take five minutes.’

‘Impossible! It must be by and by. Annette, I shall be
ready directly.’ Myra pushed away her cup, turned to the
glass to arrange her hair and her dress, and make herself look,
as Annette said, presentable, and hurried downstairs.

‘Shall we wait for Mrs. Verney?’ said Annette, as they
paused before the drawing-room door. Myra made no
answer; her nervousness had become desperation, and they
went in.

The room, which was not large, was well filled and well
lighted; and as Myra entered, a brilliant duet on the harp
and piano was just beginning; and the general attention
being thus pre-occupied, she contrived to reach the middle
of the apartment without notice. Then a cousin perceived
her, and came up and spoke; then an aunt, and a friend,
her father, and Rosamond, and, in a few minutes, she was
the centre of a little circle, all making eager and loud inquiries, under the protection of the clanging chords of Doni-
zetti's opera. But where was Mr. Verney? Still not seeing
her, but talking in a distant corner to General Mainwaring,
who, being an old man with grey hair, and a Member of
Parliament besides, had been looked upon by Myra with
awe from her infancy. To interrupt such a conversation
would have been an unpardonable disrespect. The music
ceased. Myra hoped Mr. Verney would move, and he did
move; he turned round, saw her, came up to her, shook
hands heartily, said a few kind words—so kind indeed,
that Myra felt herself the basest of hypocrites—and then

went back again to his politics. What else could she have expected? Her anxiety to speak to him alone became all but unsupportable. One or two of the party who were to have beds in the village were preparing to take their leave. Mrs. Verney came up and begged her to go to bed also. Rosamond urged the same request, promising to come to her room for a few minutes' chat. Her father made a remark upon her pale face, and told her she was foolish in remaining; and Myra felt tired, so that she could scarcely stand; and bewildered and feverish, so that she could with difficulty bring herself to make a rational answer to anything that was said; and still lingered, and persisted in lingering, until Mr. Cameron sternly ordered her to go at once, and the die was cast.

Myra wished a general 'good night,' and, walking up to Mr. Verney, interrupting him in the middle of a sentence, said, in a very low trembling voice, 'I have something to say to you. Will you come with me to the schoolroom?'

'Certainly, if you desire it;' but the expression of his face at that moment Myra never forgot.

'A private *tête-à-tête*,' said Mrs. Verney, as they passed her in the corridor. 'That is not at all proper; but I suppose you are forestalling the privilege of brother and sister. Good night, dear Myra; we meet at ten to-morrow. Charles, the Colonel wishes to go; are we to wait and take you home, or send the carriage back?'

'Send it back, if you will; I like to be independent.'

'And to have a few last words with Rosamond. Well, it is very natural! Good night, once more, dear;' and Mrs. Verney kissed Myra. 'How burningly hot your forehead is! Pray go to bed soon, or you will be ill again.'

CHAPTER XLIV.

THE schoolroom was but dimly illuminated by the one candle which Myra placed upon the centre table. Mr. Verney threw himself into a chair, his face turned partially away from the light. He was the first to speak.

'Well, dear child, it is late; you must say your say quickly.'

'As quickly as I can; but, oh, Mr. Verney! I think you know!' And Myra drew near, and raised her eyes to him timidly.

'Know! I know a good many things. You must really speak plainly, if I am to understand you.'

'You will be angry; it may not be my business, but it has made me so very unhappy. I saw Miss Stuart and Mrs. Tracy at St. Wolfgang.'

He turned round and looked her full in the face. 'Really! and I suppose they inquired after me?'

No answer. Myra was too much amazed to speak.

'They are old acquaintances of mine,' he continued. 'Perhaps they talked about me?'

'Yes, they talked; they said—but Mrs. Tracy did not wish me to repeat it all, only I must.'

'My dear little girl, this is too silly. What do you mean by keeping me here, after ten o'clock at night, to tell me what some lady would not like me to hear. You have some senseless conscience-crotchet in your head, Myra; but you are growing too old to indulge such folly.'

'It is not a conscience-crotchet,' exclaimed Myra, recovering her self-possession, as her pride was roused by Mr. Verney's tone; 'it is truth and right.'

'Indeed!'

That 'indeed' was generally too much for Myra's self-confidence, there was such absolute superiority in it. Yet she continued, boldly : ' Mr. Verney, if you were engaged to Miss Stuart, you had no right to engage yourself at the same time to Rosamond.'

' Oh ! you have heard that folly, have you ? Dear child, I quite agree with you. If I am engaged to Miss Stuart, I cannot at the same time be engaged to your sister Rosamond.'

' But Miss Stuart considered you were engaged to her.'

' What a young lady considers is one thing ; what is actually the fact, another. My dear Myra, take my advice, and go to bed, and don't trouble yourself any more with matters which don't concern you. Rosamond and I quite understand each other, and any interference with us will only produce mischief.'

' But Mrs. Tracy said the same—at least, that it had been an engagement; she did not say it was actually so now.'

' Mrs. Tracy knows the state of things too well to make any such absurd assertion.'

' There is no absurdity in it, Mr. Verney,' said Myra very gravely. ' I don't know how things are at this moment, but I do know that you were engaged, and as a proof '—— She paused, and laid upon the table the little case containing the ring and the lock of hair.

As he took them up she saw his colour change. ' I have a message for you,' continued Myra. ' Miss Stuart bids you take your choice between the two. You asked for the hair ; if you keep it she feels that you will return to her. You gave her the ring ; if you accept it back again, she will know that you are gone from her for ever.'

' Rosamond will thank you for this,' was the answer.

' I know it may seem treacherous, but they were given me. O Mr. Verney ! I have been very wretched.'

' Because you have interfered with affairs which are quite out of your province,' continued Mr. Verney sternly. ' I did give this ring; I did ask for this hair. I was like other men. Rosamond knows it; she is satisfied. You need ask no more.'

'And Miss Stuart is miserable,' said Myra.

Mr. Verney leaned his head upon his hand, as he said, in an undertone, 'And I have been miserable also.'

'I may return the hair?' asked Myra.

There was no reply.

'And I may tell my father all that I know,' she continued.

'Tell your father!' Mr. Verney started from his seat. 'Myra, do you think I am a man likely to endure this monstrous, this unheard-of interference. Tell your father! Yes, tell him at your peril.'

'I must tell him,' was Myra's firm answer.

Mr. Verney's tone changed. 'Even so—tell him if you will,' he said. 'Go to him, let him know how you have forgotten your duty to your sister—how you have striven to mar her happiness—hear what he will say.'

'I must tell him all that Mrs. Tracy told me,' persisted Myra.

'All! What all! Mrs. Tracy knows there is no engagement now.'

'Mrs. Tracy spoke of other things besides the engagement,' said Myra hesitatingly.

'Mark me, Myra, if you have been listening to lies, and are now going to repeat them, God knows how bitterly you will repent it. Let me hear what Mrs. Tracy said.'

'She told me things which I must repeat to my father,' began Myra; but Mr. Verney interrupted her.

'Then Mrs. Tracy is a false hypocrite, and if Rosamond is rendered miserable for life, it will be her doing and yours, Myra. And we trusted you; yes, we trusted you more than any other human being!'

'And I was wrong in consenting to be so trusted,' said Myra. 'That also shall I say to papa.'

Mr. Verney rose and walked up and down the room.

'I have been very unhappy,' continued Myra, 'and I cannot bear the feeling of having done wrong any longer. And, Mr. Verney, if there is no truth in what Mrs. Tracy said, you will very easily explain everything to papa.'

'Myra, listen to me. You are bound in honour to tell me the accusations made against me, before you repeat them to any one. I require you to do so.'

Mr. Verney placed himself before her, and looked at her with an expression of determination, before which she actually quailed.

'I think I am bound to do so,' she replied. 'I wished to speak to you now for that reason. I will try and remember it all.'

'Yes, all; let there be no reserve, no prevarication.'

The colour mounted to Myra's cheek, and she looked up at him indignantly. 'Mr. Verney, you have no right to use that word. I do not know how to prevaricate. Mrs. Tracy told me that you were greatly in debt, that even if you were to return to India your income would not be sufficient to set you free, and that your private fortune was all gone, because it was mixed up with Mr. Stuart's affairs, which within the last two months had become so involved there was no hope of retrieving them. And she said, also, that if it had not been for these money difficulties you would have married Miss Stuart. This is what I must tell papa,' she added; 'he must know it to-night.'

Mr. Verney had listened with a countenance absolutely impassive; when Myra concluded, a sharp, satirical, light laugh seemed to ring through the apartment, as he said, 'Is that all?'

'Yes, all.'

'Thank you, I suppose I may be allowed to spare you the trouble of communicating these important facts, or exaggerations, or falsehoods, or with whatever name they may be dignified, to your father?'

Myra gazed at him in utter perplexity.

'You have no wish, I imagine, to place yourself in an unfitting or improper position,' he continued.

'I wish to tell papa what Mrs. Tracy told me,' said Myra, 'and I intend to do so.'

'Precisely so; that is, you wish Mr. Cameron to know. If I tell him, you will be equally satisfied.'

Myra hesitated. 'I must tell him that I was wrong in sending the letters,' she said.

'We will leave your little confessions for the present. They are not exactly to the point. Time presses. I desire you simply to understand that I relieve you from your mission.'

'And you will say it all?' said Myra. 'But Mrs. Tracy, I am sure, wished me to say it myself.'

'We will forget Mrs. Tracy. The question lies between you and me.'

'O Mr. Verney! you would not deceive me,' said Myra, and she looked at him with an expression of such child-like, earnest truth, that the cold-hearted, cynical man of the world was touched by it, and he answered with a sincerity which could not be doubted—

'Myra, on the word of a man of honour, I will not marry your sister until your father knows everything that is to be known about me.'

'And I may speak to him myself after you have spoken to him?' said Myra.

He turned from her abruptly.

'I don't doubt—I can't. O Mr. Verney! forgive me!'

There was a silence of some seconds. Mr. Verney kept his face partially averted. Then he answered in a voice from which all bitterness was gone—'Say to him what you will to-morrow. Now, good night.'

Myra burst into tears.

'Poor child!' he took her hand tenderly, and she allowed it to rest in his, whilst scarcely articulate through her sobs came the words: 'If you will only say you forgive me!'

'God bless you! I am not worthy to forgive you.' The last sentence was uttered as if spoken to himself, and before Myra could add another word he had left her.

Myra listened to his footsteps along the corridor and thought he went back to the drawing-room, and after vainly trying to hide the traces of tears on her face she went up to her own room. Conyers was waiting for her with the bridesmaid's dress.

'O Miss Myra! how could you be so forgetful and stay so late? Your mamma has rung for me twice, to know if the dress fits.'

'I am so tired,' was Myra's most true answer. 'Conyers, you must leave it.'

Conyers merely replied by assisting Myra to unfasten the dress she wore, and to put on the other.

'Miss Cameron wished to come in and see it on, Miss Myra; I believe she promised your mamma she would. It looks very nice, doesn't it now?' Conyers moved the glass so that Myra might look at herself.

It was a startling contrast, that bridal attire and the pale face of distress. Myra glanced at herself for an instant, and then sat down with a look of such utter wretchedness that Conyers, interpreting it as fatigue, looked quite alarmed.

'Shall I go and call Miss Cameron?' she asked, when Myra seemed a little recovered.

'Yes, if you will. Tell her to come quickly;' and when Conyers was gone Myra walked up and down the room with her hands clasped together, repeating a few words of prayer, which, though wandering and unconnected, soothed her with the consciousness of not being left to bear her burden alone.

Cheerful, bright, good-natured, looking as if it had been morning instead of night, Rosamond came. Myra scarcely knew what she said or did; she only felt that every tone of her sister's voice went through her as if it had been the thrust of a dagger.

'You are tired, poor darling,' said Rosamond, giving a hasty glance of inspection. 'The dress does very well. Go to bed.'

'Is every one else gone? Mr. Verney?'

'Not yet, I think. Shall I take him your love?' and she laughed.

Myra sank down upon the nearest chair.

'Oh, child, to rumple your dress in that way! Take it off, Conyers, and put her into bed. Good night.'

Myra just managed to say 'good night,' and that was all. Happily, perhaps, for herself, she was by this time so utterly worn out that she could only leave herself in Conyers' hands to be undressed.

'Don't call her too early in the morning, Conyers,' was Rosamond's last good-natured speech. 'She won't be wanted till it is time to go to church.'

CHAPTER XLV.

'Eight o'clock, Miss Myra. Indeed you must be quick.'

Myra started from a heavy yet disturbed sleep, and sat up in bed, scarcely conscious where she was.

'Your sisters are very nearly ready, and the bridesmaids are all to have their breakfast together in the schoolroom; and my mistress hopes you will be able to go down and attend to them, Miss Myra; so please make haste. Can I help you?'

'Thank you, Conyers, no. I don't want help; but is papa dressed?'

'I can't say, miss, not yet though, I fancy.'

'But can I see him? Was he very late last night? Do you think I can see him?'

'Indeed, Miss Myra, if you would only dress yourself you could settle all that afterwards. Your mamma is so fidgety about the schoolroom breakfast.'

'If you will leave me, Conyers, I will be as quick as I can. Juliet must begin without me. Pray go.'

There was an intense irritability in Myra's tone. Conyers departed.

Was it then Rosamond's wedding morning? Were there no difficulties—no obstacles? Had Mr. Verney really satisfied her father? And had Myra only dreamt of some terrible discovery? She listened to the sounds in the house: all was stir, excitement, preparation. Juliet's voice was heard on the stairs—loud and merry. She wanted Conyers to alter her sash; the bridesmaids did not like the way their sashes had been made up, and must have them put on differently. Then came Annette with rather a whining voice, complaining that she should never be ready in time; then a cousin, who stood in Rosamond's doorway, called 'Conyers' in the authoritative

Z

tone which belongs to the chief confidante of the chief person age on an important occasion; and again Conyers, doubtless actuated by some secret misgiving, knocked at Myra's door, to inquire how long it would be before she was ready—and Myra started up and began to dress.

She always dressed slowly : her mind was apt to wander to subjects which interested her; and this morning she was awkward and nervous, and everything went wrong. Again and again messages were sent to hurry her, and then the nervousness increased; and she longed, oh, so earnestly! to have a quiet time for her prayers; and when she knelt down she could not collect her thoughts or express what she wanted to say; and just as she had begun to be a little composed another knock made her start up, and she had to answer some trivial question, which irritated her, and made her feel quite wicked. It was very trying; but more trying than all was a sense of unreality, which made her several times pause as if something in her mind was wrong; as if in some way she had been under a great delusion, and had not yet awakened from it.

But she was dressed at last, and went down to breakfast. A merry party was assembled. Juliet was pouring out coffee, and Annette tea. Henrietta and Elise Verney, with the other bridesmaids, making in all eight, were assembled. They were talking eagerly when Myra came in.

'Look,' said Juliet, holding up a ring to her, 'look what was found on the mantelpiece this morning. There is carefulness.

Myra turned quite white, but answered gently, 'The ring is not mine.'

'Not yours! What will you say next? You know Mr. Verney gave it you last night, and the case is on your dressing-table at this moment. Won't I tell him what a value you put upon his gifts! I wish he had offered it to me.'

'Please give me the ring, Juliet,' replied Myra; 'and will you let me have some coffee?'

'Do give her the ring, Juliet,' said Henrietta Verney, who was sitting near her. 'She does not look well enough to bear being teased this morning.'

'But she says it is not hers,' said Juliet. ''Then it must be Mr. Verney's, and I shall give it back to him.'

'Oh no, Juliet! indeed you must not. Let me have it,' exclaimed Myra. 'I know about it, only it is not mine.'

'Then there is a mystery,' exclaimed Juliet, looking round triumphantly, 'and I was right. How I will torment Mr. Verney! I could not imagine what you and he had to say to each other such a long time last night.'

The remark drew the general attention upon Myra, who sat drinking her coffee, and trying to look unconscious and indifferent, whilst the trembling of her hand and the paleness of her lips plainly betrayed her agitation.

Glances passed around. Henrietta Verney whispered to a servant to bring a little sal-volatile, but the whisper reached Myra's ears, and had a most strengthening effect. She looked up and smiled, and said she was much obliged, but she was quite well. The journey of the day before had been fatiguing, but she should be quite herself after breakfast; and then the remarks ceased apparently, but a certain feeling of curiosity and suspicion had been awakened, which was not lessened by the tone in which Myra asked whether any one had seen her father that morning.

'I see him now,' exclaimed Annette, as she turned to the window. 'He is walking across the lawn with the Archdeacon. They are going to the church, I am sure, to be sure that everything is right.'

Myra pushed aside her coffee-cup and hurried to the door.

'Myra, Myra, where are you going?' exclaimed Juliet. 'There are a thousand things we want to say and arrange. You must not go.'

'I must speak to papa,' said Myra. She hurried out of the room, and Annette watched her rushing across the lawn.

'Something is the matter,' observed Juliet oracularly. Every one else seemed to think the same, and a party gathered round the window.

'In her white dress and without a bonnet! So like Myra it is,' murmured Annette. 'I do believe she will go out into the high road.'

'The Archdeacon will think her mad,' said Juliet.

'She has not caught up with them, though,' exclaimed a young cousin. 'Just look, she is coming back.'

'I don't believe papa is going to the church,' said Juliet. 'He has turned down towards the Rectory. Can't you see him crossing the bridge ?'

Myra returned almost immediately, and said quietly, 'Dr. Kingsbury is not so well this morning, and has asked to see papa. He will be back again directly.'

'Oh ! then you did catch up with him,' exclaimed Juliet. 'What did the Archdeacon think of you ? He must have been very much astonished.'

'I did not speak to the Archdeacon,' replied Myra, and her voice grew husky as she added—'They don't think Dr. Kingsbury will live through the day.'

A general silence fell upon the party.

At that instant the door was thrown open rather widely, and Rosamond, in her bridal dress of white silk, with an orange-blossom wreath and lace veil, entered the room. A murmur of admiration passed from mouth to mouth. Rosamond's figure was exquisitely graceful. Her delicate complexion was tinged by excitement, her blue eyes, usually rather hard and cold, were softened into an expression which was almost tender in its sweetness, whilst her small mouth was brightened with a smile of the most perfect amiability. No man could have looked at her that morning without believing that he who could win her for his wife must have a prospect of perfect happiness. The more cynical of her own sex might indeed have traced an absence of perfect simplicity in her movements, and a tone of satisfied vanity in the gentle greeting which she gave her friends ; but it was surely not more than might be considered natural under the circumstances. What failing is so inherent in a woman's nature as vanity ? It is the last fault which, except in aggravated cases, the world feels called upon to condemn. It is the first which any one earnestly yearning to serve God with a perfect heart will labour to uproot.

'Mamma told me she had promised you I should come

and show myself;' and Rosamond advanced into the centre of the room. ' Myra, love, how are you this morning? You don't look as if you had slept an hour.'

Myra looked at her for an instant in silent admiration, and, kissing her, whispered—'O Rosamond! are you happy?'

' Yes, dear child, quite happy—quite. Do you doubt?' and Rosamond laughed.

Myra said not another word, but turned to go away.

' The carriages will be here almost directly, and the bridesmaids are to go first, Myra,' exclaimed Juliet, following her.

' I must wait for papa,' said Myra. She paused in the doorway.

' He may stay with Dr. Kingsbury till the last moment,' observed Juliet.

' Ah, poor Dr. Kingsbury! I am so sorry. It is dreadfully unfortunate,' murmured Rosamond. ' I should so have liked him to perform the ceremony.'

' Please, Myra, don't keep us waiting,' persisted Juliet. ' Where are you going now?'

' To mamma's room; I have not seen her this morning.'

' But Conyers is with her, and she will be worried if she is interrupted. Do stay here, and let us keep an eye upon you.'

' Please not, Juliet. I—I don't feel very well.' No one thought of asking what was the matter, and Myra shut herself up in her own room.

Those next minutes of waiting, how endless, how intolerable they appeared! One or two carriages drew up, and as each one came near Myra expected the summons. Several times she fancied she heard her father's voice. Several times she believed that she was called herself. Then came the suggestion not to worry herself any more—to forget Mrs. Tracy, to trust Mr. Verney, to believe that it was all right. Then all kinds of absurd impossible wishes entered her head,—that she could run down to the Rectory—see her father—see the dear old Rector—tell all she had to tell there. Oh! why had she

delayed ?　It must have been cowardice.　If she had not so
dreaded an interview with her father, surely she would have
sought it more.　And if all should not be right ! now, at the
very last moment !　Her heart turned sick with fear, and just
at that moment the call rang through the corridor, 'The
carriages are ready for the bridesmaids.　No time to be
lost.'

Juliet rushed into Myra's room.　Conyers also was at
hand.

'Your mamma has sent me, Miss Myra, that she may be
quite sure your dress is right.'

'I must see papa,' was all Myra could say.

'Papa !' interposed Juliet.　'Nonsense, Myra, it is impossible.'

'Indeed, Miss Myra, it won't do to wait.　Can I tell him
anything for you ?' asked Conyers.

Another impatient call for the bridesmaids, and almost at
the same instant some one was heard to say, 'The carriage is
to take Mr. Cameron up at the Rectory.'

Myra turned to her sister with sudden dignity of manner.
'Go, Juliet, I will follow directly;' and Juliet, rather awed
and repelled, though she did not know why, ran downstairs.

Myra leaned back in the carriage, and spoke not a word
till they reached the church.

The bridesmaids were to wait in the schoolroom, which
was close adjoining.　There the little procession was to be
formed, and the school-children were already in attendance,
prepared to strew flowers in the bride's path.　Several gentlemen were standing about, watching for the carriage which was
to come by the Rectory road.　Inquiries were made for Mr.
Verney, but the Stormont party had not yet arrived.

The Archdeacon drove up, and there was a feeling of
impatience and disappointment.　He went into the vestry,
and Godfrey Cameron followed him.

Still no carriage from the Rectory; but presently came a
great rumble of wheels, and the Stormont carriage and four
stopped before the west porch.　The school-children crowded
round so that no one could exactly see who got out, but it was

to be supposed that Mr. Verney was one of the number. Myra pressed to the doorway, and even went a few steps into the road. As the difficulty of approaching her father increased, the misgivings, the fears, the reproaches of her possibly over-scrupulous conscience awoke to agony.

'They are coming—yes, coming. Now then,' Juliet pulled Myra back, and the bridal carriage drew up.

Godfrey came out of the vestry and went into the school-room. 'The Archdeacon and Mr. Bathurst are quite ready; form yourselves properly—the Stormont people are in the church.'

Myra deliberately left her place, and to the consternation of every one went up to her father as he got out of the carriage, and laid her hand on his arm. 'Papa, I must speak with you.'

Mr. Cameron's face was like a thunder-cloud. 'Speak, child! Now? Folly!'

'Papa,'—she drew him aside, and her voice trembled, so that she was scarcely intelligible—'Have you seen Mr. Verney? Is it all right?'

'Seen him? He is here. Of course all is right. Go, child, go; don't think you are to arrange things.'

Myra shrank away crushed; but she joined the procession into the church. The building was crowded. All the village people were there, the farmers, and many of the neighbouring gentry, who were to be present at the breakfast afterwards.

Rosamond, leaning on her father's arm, walked composedly up the aisle, the eight bridesmaids following. Mr. Cameron glanced round for Mr. Verney, so did Godfrey, Edmund, the Archdeacon; so also did Colonel Verney and the Stormont guests. Where was he? Some one whispered, 'He must have forgotten the ring, or the license;' and the murmur was handed round, but still people looked surprised.

Mr. Cameron went up to Colonel Verney. 'Is he coming? What is the matter?'

'Coming? he must be here. Who came with him?'

No one. The Hall party had believed he was to accompany Colonel Verney. Colonel Verney had understood that Mr. Verney was gone to the Hall.

The buzz in the church became audible. One or two persons left their places and went out into the churchyard to look. Rosamond was led to a seat, still outwardly retaining perfect self-possession. Myra clasped her hands tightly together, and neither trembled nor felt bewildered, for the hour for courage was come.

Mr. Cameron, with his head erect, and insensible to the gazing crowd, walked down the aisle, and in a loud authoritative tone ordered that Colonel Verney's carriage should drive back instantly to Stormont. 'Mr. Verney had mistaken the hour.'

The coachman mounted the coach-box, and gathered up the reins, and was about to drive off, when a boy was seen running at full speed down the lane from the Hall.

'A message, sir,' said the Stormont footman, touching his hat. 'Shall we wait for it?'

'Yes, wait.' Mr. Cameron walked forward a few steps.

The footman brought back a letter directed to Myra.

'The young fellow says, sir, that he met Mr. Verney about an hour and a half ago near the railway station, and that he gave him this note, and told him to take it to the Hall.'

'An hour and a half ago!' exclaimed Mr. Cameron.

'Yes, sir; the boy say he knows it ought to have been given sooner, but he was obliged to go somewhere else first.'

Mr. Cameron took the note, examined it, almost broke the seal.

'Go for Miss Myra—bid her come here.'

The man entered the church, and went up to Myra.

All eyes were fixed upon her. Mrs. Verney came up to her, begging to be told what was the matter. So did Colonel Verney. Curiosity became intense. The congregation were leaving their seats and crowding into the aisles. Rosamond remained in her place, but she was deadly pale. Edmund Cameron alone thought for Myra, and, drawing her arm within his, led her down the church. She leaned upon him still as her father put the letter into her hands. The envelope enclosed another letter addressed to Mr. Cameron. The lines addressed to herself were few.

'You will give this to your father. I have entered into no explanations; but after the doubts expressed in your conversation last night, and which, I imagine, will be shared by all your family, it is impossible for me to fulfil my engagement. I leave it to you to comfort Rosamond, if she should require comfort. C. V.'

Myra gave the note to her brother, and tried to speak, but her voice failed her, and she almost fell to the ground. Edmund lifted her into one of the carriages and went up to Mr. Cameron.

'We must take Rosamond home, sir. Shall I fetch her?'

Mr. Cameron's face was livid with rage. He threw Mr. Verney's letter to the ground, and as he clenched his hands, for perhaps the first time in his life an oath escaped him.

'Shall I fetch her, sir?' repeated Edmund.

There was no answer; but Mr. Cameron strode up the aisle, and, without uttering a single word of explanation, led Rosamond from the church, placed her in the carriage by Myra's side, seated himself by her, and in a tone of thunder gave the order to drive to the Hall.

Then, like the rush of a storm, the congregation poured forth from the church—clergymen, bridesmaids, relations, friends, spectators—in one mingled crowd, and through them all, as they gathered at the entrance, dashed the Stormont carriage and four, with Colonel Verney shouting frantically to the coachman, 'To the Hall! to the Hall!' and Mrs. Verney, even then not forgetting her propriety, endeavouring to calm him by reminding him that it might be there was nothing really amiss.

CHAPTER XLVI.

THE whole brunt of that terrible storm for the first few hours fell upon Myra. If she had but told all that she knew public exposure might have been prevented. So it is that in this world the innocent suffer for the deeds of the guilty, and the comparatively small offence on which the public eye is fixed is exaggerated into a crime, whilst the hidden but grievous sin which God will condemn at the last day is overlooked, and even justified. But Myra was brave now. There was no surprise or hesitation, and nothing to conceal. She had been led into a difficulty by first consenting to become a party to Rosamond and Mr. Verney's deception, and circumstances had aggravated it till she could find no way of escape. So far she confessed herself in the wrong, and bore with quietness and humility the reproaches which were lavished upon her. Her brother Edmund alone defended her. A straightforward unselfish character instinctively understands the feelings of one which resembles it; and when Myra, after narrating all that she knew, left her father's study, bowed down by the thought of his anger, it was Edmund who undertook to put her conduct in its true light. Much, indeed, she needed such help. Godfrey lectured her; her mother cried, and asked how she could have kept it all from them; Juliet tormented her by triumphantly reminding her that she had known from the first there was some mystery; and Rosamond, her pride stung to the quick, turned away when Myra would have kissed her, with the cold words, 'Thank you, I require no pity,' and shut herself up in her room, till she could nerve herself to the due amount of haughty contempt which she believed her position demanded.

And whilst Myra's fault was thus exaggerated because it had brought a wound to the family vanity, Rosamond was excused, pitied, and caressed, and even Mr. Verney escaped with a less share of indignation than might have been anticipated. When Edmund endeavoured to exculpate Myra, and spoke of Mr. Verney as he deserved, Mr. Cameron sharply replied, 'The man is a scoundrel; I desire never to hear his name again. But your sister, Edmund, is a little fool.'

And this state of feeling continued, until a visit from Colonel Verney had directed Mr. Cameron's wrath into a more just and natural channel. Thoroughly shocked and distressed, the good-natured Colonel had at first vented a torrent of indignation upon his nephew, and pity upon Rosamond; and having driven away from the Hall, which he declared he could never have the face to enter again, he had stated his intention of following the missing bridegroom, and demanding a full explanation of his conduct. But Mrs. Verney, more cautious, and with a more clear comprehension of the true state of the case, quieted this fever of excitement, and the Colonel then was only anxious to go back to Mr. Cameron, and make the apology which he felt the honour of the Verney name demanded.

A most excellent intention, intrusted, alas! to most unfitting hands. The Colonel began his apology, and it was accepted stiffly, with the addition of some very cutting remarks upon the deception which had been practised. He did his best to agree, but being touchy upon the point of the family honour, he did not feel inclined to hear from another what he would have been the first to say himself, and offered a slight excuse. Mr. Cameron was bitter, the Colonel hasty. One retort followed another, and when at length the Colonel suggested that it was a pity, since Myra knew all about it, she had not had the good sense to speak, in time to prevent the unhappy exposure, Mr. Cameron turned round and proudly defended his child, and for the first time discovered that, but for her interposition, Rosamond would at that moment have been the wife of an unprincipled beggar.

The speech was the turning point for Myra, and from that moment she had no more reproaches to fear. But it was also the culminating point for Colonel Verney, and in fiery indignation he strode from the room, vowing, with asseverations which made Mr. Cameron's lip curl with pharisaical satisfaction, that he would allow himself to be torn to pieces rather than again demean himself to offer to that man the slightest shadow of an apology.

It was vain, then, for even Mrs. Verney, who sought an interview immediately afterwards, to attempt to cast oil upon the troubled waters. And, indeed, for her the effort would probably under any circumstances have been useless. There are long seasons during which insincerity and flattery have influence, but they are seasons of prosperity, when the world goes smoothly with us. Mr. Cameron was now in no mood for flattery; he had exercised his practised powers of cross-examination in discovering from Myra and Rosamond every particular of the secret engagement, and he now plainly taxed Mrs. Verney with having been a party to it at the very time when she was suggesting the marriage to himself as a perfectly new idea. When she hesitated how to reply, he put on his most repelling manner, and suggested that for the future he should prefer for his family the society of persons who were not likely to be the sharers of such secrets. He believed that parents were the best, and the only lawful judges as to what would be for their children's good. No doubt Mrs. Verney had acted with the best intentions. As a gentleman speaking to a lady, he could not suppose otherwise; but in the present instance, her interference in his family affairs had, he grieved to say, been a signal failure. And with a stiff bow, Mr. Cameron moved to the door, and Mrs. Verney had no alternative but to go. She went to Rosamond's room; and there another defeat awaited her. She offered pity and sympathy, and Rosamond was coldly indifferent, and needed no pity. Of wounded feeling she possessed very little, of wounded pride a great deal. Mr. Verney, she said, had of course at the last done the only thing which was possible to be done. She wished no excuse to be made for him. A man without principle could not be open to excuses. He had deceived and insulted her, but she left him to the world's condemnation, and certainly could only feel thankful that she had been saved the life-long disappointment which must have been hers if she had become his wife.

Mrs. Verney could say nothing in reply, and whenever this was the case, she always escaped as quickly as possible. She was still, however, full of regrets, full of affection. She only trusted that nothing that had occurred would weaken the friendly feeling which had lately been so increased between the two families. To which Rosamond replied, that whatever she might feel herself, she was afraid her father was not likely to forget or overlook the offence that had been offered; and then she sat silent. Mrs. Verney made a few commonplace remarks, and departed, without even attempting to see Mrs. Cameron, the only person whom she might really have soothed, but whose influence in her own family was so small that it was not worth her while to propitiate her. It was a very bitter disappointment to Mrs. Verney. If she could have retained the outward form of friendship with the Camerons, she might, by repudiating her nephew, have saved herself and her husband from any share in the odium of his conduct. But to quarrel with them, or to be supposed to do so, was at once to be imagined to take part with the man who had so grossly deceived and injured them. The world knows nothing of the inner working of such dissensions. It merely sees that persons are not friends; it can never tell why or how the unfriendliness has arisen, or to whom the fault is to be attributed. Mrs. Verney knew quite well that the world would talk, and that, if it talked, it would infallibly tell lies; and she would fain have stopped its mouth by a fact; the only way, indeed, by which the world can be silenced. She would willingly have pointed to the continued intimacy between the two families as a proof that the Colonel and herself were absolutely innocent; and very hard, indeed very unjust, it seemed to her, that she could not be allowed to do so. But so it was, and when she sat down to a family dinner that evening (the guests invited for the wedding having all departed), it was with the unpleasant thought that her neighbours were probably, at that moment, speculating how much or how little she and Colonel Verney had known of Mr. Verney's affairs, and deciding that, of course, they must have been aware of a good deal, as there was no doubt a decided quarrel between them and the Camerons.

For a woman who lived for the world, who basked in the sunshine of the world's favour, what imputation could be more galling?

For the first time in her life Mrs. Verney felt that she had blundered.

And at the Hall also there was a painful consciousness of the world's curious gaze, and of its unbridled tongue. But things were more simple, more open there. The feelings which were expressed were, in every case except Rosamond's, natural and real, and so there was less strain upon the party. The greater number of the wedding guests went away in the afternoon, but a few near relations remained, and as Rosamond kept to her room, and Myra waited upon her mother, who was too unwell to come downstairs, there was liberty for conversation and full expression of feeling, and this soothed Mr. Cameron by allowing him to assert his wounded dignity, and to congratulate himself more on what he had been saved from, than on what he had been called upon to bear.

Such an earthquake as the event of the morning would, it might have seemed, have upset a family for months, and yet on the evening of that same day there was a decided lull in the storm, and as the gentlemen sat together after dinner there was even something like a not unpleasing excitement in going over what they had said, and thought, and feared, and suspected. After all, they were not sufferers. To the general eye, only Rosamond was really to be pitied, and how sharp that corroding pang of wounded pride and vanity really was, she was not likely to betray.

No one thought of Myra, except to call her a silly child for having trusted to the word of ' such a fellow as Verney.' No one in the least guessed or could have understood the wreck of feeling, the blank dreariness which fell upon her, when, having left her mother nearly asleep, she shut herself up in her own room to collect her thoughts, to remember and examine all that had occurred, to see if possible how she had been led wrong, how she could have done better, and to resolve—oh! how sorrowful is that first resolve to a young heart!—that she would for the future never allow herself to be deceived by the cha..n of talent or personal kindness, but that she would suspect and be on her guard, and distrust appearances, and remember the bitter lesson which had taught her that the deeds of the life, and not the words of the mouth, are the test by which we are to judge our fellow-creatures as well as ourselves.

And at the very time when Myra made this resolve to stand alone, she had such a yearning for guidance—visible, human guidance ! It is a long time before we feel that prayer and God's help are sufficient for us ; and though Myra prayed, and found comfort in prayer, she still longed intensely for some one to whom she might go, and, as she would herself have expressed it, talk it all over, and ask what she should have done. One person there was to whom now, when one of the real trials of life had come upon her, she felt that she could have ventured, perhaps, to open her heart, but he was far away in spirit, though yet near her in the body, lingering on the borders of that silent land where the troubling of the wicked ceases, and the cares of the weary find rest.

It was in vain to think of talking to Dr. Kingsbury, and yet Myra could not resist the wish to see him once more, with perhaps the secret hope that if he had only rallied sufficiently to admit her to his room, he might say something from which she might find strength and comfort. When the dinner-bell rang, and she knew that every one was engaged, and that Conyers was waiting upon her mother with a cup of coffee, she stole quietly away, leaving word with Juliet where she was to be found, and crossed the garden and the dell to the Rectory. How everything reminded her of Mr. Verney, and that first time when she had seen him, and of the way in which her feeling for him had grown up, and been strengthened by all the quiet strolls, the pleasant conversations, the ready sympathy which had made the last summer so indescribably pleasant to her ! A man without honour, without principle, a deceiver, selfish, cold-hearted, treacherous ! Oh no ! he was not that ; he never could be that. Myra had stumbled, upon the terrible fact of human inconsistency, which is the problem of the wisest through life, and must be so till death ; and it occupied her thoughts till she found herself at the back door of the Rectory, trembling and almost repenting of her visit, as she felt what the meeting with her old friends must be when such a tale was to be discussed, such folly in herself confessed, and such evil in others to be alluded to.

The kitchen door was gently opened by Betsey. 'Is it you, Miss Myra? Master has been asking for you so many times.'

'Has he indeed?' Myra's face brightened. 'And is he better?'

'Ah! no; not better really, miss. But he has wonderful strength to last so long. We thought this morning he was going, and so did Mr. Harrison. That was why we sent for Mr. Cameron. Master had something on his mind, he was so bent upon saying to him. I suspect it must have had to do with Mrs. Patty's affairs when he is gone. Very unfortunate it was as it turned out, but we could not help it. And now he has taken some arrowroot, and Faith says she should not be surprised if he was to last out the night. But he will be very glad to see you, Miss Myra. Oh dear! he has thought a great deal of you to-day.' Betsey dared not express her sympathy more plainly, and Myra, shrinking from the least touch on the wounded spot, answered directly, 'Please, Betsey, go and tell Mrs. Patty I am here, and ask if I may come up for a minute. Tell her I must not be longer because of leaving mamma.'

'Ah! Poor Mrs. Cameron! How is she?' asked Betsey curiously.

'Pretty well, thank you. Please go quickly. I will sit down in the kitchen till you come back.'

'Oh no! Miss Myra; don't do that. Come up with me. I can be certain Mrs. Patty will be inclined to cry her eyes out with pleasure at seeing you. But here's Faith; she can tell us everything.'

Faith brought word that 'the Doctor was strangely better for the time, and had insisted upon being placed in his arm-chair by the fire, though it had been all they could do to get him there. He would be quite ready, she was sure, to see Miss Myra. He wanted sadly to hear all about it.'

Again Myra felt as though a dagger had gone through her. It was the foretaste of a pang to be repeated many many times before she could be in the least accustomed to it. She followed Faith up the stairs, determined to be brave, and endure patiently whatever might be in store for her, for doubtless she in a measure deserved it.

But the first words of fatherly greeting which awaited her were calming as an opiate. The old Rector turned round his head quite quickly when the door opened, and a smile brightened up his withered features : ' My little Myra, this is pleasant. I thank God that He has sent you. Patty, let her come near to me ; and I should like to see her alone.'

' Surely, Doctor, dear. Come near the fire, Myra. You like the low seat, and you won't disturb him. He is better just now, and waiting quietly. We are both waiting,' she added in an undertone.

' Dear Mrs. Patty, I have wanted to see you so much all day,' said Myra, as she seated herself on the low stool by the Doctor, and turned her face up to look at Mrs. Patty.

' Ah ! my dear, not half so much as I have wanted to see you.' Mrs. Patty bent down and took Myra's face between her hands, and kissed her. ' I have been sorry for a good many at the Hall to-day, but for none more than you. But tell the Doctor all you like, and if I think you are tiring him, I will come in and send you away.'

' There is not much to be told that you don't know, sir,' said Myra, addressing the Doctor as Mrs. Patty went into the next room, and closed the door behind her. ' You know that Rosamond is not married, and that Mr. Verney '——

' Is a villain,' said the old man emphatically. But seeing Myra start, he added, ' It sounds like a hard word, but it was a cruel deed to a young girl.'

' Very cruel,' said Myra, but she thought not of Rosamond, but of a broken heart in a distant land.

There was a slight pause. Then Myra added : ' I was not free from blame myself.'

' I heard it. Patty was told something about your knowing more than any one else, but I was sure you must have

been taken in. Young things like you have much to learn as
to the ways of this evil world.'

'But I might have learnt; I might have known,' said
Myra. 'It was very wrong to help them to keep the engage-
ment concealed, and that was what I did; but—I trusted Mr.
Verney.'

'No doubt you did, my dear. All little girls of your age
would have been likely to do so. But, Myra'—the old man
laid his withered hand upon hers as it rested on his knee,
and his voice was tremulous in its earnestness—'trust God
and your own heart. It is the counsel of a dying man.'

'My own heart! oh! never, never,' exclaimed Myra.

'"Keep thy heart with all diligence, for out of it are the
issues of life." My child, those are God's own words.'

But I have been deceived,' said Myra, 'and I may be
again.'

'Keep thy heart with all diligence; did you do so?' He
fixed his sunken eyes upon her, and Myra felt the glance thrill
through her.

'Perhaps I did not,' she said hesitatingly.

'God knows if you did not, and how, and why you did not.
He will pardon that sin, as He will all sin; only it must not
be repeated.'

'I deceived myself,' exclaimed Myra. 'God will not leave
me to guide myself again; will He? Oh! sir, if He would
only spare you.'

'God will help you; do not doubt it. But He may not
give you guidance—such as you seek.'

'I shall never trust my own judgment,' said Myra.

'A safe resolution, for you are young. Yet you must learn
to trust it.'

'By making blunders,' said Myra, attempting to smile.

'Even so. By making blunders, and profiting by them.
So it is we are all taught. Only there are some to whom the
teaching comes very late,' and the Doctor sighed heavily.

'You are tired, sir,' said Myra, looking at him anxiously.

'A little. But wait, child; wait.' He put out his hand
to detain her, as she would have left him to summon Mrs.

Patty. 'One word more; you have to stand alone, my little girl.'

'Yes, it seems so. Is it wrong to think it?'

'Face truth always. Never fear it.' And in his earnestness, the Doctor half raised himself in his chair, and leaned forward. 'You are alone; you want a right judgment. Take the experience of nearly eighty years. It is the balance of character which through God's grace will give you that. Do you understand?'

'Not quite—I hope I do—I will try. But indeed'—again she would have left him, for his voice was faint, and a change had come over his face.

Still his detaining hand was lightly laid upon her. 'The balance of character—proportion. No one fault, no one virtue even, allowed to get the upper-hand. It is the heart which leads the judgment astray. O God, do Thou help and tend her.'

Myra knelt by his chair, and he murmured a few more words of prayer. Then he fell back suddenly.

Mrs. Patty looked in at the doorway, and Myra beckoned to her. She came and bent over him. 'Doctor, dear.'

He opened his eyes, and gazed at her, but there was something strange in his look.

'The mischief is at the heart,' whispered Mrs. Patty; 'he has had such an attack before. Ring the bell, my dear.' She gave her orders with an unfaltering voice.

'And I made him talk,' said Myra.

Mrs. Patty folded her hands together, and said quietly, 'God's will;' and then she stooped down and kissed the old man's forehead tenderly, and spoke his name.

He knew her quite, and smiled, but he did not answer. Faith answered the bell, and Mr. Harrison was sent for.

'Shall you get him into bed?' asked Myra.

'He is more comfortable where he is. Doctor, dear, is there any pain?'

He shook his head.

'Thank God for that,' said Mrs. Patty.

'Must I go?' asked Myra.

The old Rector just raised his hand, and his lips moved.

'She will stay, Doctor, dear. Yes, she will stay. Myra, it is what we must all come to.'

Mrs. Patty was rigid in her self-control, but Myra's tears flowed fast. She continued kneeling at the Rector's feet, chafing his cold hands, but no warmth came to them.

Faith re-entered the room, and Betsey followed. They brought warm water and flannels, hoping to restore the circulation, but life was ebbing away fast. The old man spoke one word, which only Faith caught.

'He wants prayers, ma'am. Shall the curate come?'

'The commendatory prayer, Patty,' was repeated again more distinctly.

'Doctor, dear, yes;' and Mrs. Patty opened the Prayer-Book. She paused for one instant; her self-restraint entirely gave way, and she put the book into Myra's hands, and buried her face against the sofa.

And then, in the stillness of that death-chamber, the sweet young voice, through broken and faint, rose up to Heaven, commending to Almighty God the soul of him who had so long passed the term of man's appointed time on earth. It ceased, and in the pause which followed, the old Rector's voice was heard:

'Patty, there are many mansions.'

'Doctor, dear, yes. There will be one for you.'

'One for us both. Little Myra—take care of her. Jesus, Saviour—have mercy.' A sigh, a short struggle, and it was all over.

CHAPTER XLVII.

A STILL autumn evening, with a most glorious sunset, steeping the atmosphere in a tint of unearthly reddish and golden brown, like the hues of the fading leaves etherealised;—the sky in the west a burnished mirror of clear transparent gold, with crimson clouds gathering round it; the east reflecting back the gorgeous light in masses of rose-coloured vapours, rising high in the heavens. Island mists floating upwards from the valley, and catching the sunset tints as they ascend; and far away to the south-west, soft scattered clouds hovering over the summit of a steep solitary hill, and descending upon it in forms like tongues of fire.

Mrs. Patty watched that sunset from the garden of her little cottage, at the end of the lane leading from the Rectory to the Hall. Myra stood by her side. They had both been silent for many minutes. At last Mrs. Patty spoke:

'The Doctor sees something more beautiful even than that, Myra, but I can't fancy it. Anyhow, he will be glad to think I have it to look at.'

'Yes,' said Myra. 'It is always the sight that brings one nearest to heaven, is it not? dear Mrs. Patty. I wish one might never be obliged to think of anything else.'

'Which means you have something very earthly to talk about,' said Mrs. Patty. 'I knew you had by your face, but I could not bear to lose the sunset.'

Myra drew a newspaper from under her cloak, and Mrs. Patty exclaimed 'The "Times!" certainly there is nothing more earthly than that.'

'No,' said Myra gravely; 'but look;' she pointed to a paragraph in the marriage advertisements.

'Read it, my dear,' said Mrs. Patty; 'I can't find my spectacles.'

'I would rather you should read it to yourself,' said Myra. Her voice faltered, and she turned away.

Mrs. Patty searched again, brought out the spectacles, and advancing from the porch so as to gain all the advantage possible from the fading light, read half aloud : 'At Vienna, October 20, Charlotte Mary Stuart, only daughter of George Stuart, Esq., of Bombay, to Charles Verney, Esq.'

'Then he has done the right thing at last !' was Mrs. Patty's exclamation. 'But poor thing ! what a prospect of wretchedness for her.'

'No wretchedness now, as far as this world is concerned,' said Myra, drawing nearer. 'See, Mrs. Patty ;' again she pointed to the column of advertisements :

'At Vienna, four days after her marriage, Charlotte Mary, the beloved wife of Charles Verney, Esq.'

The paper dropped from Mrs. Patty's hands.

'It was too late to save her,' said Myra.

'Even so, too late,' echoed Mrs. Patty. 'God forgive me ! I could almost pray that he might never know another happy moment.'

'He will not know it,' replied Myra. 'Mrs. Patty, still I feel that there was once something noble about Mr. Verney.'

'There might have been, my dear. No doubt there was. He is God's work marred. But that he should have married that poor thing at last ! I don't understand it.'

'I think I do,' said Myra. 'It was impulse, and conscience.'

'And a bit of the world too, my dear. He knew better than you know, that when a man marries, he places himself in a new position, and then people talk less about his old one. But with the money-matters all wrong ! It was a desperate step.'

'And now he is lonely, and poor, and miserable,' said Myra.

Mrs. Patty looked at her keenly. 'Myra, child, you are not going to waste your pity upon him. The Doctor would not approve of that.' The allusion to the old Rector came out without effort. Mrs. Patty always spoke of him as conscious of her actions, if not present with her.

'Would he not?' said Myra, and she half smiled. 'Dear Mrs. Patty, he spoke more kindly of Mr. Verney than you ever did. But I waste no pity upon him, only I long to know whether, after this great shock, he will take a downward or an upward step.'

'That depends upon why he married,' said Mrs. Patty. 'If he went to that poor thing boldly, told her what he had done, keeping back nothing, and then made his offer, with an honest purpose of devoting his life to her, the marriage may have been the turning point with him ; and with this sorrow, coming so soon, he may be a different man from henceforth.'

'He would not tell her everything,' said Myra. 'He could not.'

'Why could not, child? Would not you have done it in his place?'

'Yes,' said Myra, 'but that would have been because I can never stop half way. Something always urges me on, if a thing is to be done, so that I cannot rest till it is done—fully, I mean. I don't think Mr. Verney has that feeling.'

'He wants moral courage,' said Mrs. Patty.

'So Mrs. Tracy said of him,' replied Myra.

Mrs. Patty looked very grave. 'Don't forget him in your prayers, Myra ; for he will need them now more than ever.'

'And you don't think he will improve, and grow better?' said Myra.

The words jarred upon her as she uttered them. How Mr. Verney would have smiled with contempt some few months before, if he had heard his little friend, Myra, speak of the possibility of his improving !

'I would rather not talk about him, Myra—or say what I think. The prophecy of an old woman must always sound harsh and hopeless to a young thing. I should like better to know how all is going on at the Hall with you.'

'Well, I think,' said Myra, 'very well ; only Rosamond is so altered. I cannot make her happy or satisfied, though I try to do so. And now she says such bitter things about

people ! She never used to do it. I always strive to remember, though, what she has had to make her bitter ; but I am
not much with her, for I have so many things to do.'

'Ah ! child, you have found your place now,' said Mrs.
Patty, smiling. 'Papa's head, and mamma's right hand, and
Rosamond's friend, and Juliet and Annette's example.'

Myra's face flushed, as she exclaimed : 'O Mrs. Patty !
no ; not half that. But I wonder sometimes, when so many
things go cross-wise, that I don't trouble myself about them
more. I am contented at my heart always now, in spite of
everything. Can that be because, as you say, I have found
my place ?'

'Possibly ; or, may be, you have opened your eyes to see
that you were already standing in it, only you were not aware
of it. As the Doctor used often to say : "There is a place for
every one in this world, who chooses to give up self and live
for others."'

'They are all very kind to me at home,' said Myra thoughtfully. 'Papa has quite forgotten now all the trouble at the
wedding, and mamma tells me it always does her good
when I go to her. I think that is partly owing to her not having Mrs. Verney with her as she used to have, and so being
obliged to depend upon me more. There is a pleasure in
feeling that one can stand alone, and be of use. I hope that
is not conceited.'

'I don't suppose truth ever made any one conceited,' replied
Mrs. Patty. 'You were more likely to be so, Myra, when you
set your heart upon Mr. Verney.'

'Not my heart,' replied Myra. 'It was more fancy and
imagination than anything else which made me think of him
as I did.'

'That drew you together ; but he was so clever, my dear,
and you are clever too. I don't know how it is though, Myra,
as I go on in the world, I think less and less of people who
are merely clever. I remember what the Doctor used to say
when I told him how every one admired his learning : "Patty,
the little baby who has just waked up in Paradise, is far wiser
than the cleverest man now living." It comforts me now to

think of it, because I feel that when it shall please God to bring the Doctor and me together again, I shall be better able to understand and help him.'

'I don't want to lose you yet,' said Myra, as she took her old friend's hand tenderly in her own.

'Perhaps not just yet, my dear. But it can't be very long. I am quite contented, though, to go or to stay. It is only waiting just a little while ; and meantime nothing troubles me. When the day's care comes, it is already half over, and I am so much nearer the end—the blessed end.'

'Yes,' said Myra. 'It must be pleasant to be old to feel that.'

'And pleasant too to be young, my dear ; to be strong to fight the battle, and win the crown.'

'But,' said Myra, 'one fears to be deceived, to go wrong— one cannot help fearing.'

'I don't fear. No one would fear who knew you, Myra, as I do. I once heard the Doctor say, he never trembled for those who leaned upon God, and then walked on boldly watching their own hearts, whatever blunders they might make. When he was afraid, it was for such as were always leaning upon human help. And that was why, Myra, it vexed me so to see you led by Mr. Verney I felt sure that as long as you looked up to him, you would never know what it was to find your whole strength in God.'

'I don't know it now as I ought,' said Myra.

'And you won't know it, till you can look back, and see how He has forced you to turn from earthly help, and so compelled you to rest on Him. A strange wonderful road it is that we all have to travel, Myra.'

'I could wish for nothing better than that God would bring me as quietly and safely to the end, as He is bringing you,' said Myra.

'And He will bring you there, my dear. Your way, perhaps, will not be as straight, and as pleasant as mine, because God has given you more to be anxious about, and you have a busy brain that won't be still, and take the world calmly. But step by step, hour by hour, day by day, never doubt, Myra, He will lead you. " His rod and His staff will comfort you." For surely, child, there is a prophecy for you, as well as a thanksgiving for me :

' " Thy loving kindness and mercy shall follow me all the days of my life, and I will dwell in the house of the Lord for ever." '

There was a moment's silence. Then Myra said : 'Is it only for me ? Have you nothing to hope for Mr. Verney ?'

And Mrs. Patty evasively replied : ' I know too little about him for hope or for fear. But the glory is over, and the sun has set.' And so they both went into the house.

We will take a glimpse of some in whom we may be interested, ten years after this period. And first of Mr. Verney. Mrs. Patty's doubtful words were not severe, they were prophetic. There are many men whose moral tone is kept up simply by their position in society. Mr. Verney was one of these. When he lost fortune and gained a stained name, he sank inevitably.

The cowardice which had made him a prey to circumstances through the whole of his previous career accompanied him still. The catastrophe of the eventful wedding morning was the result of no premeditation. He had left Myra prepared to face his duty, and make his confession to Mr. Cameron ; yet he procrastinated. Afraid to speak, he resolved to write, and went home for that purpose. But when he began to write, the sense of his humiliating position became overwhelming. Unable to justify himself, he felt himself, after many efforts, compelled to give up the attempt at extenuation, and after a night of utter misery, he found himself at half-past seven in the morning still unresolved what to do. In desperation he at length set out for the Hall, intending to leave the letter for Myra, and then escape the shame which awaited him by taking the railway train to London. But time was his master. The train started at half-past eight, and by going to the Hall, he ran the risk of losing it. The note was given to the first person who presented himself, and events were left to take their course.

And in like manner with all which followed. His marriage was, as Myra suspected, a matter of impulse. He was degraded in his own eyes, and he rushed to the only person who he knew would cling to him in spite of his degradation. He had made many miserable, and now that he was miserable himself, and had nothing more to lose, he could afford to make a sacrifice; not, indeed, the noble sacrifice of confession, that was the last thing Mr. Verney could think of;—he deceived even to the end; but he flattered himself that in keeping back all that had occurred, he was saving his wife from pain. He married, knowing that she was dying, but knowing also that by the act he was making her some atonement for a grievous wrong. For three days he dreamt, if not of happiness, yet of contentment; on the fourth his wife died from the effect of a shock produced by a letter unexpectedly revealing all that he had concealed from her.

And from that moment Mr. Verney began the downward course in which there is no need to follow him.

The habits from which his refined taste would have revolted when he was in prosperity, were resorted to as the only means of bringing forgetfulness of his folly in adversity; and ten years from the time when he first became acquainted with Myra, the only remark made about him by his Indian friends was, ' That unhappy fellow Verney ! what a wreck he is ! '

And what of Rosamond ? We may think of her as the wife of a man of rank and fortune, devoted to the world, but begin·ning to feel that the world is no longer devoted to her.

The brilliancy of very early youth past, and *ennui* rapidly stealing over her ; no heart interests, no true affections—weary in her secret soul, and seeking to escape from weariness by a round of petty dissipation. Disappointed in her children because the faults which she had never checked in herself were exhibited in them, and clashed with her own inclinations ; irritable with her husband because she had no principle of duty to make her obedient and forbearing with him. Friend-less in the midst of friends ; self still her idol, and self daily becoming more exacting, more tyrannous in its demands.

Hundreds there are like her :

> ' Non ragionam di lor, ma guarda e passa.'

And one last glimpse must be taken of Myra, married also ; the wife of the eldest son of the same General Mainwaring who had talked politics with Mr. Verney, on the eventful night preceding the wedding-day. Yet the same Myra still—substantially the same. In no way altered so that any one could say—' Is it possible to believe that Miss Cameron and Mrs. Mainwaring are the same persons ?' A good wife and a good mother, for had she not been a good daughter and a good sister ? A person of independent thought and clear judgment, exercising a wide and deep influence for good ; for had she not early learnt to watch and govern her own mind, knowing that each individual soul must give an account for itself, and can in nowise devolve its responsibility upon another ? Impulsive still, quick in her movements, and never having learnt to be graceful, yet infinitely attractive from the sweet loving sympathy, the kindliness which welled forth as from a never-failing fountain —the fountain of an unselfish heart. Quite simple, because living with one single motive—to do God service. So pure-minded, reverent, and earnest, that her presence was a check upon every word that verged upon evil. Yet remarkable, but in one respect—that those who knew her best could never seize upon any one striking characteristic by which to describe her until they fell back upon the cant phrase of the day, and said ' Myra Mainwaring is so true.'

PRINTED BY BALLANTYNE, HANSON AND CO.
LONDON AND EDINBURGH

MARCH 1886.

GENERAL LISTS OF WORKS

PUBLISHED BY

Messrs. LONGMANS, GREEN, & CO.

PATERNOSTER ROW, LONDON.

——◦◦⋗⦁⋖◦◦——

HISTORY, POLITICS, HISTORICAL MEMOIRS, &c.

Arnold's Lectures on Modern History. 8vo. 7s. 6d.
Bagwell's Ireland under the Tudors. Vols. 1 and 2. 2 vols. 8vo. 32s.
Beaconsfield's (Lord) Speeches, edited by Kebbel. 2 vols. 8vo. 32s.
Boultbee's History of the Church of England, Pre-Reformation Period. 8vo. 15s.
Bramston & Leroy's Historic Winchester. Crown 8vo. 6s.
Buckle's History of Civilisation. 3 vols. crown 8vo. 24s.
Chesney's Waterloo Lectures. 8vo. 10s. 6d.
Cox's (Sir G. W.) General History of Greece. Crown 8vo. Maps, 7s. 6d.
— — Lives of Greek Statesmen. Two Series. Fcp. 8vo. 2s. 6d. each.
Creighton's History of the Papacy during the Reformation. 2 vols. 8vo. 32s.
De Tocqueville's Democracy in America, translated by Reeve. 2 vols. crown 8vo. 16s.
Doyle's English in America. 8vo. 18s.
Epochs of Ancient History :—
>   Beesly's Gracchi, Marius, and Sulla, 2s. 6d.
>   Capes's Age of the Antonines, 2s. 6d.
>   — Early Roman Empire, 2s. 6d.
>   Cox's Athenian Empire, 2s. 6d.
>   — Greeks and Persians, 2s. 6d.
>   Curteis's Rise of the Macedonian Empire, 2s. 6d.
>   Ihne's Rome to its Capture by the Gauls, 2s. 6d.
>   Merivale's Roman Triumvirates, 2s. 6d.
>   Sankey's Spartan and Theban Supremacies, 2s. 6d.
>   Smith's Rome and Carthage, the Punic Wars, 2s. 6d.
Epochs of Modern History :—
>   Church's Beginning of the Middle Ages, 2s. 6d.
>   Cox's Crusades, 2s. 6d.
>   Creighton's Age of Elizabeth, 2s. 6d.
>   Gairdner's Houses of Lancaster and York, 2s. 6d.
>   Gardiner's Puritan Revolution, 2s. 6d.
>   — Thirty Years' War, 2s. 6d.
>   — (Mrs.) French Revolution, 1789-1795, 2s. 6d.
>   Hale's Fall of the Stuarts, 2s. 6d.
>   Johnson's Normans in Europe, 2s. 6d.
>   Longman's Frederick the Great and the Seven Years' War, 2s. 6d.
>   Ludlow's War of American Independence, 2s. 6d.
>   M'Carthy's Epoch of Reform, 1830-1850, 2s. 6d.
>   Morris's Age of Queen Anne, 2s. 6d.
>   — The Early Hanoverians, 2s. 6d.
>   Seebohm's Protestant Revolution, 2s. 6d.
>   Stubbs's Early Plantagenets, 2s. 6d.
>   Warburton's Edward III., 2s. 6d.
Freeman's Historical Geography of Europe. 2 vols. 8vo. 31s. 6d.

London : LONGMANS, GREEN, & CO.

Froude's English in Ireland in the 18th Century. 3 vols. crown 8vo. 18s.
—   History of England. Popular Edition. 12 vols. crown 8vo. 3s. 6d. each.
Gardiner's History of England from the Accession of James I. to the Outbreak of the Civil War. 10 vols. crown 8vo. 60s.
—   Outline of English History, B.C. 55–A.D. 1880. Fcp. 8vo. 2s. 6d.
Grant's (Sir Alex.) The Story of the University of Edinburgh. 2 vols. 8vo. 36s.
Greville's Journal of the Reigns of George IV. & William IV. 3 vols. 8vo. 36s.
—   —   —   Reign of Queen Victoria, 1837–1852. 3 vols. 8vo. 36s.
Hickson's Ireland in the Seventeenth Century. 2 vols. 8vo. 28s.
Lecky's History of England in the Eighteenth Century. Vols. 1 & 2, 1700–1760, 8vo. 36s.   Vols. 3 & 4, 1760–1784, 8vo. 36s.
—   History of European Morals. 2 vols. crown 8vo. 16s.
—   —   — Rationalism in Europe. 2 vols. crown 8vo. 16s.
—   Leaders of Public Opinion in Ireland. Crown 8vo. 7s. 6d.
Longman's Lectures on the History of England. 8vo. 15s.
—   Life and Times of Edward III. 2 vols. 8vo. 28s.
Macaulay's Complete Works. Library Edition. 8 vols. 8vo. £5. 5s.
—   —   —   Cabinet Edition. 16 vols. crown 8vo. £4. 16s.
—   History of England :—
Student's Edition. 2 vols. cr. 8vo. 12s. | Cabinet Edition. 8 vols. post 8vo. 48s.
People's Edition. 4 vols. cr. 8vo. 16s. | Library Edition. 5 vols. 8vo. £4.
Macaulay's Critical and Historical Essays, with Lays of Ancient Rome In One Volume :—
Authorised Edition. Cr. 8vo. 2s. 6d. | Popular Edition. Cr. 8vo. 2s. 6d.
or 3s. 6d. gilt edges. |
Macaulay's Critical and Historical Essays :—
Student's Edition. 1 vol. cr. 8vo. 6s. | Cabinet Edition. 4 vols. post 8vo. 24s.
People's Edition. 2 vols. cr. 8vo. 8s. | Library Edition. 3 vols. 8vo. 36s.
Macaulay's Speeches corrected by Himself. Crown 8vo. 3s. 6d.
Malmesbury's (Earl of) Memoirs of an Ex-Minister. Crown 8vo. 7s. 6d.
Maxwell's (Sir W. S.) Don John of Austria. Library Edition, with numerous Illustrations. 2 vols. royal 8vo. 42s.
May's Constitutional History of England, 1760–1870. 3 vols. crown 8vo. 18s.
—   Democracy in Europe. 2 vols. 8vo. 32s.
Merivale's Fall of the Roman Republic. 12mo. 7s. 6d.
—   General History of Rome, B.C. 753–A.D. 476. Crown 8vo. 7s. 6d.
—   History of the Romans under the Empire. 8 vols. post 8vo. 48s.
Noble's The Russian Revolt. Fcp. 8vo. 5s.
Pears' The Fall of Constantinople. 8vo. 16s.
Seebohm's Oxford Reformers—Colet, Erasmus, & More. 8vo. 14s.
Short's History of the Church of England. Crown 8vo. 7s. 6d.
Smith's Carthage and the Carthaginians. Crown 8vo. 10s. 6d.
Taylor's Manual of the History of India. Crown 8vo. 7s. 6d.
Walpole's History of England, 1815–1841. 3 vols. 8vo. £2. 14s.
Wylie's History of England under Henry IV. Vol. 1, crown 8vo. 10s. 6d.

BIOGRAPHICAL WORKS.

Bacon's Life and Letters, by Spedding. 7 vols. 8vo. £4. 4s.
Bagehot's Biographical Studies. 1 vol. 8vo. 12s.

London : LONGMANS, GREEN, & CO.

Carlyle's Life, by Froude. Vols. 1 & 2, 1795-1835, 8vo. 32s. Vols. 3 & 4, 1834-1881, 8vo. 32s.
— (Mrs.) Letters and Memorials. 3 vols. 8vo. 36s.
De Witt (John), Life of, by A. C. Pontalis. Translated. 2 vols. 8vo. 36s.
English Worthies. Edited by Andrew Lang. Crown 8vo. 2s. 6d. each.
    Charles Darwin, by Grant Allen. | Marlborough, by George Saintsbury.
Grimston's (Hon. R.) Life, by F. Gale. Crown 8vo. 10s. 6d.
Hamilton's (Sir W. R.) Life, by Graves. Vols. 1 and 2, 8vo. 15s. each.
Havelock's Life, by Marshman. Crown 8vo. 3s. 6d.
Hullah's (John) Life. By his Wife. Crown 8vo. 6s.
Macaulay's (Lord) Life and Letters. By his Nephew, G. Otto Trevelyan, M.P.
    Popular Edition, 1 vol. crown 8vo. 6s. Cabinet Edition, 2 vols. post 8vo.
    12s. Library Edition, 2 vols. 8vo. 36s.
Mendelssohn's Letters. Translated by Lady Wallace. 2 vols. cr. 8vo. 5s. each.
Mill (James) Biography of, by Prof. Bain. Crown 8vo. 5s.
— (John Stuart) Recollections of, by Prof. Bain. Crown 8vo. 2s. 6d.
—   — Autobiography. 8vo. 7s. 6d.
Mozley's Reminiscences of Oriel College. 2 vols. crown 8vo. 18s.
—   — Towns, Villages, and Schools. 2 vols. cr. 8vo. 18s.
Müller's (Max) Biographical Essays. Crown 8vo. 7s. 6d.
Newman's Apologia pro Vitâ Suâ. Crown 8vo. 6s.
Pasolini's (Count) Memoir, by his Son. 8vo. 16s.
Pasteur (Louis) His Life and Labours. Crown 8vo. 7s. 6d.
Shakespeare's Life (Outlines of), by Halliwell-Phillipps. Royal 8vo. 7s. 6d.
Southey's Correspondence with Caroline Bowles. 8vo. 14s.
Stephen's Essays in Ecclesiastical Biography. Crown 8vo. 7s. 6d.
Taylor's (Sir Henry) Autobiography. 2 vols. 8vo. 32s.
Telfer's The Strange Career of the Chevalier D'Eon de Beaumont. 8vo. 12s.
Trevelyan's Early History of Charles James Fox. Crown 8vo. 6s.
Wellington's Life, by Gleig. Crown 8vo. 6s.

MENTAL AND POLITICAL PHILOSOPHY, FINANCE, &c.

Amos's View of the Science of Jurisprudence. 8vo. 18s.
— Primer of the English Constitution. Crown 8vo. 6s.
Bacon's Essays, with Annotations by Whately. 8vo. 10s. 6d.
— Works, edited by Spedding. 7 vols. 8vo. 73s. 6d.
Bagehot's Economic Studies, edited by Hutton. 8vo. 10s. 6d.
— The Postulates of English Political Economy. Crown 8vo. 2s. 6d.
Bain's Logic, Deductive and Inductive. Crown 8vo. 10s. 6d.
    PART I. Deduction, 4s. | PART II. Induction, 6s. 6d.
— Mental and Moral Science. Crown 8vo. 10s. 6d.
— The Senses and the Intellect. 8vo. 15s.
— The Emotions and the Will. 8vo. 15s.
— Practical Essays. Crown 8vo. 4s. 6d.
Buckle's (H. T.) Miscellaneous and Posthumous Works. 2 vols. crown 8vo. 21s.
Crozier's Civilization and Progress. 8vo. 14s.
Crump's A Short Enquiry into the Formation of English Political Opinion. 8vo. 7s. 6d.
Dowell's A History of Taxation and Taxes in England. 4 vols. 8vo. 48s.
Green's (Thomas Hill) Works. (3 vols.) Vol. 1, Philosophical Works. 8vo. 16s.

London : LONGMANS, GREEN, & CO.

Hume's Essays, edited by Green & Grose. 2 vols. 8vo. 28s.
— Treatise of Human Nature, edited by Green & Grose. 2 vols. 8vo. 28s.
Lang's Custom and Myth : Studies of Early Usage and Belief. Crown 8vo. 7s. 6d.
Leslie's Essays in Political and Moral Philosophy. 8vo. 10s. 6d.
Lewes's History of Philosophy. 2 vols. 8vo. 32s.
List's Natural System of Political Economy, translated by S. Lloyd, M.P. 8vo. 10s. 6d.
Lubbock's Origin of Civilisation. 8vo. 18s.
Macleod's Principles of Economical Philosophy. In 2 vols. Vol. 1, 8vo. 15s. Vol. 2, Part I. 12s.
— The Elements of Economics. (2 vols.) Vol. 1, cr. 8vo. 7s. 6d. Vol. 2, Part I. cr. 8vo. 7s. 6d.
— The Elements of Banking. Crown 8vo. 5s.
— The Theory and Practice of Banking. Vol. 1, 8vo. 12s.
— Elements of Political Economy. 8vo. 16s.
— Economics for Beginners. 8vo. 2s. 6d.
— Lectures on Credit and Banking. 8vo. 5s.
Mill's (James) Analysis of the Phenomena of the Human Mind. 2 vols. 8vo. 28s.
Mill (John Stuart) on Representative Government. Crown 8vo. 2s.
— — on Liberty. Crown 8vo. 1s. 4d.
— — Essays on Unsettled Questions of Political Economy. 8vo. 6s. 6d.
— — Examination of Hamilton's Philosophy. 8vo. 16s.
— — Logic. 2 vols. 8vo. 25s. People's Edition, 1 vol. cr. 8vo. 5s.
— — Principles of Political Economy. 2 vols. 8vo. 30s. People's Edition, 1 vol. crown 8vo. 5s.
— — Subjection of Women. Crown 8vo. 6s.
— — Utilitarianism. 8vo. 5s.
— — Three Essays on Religion, &c. 8vo. 5s.
Miller's (Mrs. Fenwick) Readings in Social Economy. Crown 8vo. 2s.
Mulhall's History of Prices since 1850. Crown 8vo. 6s.
Sandars's Institutes of Justinian, with English Notes. 8vo. 18s.
Seebohm's English Village Community. 8vo. 16s.
Sully's Outlines of Psychology. 8vo. 12s. 6d.
Swinburne's Picture Logic. Post 8vo. 5s.
Thompson's A System of Psychology. 2 vols. 8vo. 36s.
Thomson's Outline of Necessary Laws of Thought. Crown 8vo. 6s.
Twiss's Law of Nations in Time of War. 8vo. 21s.
— — in Time of Peace. 8vo. 15s.
Webb's The Veil of Isis. 8vo. 10s. 6d.
Whately's Elements of Logic. Crown 8vo. 4s. 6d.
— — — Rhetoric. Crown 8vo. 4s. 6d.
Wylie's Labour, Leisure, and Luxury. Crown 8vo. 6s.
Zeller's History of Eclecticism in Greek Philosophy. Crown 8vo. 10s. 6d.
— Plato and the Older Academy. Crown 8vo. 18s.
— Pre-Socratic Schools. 2 vols. crown 8vo. 30s.
— Socrates and the Socratic Schools. Crown 8vo. 10s. 6d.
— Stoics, Epicureans, and Sceptics. Crown 8vo. 15s.
— Outlines of the History of Greek Philosophy. Crown 8vo. 10s. 6d.

London : LONGMANS, GREEN, & CO.

MISCELLANEOUS WORKS.

A. K. H. B., The Essays and Contributions of. Crown 8vo.
  Autumn Holidays of a Country Parson. 3s. 6d.
  Changed Aspects of Unchanged Truths. 3s. 6d.
  Common-Place Philosopher in Town and Country. 3s. 6d.
  Critical Essays of a Country Parson. 3s. 6d.
  Counsel and Comfort spoken from a City Pulpit. 3s. 6d.
  Graver Thoughts of a Country Parson. Three Series. 3s. 6d. each
  Landscapes, Churches, and Moralities. 3s. 6d.
  Leisure Hours in Town. 3s. 6d. Lessons of Middle Age. 3s. 6d.
  Our Little Life. Essays Consolatory and Domestic. Two Series. 3s. 6d.
  Present-day Thoughts. 3s. 6d.   [each.
  Recreations of a Country Parson. Three Series. 3s. 6d. each.
  Seaside Musings on Sundays and Week-Days. 3s. 6d.
  Sunday Afternoons in the Parish Church of a University City. 3s. 6d.
Arnold's (Dr. Thomas) Miscellaneous Works. 8vo. 7s. 6d.
Bagehot's Literary Studies, edited by Hutton. 2 vols. 8vo. 28s.
Beaconsfield (Lord), The Wit and Wisdom of. Crown 8vo. 3s. 6d.
— (The) Birthday Book. 18mo. 2s. 6d. cloth ; 4s. 6d. bound.
Evans's Bronze Implements of Great Britain. 8vo. 25s.
Farrar's Language and Languages. Crown 8vo. 6s.
French's Nineteen Centuries of Drink in England. Crown 8vo. 10s. 6d.
Froude's Short Studies on Great Subjects. 4 vols. crown 8vo. 24s.
Lang's Letters to Dead Authors. Fcp. 8vo. 6s. 6d.
Macaulay's Miscellaneous Writings. 2 vols. 8vo. 21s. 1 vol. crown 8vo. 4s. 6d.
— Miscellaneous Writings and Speeches. Crown 8vo. 6s.
— Miscellaneous Writings, Speeches, Lays of Ancient Rome, &c.
    Cabinet Edition. 4 vols. crown 8vo. 24s.
— Writings, Selections from. Crown 8vo. 6s.
Müller's (Max) Lectures on the Science of Language. 2 vols. crown 8vo. 16s.
— Lectures on India. 8vo. 12s. 6d.
Smith (Sydney) The Wit and Wisdom of. Crown 8vo. 3s. 6d.

ASTRONOMY.

Herschel's Outlines of Astronomy. Square crown 8vo. 12s.
Nelson's Work on the Moon. Medium 8vo. 31s. 6d.
Proctor's Larger Star Atlas. Folio, 15s. or Maps only, 12s. 6d.
— New Star Atlas. Crown 8vo. 5s. Orbs Around Us. Crown 8vo. 5s.
— Light Science for Leisure Hours. 3 Series. Crown 8vo. 5s. each.
— Moon. Crown 8vo. 10s. 6d.
— Myths and Marvels of Astronomy. Crown 8vo. 6s.
— Other Worlds than Ours. Crown 8vo. 5s.
— Sun. Crown 8vo. 14s. Universe of Stars. 8vo. 10s. 6d.
— Pleasant Ways in Science. Crown 8vo. 6s.
— Studies of Venus-Transits. 8vo. 5s.
Webb's Celestial Objects for Common Telescopes. Crown 8vo. 9s.
— The Sun and his Phenomena. Fcp. 8vo. 1s.

THE 'KNOWLEDGE' LIBRARY.

Edited by RICHARD A. PROCTOR.

How to Play Whist. Crown 8vo. 5s.   Star Primer. Crown 4to. 2s. 6d.
The Borderland of Science. Cr. 8vo. 6s.   The Seasons Pictured. Demy 4to. 5s.
Nature Studies. Crown 8vo. 6s.   Strength and Happiness. Cr. 8vo. 5s.
Leisure Readings. Crown 8vo. 6s.   Rough Ways made Smooth. Cr. 8vo. 6s.
The Stars in their Seasons. Imp. 8vo. 5s.   The Expanse of Heaven. Cr. 8vo. 5s.
Home Whist. 16mo. 1s.   Our Place among Infinities. Cr. 8vo. 5s.

London : LONGMANS, GREEN, & CO.

CLASSICAL LANGUAGES AND LITERATURE.

Æschylus, The Eumenides of.   Text, with Metrical English Translation, by J. F. Davies. 8vo. 7s.

Aristophanes' The Acharnians, translated by R. Y. Tyrrell. Crown 8vo. 2s. 6d.

Aristotle's The Ethics, Text and Notes, by Sir Alex. Grant, Bart. 2 vols. 8vo. 32s.
—   The Nicomachean Ethics, translated by Williams, crown 8vo. 7s. 6d.
—   The Politics, Books I. III. IV. (VII.) with Translation, &c. by Bolland and Lang. Crown 8vo. 7s. 6d.

Becker's *Charicles* and *Gallus*, by Metcalfe. Post 8vo. 7s. 6d. each.

Cicero's Correspondence, Text and Notes, by R. Y. Tyrrell. Vol. 1, 8vo. 12s.

Homer's Iliad, Homometrically translated by Cayley. 8vo. 12s. 6d.
—   —   Greek Text, with Verse Translation, by W. C. Green. Vol. 1, Books I.–XII. Crown 8vo. 6s.

Mahaffy's Classical Greek Literature. Crown 8vo. Vol. 1, The Poets, 7s. 6d. Vol. 2, The Prose Writers, 7s. 6d.

Plato's Parmenides, with Notes, &c. by J. Maguire. 8vo. 7s. 6d.

Sophocles' Tragœdiæ Superstites, by Linwood. 8vo. 16s.

Virgil's Works, Latin Text, with Commentary, by Kennedy. Crown 8vo. 10s. 6d.
—   Æneid, translated into English Verse, by Conington.   Crown 8vo. 9s.
—   Poems,   —   —   Prose,   —   —   Crown 8vo. 9s.

Witt's Myths of Hellas, translated by F. M. Younghusband. Crown 8vo. 3s. 6d.
—   The Trojan War,   —   —   Fcp. 8vo. 2s.
—   The Wanderings of Ulysses,   —   Crown 8vo. 3s. 6d.

NATURAL HISTORY, BOTANY, & GARDENING.

Allen's Flowers and their Pedigrees. Crown 8vo. Woodcuts, 5s.

Decaisne and Le Maout's General System of Botany. Imperial 8vo. 31s. 6d.

Dixon's Rural Bird Life. Crown 8vo. Illustrations, 5s.

Hartwig's Aerial World, 8vo. 10s. 6d.
—   Polar World, 8vo. 10s. 6d.
—   Sea and its Living Wonders. 8vo. 10s. 6d.
—   Subterranean World, 8vo. 10s. 6d.
—   Tropical World, 8vo. 10s. 6d.

Lindley's Treasury of Botany. Fcp. 8vo. 6s.

Loudon's Encyclopædia of Gardening. 8vo. 21s.
—   —   Plants. 8vo. 42s.

Rivers's Orchard House. Crown 8vo. 5s.
—   Rose Amateur's Guide. Fcp. 8vo. 4s. 6d.
—   Miniature Fruit Garden. Fcp. 8vo. 4s.

Stanley's Familiar History of British Birds. Crown 8vo. 6s.

Wood's Bible Animals. With 112 Vignettes. 8vo. 10s. 6d.
—   Common British Insects. Crown 8vo. 3s. 6d.
—   Homes Without Hands, 8vo. 10s. 6d.
—   Insects Abroad, 8vo. 10s. 6d.
—   Horse and Man. 8vo. 14s.
—   Insects at Home. With 700 Illustrations. 8vo. 10s. 6d.
—   Out of Doors. Crown 8vo. 5s.
—   Petland Revisited. Crown 8vo. 7s. 6d.
—   Strange Dwellings. Crown 8vo. 5s. Popular Edition, 4to. 6d.

London: LONGMANS, GREEN, & CO.

THE FINE ARTS AND ILLUSTRATED EDITIONS.

Dresser's Arts and Art Manufactures of Japan. Square crown 8vo. 31s. 6d.
Eastlake's Household Taste in Furniture, &c. Square crown 8vo. 14s.
Jameson's Sacred and Legendary Art. 6 vols. square 8vo.
    Legends of the Madonna. 1 vol. 21s.
    — — — Monastic Orders 1 vol. 21s.
    — — — Saints and Martyrs. 2 vols. 31s. 6d.
    — — — Saviour. Completed by Lady Eastlake. 2 vols. 42s.
Macaulay's Lays of Ancient Rome, illustrated by Scharf. Fcp. 4to. 10s. 6d.
The same, with Ivry and the Armada, illustrated by Weguelin. Crown 8vo. 3s. 6d.
Moore's Lalla Rookh, illustrated by Tenniel. Square crown 8vo. 10s. 6d.
New Testament (The) illustrated with Woodcuts after Paintings by the Early
    Masters. 4to. 21s. cloth, or 42s. morocco.
Perry on Greek and Roman Sculpture. With 280 Illustrations engraved on
    Wood. Square crown 8vo. 31s. 6d.

CHEMISTRY, ENGINEERING, & GENERAL SCIENCE.

Arnott's Elements of Physics or Natural Philosophy. Crown 8vo. 12s. 6d.
Bourne's Catechism of the Steam Engine. Crown 8vo. 7s. 6d.
    — Examples of Steam, Air, and Gas Engines. 4to. 70s.
    — Handbook of the Steam Engine. Fcp. 8vo. 9s.
    — Recent Improvements in the Steam Engine. Fcp. 8vo. 6s.
    — Treatise on the Steam Engine. 4to. 42s.
Buckton's Our Dwellings, Healthy and Unhealthy. Crown 8vo. 3s. 6d.
Crookes's Select Methods in Chemical Analysis. 8vo. 24s.
Culley's Handbook of Practical Telegraphy. 8vo. 16s.
Fairbairn's Useful Information for Engineers. 3 vols. crown 8vo. 31s. 6d.
    — Mills and Millwork. 1 vol. 8vo. 25s.
Ganot's Elementary Treatise on Physics, by Atkinson. Large crown 8vo. 15s.
    — Natural Philosophy, by Atkinson. Crown 8vo. 7s. 6d.
Grove's Correlation of Physical Forces. 8vo. 15s.
Haughton's Six Lectures on Physical Geography. 8vo. 15s.
Heer's Primæval World of Switzerland. 2 vols. 8vo. 12s.
Helmholtz on the Sensations of Tone. Royal 8vo. 28s.
Helmholtz's Lectures on Scientific Subjects. 2 vols. crown 8vo. 7s. 6d. each.
Hudson and Gosse's The Rotifera or 'Wheel Animalcules.' With 30 Coloured
    Plates. 6 parts. 4to. 10s. 6d. each.
Hullah's Lectures on the History of Modern Music. 8vo. 8s. 6d.
    — Transition Period of Musical History. 8vo. 10s. 6d.
Jackson's Aid to Engineering Solution. Royal 8vo. 21s.
Jago's Inorganic Chemistry, Theoretical and Practical. Fcp. 8vo. 2s.
Kerl's Metallurgy, adapted by Crookes and Röhrig. 3 vols. 8vo. £4. 19s.
Kolbe's Short Text-Book of Inorganic Chemistry. Crown 8vo. 7s. 6d.
Lloyd's Treatise on Magnetism. 8vo. 10s. 6d.
Macalister's Zoology and Morphology of Vertebrate Animals. 8vo. 10s. 6d.
Macfarren's Lectures on Harmony. 8vo. 12s.

Miller's Elements of Chemistry, Theoretical and Practical. 3 vols. 8vo. Part I. Chemical Physics, 16s. Part II. Inorganic Chemistry, 24s. Part III. Organic Chemistry, price 31s. 6d.
Mitchell's Manual of Practical Assaying. 8vo. 31s. 6d.
Northcott's Lathes and Turning. 8vo. 18s.
Owen's Comparative Anatomy and Physiology of the Vertebrate Animals. 3 vols. 8vo. 73s. 6d.
Payen's Industrial Chemistry. Edited by B. H. Paul, Ph.D. 8vo. 42s.
Piesse's Art of Perfumery. Square crown 8vo. 21s.
Reynolds's Experimental Chemistry. Fcp. 8vo. Part I. 1s. 6d. Part II. 2s. 6d. Part III. 3s. 6d.
Schellen's Spectrum Analysis. 8vo. 31s. 6d.
Sennett's Treatise on the Marine Steam Engine. 8vo. 21s.
Smith's Air and Rain. 8vo. 24s.
Stoney's The Theory of the Stresses on Girders, &c. Royal 8vo. 36s.
Swinton's Electric Lighting : Its Principles and Practice. Crown 8vo. 5s.
Tilden's Practical Chemistry. Fcp. 8vo. 1s. 6d.
Tyndall's Faraday as a Discoverer. Crown 8vo. 3s. 6d.
— Floating Matter of the Air. Crown 8vo. 7s. 6d.
— Fragments of Science. 2 vols. post 8vo. 16s.
— Heat a Mode of Motion. Crown 8vo. 12s.
— Lectures on Light delivered in America. Crown 8vo. 5s.
— Lessons on Electricity. Crown 8vo. 2s. 6d.
— Notes on Electrical Phenomena. Crown 8vo. 1s. sewed, 1s. 6d. cloth.
— Notes of Lectures on Light. Crown 8vo. 1s. sewed, 1s. 6d. cloth.
— Sound, with Frontispiece and 203 Woodcuts. Crown 8vo. 10s. 6d.
Watts's Dictionary of Chemistry. 9 vols. medium 8vo. £15. 2s. 6d.
Wilson's Manual of Health-Science. Crown 8vo. 2s. 6d.

THEOLOGICAL AND RELIGIOUS WORKS.

Arnold's (Rev. Dr. Thomas) Sermons. 6 vols. crown 8vo. 5s. each.
Boultbee's Commentary on the 39 Articles. Crown 8vo. 6s.
Browne's (Bishop) Exposition of the 39 Articles. 8vo. 16s.
Colenso on the Pentateuch and Book of Joshua. Crown 8vo. 6s.
Conder's Handbook of the Bible. Post 8vo. 7s. 6d.
Conybeare & Howson's Life and Letters of St. Paul :—
   Library Edition, with Maps, Plates, and Woodcuts. 2 vols. square crown 8vo. 21s.
   Student's Edition, revised and condensed, with 46 Illustrations and Maps. 1 vol. crown 8vo. 7s. 6d.
Cox's (Homersham) The First Century of Christianity. 8vo. 12s.
Davidson's Introduction to the Study of the New Testament. 2 vols. 8vo. 30s.
Edersheim's Life and Times of Jesus the Messiah. 2 vols. 8vo. 42s.
— Prophecy and History in relation to the Messiah. 8vo. 12s.
Ellicott's (Bishop) Commentary on St. Paul's Epistles. 8vo. Galatians, 8s. 6d. Ephesians, 8s. 6d. Pastoral Epistles, 10s. 6d. Philippians, Colossians and Philemon, 10s. 6d. Thessalonians, 7s. 6d.
— Lectures on the Life of our Lord. 8vo. 12s.
Ewald's Antiquities of Israel, translated by Solly. 8vo. 12s. 6d.
— History of Israel, translated by Carpenter & Smith. Vols. 1-7, 8vo. £5.

London: LONGMANS, GREEN, & CO.

Hobart's Medical Language of St. Luke. 8vo. 16s.
Hopkins's Christ the Consoler. Fcp. 8vo. 2s. 6d.
Jukes's New Man and the Eternal Life. Crown 8vo. 6s.
— Second Death and the Restitution of all Things. Crown 8vo. 3s. 6d.
— Types of Genesis. Crown 8vo. 7s. 6d.
— The Mystery of the Kingdom. Crown 8vo. 3s. 6d.
Lenormant's New Translation of the Book of Genesis. Translated into English. 8vo. 10s. 6d.
Lyra Germanica : Hymns translated by Miss Winkworth. Fcp. 8vo. 5s.
Macdonald's (G.) Unspoken Sermons. Second Series. Crown 8vo. 7s. 6d.
Manning's Temporal Mission of the Holy Ghost. Crown 8vo. 8s. 6d.
Martineau's Endeavours after the Christian Life. Crown 8vo. 7s. 6d.
— Hymns of Praise and Prayer. Crown 8vo. 4s. 6d. 32mo. 1s. 6d.
— Sermons, Hours of Thought on Sacred Things. 2 vols. 7s. 6d. each.
Monsell's Spiritual Songs for Sundays and Holidays. Fcp. 8vo. 5s. 18mo. 2s.
Müller's (Max) Origin and Growth of Religion. Crown 8vo. 7s. 6d.
— — Science of Religion. Crown 8vo. 7s. 6d.
Newman's Apologia pro Vitâ Suâ. Crown 8vo. 6s.
— The Idea of a University Defined and Illustrated. Crown 8vo. 7s.
— Historical Sketches. 3 vols. crown 8vo. 6s. each.
— Discussions and Arguments on Various Subjects. Crown 8vo. 6s.
— An Essay on the Development of Christian Doctrine. Crown 8vo. 6s.
— Certain Difficulties Felt by Anglicans in Catholic Teaching Considered. Vol. 1, crown 8vo. 7s. 6d. Vol. 2, crown 8vo. 5s. 6d.
— The Via Media of the Anglican Church, Illustrated in Lectures, &c. 2 vols. crown 8vo. 6s. each
— Essays, Critical and Historical. 2 vols. crown 8vo. 12s.
— Essays on Biblical and on Ecclesiastical Miracles. Crown 8vo. 6s.
— An Essay in Aid of a Grammar of Assent. 7s. 6d.
Overton's Life in the English Church (1660-1714). 8vo. 14s.
Rogers's Eclipse of Faith. Fcp. 8vo. 5s.
— Defence of the Eclipse of Faith. Fcp. 8vo. 3s. 6d.
Sewell's (Miss) Night Lessons from Scripture. 32mo. 3s. 6d.
— — Passing Thoughts on Religion. Fcp. 8vo. 3s. 6d.
— — Preparation for the Holy Communion. 32mo. 3s.
Smith's Voyage and Shipwreck of St. Paul. Crown 8vo. 7s. 6d.
Supernatural Religion. Complete Edition. 3 vols. 8vo. 36s.
Taylor's (Jeremy) Entire Works. With Life by Bishop Heber. Edited by the Rev. C. P. Eden. 10 vols. 8vo. £5. 5s.
Tulloch's Movements of Religious Thought in Britain during the Nineteenth Century. Crown 8vo. 10s. 6d.

TRAVELS, ADVENTURES, &c.

Aldridge's Ranch Notes in Kansas, Colorada, &c. Crown 8vo. 5s.
Alpine Club (The) Map of Switzerland. In Four Sheets. 42s.
Baker's Eight Years in Ceylon. Crown 8vo. 5s.
— Rifle and Hound in Ceylon. Crown 8vo. 5s.
Ball's Alpine Guide. 3 vols. post 8vo. with Maps and Illustrations :—I. Western Alps, 6s. 6d. II. Central Alps, 7s. 6d. III. Eastern Alps, 10s. 6d.
Ball on Alpine Travelling, and on the Geology of the Alps, 1s.

London: LONGMANS, GREEN, & CO.

Bent's The Cyclades, or Life among the Insular Greeks. Crown 8vo. 12s. 6d.

Brassey's Sunshine and Storm in the East. Crown 8vo. 7s. 6d.

— Voyage in the Yacht 'Sunbeam.' Crown 8vo. 7s. 6d. School Edition, fcp. 8vo. 2s. Popular Edition, 4to. 6d.

— In the Trades, the Tropics, and the 'Roaring Forties.' Édition de Luxe, 8vo. £3. 13s. 6d. Library Edition, 8vo. 21s.

Crawford's Across the Pampas and the Andes. Crown 8vo. 7s. 6d.

Dent's Above the Snow Line. Crown 8vo. 7s. 6d.

Froude's Oceana ; or, England and her Colonies. 8vo. 18s.

Hassall's San Remo Climatically considered. Crown 8vo. 5s.

Howitt's Visits to Remarkable Places. Crown 8vo. 7s. 6d.

Maritime Alps (The) and their Seaboard. By the Author of 'Vèra.' 8vo. 21s.

Three in Norway. By Two of Them. Crown 8vo. Illustrations, 6s.

WORKS OF FICTION.

Beaconsfield's (The Earl of) Novels and Tales. Hughenden Edition, with 2 Portraits on Steel and 11 Vignettes on Wood. 11 vols. crown 8vo. £2. 2s. Cheap Edition, 11 vols. fcp. 8vo. 1s. each, sewed ; 1s. 6d. each, cloth.

Black Poodle (The) and other Tales. By the Author of 'Vice Versâ.' Cr. 8vo. 6s.

Brabourne's (Lord) Friends and Foes from Fairyland. Crown 8vo. 6s.

Harte (Bret) On the Frontier. Three Stories. 16mo. 1s.

— — By Shore and Sedge. Three Stories. 16mo. 1s.

In the Olden Time. By the Author of 'Mademoiselle Mori.' Crown 8vo. 6s.

Melville's (Whyte) Novels. Cheap Edition. 8 vols. fcp. 8vo. 1s. each, sewed ; 1s. 6d. each, cloth.

The Modern Novelist's Library. Crown 8vo. price 2s. each, boards, or 2s. 6d. each, cloth :—

By the Earl of Beaconsfield, K.G.
    Lothair.
    Sybil.
    Coningsby.
    Tancred.
    Venetia.
    Henrietta Temple.
    Contarini Fleming.
    Alroy, Ixion, &c.
    The Young Duke, &c.
    Vivian Grey.
    Endymion.

By Bret Harte.
    In the Carquinez Woods.

By Mrs. Oliphant.
    In Trust, the Story of a Lady and her Lover.

By James Payn.
    Thicker than Water.

By Anthony Trollope.
    Barchester Towers.
    The Warden.

By Major Whyte Melville.
    Digby Grand.
    General Bounce.
    Kate Coventry.
    The Gladiators.
    Good for Nothing.
    Holmby House.
    The Interpreter.
    The Queen's Maries.

By Various Writers
    The Atelier du Lys.
    Atherstone Priory.
    The Burgomaster's Family.
    Elsa and her Vulture.
    Mademoiselle Mori.
    The Six Sisters of the Valleys.
    Unawares.

Oliphant's (Mrs.) Madam. Crown 8vo. 3s. 6d.

Payn's (James) The Luck of the Darrells. Crown 8vo. 3s. 6d.

Reader's Fairy Prince Follow-my-Lead. Crown 8vo. 5s.

Sewell's (Miss) Stories and Tales. Cabinet Edition. Crown 8vo. cloth extra, gilt edges, price 3s. 6d. each :—

    Amy Herbert. Cleve Hall.
    The Earl's Daughter.
    Experience of Life.
    Gertrude. Ivors.

    A Glimpse of the World.
    Katharine Ashton.
    Laneton Parsonage.
    Margaret Percival. Ursula.

London : LONGMANS, GREEN, & CO.

Stevenson's (R. L.) The Dynamiter. Fcp. 8vo. 1s. sewed ; 1s. 6d. cloth.
— — Strange Case of Dr. Jekyll and Mr. Hyde. Fcp. 8vo. 1s. sewed ; 1s. 6d. cloth.
Sturgis' My Friend and I. Crown 8vo. 5s.

POETRY AND THE DRAMA.

Bailey's Festus, a Poem. Crown 8vo. 12s. 6d.
Bowdler's Family Shakespeare. Medium 8vo. 14s. 6 vols. fcp. 8vo. 21s.
Dante's Divine Comedy, translated by James Innes Minchin. Crown 8vo. 15s.
Goethe's Faust, translated by Birds. Large crown 8vo. 12s. 6d.
— — translated by Webb. 8vo. 12s. 6d.
— — edited by Selss. Crown 8vo. 5s.
Ingelow's Poems. Vols. 1 and 2, fcp. 8vo. 12s. Vol. 3 fcp. 8vo. 5s.
Macaulay's Lays of Ancient Rome, with Ivry and the Armada. Illustrated by Weguelin. Crown 8vo. 3s. 6d. gilt edges.
The same, Annotated Edition, fcp. 8vo. 1s. sewed, 1s. 6d. cloth, 2s. 6d. cloth extra.
The same, Popular Edition. Illustrated by Scharf. Fcp. 4to. 6d. swd., 1s. cloth.
Macdonald's (G.) A Book of Strife : in the Form of the Diary of an Old Soul: Poems. 12mo. 6s.
Pennell's (Cholmondeley) 'From Grave to Gay.' A Volume of Selections. Fcp. 8vo. 6s.
Reader's Voices from Flowerland, a Birthday Book, 2s. 6d. cloth, 3s. 6d. roan.
Robinson's The New Arcadia, and other Poems. Crown 8vo. 6s.
Shakespeare's Hamlet, annotated by George Macdonald, LL.D. 8vo. 12s.
Southey's Poetical Works. Medium 8vo. 14s.
Stevenson's A Child's Garden of Verses. Fcp. 8vo. 5s.
Virgil's Æneid. translated by Conington. Crown 8vo. 9s.
— Poems, translated into English Prose. Crown 8vo. 9s.

AGRICULTURE, HORSES, DOGS, AND CATTLE.

Dunster's How to Make the Land Pay. Crown 8vo. 5s.
Fitzwygram's Horses and Stables. 8vo. 10s. 6d.
Horses and Roads. By Free-Lance. Crown 8vo. 6s.
Lloyd, The Science of Agriculture. 8vo. 12s.
Loudon's Encyclopædia of Agriculture. 21s.
Miles's Horse's Foot, and How to Keep it Sound. Imperial 8vo. 12s. 6d.
— Plain Treatise on Horse-Shoeing. Post 8vo. 2s. 6d.
— Remarks on Horses' Teeth. Post 8vo. 1s. 6d.
— Stables and Stable-Fittings. Imperial 8vo. 15s.
Nevile's Farms and Farming. Crown 8vo. 6s.
— Horses and Riding. Crown 8vo. 6s.
Steel's Diseases of the Ox, a Manual of Bovine Pathology. 8vo. 15s.
Stonehenge's Dog in Health and Disease. Square crown 8vo. 7s. 6d.
— Greyhound. Square crown 8vo. 15s.
Taylor's Agricultural Note Book. Fcp. 8vo. 2s. 6d.
Ville on Artificial Manures, by Crookes. 8vo. 21s.
Youatt's Work on the Dog. 8vo. 6s.
— — — — Horse. 8vo. 7s. 6d.

London : LONGMANS, GREEN, & CO.

SPORTS AND PASTIMES.

The Badminton Library of Sports and Pastimes. Edited by the Duke of Beaufort and A. E. T. Watson. With numerous Illustrations. Crown 8vo. 10s. 6d. each.

> Hunting, by the Duke of Beaufort, &c.
> Fishing, by H. Cholmondeley-Pennell, &c. 2 vols.
> Racing, by the Earl of Suffolk, &c.

Campbell-Walker's Correct Card, or How to Play at Whist. Fcp. 8vo. 2s. 6d.
Dead Shot (The) by Marksman. Crown 8vo. 10s. 6d.
Francis's Treatise on Fishing in all its Branches. Post 8vo. 15s.
Jefferies' The Red Deer. Crown 8vo. 4s. 6d.
Longman's Chess Openings. Fcp. 8vo. 2s. 6d.
Peel's A Highland Gathering. Illustrated. Crown 8vo. 10s. 6d.
Pole's Theory of the Modern Scientific Game of Whist. Fcp. 8vo. 2s. 6d.
Proctor's How to Play Whist. Crown 8vo. 5s.
Ronalds's Fly-Fisher's Entomology. 8vo. 14s.
Verney's Chess Eccentricities. Crown 8vo. 10s. 6d.
Wilcocks's Sea-Fisherman. Post 8vo. 6s.
Year's Sport (The) for 1885. 8vo. 21s.

ENCYCLOPÆDIAS, DICTIONARIES, AND BOOKS OF REFERENCE.

Acton's Modern Cookery for Private Families. Fcp. 8vo. 4s. 6d.
Ayre's Treasury of Bible Knowledge. Fcp. 8vo. 6s.
Brande's Dictionary of Science, Literature, and Art. 3 vols. medium 8vo. 63s.
Cabinet Lawyer (The), a Popular Digest of the Laws of England. Fcp. 8vo. 9s.
Cates's Dictionary of General Biography. Medium 8vo. 28s.
Doyle's The Official Baronage of England. Vols. I.-III. 3 vols. 4to. £5. 5s. ;
     Large Paper Edition, £15. 15s.
Gwilt's Encyclopædia of Architecture. 8vo. 52s. 6d.
Keith Johnston's Dictionary of Geography, or General Gazetteer. 8vo. 42s.
Latham's (Dr.) Edition of Johnson's Dictionary. 4 vols. 4to. £7.
   —   —   —   —   —   Abridged. Royal 8vo. 14s.
M'Culloch's Dictionary of Commerce and Commercial Navigation. 8vo. 63s.
Maunder's Biographical Treasury. Fcp. 8vo. 6s.
   —   Historical Treasury. Fcp. 8vo. 6s.
   —   Scientific and Literary Treasury. Fcp. 8vo. 6s.
   —   Treasury of Bible Knowledge, edited by Ayre. Fcp. 8vo. 6s.
   —   Treasury of Botany, edited by Lindley & Moore. Two Parts, 12s.
   —   Treasury of Geography. Fcp. 8vo. 6s.
   —   Treasury of Knowledge and Library of Reference. Fcp. 8vo. 6s.
   —   Treasury of Natural History. Fcp 8vo. 6s.
Quain's Dictionary of Medicine. Medium 8vo. 31s. 6d., or in 2 vols. 34s.
Reeve's Cookery and Housekeeping. Crown 8vo. 7s. 6d.
Rich's Dictionary of Roman and Greek Antiquities. Crown 8vo. 7s. 6d.
Roget's Thesaurus of English Words and Phrases. Crown 8vo. 10s. 6d.
Ure's Dictionary of Arts, Manufactures, and Mines. 4 vols. medium 8vo. £7. 7s.
Willich's Popular Tables, by Marriott. Crown 8vo. 10s.

London : LONGMANS, GREEN, & CO.

A SELECTION

OF

EDUCATIONAL WORKS.

—•◦•—

TEXT-BOOKS OF SCIENCE, MECHANICAL AND PHYSICAL.

Abney's Treatise on Photography. Fcp. 8vo. 3s. 6d.
Anderson's Strength of Materials. 3s. 6d.
Armstrong's Organic Chemistry. 3s. 6d.
Ball's Elements of Astronomy. 6s.
Barry's Railway Appliances. 3s. 6d.
Bauerman's Systematic Mineralogy. 6s.
— Descriptive Mineralogy. 6s.
Bloxam and Huntington's Metals. 5s.
Glazebrook's Physical Optics. 6s.
Glazebrook and Shaw's Practical Physics. 6s.
Gore's Art of Electro-Metallurgy. 6s.
Griffin's Algebra and Trigonometry. 3s. 6d. Notes and Solutions, 3s. 6d.
Jenkin's Electricity and Magnetism. 3s. 6d.
Maxwell's Theory of Heat. 3s. 6d.
Merrifield's Technical Arithmetic and Mensuration. 3s. 6d. Key, 3s. 6d.
Miller's Inorganic Chemistry. 3s. 6d.
Preece and Sivewright's Telegraphy. 5s.
Rutley's Study of Rocks, a Text-Book of Petrology. 4s. 6d.
Shelley's Workshop Appliances. 4s. 6d.
Thomé's Structural and Physiological Botany. 6s.
Thorpe's Quantitative Chemical Analysis. 4s. 6d.
Thorpe and Muir's Qualitative Analysis. 3s. 6d.
Tilden's Chemical Philosophy. 3s. 6d. With Answers to Problems. 4s. 6d.
Unwin's Elements of Machine Design. 6s.
Watson's Plane and Solid Geometry. 3s. 6d.

THE GREEK LANGUAGE.

Bloomfield's College and School Greek Testament. Fcp. 8vo. 5s.
Bolland & Lang's Politics of Aristotle. Post 8vo. 7s. 6d.
Collis's Chief Tenses of the Greek Irregular Verbs. 8vo. 1s.
— Pontes Græci, Stepping-Stone to Greek Grammar. 12mo. 3s. 6d.
— Praxis Græca, Etymology. 12mo. 2s. 6d.
— Greek Verse-Book, Praxis Iambica. 12mo. 4s. 6d.
Farrar's Brief Greek Syntax and Accidence. 12mo. 4s. 6d.
— Greek Grammar Rules for Harrow School. 12mo. 1s. 6d.
Hewitt's Greek Examination-Papers. 12mo. 1s. 6d.
Isbister's Xenophon's Anabasis, Books I. to III. with Notes. 12mo. 3s. 6d.
Jerram's Graecè Reddenda. Crown 8vo. 1s. 6d.

London: LONGMANS, GREEN, & CO.

Kennedy's Greek Grammar. 12mo. 4s. 6d.
Liddell & Scott's English-Greek Lexicon. 4to. 36s.; Square 12mo. 7s. 6d.
Linwood's Sophocles, Greek Text, Latin Notes. 4th Edition. 8vo. 16s.
Mahaffy's Classical Greek Literature. Crown 8vo. Poets, 7s. 6d. Prose Writers, 7s. 6d.
Morris's Greek Lessons. Square 18mo. Part I. 2s. 6d.; Part II. 1s.
Parry's Elementary Greek Grammar. 12mo. 3s. 6d.
Plato's Republic, Book I. Greek Text, English Notes by Hardy. Crown 8vo. 3s.
Sheppard and Evans's Notes on Thucydides. Crown 8vo. 7s. 6d.
Thucydides, Book IV. with Notes by Barton and Chavasse. Crown 8vo. 5s.
Valpy's Greek Delectus, improved by White. 12mo. 2s. 6d. Key, 2s. 6d.
White's Xenophon's Expedition of Cyrus, with English Notes. 12mo. 7s. 6d.
Wilkins's Manual of Greek Prose Composition. Crown 8vo. 5s. Key, 5s.
— Exercises in Greek Prose Composition. Crown 8vo. 4s. 6d. Key, 2s. 6d.
— New Greek Delectus. Crown 8vo. 3s. 6d. Key, 2s. 6d.
— Progressive Greek Delectus. 12mo. 4s. Key, 2s. 6d.
-- Progressive Greek Anthology. 12mo. 5s.
— Scriptores Attici, Excerpts with English Notes. Crown 8vo. 7s. 6d.
— Speeches from Thucydides translated. Post 8vo. 6s.
Yonge's English-Greek Lexicon. 4to. 21s.; Square 12mo. 8s. 6d.

THE LATIN LANGUAGE.

Bradley's Latin Prose Exercises. 12mo. 3s. 6d. Key, 5s.
— Continuous Lessons in Latin Prose. 12mo. 5s. Key, 5s. 6d.
— Cornelius Nepos, improved by White. 12mo. 3s. 6d.
— Eutropius, improved by White. 12mo. 2s. 6d.
— Ovid's Metamorphoses, improved by White. 12mo. 4s. 6d.
— Select Fables of Phædrus, improved by White. 12mo. 2s. 6d.
Collis's Chief Tenses of Latin Irregular Verbs. 8vo. 1s.
— Pontes Latini, Stepping-Stone to Latin Grammar. 12mo. 3s. 6d.
Hewitt's Latin Examination-Papers. 12mo. 1s. 6d.
Isbister's Cæsar, Books I.-VII. 12mo. 4s.; or with Reading Lessons, 4s. 6d.
— Cæsar's Commentaries, Books I.-V. 12mo. 3s. 6d.
— First Book of Cæsar's Gallic War. 12mo. 1s. 6d.
Jeffcott & Tossell's Helps for Latin Students. Fcp. 8vo. 2s.
Jerram's Latiné Reddenda. Crown 8vo. 1s. 6d.
Kennedy's Child's Latin Primer, or First Latin Lessons. 12mo. 2s.
— Child's Latin Accidence. 12mo. 1s.
— Elementary Latin Grammar. 12mo. 3s. 6d.
— Elementary Latin Reading Book, or Tirocinium Latinum. 12mo. 2s.
— Latin Prose, Palæstra Stili Latini. 12mo. 6s.
— Subsidia Primaria, Exercise Books to the Public School Latin Primer. I. Accidence and Simple Construction, 2s. 6d. II. Syntax, 3s. 6d.
-- Key to the Exercises in Subsidia Primaria, Parts I. and II. price 5s.
- - Subsidia Primaria, III. the Latin Compound Sentence. 12mo. 1s.
— Curriculum Stili Latini. 12mo. 4s. 6d. Key, 7s. 6d.
— Palæstra Latina, or Second Latin Reading Book. 12mo. 5s.

London : LONGMANS, GREEN, & CO.

Millington's Latin Prose Composition. Crown 8vo. 3s. 6d.
— Selections from Latin Prose. Crown 8vo. 2s. 6d.
Moody's Eton Latin Grammar. 12mo. 2s. 6d. The Accidence separately, 1s.
Morris's Elementa Latina. Fcp. 8vo. 1s. 6d. Key, 2s. 6d.
Parry's Origines Romanæ, from Livy, with English Notes. Crown 8vo. 4s.
The Public School Latin Primer. 12mo. 2s. 6d.
— — — — Grammar, by Rev. Dr. Kennedy. Post 8vo. 7s. 6d.
Prendergast's Mastery Series, Manual of Latin. 12mo. 2s. 6d.
Rapier's Introduction to Composition of Latin Verse. 12mo. 3s. 6d. Key, 2s. 6d.
Sheppard and Turner's Aids to Classical Study. 12mo. 5s. Key, 6s.
Valpy's Latin Delectus, improved by White. 12mo. 2s. 6d. Key, 3s. 6d.
Virgil's Æneid, translated into English Verse by Conington. Crown 8vo. 9s.
— Works, edited by Kennedy. Crown 8vo. 10s. 6d.
— — translated into English Prose by Conington. Crown 8vo. 9s.
Walford's Progressive Exercises in Latin Elegiac Verse. 12mo. 2s. 6d. Key, 5s.
White and Riddle's Large Latin-English Dictionary. 1 vol. 4to. 21s.
White's Concise Latin-Eng. Dictionary for University Students. Royal 8vo. 12s.
— Junior Students' Eng.-Lat. & Lat.-Eng. Dictionary. Square 12mo. 5s.
Separately { The Latin-English Dictionary, price 3s.
{ The English-Latin Dictionary, price 3s.
Yonge's Latin Gradus. Post 8vo. 9s.; or with Appendix, 12s.

WHITE'S GRAMMAR SCHOOL GREEK TEXTS.

Æsop (Fables) & Palæphatus (Myths). 32mo. 1s.
Homer, Iliad, Book I. 1s.
— Odyssey, Book I. 1s.
Lucian, Select Dialogues. 1s.
Xenophon, Anabasis, Books I. III. IV. V. & VI. 1s. 6d. each ; Book II. 1s.; Book VII. 2s.

Xenophon, Book I. without Vocabulary. 3d.
St. Matthew's and St. Luke's Gospels. 2s. 6d. each.
St. Mark's and St. John's Gospels. 1s. 6d. each.
The Acts of the Apostles. 2s. 6d.
St. Paul's Epistle to the Romans. 1s. 6d.

The Four Gospels in Greek, with Greek-English Lexicon. Edited by John T. White, D.D. Oxon. Square 32mo. price 5s.

WHITE'S GRAMMAR-SCHOOL LATIN TEXTS.

Cæsar. Gallic War, Books I. & II. V. & VI. 1s. each. Book I. without Vocabulary, 3d.
Cæsar, Gallic War, Books III. & IV. 9d. each.
Cæsar, Gallic War, Book VII. 1s. 6d.
Cicero, Cato Major (Old Age). 1s. 6d.
Cicero, Lælius (Friendship). 1s. 6d.
Eutropius, Roman History, Books I. & II. 1s. Books III. & IV. 1s.
Horace,Odes,Books I.II.& IV. 1s. each.
Horace, Odes, Book III. 1s. 6d.
Horace, Epodes and Carmen Seculare. 1s.

Nepos, Miltiades, Simon, Pausanias, Aristides. 9d.
Ovid. Selections from Epistles and Fasti. 1s.
Ovid, Select Myths from Metamorphoses. 9d.
Phædrus, Select Easy Fables, 9d.
Phædrus, Fables, Books I. & II. 1s.
Sallust. Bellum Catilinarium. 1s. 6d.
Virgil, Georgics, Book IV. 1s.
Virgil, Æneid, Books I. to VI. 1s. each.
Book I. without Vocabulary, 3d.
Virgil, Æneid, Books VII. VIII. X. XI. XII. 1s. 6d. each.

London : LONGMANS, GREEN, & CO.

THE FRENCH LANGUAGE.

Albités's How to Speak French. Fcp. 8vo. 5s. 6d.
— Instantaneous French Exercises. Fcp. 2s. Key, 2s.
Cassal's French Genders. Crown 8vo. 3s. 6d.
Cassal & Karcher's Graduated French Translation Book.   Part I. 3s. 6d.
    Part II. 5s. Key to Part I. by Professor Cassal, price 5s.
Contanseau's Practical French and English Dictionary. Post 8vo. 3s. 6d.
    —   Pocket French and English Dictionary. Square 18mo. 1s 6d.
    —   Premières Lectures. 12mo. 2s. 6d.
    —   First Step in French. 12mo. 2s. 6d. Key. 3s.
    —   French Accidence. 12mo. 2s. 6d.
    —   — Grammar. 12mo. 4s. Key, 3s.
Contanseau's Middle-Class French Course. Fcp. 8vo. : —

Accidence, 8d.	French Translation-Book, 8d.
Syntax, 8d.	Easy French Delectus. 8d.
French Conversation-Book, 8d.	First French Reader, 8d.
First French Exercise-Book, 8d.	Second French Reader, 8d.
Second French Exercise-Book, 8d.	French and English Dialogues, 8d.

Contanseau's Guide to French Translation. 12mo. 3s. 6d. Key, 3s. 6d.
    —   Prosateurs et Poètes Français. 12mo. 5s.
    —   Précis de la Littérature Française. 12mo. 3s. 6d.
    —   Abrégé de l'Histoire de France. 12mo. 2s. 6d.
Féval's Chouans et Bleus, with Notes by C. Sankey, M.A. Fcp. 8vo. 2s. 6d.
Jerram's Sentences for Translation into French. Cr. 8vo. 1s. Key, 2s. 6d.
Prendergast's Mastery Series, French. 12mo. 2s. 6d.
Souvestre's Philosophe sous les Toits, by Stiévenard. Square 18mo. 1s. 6d.
Stepping-Stone to French Pronunciation. 18mo. 1s.
Stiévenard's Lectures Françaises from Modern Authors. 12mo. 4s. 6d.
    —   Rules and Exercises on the French Language. 12mo. 3s. 6d.
Tarver's Eton French Grammar. 12mo. 6s. 6d.

THE GERMAN LANGUAGE.

Blackley's Practical German and English Dictionary. Post 8vo. 3s. 6d.
Buchheim's German Poetry, for Repetition. 18mo. 1s. 6d.
Collis's Card of German Irregular Verbs. 8vo. 2s.
Fischer-Fischart's Elementary German Grammar. Fcp. 8vo. 2s. 6d.
Just's German Grammar. 12mo. 1s. 6d.
— German Reading Book. 12mo. 3s. 6d.
Longman's Pocket German and English Dictionary. Square 18mo. 2s. 6d.
Naftel's Elementary German Course for Public Schools. Fcp. 8vo.

German Accidence. 9d.	German Prose Composition Book. 9d.
German Syntax. 9d.	First German Reader. 9d.
First German Exercise-Book. 9d.	Second German Reader. 9d.
Second German Exercise-Book. 9d.	

Prendergast's Mastery Series, German. 12mo. 2s. 6d.
Quick's Essentials of German. Crown 8vo. 3s. 6d.
Selss's School Edition of Goethe's Faust. Crown 8vo. 5s.
— Outline of German Literature. Crown 8vo. 4s. 6d.
Wirth's German Chit-Chat. Crown 8vo. 2s. 6d.

London : LONGMANS, GREEN, & CO.

Spottiswoode & Co. Printers, New-street Square, London.